KILL ALL THE
LAWYERS

KILL ALL THE
LAWYERS

A novel by

William Deverell

Ballantine Books
A Division of Random House of Canada Limited

Ballantine Books 1995

Canadian Cataloguing in Publication Data

Deverell, William, 1937–
  Kill all the lawyers

ISBN 0-345-39817-3

I. Title.

PS8557.E8775K5 1995   C813'.54   C95-931213-7
PR9199.3.D48K5 1995

Printed and bound in Canada.

9 8 7 6 5 4 3 2 1

Dedicated to the defenders of the Clayoquot.

JACK CADE: I will apparel them all in one
          livery, that they may worship me their
          Lord.

DICK THE BUTCHER: The first thing we do, let's
          kill all the lawyers.

JACK CADE: Nay, that I mean to do.

Henry the Sixth, Part Two
— William Shakespeare

1

The Last Summer
of Arthur Besterman

Arthur P. Besterman was a reformed alcoholic and a criminal lawyer. He had been droning away for so long at 222 Main Street that he was regarded by the court staff as a fixture, like one of the cement waste bins or water fountains. If the Provincial Court Building were ever to be sold, Besterman would go with it, still passing out his cards.

He was a dogged lawyer but not very gifted, losing most of his cases. Two failed marriages and a nebulous sense of his own incompetence had led him to seek solace in alcohol, but a few years ago he took the cure and joined the Vancouver Trial Lawyers' chapter of Alcoholics Anonymous.

Most of his clients were persons for whom crime had not paid, shifters and grifters assigned to him through legal aid. He earned enough to keep a small office in the Gastown area and a half-day secretary.

An accused person who applies for legal aid often does not know who his lawyer will be. The Legal Services Society might assign a very good lawyer, or at least one of middling skills. Or an accused might get Arthur Besterman. It is a lottery.

Thus, did Arthur acquire the file of O.D. Milsom, a dull-witted middle-aged loner who had confessed to the random stabbing deaths of three young women in the previous fall. By the time the trial began the following July, the media had already convicted Milsom, and the court was packed daily with outraged citizenry.

For Besterman, a very unusual thing happened. He won.

A hearing was held to determine the admissibility of Milsom's confession — and though Besterman hadn't argued it well, he did raise a point which interested the judge. O.D. Milsom had been apprehended by a group of citizen vigilantes known as the White Angels, the leader of which threatened to emasculate him unless he confessed. Did that make the following outpouring of guilt inadmissible?

Counsel for the Crown, the wily Leroy Lukey, Q.C., argued through two days that Milsom's confession was not induced by threats or fear of violence.

The judge sat silent through all of this, then ruled the confession inadmissible. Since there was little other evidence against Milsom, the judge then ordered the jury to acquit him. An appeal was filed on the same day. Milsom packed up his few belongings and disappeared into the void.

Arthur P. Besterman, enjoying the best day of his life, drove straight from the courthouse to a bar in the Gastown area of Vancouver, near his office, where he ordered his first whiskey in three years. He stayed there until midnight, when he was observed stumbling out the back door to the parking lot.

At five a.m. on the next day, the twelfth of July, his body was found in the parking lot behind his office, his skull caved in. A fan of blood was spread across the pavement and on nearby cars, leaving a shadow where the assailant had stood. The coroner guessed a baseball bat, or something similar.

A mugging was ruled out, since Besterman's wallet, still in his jacket pocket, contained four hundred and fifty-five dollars. Vancouver homicide visited the families of the murdered women, but no anguished father, no vengeance-lusting brother or cousin was found to be without alibi. The leader of the White Angels was questioned, too, but his witnesses confirmed he was snug in his bed at the group's downtown barracks all night.

For a while the Bar Association maintained pressure on the authorities to solve this crime. Lawyers don't get killed. Lawyers were members of a professional elite, safe, sacrosanct, removed from the battle. Police and criminals get killed, not lawyers.

After several weeks of failed leads, investigators became apathetic. Soon Besterman was earning, at best, only the occasional paragraph in the back pages.

The memory of Arthur P. Besterman seemed to slowly dribble away with the coming of the winter rains...

"...those ceaseless, sullen rains of winter. Little did Lance Valentine know, as he stared out into the grey watercolour wash outside his window, that he had also been chosen to die."

Brian Pomeroy punched the period key, then scanned his opening paragraphs with a critic's stern and cautious eye. Imperfect, yes, but surely you must agree, Mr. Widgeon, that the yet unheralded author of these virgin paragraphs has obeyed the do's and don'ts, the edicts and statutes that you have promulgated.

We have a corpse. The law according to Widgeon: waste little time in wasting your first victim.

But first, please: know your victim. "The writer must always retain a photograph of this unfortunate soul at an earlier time — while still in the flower of life. Take a few snapshots to remember him by, but do not dwell on him; the reader cares not whether the victim collected stamps or picked his nose or grew prize pumpkins (unless indeed it turns out he was felled, in a jealous rage, by the loser of the annual Southampton Fall Fair)."

Mr. Widgeon (*The Art of the Whodunit*, $24.95, Cheltenham Press) also instructs: immediately create an air of mystery. "Something about this death must engage the reader: the senselessness of it, the apparent lack of motive, the odd choice of modus."

Had Brian sufficiently complied? Is a blunt instrument too blunt a device? Does it limit one's options? Poison, says Widgeon, is so much more subtle, and one should never ignore the possibility of suicide.

The hunt must be taken up quickly, and the protagonist more formally introduced. But who *is* Lance Valentine? Alas, the author has never met this shadowy figure with the brave and romantic name — is he a private eye with caustic tongue, a pipe-smoking homicide inspector in rumpled tweed, some kind of nosy, cozy Hercule Poirot?

Which brings us to that annoying rule number one: Know where you are going.

Brian examined the typewriter keys, as if seeking coded answers there. No suspects, no motives. One victim. Crushed to death beneath an enormous writer's block.

Three pages of manuscript, the fruit of two weekends and twelve evenings of creative labour. Why had he boasted to Caroline and, worse, to his snide confreres at the office that he was writing a mystery?

The phone rang. He waited for Caroline to pick it up in the living room. It rang again, jangling in his brain, breaking up the knots of concentration. Oh, for sanctuary, a place unwired to the pestering world.

"I'm feeding the owl, Brian," Caroline called. Turning to the window of his den he could see her, under the pear tree, tending to the ever-voracious Howland.

Stubbornly, he refused to answer the phone, and after the fourth ring he heard his own polite voice from the answering machine, apologizing for his absence.

"Brian, it's me." Augustina. "Yoo-hoo. Brian? Caroline? Come on, I know you're…" Her voice suddenly went tense. "Brian, I'm scared." Then shrill with terror. "Oh, my God, he's coming through the door now! He has a knife!"

Brian knocked over his chair going for the phone.

"Augustina?"

"That's sweet, Brian, because there could have been somebody with a knife. Guess what? We've got the Kitswuk Five."

2

The Case of
the Kitswuk Five

Wentworth Chance was in hog heaven on this sodden mid-December
Friday. Here he was, at twenty-three, six months out of law school,
helping win a big Tony Award-winning West Coast trial, the case of
the Kitswuk Five.

It was *he*, Wentworth, the lowly articling student, who had stumbled upon that obscure case from Manitoba which had convinced the
judge to turf the wire taps.

"That just leaves the fink," Brian Pomeroy said. "I'm going to take
him off at the knees."

They were in the office girding for battle, the tenth day of the
trial of five braves of the Kitswuk Nation who were accused of
planting dynamite near a salmon ladder beside the newly built Knot
Lake Dam. Power for a smelter; silt to kill the spawning streams.
A popular politician — mayor, Legion president, and prime booster
of the Town of Knot Lake — had been touring the site with the
construction superintendent when the blast caused the dam to breach
on one side. The two men were carried off with the torrent, and met
their deaths by drowning. The Kitswuk Five were charged with
manslaughter.

Brian had won a change of venue for the trial: Vancouver, far away from Knot Lake, where the townspeople were hostile toward the accused.

"What did I do with the sheets on the informer?" Brian asked.

Wentworth handed him a skimpy file: a few stolen cheques, an assault, a false pretences.

"Not much of a record," Brian said. "Need some props." He told Wentworth to go to the closed-files locker and bundle up about thirty pounds of paper. Wentworth didn't ask why. One doesn't question. One just does. Happily.

Wentworth was a somewhat emaciated-looking young man whose face was pitted with teen-aged wounds. He was astigmatic, given to wearing half-moon reading glasses, which he thought made him appear mature and learned. He had grown up in a village on the Alaska Highway — a filling station, basically — and had hungered for the lights. Now he was living in a great port city, a connection town full of crooks and flakes — which the West Coast of Canada seemed to attract in unusual abundance — and articling for a firm that seemed to be at the centre of all its action.

Wentworth had been near the top of his graduating class and was entertained by scouts from several large firms. But he was idealistic and wanted to fight for people's rights. For law graduates set upon this course, there was only one firm in Vancouver, that holy shrine of the underdog, the office of Pomeroy, Macarthur, Brovak and Sage. Brian Pomeroy, defender of Greenpeaceniks, Sea Shepherds and Earth Firsters (though for some unfathomable reason he wanted to be a mystery writer). Maximillian Macarthur III, who seemed to get every big civil liberties case in town. John Brovak, the abrasive Rambo of the criminal courts. The scandal-haunted beauty Augustina Sage, champion of aboriginal rights.

These were bold and doughty barristers, not simpering solicitors. These were guerrilla fighters in the Great War of Justice.

So Wentworth Chance applied for articles with the offices of Pomeroy Macarthur — as did thirty-seven other classmates. The offices were located in Gastown, Vancouver's old section, at the neck of the downtown peninsula, near the docks of Burrard Inlet. The city had attempted to restore the area but had failed, and its streets counted many junk import shops and tourist traps. The area is near Chinatown and merges with skid road, whose derelicts often migrate into Gastown to solicit spare change and frighten tourists.

Pomeroy, Macarthur and Company were on the second floor of a nineteenth-century red brick building between the CPR tracks and the bronze statue of Gassy Jack Deighton on Maple Tree Square. Deighton, a lush, was one of the spiritual founders of Vancouver, a pioneer oddball of the Left Coast.

On the ground floor of the building was the New Age Awareness Centre, where seekers were massaged, enlightened and made whole. Formerly, the space had been rented out as a rock and roll club. The new downstairs tenants were much quieter, except for the primal screamers.

When Wentworth Chance had arrived for his interview with the firm, at first he couldn't get up his courage to go inside, and instead wandered through the New Age Awareness Centre seeking strength. In one of the rooms, according to the sign outside the door, someone was doing a workshop on "Dreamwork, Trance Channeling, and Past Life Regression."

The hell with this new age stuff, he decided, criminal law was his dreamwork. He went upstairs and, after waiting with numerous law school peers, ultimately found himself in the library-boardroom looking upon his gods. They seemed out of sorts, as if hung over, especially John Brovak. Brian Pomeroy appeared bored with the process and spent the whole time standing, staring out a window.

The interview went something like this:

Brovak: "How many more eager beavers are out there?"

Sage: "I counted five anyway."

Brovak: "Aw, God help me. I need to go home and conk off."

Macarthur: "Yeah, I have brain-fade. Let's just take this guy and get it over with."

Brovak: "You got a car?"

Chance: "I can't afford a car."

Macarthur: "Well, you better buy a bicycle because you're going to be pedaling a lot of paper around."

Wentworth had heard he would see lots of paper during his year-long internship before being called to the bar. Running back and forth to court registries, filing documents, work which they could hire a grade one dropout to do. Except they would have to pay the mini-mum wage and comply with the Fair Labour Practices Act.

Since signing on with the firm last June, Wentworth had been toiling something like a hundred hours a week. He was not getting overtime, unless one counted his share of the tab the firm picked up for the drunken debauches that Friday lunches at Au Sauterne often evolved into. Au Sauterne being a restaurant across the square where individual entrees cost as much as the monthly payments on his new Outback 310 twenty-one-speed bike.

Ah, but there were perquisites. Had Wentworth accepted articles with the firm of Staid, Stolid, Boring and Sober, he would rarely have seen the inside of a criminal courtroom or witnessed the slash and duel over the rights of the accused. Though he was on overload, and his nickel-nursing bosses barely paid him the interest due on his student loans, he loved this firm. Would they keep him on when he was called to the bar next year?

Laden with a box of old files, Wentworth followed Brian and Augustina Sage into the courtroom. They took a seat at a crowded counsel table and turned to look at their clients: buckskin and feathers, noble, proud, and probably guilty, though that, Wentworth had learned, was not important to a lawyer. From the gallery, several witnesses from Knot Lake were staring at these haughty savages with abhorrence.

The Kitswuk Five had originally retained Augustina Sage, the junior partner, but she had asked Brian Pomeroy to lead the defence. He was a tree-hugger; the case was right up his ecological alley. Wentworth's black-robed hero was six-foot-one and ungainly, with a bony face, an untidy Mark Twain moustache and a blond thatch roof, unruly tufts of straw. Wentworth knew from tales told in the office coffee room that Brian suffered a tendency to complicate his personal life with flubs and footshots, but in court he was cool and quick-witted.

Conferring in whispers beside him sat Augustina Sage, slim, slinky, with teased curls, dark almond eyes and tawny skin from a Métis mother. Wentworth had a crush on her.

"Your witness," the judge said.

Brian studied with distaste the slick-haired young man slouching in the witness box. "Bring out the props," he whispered to the student, who heaved several thick files onto the counsel table with a loud thunk, papers spilling from them.

"You have quite a criminal history," Brian said, opening one of the dead files — some old expropriation matter, he didn't remember it. He pretended to study a page, then opened another file, frowning. "Bunch of stolen cheques." He picked up another file, ten-year-old financial statements for Pomeroy, Macarthur and Company, and flipped through the pages. "False pretenses, assault, let's see…" Riffling through records of office disbursements for 1983, he shook his head sorrowfully. "My, my." Another file. "Goodness."

The prosecutor rose to complain. "If counsel wishes to put a criminal record to the witness he knows how to do it."

Brian decided he had milked what he could from these minor offences and abandoned the files and strolled toward the witness until he was within intimidation distance, close enough to smell the staleness of his breath. "You want us to believe that you overheard Mr. Eagle Talon say they were going to dynamite the dam?"

"Yeah."

Juror Eight, the retired United Church minister, was still looking at all those files on the counsel table. Brian waited until he could make eye contact, then picked up the worn copy of the Bible. Until recent years, the archaic practice had been to require witnesses to kiss this book. Brian thought of all the lying, unsanitary lips that had touched it.

"You swore on this holy book to tell the truth, didn't you?"

"Yeah, I did."

"Just as you did last June."

"What do you mean?"

"When you were on trial for dealing in stolen cheques."

"Yeah, I guess I swore on the Bible then."

"And you lied through your teeth at that trial. Just as you've been doing at this one."

"Counsel might like to reword his pronouncement as a question," said the judge. Her tone, though, was of friendly admonition — she had quietly joined the camp of the defence.

"You were found guilty."

"I shouldn't of been."

"Your jury was mistaken, or just stupid?"

"They blew it."

Too late, the prosecutor yelled, "I object!"

Brian sighed. "My learned friend doesn't want the truth to come out."

"Counsel, please refrain from making editorial comments," said the judge.

"And he should back away from the witness," said the prosecutor.

"I don't like being that close to him myself," Brian said.

He returned to the counsel table, and whispered to Augustina: "How am I doing?"

"Cut it to the bone and avoid that sneering tone," she said.

Brian had a sense the jury wanted to get out of here to do their Christmas shopping. He diced the witness up a little more, got him stammering over some minor contradictions, and suddenly sat down, announcing he didn't find it necessary to call any evidence.

The jury acquitted the Kitswuk Five at twenty-three minutes past noon on Friday, December 11.

Outside the courthouse, Brian and Augustina, their arms around their happy clients, spent a few humble minutes before some microphones and cameras, as the stone-faced folks from Knot Lake walked sullenly from the courthouse.

Winners buy lunch at Au Sauterne; that was the custom. Wentworth, ever eager for a free meal, volunteered to get there early and hold a table. He was half-way through a basket of hot crispy rolls when Brian and Augustina joined him, soon followed by wiry, balding Max Macarthur — he was five-foot-five, and Wentworth had oftentimes heard him complain of heightist attitudes on the part of his jocular partners. But they were always jabbing at each other.

Max said, "Cops screwed it up, eh?"

"Augustina, tell him how I held the fink's feet to the fire."

"Guess this means you can get ready for the Hullipson trial on Monday," Max said.

"I have earned some time off. I have just won a trial of mythical proportions. The jury was out *half an hour*. Wentworth, tell this pod person how I decimated the squeal."

Brian began to replay highlights from the Kitswuk trial, but Max continued to treat his victorious partner with an air of casual indifference.

"Hate to be a drag," said Max, "but before you finish pumping yourself up and float off like a balloon, can we talk about Hullipson?" This was a two-dayer — a minor-league monkey-wrencher was charged with removing surveyors' ribbons. Max had been baby-sitting it for Brian, who had picked up the case while in Knot Lake last summer, doing the Kitswuk preliminary.

"You said you'd take Hullipson if your trial didn't run over."

"Aw, for the love of God," Brian said, letting Max get to him, "I've just fought the hardest trial of my life, and I'm a helpless *wreck*! Hullipson's a mischief-under-two-hundred, a summary trial; any idiot can handle it."

"Good, that's settled," Max said.

Brian saw that he was stuck with Hullipson. Well, it was Friday. That meant the weekend to prepare. Call up the prosecutor and ask for a late start, fly up to the Chilcotin on Monday morning, maybe take his notes for The Novel with him, and seek inspiration in the winter wilderness. Maybe take Charity, too. Or take Charity instead of his notes. Or maybe not take Charity, because maybe the idea is crazy.

The affair with Charity Slough was, after all, only a casual four-month amourette, and Brian had been promising to write the final chapter to it. Hippie poet from his creative writing group. Big, beauti-ful, bosomy, and boring out of bed. His wife Caroline was, of course, ignorant of this relationship. Damage would be caused to precious parts of his body if she were to learn of it.

They were into a second bottle of Bordeaux when John Brovak arrived. His drug case had run late.

"I'm bagging ass for the rest of the day," he said. "If Leroy wants to sit Friday afternoons, he can sit without me. Instead of on top of me — the fat man's preferred position."

Mr. Justice Leroy Lukey, newly appointed to the bench, was Brovak's bête noir, and for the next several minutes he related a long list of this judge's latest atrocities, before launching into a ramble about his skiing plans this weekend.

Brovak had once served, though not with distinction, on the Canadian Olympic ski team. He had an athlete's body, fluid and mus-cular, and women thought him unbearably handsome, despite his scars and marks of dissolution.

He paused to order another bottle of wine, lit a smelly cigar, then turned to Brian with a supremely bored look.

"So what's new?"

"Won the Kitswuk Five, guess you heard."

"Coulda won that one blindfolded and gagged." He turned to Wentworth. "Want you to run down after lunch and ask one of the guys to sit in for me. It's Friday, and I ain't gonna be chained up in a courtroom."

Brian and Brovak stayed on after the others returned to the office, and, celebrating too much, Brian lost count of the many cognacs consumed. He was alerted to the lateness of the day when dinner customers began arriving.

Navigating from the restaurant and down the street, Brian realized he couldn't remember where he had parked his car. He observed that December's early night had fallen, and mists obscured the towers of glass to the west, the city's uptown hub. In the harbour, a massive freighter was being prodded toward the cranes of Centennial Pier, tugboats clinging to her like pilot fish. The lights of the North Shore Sea-Bus twinkled then faded into the distant gloom.

For a while Brian wandered aimlessly through the streets of Gastown among old brick warehouses converted to loud, cheap bars, among shops with Christmas-lit window displays of tawdry souvenirs. He finally found his little energy-conserving Honda at a meter with a clutter of tickets on the windshield.

He worried about negotiating the Lion's Gate Bridge to his house in North Vancouver. Maybe he should stop by Charity's for a coffee.

No, he told himself. N-O.

3

Affair with
a Bad Poet

Caroline Pomeroy returned home from the campus bleary-eyed after a hopeless afternoon of grading papers for her English Lit 403s: Thackeray, Trollope and Brontë, The English Novel in the Age of Vanity. When she heard the news of Brian's victory on the radio, she felt some of her tension ease. It was blue hell around the house whenever he lost. The moping, the gnashing of teeth.

She went out to the back to feed Howland, the screech owl, who was yawning himself awake on his pear-tree perch beside his nesting box.

"Come on, sack artist, time to get up and go to work. Heavy night of hooting ahead."

One morning last spring, Caroline and Brian had heard a great cawing and scolding of crows behind the house, and found Howland broken-winged after battle with them. The Pomeroys were rabid birders (Brian had actually taken an Audubon Society course called "Bird Aid"). They put a splint on the wing, and it mended. Spoiled by the good life in North Vancouver suburbia, Howland spurned the woods beyond his pear tree, and now he was simply there, a kind of lazy relative hanging around the back yard, waiting for a little action, waiting for the night.

"You're on your own tonight, Howland. We have tickets to *Candida* at the Playhouse."

Howland nodded wisely.

"I just bloody hope Brian hasn't forgotten."

Howland winked at her knowingly.

"Pretend it's a fresh kill, Howland." Caroline passed him up a strip of butchered rabbit.

What for their own dinner? She returned to the house and poked around in the fridge, then began to prepare a quick casserole d'leftovers — they would just have time to gulp and go.

She and Brian really must start spending more time together. He'd been working too many evenings, in the law library…And when he did spend an evening at home, he locked himself away in his little den with that beastly murder mystery he claims he's writing, his shelves full of soft-boiled Father Browns, hard-boiled Marlowes and medium-boiled Archers, and Inspector Maigret and Inspector Migraine and Inspector Diddle, and Inspector Fiddle, and Inspector Piddle.

She'd give more credence to his pretensions of literary creation if he ever summoned the courage to show her this masterwork. She didn't hear those typewriter keys clicking all that much.

It never occurs to him that *she* might like to write. They had even taken the same creative writing class together and *she* was the one with the Ph.D. in English literature.

Caroline put the casserole in the oven and went to the bedroom to dress. A simple huggy semi-mini of the ecologically correct hue: green to match the emerald of her eyes. Let the theatre-going public know that Caroline Pomeroy still has curves and legs. Maybe Brian might notice, too. His love-making recently had been, so to speak, a little flaccid. She tried to suppress thoughts that she was to blame. (Still childless after five trying years: her fault?) Incorrect thinking, is what her feminist pal Abigail Hitchins would say.

Anyway, she had an appointment with her gynecologist on Monday. She hadn't yet told Brian she'd had tests done. She was thirty-one, deteriorating, soon to be geriatric. Now or never. Never, she feared. Barren — the cruellest adjective.

Brian was grievously late. As the minutes dragged by, Caroline found herself adding to the list of her husband's shortcomings. Why is *his* career more important than hers, why does he always *compete*? Even when they're out birding, it's "There's a White-Tailed Ptarmigan, that's mine, saw it first." Don't marry a criminal lawyer, Abigail had warned.

The casserole had almost dried out when Brian finally arrived, just an hour before opening curtain. Caroline quelled her temper momentarily, kissed him at the door, and could barely stand the smell of him.

"You're drunk," she said.

"Hey, can't a guy celebrate? You heard, I…"

"I heard."

"So whatta you say, letch…let's go out tonight, maybe down to the Lion's Arms for a drink after dins. I'm starving. What's on the menu?"

"A former casserole."

Brian watched with amiable confusion as she dumped the casserole into the organic waste, put on her coat and strode to the door.

"You've quite obviously forgotten." Green-fire eyes threw darts at him. "You're a self-centered, immature, thoughtless bastard." She marched out of the house and went alone to the play.

Brian poured himself two fingers of rum and drag-tailed to the backyard to seek consolation from Howland. The owl gazed down upon him with disgust.

"I plead not guilty, m'lord."

But no acquittals were to be won in front of Mr. Justice Howland Owl. Odd how he resembled the chief of the trial division. Those big ear tufts. The yellow eyes. The scowl, the censorious play of feature.

Howland swivelled his head away, as if he could no longer stand to look at the miscreant.

"I won the Kitswuk Five!" he declaimed, then muttered, "Bigges' night of my life, I come home, I'm treated like a piece of shit by the wife and the owl."

He downed his rum. "I'll show her. I'll *write*." He'd be hard at work on his masterpiece when she returned from her frivolous evening at the theatre.

"You're s'posed to be wise, Howie. So give me a plot."

Howland wouldn't look at him. Brian whistled. The owl turned and sent him a dirty look and whistled back.

"Who killed the criminal lawyer with a blunt instrument in the parking lot? Whodunit, Howland?"

"Hoo," said Howland.

"Yeah, who. And why and how. Give me the perfect murder."

He took a stagger step to his left, and, trying to regain balance, found himself entwined in a folding aluminum chair.

Suddenly Howland was airborne, swooping on a field mouse making a run for it across the grass to the woodshed.

The mouse didn't stand a chance.

"*You* dunit, Howland."

The next morning, Brian awoke to find himself on top of the covers of the bed, with his shirt off but his pants on, and Caroline snoozing beside him under the sheets. Though it was Saturday, and a brutal hangover was settling in, Hullipson had to be prepared for. He avoided further marital discord — imminent, because Caroline seemed to be stirring awake — by retrieving the balance of his clothes and heading out the door.

He pouted. He felt wronged. His Honda didn't seem to want to stop at the office; it continued on into East Chinatown, among the lap-sided gingerbread houses, with tiny green patches of lawn, skeletal trees and winter gardens. He stopped in front of a rooming house with its roof canting wearily to one side. There lived Charity Slough.

He found her at her desk, sitting beneath a chart of the constellations. Tall, voluptuous Charity Slough. Ursa Major.

He heard himself asking her to join him on a trip to the Chilcotin.

"Well, that sounds positively cuspy," said Charity.

Cuspy. What the hell did that mean? He stared through hangover eyes at her chart of the constellations: bear, ram, crab, unicorn. Snake.

She kissed him. "Pee-yew. Brian, you look like someone dragged you through a bush. What rhymes with meander?" She was working on a poem.

"Philander."

Driving to the office, he thought: that was barmy, inviting Charity to Knot Lake, what an imprudent thing to do. He felt himself being watched by all the Santas and Rudolphs in the windows, felt besieged by jingle bells and twinkle lights, the total effect of which was to plunge him into deeper gloom and shame.

In Knot Lake, in the cold and wintry Chilcotin foothills, he would tell Charity that it was over, this immature effort to assert his manhood at mid-life, this ridiculous liaison with a mystic poet of indifferent talent.

He and Caroline spent Sunday trying to repair the damage of Friday night's altercation, counting wintering loons at the Reifel Waterfowl Refuge. He was the first to spot the Green Heron wading among the reeds; a find, a rarity on the Coast, well beyond its wintering grounds, and he beat Caroline to it with his camera. She congratulated him, but rather coolly. The heron may have sensed the chill, too. It swivelled its head at them, frowning, and took wing.

The circuit judge presiding at the Knot Lake courthouse — the local Legion Hall except on every second Monday — was a bawdy old fellow before whom Brian had appeared a couple of times. As court opened, he congratulated Brian on the Kitswuk Five win. Brave of him, thought Brian, here in Knot Lake, unfriendly terrain.

The young prosecutor, perhaps unnerved by the respect Brian was being afforded during the first hour of the trial, drew him aside during the morning break to say that she would be happy if he pleaded to just two of the eight counts. They finally bartered Hullipson down to one count of mischief, the prosecutor agreeing not to oppose a conditional discharge.

Court was recessed, Hullipson went home smiling, and the judge ambled down from his bench to ask if he could buy Brian lunch.

"You're alone?" he said.

Brian glanced at Charity, who was sitting in the back row, smiling a little too omnivorously at him. "Ah, no, not quite."

He tried to think of an excuse for lunch, but the judge saved him the trouble.

"I can see you may have already eaten." The judge had spotted her.

Brian suddenly remembered that this judge had met Caroline. A law retreat a few years ago.

"Enjoy your dessert," said the judge with a slow, fat wink.

On their way back to the motel in the rented car, Charity looked at Brian with eyes that seemed to seek too much connection.

"We're paired?" she said. It wasn't a question; she tended to inflect her voice at the end of sentences. "We met in superior conjunction, you know. Between Mercury and Venus?"

This *has* to end, he thought.

They made love energetically in their room, and after dinner made love again, she indefatigable, he with increasing effort and bravery as he grew more concerned about her staring moony eyes that searched for his own eyes, for accord, completion, astral connection.

Next morning, driving to the airport, he tried with all the steel in his soul to bring himself to tell her he wanted out of this. He steered his car into the parking area of a lookout point over frozen Knot Lake, stopped and stared at the brittle whiteness of the valley and its sled-scarred lake, trying to rehearse an opening line.

"Charity, I really like you…" He struggled to find the appropriate qualifying clause, but stalled. It never emerged because Charity smothered him with her mouth, then drew back, murmuring, "I know, I know. I love you, too."

He tried to evade her thrusting tongue, her hands reaching, searching, kneading an unbidden erection to life.

She pressed herself to him. He didn't undo his seatbelt.

"Let's make love. Now. While we have the world spread below us."

Fortunately — he thought at the time — another car drove in behind them just then. He paid it little heed. Dark blue, he recalled later, nondescript, an old Chevrolet or something; he didn't know his cars.

"Not here, we have company." But she was at his belt, tugging with powerful Amazonian hands. She freed his cock, stared at it for a second as if planning strategy, then abruptly went down on him. Hot but frantic, Brian swivelled his head, saw with relief his windows were fogging fast. Where was that car? Starting to drive off.

All resolve lost, he gave into her driving hands, her urgent, searing tongue, and closed his eyes and felt himself building within. He arched his back spastically, and exploded. As she pumped him into her mouth, the windshield exploded, too.

They were showered with glass pellets, and Brian dizzily realized that no orgasm is powerful enough to shatter glass. He felt the rush of freezing air from outside, and realized Charity was screaming.

Afterwards he remembered his confusion: was the explosion the sound of a gunshot or only the sound of his window shattering? But does windshield glass just shatter?

He looked at the wide, wet mouth of Charity; she was gasping, catching her breath, semen on her blouse, glass in her hair. But no blood, no blood. Shouting at her to keep calm, Brian accelerated hard, the tires screaming on the salted pavement. With the wind scalding him through the shattered window, his pants halfway to his knees, he urged his car over the brow of a hill and down a straightaway which he took at dangerous speed.

In the valley, he went through a radar trap, heaving a sigh of relief when he saw the wigwag lights behind him and heard the bleat of the siren: an RCMP cruiser closing in. He braked and pulled onto the shoulder.

When the police car stopped behind him, Brian hurried out to the driver, who was scribbling in his pad, not looking up.

"May I see your licence, sir?"

"Someone took a shot at me!"

The officer glanced up, saw the bits of glass decorating Brian's jacket, and glanced down.

"Your fly's undone, sir," he said, getting out of the patrol car.

Brian fumbled at his zipper with numb fingers as the officer walked over and looked at the rent-a-car's demolished windshield. Charity was out of the car by now, shivering in the cold.

"Could've been a rock," the officer said.

"Could've been a bullet," Brian said.

The policeman spent a minute probing around the rented car and finally came up with a lead slug imbedded in the panelling.

As he was calling his detachment office, he asked Brian, "Know any reason someone'd want to shoot at you?"

He thought. A prurient sicko who objected to the giving of head in a public place? No: a Knot Lake redneck...the Kitswuk Five trial... someone had followed him from town...

All he said was, "I'm a criminal lawyer."

The officer nodded as if that were motive enough.

"What about her?" He gave an appraising look at the criminal lawyer's bouncy-breasted paramour, standing in the cold, shivering. "Maybe we got a jealous boyfriend or husband or something like that here?"

"I don't think so."

The officer invited Charity Slough to get into his car. "We'll have to take full statements from the both of you."

Brian felt sick. He knew of a person who would want to kill him, all right. How the *hell* was he going to explain this to Caroline?

4

Tears in
the Tamales

January 4

Dearly beloved,

Though these greetings come unseasonably late from so
compulsive a letter writer as I, may I belatedly offer one figgy
pudding to you, Max, tons of sugarplums to you, Augustina,
and a bucket of blood for the pagan Brovak. To you all a
happy though doubtless soggy New Year.

It rains in Vancouver? That soundless weak pizzle of
winter? Visit the Osa Peninsula in December. Here the rain
roars, trillions of drums and cymbals upon the roof of
corrugated zinc under which I cravenly cower.

But five days ago, His Highness the Emperor of the Sun
rose like a wrathful avenger from over the Golfo Dulce and
put the clouds to flight. The dry season has arrived faster
than cops through the door of a crack house, and now I can
see the view. Had I the soul of Keats or the voice of Shelley I
might find some means of describing it to you.

Oh, all right, I'll try. Picture me at my typewriter on my
shady but windowless porch. Imagine me reaching out and

picking a starfruit from an overhanging bough, yellow, plump and tart. From time to time, one of the papaya trees drops a sweet orange turd onto the grass of the yard.

A crested flycatcher (the Yellow-Bellied though not cowardly Elaenia, or *elaenia flavogaster*) sings sweetly from the sour orange tree. At night the crickets lull me to sleep (a dreamless sleep, unCarolined) and at dawn the howler monkeys hoot me awake from the mango trees. I rise and pee and brush my teeth and ready myself to confront the terrifying beauty of another sunrise.

To the East, to the East: there rises the sun, there, beyond the Golfo Dulce, that bottomless bay of sweetness between me and the nearest fax machine; beyond the prickly spine of the Central American isthmus rises the sun, painting butterscotch mountains in a lilac haze, the sea iridescent below.

To the west, where sets the sun with even more spectacular consequences, lies boundless ocean, blue and green and infinite.

Where sea meets land are beaches ringed with wild almonds and palms and manzanillo trees. I will not bore you with a description of these beaches (two minutes away by sandaled foot), but I should advise you that the sand, in addition to being soft and golden, is virgin: no imprints of foot or beachball or carcinogen-skinned sun-and-fun-seeker body mar it.

To the north, and spreading feverishly all about the house, is the most impressive sight of all: tropical jungle. Massive and green, birthing, living, dying, scented, ringing with birdsong and insect chirp, pumping out the oxygen that man greedily devours in his engines and his fires.

Enough, enough.

So. For me, all is well, as you can see by the ebullient spirit of this letter. I'm sure you are surprised to find me in this much-changed state, recalling as you might my panicky behavior of three weeks ago (as I recall your whispered confabulations about my so-called nervous collapse).

Okay, I am not quite whole, but I *am* recovering from Caroline's extravagant censure (not to mention the firestorm

of hurtling potware that greeted me on my return home
from Knot Lake) that temporarily scrambled my brain and
left me hopelessly weeping and ranting in your kitchen, Max.

But spans of distance and time seem to have given salve
to my wounds, and I am encouraged by this and grow
stronger daily. I will be Pomeroy of old soon. Or at least a
carefully reconstructed version of that once priceless artifact.

I don't exactly think of her every moment of the day any
more. (Oh, when I happen to i.d. a new bird, she quickly
comes back, and I remember that she still has my good
binoculars.) Anyway, have any of you heard from Professor
Pomeroy?

When I phoned her from Knot Lake she seemed so concerned for me…If only I'd told her about Charity then, over
the phone, but I didn't have the *cojónes*. And, well, I guess it
was an awkward scene for her, the reporters barging into the
English faculty lounge, explaining how her husband had
nearly been murdered, and making indelicate inquiries about
the woman who'd been with him.

I still can't believe I almost got my brains spattered all
over that rented car. If someone wanted to take a shot in my
direction, why didn't they have the decency to do so when
Charity Slough was not around?

Try as I can, I remain absolutely blank as to how many
were in that other car. And despite all the speculation, I really
don't buy the idea that Someone Was Out To Get Me. A
deranged supporter of the late and much-mourned mayor of
Knot Lake. Are the police still interviewing his cronies? Or
have they simply given up, as I suspect?

The event, however, has its up side. You will remember
our speculation about some weird sort of link between
Arthur Besterman's murder last summer and the attempt
on the life of my own good self — the common denomina-
tor being we'd both just come off big wins — and our
fanciful conjecture that a lawyer-hating lunatic was on the
loose.

It may be the stuff of fiction, but it's the stuff of tran-
scendent and indelible fiction. As you know, Besterman's

murder inspired my first hesitant plunkings upon a type-writer keyboard; now I have performed radical surgery upon my previous novel outline, and a lawyer-hating dingbat will now grace the kill-and-thrill-filled pages of the manuscript.

(Yes, you scorning scoffers, Brian Pomeroy WRITES. Pages fly from Twelve-Finger Watson's elderly upright Underworld typewriter.)

Anyway, as to the Bad Day at Knot Lake, I prefer the cops' main thesis. A couple of sauced-up rednecks driving around with a rifle.

If the shot came from their car at all. I'm more and more inclined to the theory that someone mistook my rental car for a moose. It was, after all, hunting season.

(At night here, I am sometimes awakened by the thrash-ing sounds of a fresh kill in the jungle, a scream of perishing parrot in the claws of a hunter owl, a kinkajou screeching for mercy as the ocelot sinks fangs to the throat. It is at these times, as I lie under my white shroud of a mosquito net staring into humming jungle darkness — my murder plot spinning through my head — that I wonder: Maybe there is a homicidal maniac out there.

One who has broken the office code of silence as to the current whereabouts of this fellow Pomeroy.

But those minor night-time shivers soon pass, and I am again secure in the enveloping, mothering blanket of the jungle.)

Everything, I hope, goes swimmingly at the office? The income taxers haven't demanded to audit the books? Brovak has not been secretly meeting Judge Lukey in the steam baths?

John, I forgive your obscene caterwauling on the subject of my leave of absence ("What? So you can jack off in front of a typewriter for six months just because you got your nuts caught in a ringer over a little pussy?"), and I ask you again to thank Twelve-Fingers Watson for giving me free rent of his curious villa down here.

The landlord's taste is as garish as one would expect of a coke dealer. The purple plastic bar stools have to go. The stuffed Jaguar already has. But everything works, including the toilet, although I had to tease out a small green snake from behind the float.

Since there are no nuclear plants or hydroelectric dam developments nearby I am (mercifully) without electricity, but the propane stove and fridge suffice. Fresh water is gravity-fed to me from a pulsing stream which passes under a little bridge, and empties into the ocean near a sandbar.

I'm afraid everything was a little fuzzy with mildew and fungus when I first moved in. I hired Señora Róbelo to come up from next door to clean. She brought along only six of her children, leaving I forget how many others under the care of her oldest girl, whom I will come to.

Señora Róbelo and her flock of tumultuous angels are my neighbours down the road. Señor Róbelo is nowhere to be found. I gather that he ran away a few months ago to join his mistress in Golfito, the old banana port across the Golfo Dulce.

Despite this betrayal, Señora Róbelo remains buoyantly, chirpily cheerful, a squat mass of muscle and bustle and love, the mother of all mothers. Here's a woman unembittered, a woman for whom life goes on. Caroline, childless, poisons her mind with thoughts of vengeance against her (soon-to-be) ex-husband. Oh yes, she has seen a lawyer, one Abigail Hitchins who boasts of her collection of pelts of errant husbands. Tell Caroline — I shall not be writing to her — it was a mistake to hire Abigail.

Tell her if she does divorce me I intend to marry Señora Róbelo's nineteen-year-old daughter, who bears the unbearably lovely name of Leticia and smites all who cross her path with her beauty. She has hot copper skin, eyes that flash like distant stars and a smile of molten gold.

Leticia had a year of college (her noble ambition is to become a botanist) but, sadly, had to abandon her studies to help support the family, and is now working for the National Parks Service.

Let me pause awhile at my typewriter. Let my eyes trail down the rutted road up which three Róbelo tots pad along as bare of foot as their skinny dog. What do I see behind those almond trees? A tongue of ocean lapping at the sand. The Golfo Dulce, sweet and warm, warmer than a mother's womb.

It calls me, it calls me.

Your humble servant,
Ernest Hemingway

January 4

Dear Caroline,

I just finished a letter to the firm, so I thought I should add a note to you. Relax, I won't make it a habit, and of course I will honour your gracious request upon our final, touching parting.

("I'll write you," Pomeroy said softly.

"Don't bother," snapped Caroline as she held open the door.

Pomeroy walked toward the waiting taxi with his suit-cases, unaware that he had left his favorite binoculars behind.)

But in the infinitesimally unlikely possibility that you care to hear how I've been doing for the last three weeks, I shall hunt and peck for some appropriately non-volatile words to transmit to you.

Let me first assure you (since I know you've been dis-traught with worry) that I am well. My mind is whole. My body is strong. My sudden dismissal from your life after five years of unblemished matrimony has not caused blade to hover above wrist. Writing is therapy.

A brief writer's block conquered, Pomeroy has become known hereabouts as "El Escritor," The Writer. Daily must he reject invitations to literary teas. Cruelly he refuses autographs. His muse is his only master.

I should mention before I forget. Saw a Rufous-Crested Coquette (very rare) near here yesterday. Of course it flitted off before I could find the right lens, so you'll just have to take my word. Others I have captured on Fujichrome include a family of Spectacled Foliage-Cleaners, and a solitary Scaly-Throated Leaftosser.

A shrieking flycatcher called a Yellow Tyrannulet also hangs around here — which reminds me: Ms. Abigail Hitchins. You might advise your pal I have just received her letter, wherein that Great Humourless Champion of Women's Rights proposes to take from me everything but my undershorts. I know she is your long-time bosom (silicon-enhanced, I suspect) buddy, but she also happens to be a grasping, greedy, malevolent cunt.

Let's keep the lawyers out of it.

Merry Christmas, by the way.

("How did you spend yours?" she asked with an irritating politeness.)

Alone, alone.

Until my cleaning woman came up from down the road with a gift of Christmas tamales. At which point, for some unaccountable reason, I started to cry. Señora Róbelo took a Kleenex to my nose like a child and made me blow it.

Her husband ran off with a whore and left her with ten thousand kids. Her sister died, leaving her three more. She is happy. She copes. She forgives. She doesn't run out and hire Abigail Hitchins.

Expecting not to hear from you, I remain,

Yours sincerely,
Brian.

P.S., is it fair, Caroline? One little fling with a woman I hardly knew, and I'm sent packing? She was in my writing group, as I think you know, and we had coffee after one of the readings and I got foolish and we decided to have this little one-night thing in Knot Lake. That's it. A one-night stand. Very casual acquaintance.

B.

5

The End
of Brovak

On the second Tuesday of February, Wentworth Chance arrived at the office ashen-faced and out of breath.

"John Brovak just snapped in Court 54," he announced.

The firm convened an emergency meeting in the library, where Wentworth delivered a breathless summary of Brovak's last moments before being taken to the cells. When he finished, Max Macarthur and Augustina Sage sat looking at each other in silent wonder.

"Cocaine psychosis," said Max grimly.

"Cerebral meltdown," Augustina said softly. "The Monster finally did him in."

Regina versus Watson and Twenty Others — more commonly referred to as the Monster — was a case Brovak had been fighting for half his career. Mistrials, retrials and appeals, the case sputtering, stalling, reviving itself, wheezing forward — for six years.

Over that span, attrition had reduced the ranks of the lawyers from an original high of twelve to a current low of four. Brovak, who had started with two clients, had inherited seven more from lawyers who had dropped out to preserve their marriages or their sanity.

When the appeal court ordered yet another new trial last year, the Justice Department, wearying of the battle, had wanted to halt proceedings. But Staff-Sergeant Everit Cudlipp of the RCMP insisted on one last go-round: he had smashed the West Coast's biggest cocaine ring, and he wanted satisfaction. So the Monster had commenced in September and had been plodding along before a jury at the Vancouver courthouse for the last five months.

Appointed to direct this latest rerun — it was as if a macabre joke had been played on Brovak — was Mr. Justice Leroy Lukey, newly elevated to the bench despite his failed efforts to prosecute O.D. Milsom for four serial murders. He and Brovak had been mauling each other from opening bell. Today was day eighty-eight of this sweaty match. The Hunk Meets the Hulk.

"From the top," said Max.

He and Augustina sat in morbid silence as their articling student related his story once more. Wentworth, who had been junioring His Satanic Majesty, was nervous, flustered. The mirthless expressions on his bosses' faces did little for his equanimity.

"So John was cross-examining this cop, and at some point the judge turned his back to him and said, 'You've asked that question five times.' And John said, 'Are you speaking to me or to the wall?' And then everything kind of went still. The judge just said, 'You heard me, you've asked that question five times.' And John said something like, 'I got five different answers, and at least four of them are lies.'

"And when the judge said he thought the witness was doing his best, John accused him of coddling all the cops like they were his personal troop of Girl Guides. Then he kind of muttered to us, 'Asshole flogs his meat at the sight of a uniform.'"

Augustina's dark eyes widened in alarm as she snubbed out one cigarette and lit another.

"The judge heard all the laughter and asked, 'What did you say?' and then Mr. Boynton, the prosecutor, stood up and said…'My lord, counsel made a remark in the most execrable taste.' And John turned to the prosecutor and, I don't know, it's like John just blew up, and that's when he called Mr. Boynton…" Wentworth looked through his notes. 'A dicksucking little pansy fink.'"

The judge, he recounted, leaned forward and almost screamed at Brovak: "You are in contempt!"

"And John said, ah, okay, he'll withdraw the word dicksucking because it's only hearsay."

"And then?" said Max, looking very bleak and worn.

"Well, Mr. Justice Lukey kind of half stood up, grabbed his ledger, and slammed it down on the desk, and told John to leave court. He said, and this is a quote, 'I want to see the goddamn end of you, Brovak!'" Wentworth looked up from his notes, and shrugged. "And that's when John turned around, raised his robe, and pulled down his pants." He paused and added, "Full harvest moon."

The library was plunged into silence, just the faint clicking of keyboards outside and the muffled words of a secretary urging patience upon a waiting client. Augustina seemed to be meditating. Wentworth noticed that Max Macarthur's facial muscles were becoming more and more taut.

Finally came a sound from Max, a small, choked-back "mrmph" noise. He began to struggle with himself, physically, holding his chest with his arms. Wentworth felt a wave of fear. All that long-distance running Macarthur was into, those six daily miles around Stanley Park: it was his heart.

Max's cheeks extended, then collapsed, and he expelled air with sudden unleashed energy. He leaned forward, helpless in the grip of his affliction, and emitted an uncontrollable roar of laughter.

He threw his head back, pealing, hooting, banging the table with his fists.

"Oh, shit," said Augustina Sage, her cheerless look dissolving in the face of Max's anarchic laughter. Blowing out a stream of cigarette smoke, she, too, started laughing. Infecting each other, she and Max were unable to get a grip on themselves.

Wentworth Chance, who never quite knew what to make of his bosses, was unsure just how funny this whole thing was. He tried a grin; it seemed to relax him, and he soon found himself laughing, too.

"I want to see the goddamned end of you," Max Macarthur roared with fair mimicry of Leroy Lukey.

The phone rang and Max got himself under control and picked it up.

"This is my one phone call," said Brovak. "The screws are listening on the jailhouse tap, so be careful. All right, these are your instructions. Go directly to jail. Do not pass go. Collect three thousand dollars."

"Leroy gave you bail?" Max asked.

"To be sure."

"What's the catch?"

"I am instructed that tomorrow I am to be brought before his eminence, His Lardship, the porcine prince himself, Mr. Justice Leroy Lukey, where I am to fall prostrate before him and weep for his forgiveness."

"How did you get this deal?"

"Because he knows if he throws me off the Monster I win another mistrial."

"You are going to do this?" said Max. "You are going to snivel and suck?"

Brovak responded with a tone of utter serenity. "Leroy misinterpreted how I, in my awkward way, was trying to express my feelings of admiration for him. Among the baboons of the African veldt, a baring of the buttocks is a gesture of submissiveness, of surrender to a more powerful authority. It is a gesture reflecting the esteem in which the more powerful baboon is held. I am going to explain this to Leroy."

Max was suddenly impatient. "You've pulled a lot of dumb stunts, John, but calling Boynton a suck…"

"Pansy, Max, a pansy fink."

"…that's bad enough, but John, John, mooning Lukey, why in God's name…"

"Simple. I'm gonna get thrown off this case. And that's gonna cause the Monster to miscarry again. Leroy will have buggered up his first big case as a judge. The feds don't have enough muscle in their combined dicks to get it up for a fourth run at my guys. They'll throw it in."

"And you'll be in jail," said Max.

"Aw, Leroy won't do that to me. Hell, I bent over backwards for that guy. Tell the student to get on his bike and pedal on down here with the three grand."

He disconnected. Max brushed some hairs over his bald spot. "What do we get him, a shrink, a lawyer or an exorcist?"

"How about a drug counsellor?" said Augustina.

"Okay, we can't mention the drugs," Max said, already workin up the defence. "Nervous breakdown. Caused by the pressure of practising criminal law after an assassin almost murdered his partner."

As Max and Augustina discussed retaining a doctor to testify for Brovak, Wentworth Chance went to his telephone booth — a tiny office he shared with the copying machine — and did a Clark Kent from shirt and tie to cape and rain jacket, then hurried from the office with a cheque for three thousand dollars.

When bicycling to the courthouse, Wentworth usually avoided the long diagonal across the parking lot where Arthur P. Besterman had been murdered last summer, half a block from the offices of Pomeroy, Macarthur. But this afternoon he was in a hurry and cut across it, past the spot where the body was found. He felt an extra chill, cutting more keenly through him than the February rain.

6

The Parlour
of Love

Soon after Wentworth Chance handed over the bail moneys to a clerk at the courthouse, Brovak was brought up from the cells carrying his shoelaces and buckling his belt.

"They wouldn't let me kill myself. Oh, well, think I'll go out and get laid."

He disappeared into a taxi, and Wentworth bought a $2.49 special, soup and sandwich, in a nearby greasery, then pedaled off toward the Granville Bridge. He had a date with a client, the beauteous Minette Lefleur. His first big case.

He had waited a long time for this one. Seven months in the trenches with jaywalkers and runners of traffic lights and juvenile candy bar thieves. But a few days ago he got Minette Lefleur. She was an alleged keeper of a houseboat of prostitution — tied up at Granville Island, below the downtown area. She ran an escort service from there, and advertised it in the classifieds.

Wentworth had met her a few days ago in Brovak's office. She was young, maybe Wentworth's age, and looked stunning in red lips and red mini. Brovak had introduced Wentworth as his brilliant associate.

"Minette has been falsely accused of being a whore," Brovak said. "Debrief her."

"Debrief her," Wentworth repeated, staring at her, only dimly registering the command.

"Get the whole story, witnesses' names, her personal history, what she said to the pigs, everything."

Lefleur looked Wentworth over doubtfully, and turned to Brovak. "But *you* are going to handle the case."

"Yeah, eventually, but I'm up to here now. Wentworth's a specialist in your type of situation. We'll need a five thousand retainer by next week."

She opened her purse and paid it in large bills.

"Business must be booming," Brovak said.

"I have a very good defence," she said.

Brovak drew Wentworth into the corridor. "She's dead on the facts. You may have to cop her out."

The facts, earlier conveyed to Brovak by the prosecutor's office, had an undercover cop answering her advertisement, attending at her floating boudoir, and being offered oral stimulation of the penis for three hundred dollars. Which was more than six monthly payments on Wentworth's Outback 310 twenty-one-speed bicycle.

She wouldn't tell him right away what her very good defence was, but wanted him to visit the scene of the crime. With throbbing heart in throbbing throat, he was on his way to debrief this sinful siren in her floating bawdy house.

Pedalling by the trendy metal storefronts of Granville Island, past the public market, over bumpy cobbles, Wentworth found the waterfront and a neighbourhood of houseboats. Minette Lefleur greeted him at the door in a thigh-high peignoir, her hair wet. She said she had to dress soon to meet a Japanese businessman for dinner.

Wentworth sneaked a nervous peek at the curve of a leg. He felt a little wobbly in the knees, but decided it was the gently rocking houseboat. The place was dangerously cozy, the furnishings and decor unerringly tasteful. Lazy Matisse nudes on the wall. On the table, a pile of glossy slicks, magazines called *Allure*, *Shape*, *Glamour*, *Flare*.

"What's your very good defence?" Wentworth asked.

She gestured toward the bedroom door. "Come into my parlour of love."

Wentworth gulped. He felt his testosterone start to simmer and bubble. He feared her wicked smile.

✝ ✝ ✝

Augustina Sage returned to the office late that day after an afternoon in pre-trial discovery. The case involved the rector of a boarding school for native boys, Rev. Arnold S. Doyle, and his roster of victims and his portfolio of crimes: verbal, physical and sexual abuse of the eighteen clients who had dared to come forward. Two hundred thousand dollars for each; she wouldn't settle for less.

Perspiration had eaten through her roll-on; her armpits were just a little clammy, and scented with tired body flavour. She decided to do a stint in the recovery room, the office steam sauna. A showering away of Father Doyle, and of his almost equally offensive lawyer, Martin Wessel.

The office staff had gone; and it looked as though the lawyers had fled, too. Just as well, she didn't need any more heavy male energy. When Augustina had joined the firm then known as Pomeroy, Marx, Macarthur and Brovak, seduced (literally) by John Brovak from her legal aid clinic, she'd had a friendly female ear to talk to and a shoulder to cry on. She missed Sophie Marx so much. She'd been like a den mother. Now Sophie was two years gone to the provincial bench.

Augustina mostly did the civil side now. She had stopped doing much criminal work after a bizarre romance, a farcical infatuation, really, with an Errol Flynnish robber of banks.

God in Her wisdom had made Augustina, endowed with good taste in all things else, a poor connoisseur of men. John Brovak. Sweet lord. That had lasted all of five weeks. Then that doctor from the abortion clinic: all hands no heart no brain no soul. And she should have reported him for sexual abuse of patients. For some reason, Augustina was attracted to men like that. Men with handsome outer packaging but either crazy like Brovak or empty inside of all but muscle-preening male vanity.

But let's face it, there's not much out there. Or they're all taken, or hiding in a cave somewhere. Wanted: sensitive, fun-loving male person who isn't suffering from (a) delusions of grandeur, (b) anxiety neurosis, or (c) identity crisis, and who doesn't look like a warthog.

Augustina was thirty-five. A spinster — why was that word so hopelessly depressing? Men get to be bachelors, why couldn't she?

She turned the steam timer on. Converted from a dry sauna, the recovery room was a minor indulgence the firm had granted itself: a reward for Max Macarthur's runs to Stanley Park and back, Brovak's hangover sanitarium.

On her way to her office, where she kept a change of clothes, Augustina passed by the library and saw a light under the door. When opened, it revealed Wentworth Chance, glassy eyes peering above a stack of books.

"How boring, Wentworth. Life is too short."

"You seen John? I have to talk to him."

She shook her head. "Come and have a steam."

"Uh, I don't know."

"I may need you to scrub my back."

Wentworth blushed purple. She took him by his collar and playfully pulled him, unresisting, to his feet.

"You can wear a towel."

Modestly, he did. But sybaritic Augustina, who loved the sense of her pores opening to the hot mist, sat naked in the billowing, hissing steam. Wentworth lay prone on a bench with his eyes closed, not daring to look at her.

"What do you do for fun, Wentworth? You *do* have a life away from the office?"

"Don't get out much. A movie costs a half a day's wages."

"Got a girlfriend?"

"Who's got time for girls?" He paused. "I think I'm off sex for life."

"Sounds traumatic."

"You wouldn't believe."

He didn't explain.

Soon after getting sprung from the courthouse lock-up, John Brovak happened upon a too-hip tourist from Holland in a happy hour bar. Everything about her said she was in the trade — the gold, the argot, the sweet odour of danger. She had acid, and Brovak decided what the hell. They dropped a couple of dots each and, with Brovak clinging zombie-eyed to the steering wheel of his Mercedes SL coupe, they sped laughing through the electric garish forest of Stanley Park, over twisty, wobbly Lion's Gate Bridge, up the tree-clawed heights of Hollyburn to the Ridge, where they had clumsy, psychedelic sex in Brovak's hot tub.

The next morning he found she had slipped away, but not before boosting three hundred dollars from his wallet. He was disappointed in her and decided not to try to look her up again.

Why couldn't he ever meet anyone...just nice? Despite being in his thirty-eighth year, Brovak had never known the rapture and the pain of love, was still a virgin of the heart, and it worried him that he might forever be. What *about* love? What does it feel like?

Well, he would be off women for a while. During his vacation in the slammer. This was Day Eighty-Nine of the sixth annual production of Regina versus Watson and Twenty Others, the Monster, the Rocky Horror Trial. Closing performance.

Not wanting to leave his car downtown while he was in jail, he called Twelve-Fingers Watson, who came by in his Range Rover, and they headed off to court. A cold day, the rain like frozen slush, the skies a monotony of grey — the eternal damp of a Wet Coast winter. It makes people suicidal, thought Brovak. *He* was suicidal. Leroy Lukecidal. Well, Leroy can stick it where the sun don't shine.

From the passenger window, he looked north to where the mountains should have been. They must be hidden behind that grey curtain. People were skiing up there in the soft, falling snow. Brovak should be skiing. Brovak should not lose an excellent day of trackless snow to face a bum rap.

Watson snuffed up some blow from the back of one of his six-fingered hands — two extra little nubbins, with one knuckle each — and asked Brovak if he wanted a little. Brovak declined.

Watson looked shocked. "You okay?"

"Yeah, I'm deliriously okay."

"You need any protection, you know...in there, I can look after it." Watson had friends in there. *In there* meant prison. Watson didn't like to use the word, knowing it made his lawyer feel bad.

"Don't know why I'm doing this for you guys," Brovak mumbled.

"Thought you were doin' it for the hundred grand."

That was the deal. A big bonus if Watson got off. Let his partners continue to think he was loony until he lays out a hundred big ones upon the boardroom table.

The deal wasn't in writing, but Watson was one of those rare entities, an honourable dealer of Bolivian whiff. Anyway, Brovak held security: title deeds to Watson's finca in Costa Rica, current home of his bird-watching partner Brian Pomeroy.

Watson was this town's big actor when it came to cocaine, and though he also handled a full line of cannabis products, plus ludes, drivers, lid poppers, nebbies and downs, he didn't deal in tragic magic. The smack business was run out of the East End by Tony d'Anglio's people, an old-style mob with a lot more muscle. They were also starting to move a fair bit of coke, to Watson's distress.

While Watson sought a place to park, Brovak sloshed up the steps to the cantilevered courthouse, all concrete and glass, aluminum tubing, and computer-watered plants, along with several dozen court-rooms done up in red and beige and human sweat.

The one thing Brovak would miss during his bit in the jug (a couple of weeks, a month? — he needed the rest), would be the Leroy Lukey party two weekends hence. Leroy's roast by the East Side Bar, in honour of his disappointment to the bench last year. Brovak liked these drunkaramas, and was usually one of the last standing at the end.

He would have enjoyed blowing an obese joint of Cambodian flower before the show, then getting into the whole Caesarian spectacle, maybe offering his own little toast to Lukey in recognition of his Lordship's sadistic excesses in the courtroom. But he would be denied the pleasure of making this toast, because he was now toast himself, toast and peanut butter jam which he would soon be enjoying for breakfast in the joint.

Staff-Sergeant Everit Cudlipp advanced upon him as he entered the courthouse.

"You trying to gum up the system again, Brovak?"

Cudlipp was tall and fit but big in the kitchen, his upper lip decorated by a trim, clipped moustache. He had spent six months preparing a case that had so far taken six years to prosecute, and so was cynical about due process.

"You want to get thrown in jail for these pissers? You love them so much? Or is it all the free coke?"

"I took the taste test, switched to Pepsi." Striding to the barristers' room, Brovak tried to ignore him, but Cudlipp stayed in lock-step.

"If you think you're going to try to mistrial us again, smartass, think again. Leroy is gonna bury 'em all. Watson — he's goin' down for the big one, life."

"I take it you've discussed this with His Lordship."

"Just take it I know. Nobody is walking."

Upon hearing the ring of absolute assurance in Cudlipp's voice, Brovak stopped and scowled at him. But the sergeant smiled and carried on down the corridor. A badly bent cop. He should dig a little more into his past. And Cudlipp and Lukey probably *had* got next to each other over this one. They were tight. Trout-fishing buddies.

Brovak went into the changing room. Black robes for the Spanish Inquisition. He paused, then searched his pockets, bringing out a little packet and snorting some of its contents. He wasn't going to, but he did. He needed euphoria. Cudlipp had upset him.

Court 54 was jammed when he got there: including about twenty lawyers taking time off to witness the Ayatollah ordering the infidel stoned to death. It was the way Brovak wanted to go. Stoned.

He was pleased to see that his partners had obeyed his dictum not to show up. Max had pleaded with him on the telephone last night, but Brovak had declined his services. No, Brian Pomeroy's brush with death had not rendered Brovak temporarily insane. He hadn't had a nervous breakdown. Sorry, pal, he wouldn't know what one even looked like. Nor had he been bending over to retrieve the trousers the belt of which he had embarrassingly forgot to buckle.

So, when court opened, the office was represented solely by Wentworth Chance, who Brovak noticed appeared a little more wan and sleepless today than usual.

Leroy Lukey carried his two hundred and sixty pounds up the stairs to the judge's bench and, in an oddly pleasant voice, said, "Where are we now?"

Prosecutor Jack Boynton was conferring in whispers with Sergeant Cudlipp at the Crown counsel table. He looked up. "Sir?"

"Should we have the jury in?"

Boynton looked flustered. "With respect, ah, isn't there an issue left over from yesterday?"

"Oh, Mr. Brovak," said the judge. "Of course."

Brovak doodled on his pad. Here was Lukey, he observed, pretending the incident had hardly fazed him. A little matter left over from yesterday's business.

"Mr. Brovak," said the judge.

Brovak took an eternity to stand. "M'lord."

"I'm not going to cite you for contempt."

Brovak thought about that for a second. "Very kind of you, m'lord."

"Normally, I'd accommodate you. A term of three months would be about right, but that would cause another mistrial, wouldn't it? It would leave your eight people unrepresented, and we'd never find another lawyer on short notice."

"Pretty well impossible, I agree, m'lord."

The civility of Brovak's tone finally seemed to grate on Lukey, whose voice acquired an edge.

"You're not off the hook, Brovak. The Benchers will decide after this trial is over whether you will ever be allowed to practise law again. I am instructing Mr. Boynton to prepare a report for them."

Brovak looked across at the man he had called a dicksucking pansy, and smiled with affection. "I know Mr. Boynton will try to be fair," he said.

"But in the meantime we will finish this trial," said Lukey. "It is going to proceed. To a conclusion."

Brovak looked across to Staff-Sergeant Cudlipp, who met his eyes without expression.

"Bring the jury in," said the judge.

Brovak sighed and slid back onto his chair and leaned toward Wentworth Chance. "The fix is in," he said. "They're gonna kangaroo us."

"When you have a minute, can we talk?" asked Wentworth.

"You look a little tormented, kid, what's up?"

7

The Seeker
of the Green Flash

February 22

Dear Ms. Hitchins,
            <u>Re: Pomeroy v. Pomeroy</u>

In answer to your telegram, I thank you for your advice
that I not further correspond with my wife. No, I certainly
would not wish to exacerbate the situation.

But I regret that I can neither accept service by mail
of your petition for divorce nor instruct anyone else to do so
for me. With respect to any legal documents that must be
personally served, may I cordially suggest you personally
serve same by sticking them up your ass.

Yours very truly,
Brian W. Pomeroy, Esq.

✠ ✠ ✠

February 23

Dear fellow earthlings,

It is now seven p.m. Paradise Standard Time, the vesper hour, when the nightjars begin to whoop, and the Common Potoo chants her haunting, wailing dirge. The sun is just bailing out for the day, purpling the clouds, flattening like a tired testicle against the ocean.

I wait for the green flash which aficionados of sunsets often claim they see. I have never seen the green flash. I want to believe in the green flash.

And again the light blips out with no green flash.

Is it myth?

I have just lit the coal oil lamp. It gets dark in an instant here. Often I work on my novel into the night, beneath a turmoil of moths. At night, frankly, it gets lonely here, and for fear my thoughts will wander north to cold, cruel Canada I plunge into my world of fiction, my array of twisted odd-ball characters, my serpentine plot that extends its octopean tentacles to too many different compass points. Not enough suspects, so I must devise a few more treacherous dastards and give them motive. ("The author," says Mr. Widgeon, "must offer an array of suspects, and dress them up with strong motive — or at least clothe them with the proper accoutrements of suspicion.")

Sadly, I can't think of very many motives for wanting to kill a lawyer. So my array of suspects will comprise mostly brainless zoids and goops.

By the way, your letter was just received, Max, and thank you for that delightful attempt to send me up with your story about Brovo giving His Lordship the moon. Nice try. I know you guys sit around over your end-of-the-day beers and concoct poppycock, with the idea of taking the mickey out of this guileless, simple-minded beach bum.

Tell me it's not true.

But your story, Max, about Brovak and Lukey — apocryphal though it sounds — has served to feed the hungry dogs of inspiration: why not add such a judge to the wicked cast?

But what murderous motive could so blacken the heart of such a respected jurist? A full moon at counsel table seems an insufficient incitement to kill.

I have it! Yes, after my Brovakian character is offed, I shall point a finger (more accurately, sphincter) of suspicion at a Lukey-like judge who becomes twisted up inside at the sight of those hairy, masculine buttocks and murders Brovak in order to deny his infatuation with them.

But perhaps I should seek a more sombre tone. Avoid excessive levity, says the author of *The Art of the Whodunit*: "Humour has its place in mystery novels in the same way in which a well-mannered child has his place in the home: unobtrusive, but permitted an occasional giggle." (Widgeon's own novels follow that precept, though I find his humour a wee vapid.)

Life remains placid here. No electrifying events beyond the occasional sensarama thunderstorm far out at sea. Well, one electrifying event. The episode outside the church when the girl next door, divine Leticia, took my arm...

While I have you at my mercy, let me escort you to town, a thrice-weekly excursion I make for my health and to get the mail. Puerto Próspero is what passes for civilization in this hidden back pocket of our stricken planet. It is five miles up a jeep road from Watson's villa, along the coast behind the almond trees.

Próspero is famed only for being the starting point of the old Back-Packing Gringo Trail into the Corcovada. Ecotourism. It's in. The jungle as zoo. Many of these pilgrims in search of our vanishing wilderness pause in town, and put up at Hotel El Grande (four dollars a room, sharing) or, changing their minds when shown the room, string up tents by the beach.

Located in Puerto Próspero are, in addition to the hotel, one school, one bank, one not-so-supermarket, one whore-house, fifteen bars, and the local chapter of Alcoholics Anonymous.

Affordable drinking is the major entertainment in this town, which unfortunately lacks the usual diversions, such as art galleries, opera houses, and hockey arenas. The cream of local society, however, assembles at Horvath's Bar. This picturesque little establishment, set on piles by the edge of a mangrove swamp, is famous for the odour which comes from the emptying of fecal matter from the toilet above. This, in combination with other offal things deposited there, creates hydrogen sulfide gases.

These combine (to delight the connoisseurs of effluvium) with the smells of stale piss, beer and smoke, plus the particularly pungent aromas of Horvath himself. He is a refugee from the former Communist government of Hungary and hasn't heard that the Cold War is over. Horvath, who is about 70, wanders around the bar with giant folds of fat hanging over his filthy shorts and complains about the commie squatters. (Costa Rica has this odd law: you squat in somebody's yard long enough, you get to keep it.)

There is also, to be fair to Puerto Próspero, one church here but, alas, it's poorly attended. Not that there aren't believers. Señora Róbelo regularly leads her undisciplined mob, dressed in their Sunday best, the eight clicks to town for early mass. I went with them to the church once (I did, after all, grow up as a casually High Anglican and still enjoy the ornaments of ceremony) and relished the exquisite, almost spiritually erotic thrill of Leticia Róbelo putting her arm in mine as I led her mother and the rest of the brood out the door.

Leticia is a pious young woman, yet spirited, a kind of Brontë heroine. Quite tough-minded and picky, though: she has tried and discarded various young suitors, and remains the only nineteen-year-old virgin in Costa Rica. We feel intense affection, but it is as with little sister and big brother.

Her real brother, Léo, is my new chopper. This is a Spanglish word. No, Léo is not a motorcycle or a helicopter (more on that later); he is a weed eater. How grass gets cut hereabouts is simple: a guy walks around with a machete and swacks it.

As to the other sort of chopper, I am often driven to

wonder if some sort of air traffic control system might not
be useful in this area. Almost every night my blissful solitude
is impaired by their clatter as they pass by, usually a distance
out to sea.

It is my suspicion they are up to no good. Evidence: (1)
Several big movers like Twelve-Fingers Watson have also
bought properties near here. (2) Panama is only ten minutes
away by air. (3) Panama is where the major dope comes from
these days. (4) There are a lot of flat and empty beaches
around here.

It is all fuel, I suppose, for the muse. I am importing a
little Colombian coke into my story.

To the point of this windy letter (all of the above is
not merely avoidance, but also a summoning of strength):
Caroline.

Again I broke into tears last week. It was when Theresa
Róbelo, aged eight, came to my house with a gimpy-legged
Red-Legged Honeycreeper. I rigged up a little splint with her,
and as I was doing so — feeling quite okay, thank you — this
incredibly unwilled water started to flow from my eyes.

Now, this has happened several times, twice in public,
and is becoming embarrassing, and it's all Caroline's fault.

Having won the big one, having sprung the Kitswuk
Five, and in as merry a mood as can be, I was greeted at
home with all the courtesy due a bag of last week's garbage.
In reaction, I made ONE mistake. I took a young woman
I barely knew to Knot Lake. Nothing between us. I never
planned to see her again. Research, that's all it was: a writer
must endure life's excesses to bring them alive on his pages.

Caroline's reaction: she pulls the tantrum of tantrums,
sends me bag and baggage from the matrimonial home, hires
a lawyer, and sues for divorce.

Now I ask you: is that not over-reaction?

I cry. Because like Theresa's Red-Legged Honeycreeper, I
am wounded.

Max, Augie, one of you: tell Abigail Hitchins I regret the
impolite tone of the letter I sent her. Tell her some carefully
worded lie about how much I truly respect her. Tell her

there's no need for court action; I'll give Caroline everything anyway, even the binoculars. In exchange for one thing: a chance to talk to her. Twenty minutes of open mind and undivided attention.

I am prepared to forgive.

Yours, etc.
El Escritor.

8

Angels in
White Berets

"The ignominy, the shame," Brovak bellowed at Max Macarthur upon learning he'd accepted the retainer of the Attorney General. "That the noble house of Pomeroy Macarthur would stoop so low — that my partner can be bought with the Queen's coin to do the dirty work of sending her citizens to jail…"

"This is O.D. Milsom we're talking about," Max said.

"Goddammit Max — we have a devoted clientele. They trust us; we've *never* sold out to the other side."

Augustina declared herself for Max. "We're dealing with a serial killer here."

"I talked it over with Ruth," Max said. "She said to do it."

"Or what, she's gonna cut you off?" Brovak roared: "You little pussywimp…"

Max broke in, trying to head off the tirade. "Look, Brovak, your pal Lukey blew it when he prosecuted this thing, and I'm going to repair the damage. I'm going to save the lives of certain women in this community who aren't keen on finding a slavering sicko in their bedroom with a knife. Okay?"

But why did he feel something akin to a fall from grace? Many times he had been asked to take on a prosecution, and each time had stoutly refused. He was a civil libertarian, the feisty little guy against the system — he'd made his name that way.

"I'm just going to do this one little appeal for them."

"I say it's the thin end of the wedge," said Brovak, "and next you're gonna be taking trials for them, yeah, prosecute a few helpless kleptos and junkies. Maybe it'll get you off, sending guys to the can. It's the road to a judgeship, ain't it, Augie? He's a power-hungry hack, it's been in his genes all the time."

He clapped a sarcastic hand on Max's shoulder. "Yes, sir, m'lord Chief Justice Max Macarthur the third, scion of three generations of judges. Your old man finally got to you, eh?"

"I am *not* interested in being a goddamn judge," Max shouted. Brovak had hit a tender spot. That *had* been his father's route — defend a little, prosecute a little, show you can play both offence and defence, then quickly up the ladder to the top. Not for Max. No way.

Augustina gave Max a little hug. "You nail that Milsom creep, okay?"

"Course he will, Augie. Why do you think they picked Max for this hatchet job? His dad is Chief of the Court of Appeal, how can his brethren say no to his ambitious son?"

The files that were delivered to the office included a curious account of O.D. Milsom's arrest by Roger Turnbull, who was well known to Max; a thirty-five-year-old lay gospeller whose former employment involved curb-selling used cars. He was now a crime-fighter, leader of a group of devotees called White Angels — all wore white berets.

They were young men, athletic: Turnbull himself was tall and lithe, though portly. The Angels patrolled the downtown streets in squadrons of three or four, seeking muggers and drug traffickers and perverts.

A year ago last November, following three random stabbings of Vancouver women, Turnbull publicly pledged to bring their murderer to justice. Four days later, he did so.

Turnbull and two colleagues had been enjoying tomato juices in a neighbourhood pub when, at final call, a young woman left a table of friends and headed for the door. The man who turned out to be O.D. Milsom was slowly walking up behind her in the parking lot when

Turnbull and his two comrades pounced on him, pinned him, and searched him for weapons. They found none. But Turnbull threatened Milsom with the forcible removal of both testicles unless he confessed to the three murders, and Milsom promptly did so.

The police were called. O.D. Milsom confessed to them as well, and was charged with three murders in the first degree. Single, on social assistance, possessed of an I.Q. of 83, he lived in a small rented room, a search of which turned up several newspaper headlines about the murders, clipped out and hidden in a cardboard box.

At the subsequent press briefing Turnbull recounted how he deduced the killer's modus operandi. All three of the women had been known to have been drinking beforehand, as singles in public bars. Turnbull guessed the killer selected his victims in these bars.

When Milsom's confession was ruled inadmissible and the case for the state fell apart, Turnbull stormed out of court berating the legal system. So when Milsom's lawyer, Arthur P. Besterman, was bludgeoned to death behind his office, suspicion fell on the leader of the White Angels. But his comrades vowed that at the time he had been in his barracks, as they called their downtown quarters. No bloodied clothing was found there.

In the meantime, Milsom had vanished into the void. Police and social welfare agencies had been alerted to watch for him but he hadn't surfaced, though it was known he had bought a bus ticket for Toronto.

Turnbull was obsessed with overturning Milsom's acquittal, and so part of the baggage that arrived at Max's office with the Milsom appeal was Mr. Turnbull himself.

He would be in the office when it opened. "Mind if I ask, my friend: is the appeal court going to convict him or just order a retrial?"

He would be in the office when it closed. "And how is my friend Max Macarthur today? Max, I've another idea about how he got rid of the knife."

He would phone. "The fact that Milsom has disappeared off the face of the earth means something, doesn't it? If he was innocent, he'd show his face. You'll explain that to the court?"

Max would tell him, "The court can't convict anyone, and can only order a new trial. The appeal doesn't ride on how Milsom got rid of the knife. The fact that Milsom was free and no other women had been attacked would argue in his *favour.*"

Turnbull gave Max an acid stomach: his gotch-eyed look — those protruding, intense eyes — and his saccharine third-person manner of greeting him. ("And how is my friend Max, tonight?" "A little sick in the gut, Roger.") Moreover, he couldn't get rid of the thought that Turnbull may have wielded the bat that beat out the brains of Arthur Besterman.

He knew, from talking to the detectives in charge of the Besterman case, that the file on Turnbull had not been closed. But if he was a murderer, he was acting strangely: instead of retreating into the woodwork, away from the glare of suspicion, he was out front and centre, openly consumed with Milsom's appeal. But maybe that hinted he *was* the assailant. The Raskolnikov effect, a man fascinated by his own crime...

When the appeal opened on Wednesday, February 24, Turnbull was waiting for him at the courthouse along with big Jack Calico, his second-in-command, an iron-pumping gargoyle on steroids.

"And how is Max today?"

He didn't respond.

"So, Max — what should I be saying in court?"

"You are to say nothing."

Turnbull seemed taken aback.

"But Max, hey, I've got to explain that that trial was a complete farce."

"Look, Roger, I have work to do. Get off my case. Literally."

Turnbull turned unfriendly, and fixed Max with his big buggy eyes, and growled: "Know what I think? I think lawyers administer their own so-called justice, not God's." Then he added: "There'll be quite a few people watching you in there today."

Max picked up a note of menace. "If you're making some kind of threat..."

Turnbull switched modes, took Max's elbow in a friendly salesman's grip. "Oh, gosh, no, I only mean it's...a great chance for you, Max, wonderful chance."

Max told him if he opened his mouth once in court he would put a bag over his head.

The absent Milsom was represented by his court-appointed counsel, a semi-retired lawyer who, though courageously filling a dead man's shoes, was not much of a cut above Besterman in ability and who impressed Max as not giving a damn whether he won or lost.

This meant, however, that Max Macarthur would have to work even harder. An idealist, he held to the canon that Crown counsel must be unimpassioned, scrupulous and fair, must ensure that the appellant receives his day in court — despite his lack of vigorous representation.

Max had drawn a good coram, three pleasant judges whose experience was mostly on the civil side and who didn't know much about criminal law, and who were notoriously skeptical about criminals being allowed to hide behind rules of evidence. Odd how the same three judges seem so admirable when you're prosecuting, and so obstinately wrong-headed when you're on the other side.

Max's most formidable argument, though he would have to couch it carefully because it was irrelevant, was that Milsom's confession could not have been fabricated. He remembered too much; he had given reasonably accurate descriptions of the women he had killed, of the two apartments he had entered. Though he could have gleaned much of this from the media, he simply could not have known — if he were innocent — two inconsequential items of data the media hadn't been told about: the pair of caged lovebirds in one victim's bedroom, the Rolling Stones album that had been playing in another's suite, appropriately if gruesomely titled, *Let It Bleed*. Without prompting, Milsom had recalled these details.

"As your lordships well know," Max began, "the rule that confessions are inadmissible if obtained through threats is subject to a proviso: the threats must have been made by a person in authority. Mr. Turnbull and his friends, though acting like officers of the law, held no more authority than a self-appointed posse on the Western frontier."

The senior judge smiled and turned to one of his point men, and they shared a whispered joke. This was going well already, thought Max.

He had all but completed his argument by the end of the first day, and after court recessed he glanced behind him. There they were, Turnbull and Calico, sitting on the back bench. He waved Inspector Nordquist over, the stoic, droopy-eyed chief bloodhound from homicide.

A tall, spare man, almost skeletal — his friends called him "Bones" — Lars Nordquist was Max's favourite cop. In his late fifties, he was of the old breed, formal in manner and expression, gentlemanly. Max looked over at the Angels filing out.

"What's with these dumbos?" Max said.

"They watch too many police shows. They think it's fun being a policeman."

"Do you think Turnbull bopped Besterman? Him or one of his goons?"

"Make out a case for me."

Max mused, then said, "Where was he last December fifteenth?"

Nordquist looked blank.

"The day somebody took a shot at my partner."

"Oh, yes, Brian Pomeroy." Nordquist smiled his gloomiest smile. "Your partners keep getting caught with their pants down, don't they? Why Pomeroy?"

"I don't know, Bones, there's just something too weird about Roger Turnbull. I just wonder if he's not on some spiritual crusade against lawyers. Maybe he thinks he's been appointed as God's little helper."

"Max, I think you've been working too hard."

9

Bent
Copper

Day One Hundred and One. Brovak felt himself being slowly devoured by the Monster, limb by limb, his bones ground to dust in its teeth. What made it worse was that Mr. Justice Lukey no longer seemed to rise to his bait. For the two weeks since his failed attempt at being cited for contempt, the judge had treated him with utter sang-froid, ignoring his taunts and giving a civil hearing to all his objections, even allowing some minor ones.

Brovak assumed Lukey wasn't going to make him the gift of any grounds of appeal. At the end of the trial, he obviously intended to coach the jury into convicting.

Watson and Twenty Others were not the only conspirators in this courtroom. The true conspiracy, one which made the trial a sham, had been hatched between Lukey and his buddy Staff-Sergeant Cudlipp: a quiet little understanding that no smuggler shall go free.

If only Brovak could pull something out of his ass and rearrange this stacked deck.

Cudlipp himself was on the stand today, and Brovak was armed. In the meantime, he listened with acute discomfort as one of his fellow counsel, Wayne Buruda, a long-haired Legal Aid lawyer, made a rambling, incoherent submission about some point of evidence.

"You lost me again, Mr. Buruda," said Lukey amiably. "Try again."

Brovak wondered: would he be so unflappable at his roast tonight?

Buruda abandoned an argument he himself didn't understand, sat, and rendered Cudlipp to Brovak's tender mercies.

He rose wearily from his table, and strolled to a position near the jurors. He liked to be close to them.

"Now, you're telling us that my client, Mr. Watson over there, made some statements to you."

"Yes, sir, that was my testimony."

"You're telling us he admitted to operating this small plane that was found on that airstrip."

"Yes. The aircraft from which we subsequently confiscated 309 kilograms of cocaine."

"Uh-huh. And yet you can't trace its ownership."

"All I can say is we believe the proprietor is a dummy company out of Panama."

"And this little talk you say you had with Mr. Watson — it took place after you called him over to your car?"

"Yes, sir."

"And of course there were no witnesses to this conversation."

"I believe surveillance members were attending."

"Couldn't hear what you were saying."

A hesitation. "I don't suppose so, no."

"So just out of the blue he says he owns the plane."

"I proceeded to ask him, and he said yes."

"You expect this jury to believe that?"

Jack Boynton jumped to his feet. "That's argumentative."

"Continue, Mr. Brovak," said Lukey.

"You make a note of his words?"

"Afterwards, yes."

"*Two* days after, according to your notebook."

Another pause. Cudlipp frowned. "Um, yes, affirmative on that."

"Kind of an afterthought, wasn't it? Too unimportant to jot down at the time. This little admission that magically keeps the whole Crown case from falling apart."

"My lord — " Boynton began.

"I wouldn't wish to offend Mr. Brovak by directing his attention to the rules of cross-examination," said the judge. "Proceed, counsel."

"Why, thank you, m'lord. Nice to see us all in a good mood this afternoon."

Brovak looked around at the people in the gallery. There was his number one fan, Joe Ruff, sitting near the front with his encouraging smile. The guy was always in court: tall, portly, about fifty, somewhat graceless in his movements. Ruff had no law degree but affected the manner of a barrister — three-piece suit and bulging briefcase. A kind of trial-lawyer groupie. He especially revered the lawyers from the firm of Pomeroy Macarthur.

Brovak returned to Cudlipp. "Well, staff-sergeant, I want to suggest you fabricated this evidence."

"Excuse me, counsel, is that a question?" Cudlipp said.

"No, it's a statement of fact."

"If it please your lordship, this type of — "

"Please sit down, Mr. Boynton," Lukey said.

"Now, I'm going to give you this chance, sergeant, to admit you spoke a little white lie about this so-called conversation with Mr. Watson, and then I won't carry it any further than that. Fair?"

"I don't commit perjury that easily, Mr. Brovak."

"No, I know. You usually put some real effort in it."

Boynton was up again, "If your lordship *please* —"

"What's with this constant knee-jerk reaction?" Brovak complained. "My learned friend got a nervous disorder?"

"Let him go on with his business, Mr. Boynton. The sooner we get done."

"Ever give evidence before the police commission?" Brovak asked the sergeant.

Cudlipp's expression went blank, unreadable. After all those dress rehearsals — three previous trials and a preliminary hearing — here was something new being dredged up by Brovak.

"I have, yes."

"Back about fifteen years ago when you were charged with stealing some heroin from the RCMP exhibit locker, correct?"

"That was…incidental to an undercover investigation."

"Yeah that's what you told the police commission when they were investigating you — "

Cudlipp interrupted. "I was cleared."

"— but no one else supported you."

"I was cleared."

"And then there were those charges of taking bribes from Dr. Au P'ang Wei, who just happened to be one of the biggest heroin pushers in North America — "

"All part of the same hearing. I gave evidence that I was running an undercover sting against that individual."

"Yes, God forbid you'd lie to save your skin."

"It was all a mistake." Cudlipp tried to puff himself up a little. "I've since been made staff-sergeant."

Brovak strolled back to the table, and riffled through some files. Cudlipp stared at them, his face now clouded and hard.

"Let's see…" said Brovak. "And then five years ago, here it is…there was another complaint about you made to the police commission."

"I don't know what you're in possession of," Cudlipp said.

"Ah, just some stuff I got under the Freedom of Information Act. Says here: complaint of beating up on a citizen."

"Again I was exonerated. That was a matter of self-defence."

"Yeah, some sick, puking junkie you said jumped you in an alley."

"In all fairness, my lord," said Boynton, rising once again, "how can he be allowed to bait the witness this way?"

"My temper *is* getting close to the edge," said Mr. Justice Lukey. "What does this have to do with anything that is before the court, counsel?"

"Goes to his credibility. I am attempting to show he is a liar. Now, the court can stop me — "

"Proceed," Lukey said brusquely.

Brovak picked up another file. "Two years ago, *after* you were made staff-sergeant, yet another complaint, this one to do with some missing exhibit money."

"I borrowed that for an on-going investigation, then proceeded to replace it."

"After someone raised the alarm, right? And again you went before the police commission. Reprimand this time."

"Yes," Cudlipp said weakly.

"Commission didn't believe your evidence."

"Uh…maybe some of it."

"Given under oath, after you swore on the Bible just as you did here today...They decided you lied on the witness stand."

"They...well, that's a matter of opinion, sir. They obviously didn't regard it as very serious."

"Not serious, eh? Guess it comes down to this: you perjure yourself whenever it suits you." Brovak watched Boynton once more do his jack-in-the-box number, and then sat before he could open his mouth. "Thank you. No more questions."

Lukey addressed the jury, offering an attempt at a smile. "Ladies and gentlemen, I think we'll retire now for the day. A little occasion tonight demands my presence, and I have to prepare a few words for it."

After dismissing them, he switched off the smile. "Mr. Brovak, your insolent manner of cross-examination will not go unregarded. I will be asking Mr. Boynton to make comment on it in his report to the Benchers."

"I would appreciate that, my lord," said Brovak. "Very important cross-examination."

The judge paused as if he wished the last word, then gathered his robes and marched from the bench.

The defendants and audience all filed out, while Brovak remained at the counsel table, enjoying the look of discomfiture on Cudlipp's face as he conferred with Boynton in a corner.

The pretend lawyer, Joe Ruff, slung his briefcase onto the counsel table, and sat beside him. "Brilliant, old boy, absolutely brilliant." Ruff had learned the speech mannerisms of an English toff at a Vancouver Island boarding school.

"Why, thank you, Joe."

"Freedom of Information Act. I use it myself, what? Involves a cracking lot of paper, but it's worth it."

Though not a lawyer, Ruff was always suing somebody: neighbours for slander, public servants for negligence, the civic government for cracks in the sidewalk. A litigious neurotic, he defended his own parking and jaywalking tickets with a tenacious vigor, and lower court judges lived in fear of him.

As Brovak was gathering his files, a note fluttered from one of them. Ruff picked it up, looked at it and frowned.

"Besterman?" he said.

"Besterman…" Brovak hadn't remembered looking at this note, which must have been loose in one of the Freedom of Information Act files.

He studied it. A memo from the police commission's files: "Call re: Sergeant E. Cudlipp July 10th. Send complaint form to Arthur P. Besterman."

That date was four days before Besterman died.

"Don't tell anyone about this, okay?" Brovak said.

"Mum's the word," said Ruff. "Well, I must trundle off to the Provincial Courts."

Max Macarthur glanced up at the clock. Eleven-thirty. His turn to buy lunch at Au Sauterne. That he must pay this penalty was seeming ever more likely: the judges had told him they didn't wish to hear from him further, a coded message for which the true meaning was, "We have already made up our minds, but propriety demands that we go through the motions of listening to the opposing counsel."

The judges finally bludgeoned Milsom's lawyer into a sullen silence. The court announced that the appeal was being allowed and a new trial being ordered — with reasons to be delivered later.

"See you in Ottawa," Milsom's lawyer said in a peeved tone. The Supreme Court of Canada, the appeal court of last resort.

Inspector Nordquist shambled off to apply for a tag for Milsom, an all-Canada warrant.

From the gallery, Roger Turnbull smiled at Max, and gave him a victory fist. Max remembered that curious comment: *Lawyers administer their own so-called justice, not God's.*

In another courtroom, Wentworth Chance, feeling transported within the translucent mist of Minette Lefleur's overpowering perfume, heard the Provincial Judge, as if in the distance, asking for time estimates for her trial.

"Mr. Chance, are you there?"

"Uh, oh, yeah. Gee, half a day?"

Afterwards, the prosecutor said to Wentworth: "Why aren't you copping her out? This is cut and dried. You know something I don't know?"

"I don't know anything." He blurted that lie, and turned red, and left court bowed with the weight of his terrible secret.

During lunch at Au Sauterne, John Brovak withheld from his gossipy partners his discovery that Arthur Besterman had been contemplating the filing of a complaint against Staff-Sergeant Everit Cudlipp. Charging him with...what? Word must not get back to Cudlipp before Monday, when, God and Leroy Lukey willing, Brovak would reopen his cross-examination of the officer and ask some probing questions.

He was feeling peppy, he had almost decimated Cudlipp on the stand. Maybe on Monday he would find ammunition enough to unfix the fixed verdict, and to persuade the jury not to be browbeaten into convicting.

When Wentworth Chance arrived at their table, he congratulated Max Macarthur on the Milsom win, and Brovak told him not to be a suck.

"He gets a coram of three judges so hard-nosed they make Attila the Hun look like Caspar Milquetoast," he declaimed. "Made up their minds before they heard a word Max said. He was just window dressing in there."

"O.D.'s lawyer was pretty miffed, so it's going upstairs," Max said. "A.G. wants me to argue it in Ottawa. Money is no object."

Brovak snorted. "Didn't I say? Oh, yeah, he was just gonna do this one appeal for the Crown. The state has its meat hooks in him now, they're gonna remove part of his brain and make him a snivel servant." He was puffing on a big, ugly, after-lunch cigar.

"I hope you're going to be on your best behaviour tonight, John," Max said.

"No problem," he said.

Through all this, Wentworth Chance sipped gingerly at his wine and worried about his future with this firm. Never mind that — his future as a lawyer was at risk. Also, John Brovak had warned he was going to get him drunk tonight. Wentworth had a fetishistic fear of making a fool of himself.

At the end of the working day, after the secretaries had fled, the lawyers retired to the coffee room for one of their interminable partnership meetings.

Brovak kept cracking open beers, interrupting the agenda with caustic asides about the Lukey dinner that night, about how he had decided to make his own special toast to the judge. He raised his bottle of Molson's Dry in the air. "Will you all please stand. Will you join me in throwing up in honour of that fat blob of flatulence, Mr. Justice Flukey."

"You'll be making no toasts, John," said Max.

"I'm *making* a toast. Anything goes at the East Side Bar."

"John," said Augustina, "don't embarrass us."

"Ah, yes, Ms. Goody Two-Shoes. I am partnered to milksops." Brovak left the room in search of Wentworth Chance, and found him at his post in the library.

"We're gonna get pissed up tonight, kid."

"Two drinks and I pass out."

"What kind of fuzz-nutted Yuppie cream puffs are coming out of law school these days?" He patted his pockets and came out with a bent joint. "C'mon, let's blow one up. It's six o'clock on a Friday, take the night off."

Wentworth didn't like John Brovak thinking of him as a Yuppie cream puff. After high school he had given up marijuana with his childhood, but he would take a little toke to prove his cream puff-lessness.

Following Brovak to the balcony above the back fire escape, he quelled an unmanly urge to ask Brovak from what part of the world came this cannabis. He observed that the joint, though fat, was rolled crookedly, carelessly. It seemed non-threatening, limply impotent.

He inhaled. The smoke was sweet, and he held it in, and did not embarrass himself with a coughing fit in front of Brovak. He expelled. Nothing. Could have been dry cuttings for all the effect it had on Wentworth. They each took another hit, then Brovak tamped it out.

"Don't want you to o.d., kid."

Wentworth enjoyed a slight calming. But he was afraid of what might happen tonight. How had he got roped into this?

10

Here Comes
the Judge

The full force of Brovak's resinous Asian jungleweed didn't hit
Wentworth Chance until about twenty minutes later as he was getting
into a taxi to go to the Tropicana Hotel. As he stared into the muffled
winter street light of Maple Tree Square, he felt himself becoming
rigid with fear.

Paranoia. Guilt. He had to fight the premonitions of disaster that
sought to overwhelm him. A memory of Minette in her parlour of
love…

"C'mon, kid, get in."

He joined his bosses in the taxi, urging calmness on himself, and
they floated down Hastings Street to the East End.

This would be Wentworth's first meeting of that inner sanctum of
criminal lawyers, the Downtown East Side Trial and Error Society,
tales of which had been told in the law school lounge. Tales of
debauchery, of calumnies hurled like javelins across the room. Stories
of fist fights between judges and lawyers.

The situ for this event was the dining hall of a small hotel in the
blue-collar East End, the Tropicana. Just judges and lawyers allowed.
No spouses. No press. No tape recorders. No cameras. No outsiders
but the waiters with their trays of rubber chicken.

Here the judges held no rank. It was a tradition of the Society that anything could be said at these events, defamatory, scandalous, obscene. Nothing must be remembered the next day, even by a judge, however gravely slighted.

When Wentworth walked in, the place was already teeming, a melee of standing, gabbing lawyers near the cash bar. The uproar of voices against the room's Polynesian backdrop of paint-flaking palms seemed to unsteady him, and he tried to melt unseen into the mingle of men and women, although not before Brovak thrust a double whiskey into his hand.

Wentworth tried to focus. Here, here in this banquet hall, here were all his heroes. Cyrus Smythe-Baldwin, the venerable don of the criminal bar, perky at 81, still in harness. And there, the honey-throated seducer of juries, Arthur Beauchamp, talking to Foster Cobb of the rapier cross-examination.

And here was Wentworth Chance, defender of traffic violators, woozy with weed, already corrupted beyond redemption.

Max Macarthur was in a corner of the banquet room, where his father had buttonholed him.

"Your mother was dreadfully hurt when you phoned to cancel dinner."

"I was feeling wrecked, Dad."

"She thinks it was Ruth's doing."

"It was *my* doing." Max tried to change the subject. "Heard from Ottawa?"

"I'm on the short list," his dad said.

There was a vacancy in the Supreme Court of Canada and Max knew his father — whom everyone called Max Mac Two — was angling hard, using all his connections, to win elevation to this highest judicial pinnacle. No Macarthur had yet made it to the Supreme Court.

"We had Tom Hosegood over to the dinner you so inconsiderately missed. You know he's retiring."

"No, really?"

"Upshaw, Pendergast, Hosegood. There'll be an opening there, a full partnership. I heard four hundred thousand a year being bruited about for starters."

"Dad, I like the firm I'm in."

"Oh, yes, fine firm. With Brian Pomeroy defending terrorists and getting his name plastered all over the papers with that discreditable young woman, and John Brovak putting on one of the most unutterably obscene displays in the history of our courts."

Max excused himself and sought more congenial company.

Abigail Hitchins was about the only person in the universe who made Augustina Sage feel outré and unstylish. Abigail was garbed tonight in something ultra-swoopy that might once have adorned a Paris model, *trés décolleté*.

Somehow they got onto the subject of one of Abigail's current divorce cases: Pomeroy versus Pomeroy. Augustina found herself defending Brian, but Abigail impaled her with one raised, fierce eye.

"I know more about Mr. Pomeroy's history of dicking around than you do, honey. He's a quickie artist, he's been double shuffling around Caroline since they were engaged."

"All he wants — "

Again, Abigail cut her off. "Is a chance to worm his way out of it. Caroline showed me his letters. I have absolutely *forbidden* her to write back to him."

Abigail, a banner-waving marcher against abusive men, was herself a veteran of two failed marriages. Augustina feared this narcissistic woman was exacerbating the anger between the Pomeroys, feeding the flames.

"My God, you'd think *you* were the scorned spouse."

Abigail chilled her with a smile. "I like to identify with my clients." She gave Augustina a perfumed kiss and flew off like a butterfly.

"Lemme help you with that," Brovak said to Jack Boynton, prosecutor of drug importers. Boynton had just entered the Tropicana dining hall, weighted down with video projector, tapes, camera, cables.

"I have everything under control."

"Help you set up," Brovak said, seizing the roll-up screen.

"Don't touch *anything*." Boynton wrestled for possession of the screen, and dropped a bunch of cables and a few video cassettes. "*Damn* it."

"Hostility. I sense hostility." Brovak helped gather up the dropped articles, still with firm grip on the screen. "Jack, that stuff I said in court about you, you know that was all play-acting; it's for the galleries. C'mon, pros like us don't carry any personal feelings with them out of the courtroom." Boynton loosened his grasp on the screen, and Brovak easily pried it from him.

"I'll take that as an attempt at an apology."

"It's the East Side Trial and Error Society, Jack. We're all just friends working the law for a living here; we're brothers and sisters and fuck the rest of the world."

They walked together to the front of the banquet hall.

"I agree that counsel must leave their ill humour behind them in the courtroom," Boynton said. "But what you did transgressed all bounds. Don't ask for any favours when I write the benchers a report on the incident."

"Tell them the bare facts, Jack." He unrolled the screen. "I got one of these setups myself; I know how to do this shit. Hope these tapes aren't going to cause Leroy to puff up any more than he has."

"Don't worry." Boynton waxed proud. "I winnowed through hundreds of his interviews. I have slips of the tongue, I have footage where he belches right before a camera, and I have his interview after he lost that Shiva mass murder, when he was a little drunk. I have some howlers."

"Boy, you must've spent hours."

"Try three weeks. Every spare moment."

Brovak shook his head. Such dedication.

"I wonder if you might afford me the pleasure of buying you a drink after this horror show is over…if you're not doing anything…"

Augustina Sage let Mr. Justice Quentin Russell's invitation just dangle there. He was attractive (silver-streaked long hair) and he was charming (and also rich and very single-o), but Augustina couldn't quite escape the thought that he felt her to be easy.

"I may become suicidal if you say no."

He had been hitting on her for the last fifteen minutes, smooth as velvet, with that roguish grin. He used to act for the mobs, big money people, and she'd heard he'd turned his hefty fees into good investments (real estate, a chain of chic hotels). One of her best friends had had an affair with him, Olive Klymchuk, an attractive, brassy criminal lawyer from Victoria. Olive had gotten a royal runaround from the cad — at least that was *her* version.

"Maybe I'm pressing too hard," Russell said with a sad-little-boy look.

"I'm thinking," she said.

"While the jury deliberates, I'll freshen these drinks." He took her glass, melted her with his smile, and departed.

Her former partner, Sophie Marx, a woman whom the Sears catalogue would describe as being full-figured, joined her, giving her a warning look as Russell smoothed up to the bar.

"He's been coming on like hot cakes," Augustina said.

"Keep your legs crossed."

"Is he all that bad?"

"Beneath the gleaming surface lurks a lech. A *rich* lech, though."

"Yeah, but he's…interesting."

At a table in the back, Brovak gently slapped Wentworth's fingers as he was going for a bread roll. "Save your buns," he said. "We throw them at Lukey later. Leroy likes buns." Brovak seemed to be in astonishingly good spirits. Or very high.

Smoke from his hand-rolled Cuban corona drifted heavily past Wentworth's nose and nauseated him slightly. He remained stoned and silent, slowly imbibing yet another double scotch. He should have told the other partners. His chances of staying on after articles were worth squat now. Maybe, if he wasn't disbarred, he could go back home and open a practice in Tlaksis Creek.

Brovak babbled. "That sycophant Boynton has probably got some sucky kowtow shit mixed in with the funny videos. But he's gonna show that interview after Flukey lost the Shiva case to you, Max, where he was slurring and hiccupping." He paused for a swallow of wine. "Check the stems on that sweet new centrefold in the persecutor's office. Eatin' stuff. I'd be an easy win for her." More wine.

Wentworth Chance lost a half-hearted battle with his chicken and left most of it untouched.

Sophie Marx, as chairperson, was at the head table, with Max Mac Two on her right, Leroy Lukey her left, and assorted nabobs on either wing.

At the end of the main course, she stood up and asked for silence.

"I would appreciate a few moments of quiet memory for a comrade who was taken away from us last year. Arthur P. Besterman."

"Yay, Arthur," came a somewhat inebriated voice.

One or two lawyers looked puzzled before remembering who he was.

As everyone stood, Wentworth Chance felt the weight of morbid silence and remembered the parking lot where a drunken lawyer died.

After mentioning a couple of other veterans of the bar who had passed away under more reposeful circumstances, Sophie asked everyone to get unserious; there was a long list of speakers wishing to pay homage to Justice Lukey and a movie to be watched about the highlights of some of the more awesome moments in his glorious career.

"Boynton, get up here and let's see this profile you did of his lordship. Hope that screen's going to be wide enough to get all of him in."

Boynton went to his post.

"All speeches have to be under five minutes," Sophie announced. "We've got an unusually long list. I guess that's because you're really popular, Leroy."

Hoots of laughter followed that.

"Just kidding. I know how you pride yourself on being generally disliked." Lukey made a show of laughing with the others. "One other agenda item. Following the toasts there will be a public display by John Brovak."

She waited again for the laughter to subside.

"Okay, Boynton is ready. We're going to show you a few entertaining moments in Leroy's otherwise lackluster career."

Leroy Lukey sat through Sophie's introduction composed, almost benign in bearing, laughing at himself with good grace when the occasion demanded, accepting the arrows. Normally a robust reveller, tonight the judge was declining drinks, keeping up a guard.

"Lights," said Boynton.

First he played a portion of a tape showing a much younger Lukey, before he'd acquired much of his excess baggage, announcing his candidacy for the Liberals in a federal election; a somewhat bombastic performance which was followed by an interview in which he was asked how it felt to lose his deposit.

Boynton had indeed done a caring job, and though much of his stuff was tumid, more of it, including the belch, had the viewers cheering.

He switched tapes. "And now for his lordship's greatest triumph."

Whatever awkward moment Boynton had intended the screen to display, only he would know. The screen showed black for a moment...

And then came into view the parlour of love on the houseboat of Minette Lefleur. Minette was on the bed, head down and rump up, squealing with either counterfeit pain or counterfeit joy, giving entry to Mr. Justice Leroy Lukey behind her, who was naked but for a pair of socks held up by garters.

The room went soundless except for the squeals and the grunts of exertion from the video sound system. Boynton looked as if he had been quick-frozen. He stared unblinking at the screen for the entire act of penetration and for several moments of sexual rhapsody afterwards.

"Lights!" yelled Boynton, his mind garbled, unable to find a quick solution. No one turned on the lights.

As Lukey battle-cried his orgasm, Boynton finally found the off-switch, and the room went into a darkness made ghostly by the frozen glow of candles on the tables.

The stillness of this moment was suddenly broken by the sound of Leroy Lukey crashing like a rhinoceros through the tables en route to John Brovak, unerring in his choice of culprit.

"I'll kill you, you fucking son of a bitch!" Lukey bellowed. Arms grabbed at him, slowing his progress. Brovak sat there unperturbed, relaxed, relighting his stogie.

As the lights went on, Lukey broke free and changed direction for the stairs outside, running out to his Chrysler, where he found Wentworth Chance throwing up over the hood. Wentworth had missed the show.

11

Ghostwriters
in the Sky

February 26

Dear Macarthur, Brovak and Sage,

Since I have run out of batteries for my shortwave, I have
no way of knowing what the weather is like back home, let
alone the climate for my intended brief return there (no mil-
itary brass bands, *please*; I intend to sneak in and out,
avoiding all deer hunters).

The purpose: I shall be seeking audience with Caroline.

She has written to me! She has done this without the
knowledge, advice or consent of her lawyer — which surely
means she is emerging, somewhat ruefully and perplexed,
from beneath the domineering sway of the psychopathic
harpy Abigail Hitchins. Caroline's letter was stern in manner,
written in the tone one might use in complaining to the
parks board about the spraying of dangerous herbicides on
the boulevards, and although she indicated that there was no
chance of reconciliation, what else could she mean but the
opposite? Why else this sneaking around behind Abigail's
back?

I am encouraged to believe she will grant me a hearing of some sort. "There remain matters to be straightened out," she wrote.

Maybe all she has in mind is discussing how we might divide up the photos in the wedding album. (Or, black thought, maybe it's a ruse between her and her lawyer to seduce me back to Canada, there to be served with the divorce petition. No, I shall *not* believe that of Caroline.)

Now here is what we'll do. I will return for her birthday which is March 13, and you will reserve that table by the fireplace at Antoine's, where they usually have a chamber trio on Saturdays. I don't care what gambit you use to get her there — it's her birthday, Augustina can invite her out for dinner, girl talk, one on one.

("Who's the other chair for?" Caroline asked, a lingering sadness in her voice.

"It's for someone who loves you," said Augustina.

Caroline looked puzzled, but then turned her emerald-green eyes to the sun-bronzed Adonis walking toward their table. "Brian," she said through her glistening tears.

"Caroline," he said gently, his voice breaking with emotion.)

Then you will lecture both of us as to the asininity of our ways, and discreetly depart to the strains of a Mozart allegretto.

Make sure they have a good chilled Chardonnay, you know the stuff Caroline likes. Reserve their best champagne. Ensure they have sole almondine on the menu.

A single, perfect rose on the table.

Thus we trap and band the elusive Hermit Thrush.

And then, with controlled emotion, I begin an address to this set-faced frowning one-woman jury that would bring tears to the eyes of Lucifer himself. Knowing my client's case is not well served by casting even one iota of blame in any direction but my own, I fulsomely apologize for my weakened moment with a bad poet whom I plan neither to see or hear from again, and for whom I, at no time, felt any emotion beyond a kind of adolescent sexual curiosity.

Later today I shall amble merrily down the trail to town and mail this secret plan to you, and I will telephone you from the San José airport on the day before I arrive. (The telephone system in Puerto Próspero has been shut down as a result of a recent earthquake, and only God knows when the lines will be up again.)

For some reason, ever since I received Caroline's letter, the fires of creation have been raging out of control, and suspects galore are running from the forests. But now I am short on bodies. Enough deathless prose: I must now indulge in the sweet agony of the kill. The snuffing out of another hapless victim or two. The power, the power.

I fear, however, I have lost sight of my protagonist. No, not quite. He has multiplied amoeba-like; each version of my once beloved and Pomeroyic hero going off upon his (or is it her?) own conquests of the Grail. Mr. Widgeon, I know, does not approve. Mr. Widgeon: *The Art of the Whodunit*, who sits sneering at me as he stands there between Mr. Webster and Mr. Fowler, who makes caustic asides to Messrs. Strunk and White near the other bookend. Mr. Widgeon, whose bible admonishes that there shall be no protagonists but one in the successfully conceived mystery novel.

Schizophrenically, I defy Mr. Widgeon. Protagonist by committee.

In the meantime, for some occultish reason, the book seems to be proceeding authorless, like a galloping racehorse that has lost its rider. I am no longer sure where this story comes from, and, even more worrisome, know not how it will end. It is as though a creative demon enters my skin each day and flexes my fingers before the keyboard and weaves this ragged, loose-ended plot. I am this demon's amanuensis, his copier, his scribe. I am my own ghostwriter.

With all main characters and suspects now in attendance, I have embarked on that part of the book Widgeon calls "thematic development." Motives must be clarified. Inquiries must be made. Clues must be found. Leads must dry up. Reversals must occur. New victims must be brought by the demon to my sacrificial altar.

Enough, a different demon growls within and bids me do its bidding. (Or is that my stomach? I think I forgot to eat today.)

Edgar Allan Poe.

March 1

Dear Charity Slough,

I must say your letter came as a surprise. I am astonished that you went to such great pains to write me so ornate an epic of prose, and while I do appreciate the poems included and the little drawings, I am afraid I will have to be a little more curt and plain in response.

I am piqued to find that someone in my office let it be known where I was, and frankly I'd love to find out who. I gave strict instructions. Not with special reference to you, Charity, but to the world generally, because I really need to be alone to write this novel, a project which I think I mentioned to you.

While I am really overwhelmed by your expressions of regard for me, I think it would be most unwise for you to come down here. I am afraid it's quite dangerous, and I dare not often stir from the house for fear of the terciopelos which slither around outside my door. More commonly known as the fer-de-lance, this viperous snake, unlike the other less-sociable poisonous species which abound in Costa Rica, seems to prefer hanging around outside people's houses (the scorpions and tarantulas, however, usually choose to stay inside).

The tiny spiders, though, are the worst. One does not see them until too late, when paralyzed by their venomous bite. The fire ants and killer bees and vampire bats — well, one simply lives with nature here, and prays.

There are a couple of matters you raised in your letter which I think I should comment upon.

I'm afraid I don't see that there are matters of the heart

that remain "unrequitted" (sic). (Unrequited, Charity, it rhymes with uninvited.) I agree some kind of therapy might be useful, but I think you should seek a more mainstream type of help than those treatments, or whatever you want to call them, that you're taking at the New Age Awareness Centre. I don't think going into trances or into past-life regression is the route to take. Also, that route brings you a little too close to my office, which is a little too close for comfort.

The other thing: I don't recall ever coming to the announced conclusion that I had fallen in love with you. One says a number of things when one is in a state of altered sensibilities, but I really don't think I would have got carried away to that extent. I really wish you hadn't mentioned that in your letter to Caroline.

In fact, I really wish you'd never written the letter at all. I think it wise if we don't maintain communication.

Yours sincerely,
B. Pomeroy.

March 1

Dear Suspects,
This is a P.S. to my letter of Friday, which I was unable to mail as a result of my having been frozen into a catatonic state shortly upon my entry into the post office. A large item of freight had been mailed to me, smelling as if dunked in some kind of herbal perfume.

I would sincerely like to know which one of you is the yellow singing bird. Reception doesn't even have a forwarding address for me: only you four know (plus Caroline). But someone, somehow, and I suspect not all that innocently, tipped off Charity Slough, who has written me a letter as long as the complete works of Rudyard Kipling, garnished with illustrations of flowers, kissing lips and delightful little dancing elves.

And bearing a threat to come to Costa Rica to be at my side in this time of my despair because she knows I have been evicted from my home by a wife who is divorcing me.

Pause here. And how did she know that?

Forgive me my suspicions, I wronged you guys.

Of course. It was the hell-witch herself, wasn't it? Who may have just called upon Charity Slough in her ashram, or wherever she nows lives, to take a brief of evidence about the acts of adultery and other assorted depravities indulged in by the defendant Pomeroy, and who doubtless hinted that said defendant had left his wife and was in Costa Rica pining for the woman he truly loved, to wit the co-respondent Charity Slough.

God save me if she ever comes down here.

But worse: this confused victim of Abigail's machinations has just written a letter to Caroline.

I am numb with despair. I have been caught up in an embarrassing white lie, for I regret to say I erroneously advised Caroline that the affair involved only a single night in Knot Lake. Moreover, and this is the kicker, I am accused in this letter of having told Charity I was in love with her. I don't remember this, although it is possible I went brain dead at a critical moment of heat. She may have misunderstood me to say, "I love you," when I was actually saying, "I love this." Anyway, she has asked Caroline to kindly render her husband up. "I asked her to give us the gift of love," Charity writes, "for I know she is not a heartless woman."

This is Abigail Hitchins's doing. Please be instructed that I am retaining your firm to take appropriate proceedings. I shall want damages for alienation of affections and I shall want Ms. Hitchins deported to her native Transylvania so she can be resettled among her fellow vampires.

Brian.

P.S. I'm cancelling all plans to come back. I can't handle it.

12

Pineapple
Surprise

Wentworth Chance toiled in the office library all weekend, but with a nerve-frazzled lack of concentration. Brovak was nowhere to be found. Brovak who should be here to advise him, Brovak who had promised that "nothing will happen to you, kid," if he borrowed that video tape from Minette Lefleur. Upon these assurances, Wentworth gave him one of the tapes that he'd viewed in Minette's parlour of love, whose concealed video camera had also captured several other prominent citizens in various states of abandon.

Minette Lefleur had a *very* good defence.

On the morning of Monday, March 1 — Day One Hundred and Two of Regina versus Watson and Twenty Others — as Wentworth hurried into Court 54 seeking to confer with John Brovak, he observed that Sergeant Cudlipp was waiting to reenter the witness stand. Their eyes met, and Cudlipp's shot flames. Wentworth felt fibrillations of dread in his thumping heart.

Cudlipp knew. How could he know? He had traced the video back to Minette Lefleur. The police would extort a statement from her, implicating Wentworth Chance. Regina versus Chance, conspiracy to commit public mischief. End of career.

But there, winking at him, was John Brovak at the counsel table, basking in the admiration of his fellow defenders, but shaking his head and telling all: "Can't figure out how Boynton got ahold of that pointless, disgusting film."

And there was Jack Boynton, an island of grief in a sea of good cheer.

"Terrible thing," Brovak said to him. "You must feel just sick inside."

"You rotten slime," Boynton hissed. "You switched the tapes."

"So sue me."

Brovak was showing remarkably few scars from a non-stop wanton weekend.

He had proceeded from the Tropicana Hotel that Friday night bounding merrily from bar to bar, and even when the sun rose, Brovak didn't go down. Instead, he hailed a taxi and by noon was on the upper slopes of Whistler Mountain, slicing down the diamond-rated Rattlesnake Trail at stomach-churning speed, shrieking like a banshee. He drank his way back to Vancouver where he continued until two o'clock this morning before collapsing. When one really wants to party, the drug of choice is alcohol.

Despite his inordinate consumption of this drug, he had risen above the Monday-morning pain of it all and had arrived in Court 54 only a few minutes late. The Monster had not yet gone into session, and now, twenty minutes later, everyone was still standing about, waiting. It was assumed that a crisis session was in progress in the chambers of the Chief Justice of British Columbia, Max's father.

A giggly, nervous energy filled the courtroom. The clerks and court reporters had heard the gossip, of course.

Had the press? Brovak saw they were here in numbers. But nothing had appeared in print.

"Another day, another dollar, eh, Staff?" Brovak said to Cudlipp. The policeman seemed to be sizing his tormentor up for a wheelchair.

Brovak was interested in asking this officer some questions about whatever bad information Arthur Besterman had about him, and so, though he yearned to see the end of Lukey, was of divided mind as to whether he wanted the trial to continue. In a case with a jury, there was always the chance another judge could be called in from the bullpen, to replace a bench-mate who has been run over by a truck, so to speak.

Finally, the court clerk was summoned outside, where she conferred with someone. A few minutes later, she returned and called the court to order. "Regina versus Watson and Twenty Others," she bawled. "Mr. Justice Quentin Russell presiding."

Brovak felt a warmth suffuse him. Good old Quent the acquitter, former counsel to the mobs. Russell had been at the East-End party Friday night, Brovak recalled, and had slipped out with Augustina, the last he saw. He hoped they'd had a pleasant time.

The judge took his seat and nodded to counsel.

"Gentlemen," said Russell, "I regret to say that Mr. Justice Lukey cannot be with you today. He has been stricken with a sudden ailment that his physicians tell us will have him bedridden for quite some time. As a result, having given some consideration to the matter — and of course I will hear from counsel — I am minded to declare a mistrial of this case. I think it quite unlikely that I or any judge in Mr. Justice Lukey's stead would be sufficiently able to pick up the threads...Mr. Brovak?"

Brovak was standing. "M'lord, may I be included among the many who pray that the good Lord will engineer Mr. Justice Lukey's speedy recovery?"

Quentin Russell smiled, a little too broadly. "Thank you, counsel."

"But I wonder if, before there's any mistrial declared here, we could just conclude the evidence of Staff-Sergeant Cudlipp, who was on the witness stand at Friday's break."

Russell looked puzzled. "Why?"

"Involves a matter that's just come to light, m'lord."

A little matter pertaining, perhaps, to Besterman's murder. As Brovak was reaching into his stash of Freedom of Information Act folders, he saw Cudlipp in urgent whispered conference with Jack Boynton.

"That seems an odd request, Mr. Brovak, but — " the judge began.

Boynton interrupted. "Excuse me, my lord, I think it will save a good deal of trouble and time if I simply stay this case — "

"Well, just a sec, here," said Brovak.

But Boynton plowed ahead. "Crown does not intend to proceed further against any of the accused. I direct the clerk of the court to enter stays of proceedings against each of them."

After a moment, Brovak asked: "What's the rush all of a sudden?"

"Not much we can do about it, Mr. Brovak, is there?" said Russell. "The Crown has dropped the charges."

"Yeah," said Brovak. "Right." He looked speculatively over at Cudlipp and Boynton as the clerk announced the formal closing of the court and the judge departed.

A moment of silence. No one stirred.

Watson leaned toward Brovak. "Does this mean we won?"

"Yeah. We won."

Watson and Twenty Others rose to their feet in great jubilation, and Brovak was buried among hugging arms.

Twelve-Fingers Watson came over to Brovak's office about an hour later to invite him to the victory party the next night. He was carrying a heavy attaché case.

Brovak led Watson into his office and locked the door.

"Fifty large now," said Watson, bringing three rubber-banded wads of bills from the briefcase. "I got some current operating expenses. I ain't gonna stiff you for the other fifty."

"Perish the thought."

"I gotta get some new stock in. I'm gonna do the big one. Put everything I got into it."

"How about instead of the fifty K's," Brovak said, pocketing the bills without even a riffle count, "your finca in Costa Rica?"

Watson thought about that. "Yeah, okay, give me a month."

"Why a month?"

Watson shrugged. "Gotta go down there to a lawyer's and sign the papers."

"You're not doing a drop down there on the property. I got my pal there."

"Brian — he's cool isn't he?"

Brovak became very agitated. "No fucking way."

A hush fell.

"Okay. There's other strategies. I'll talk to you tonight. Sayonara." He left with his empty attaché case.

Twelve-Fingers Watson reserved the entire back room of Archie's Steak House for Tuesday night, a restaurant on Kingsway owned by one of Watson's regular customers. Brovak prevailed on Wentworth

Chance (with little resistance — beans and toast being the alternative) to join in this victory feast, though he planned to eat and run — he had to study for bar exams next month.

Wentworth had a client in an out-of-town courtroom that afternoon, someone who had poisoned his neighbor's noisy dog, and it was a long pedal back from Port Moody to Archie's Steak House. As he entered he could hear ribald laughter from the back room. The front area of the restaurant was busy, too, and when Wentworth looked around he recognized two men at a table for two; he'd seen them at Brovak's trial: narcs, two of Cudlipp's drug squad. They didn't look at him, and he continued on to the back room.

He arrived just in time for entrées. He was going to sit in a far corner, but Brovak ordered him to take a place of honour beside him at the centre of a long table, where Brovak was presiding over this assemblage. Wentworth ordered a fourteen-ounce New York, and watched his hero hold court.

Brovak rose with his glass, which had obviously been refilled more than a few times. "Ladies and gentlemen, the Queen."

"The Queen," voices returned.

"May she continue to reign until the forecast calls for snow." Again he raised his glass. "And to the vanquished enemy who fought so brave and bold, the great upholders of our noble institutions of law and order, without whose dedicated efforts I would not be able to make a living. And thank you to my director, my producers, my co-stars and all the cast and crew, and of course to the wonderful people of my home town of Turtleford, Saskatchewan."

He paused to catch his breath. "And here's to the fighters for independence in my ancient homeland of Slovenia, not to mention Slovakia, Slavonia, and Slobovia, and to the entire membership of the International Brotherhood of Nose and Goober Pickers."

Brovak continued calling for toasts until Watson presented him with a beribboned box containing a magnum of Moët Champagne. Brovak popped the cork and it bounced off the windows behind him. He filled glasses at his table, tilted the bottle and finished it.

"To...to..." He looked down at Wentworth, gave him a brotherly smile. "To Wentworth Chance, my main man, who, ah, discovered a big loophole in the case against us. A big *wet* loophole."

Don't blow my cover, Wentworth silently asked.

A waiter came up to their table and gave Brovak another gift-wrapped box, too small and square to hold a bottle.

"Compliments of a gentleman out there," said the waiter, nodding in the direction of the door to the front.

Brovak slipped the ribbon off.

Wentworth — as he later remembered — had this odd, prickly intimation of calamity. He had no idea where it came from, and felt stupid in warning Brovak.

"John, better check who that's from."

But Brovak was already prying open the stiff cardboard lid on the box inside the wrappings. As he did so, both he and Wentworth observed that it contained a hand grenade. They also observed that Brovak's action in prying open the lid had pulled from the grenade a pin which had been taped to the lid.

"Everybody DOWN!" Wentworth hollered at the top of his voice.

In the turmoil of screams and yells and scrambling bodies, Brovak seemed suddenly to become monumentally sober. He took the grenade out of the box. With his other hand, he sent the empty champagne bottle smashing through a window above and behind him. He then tossed his admirer's gift high toward the broken window, a perfect basket through the hoop of broken glass. The grenade cleared some imitation Greek statuary in the terrace, and exploded on impact with the trunk of a potted tree.

A burst of flame and glass as windows imploded. A moment of utter silence, and a final, quiet tinkle of glass.

Wentworth looked up from under his table. Brovak was still standing, a cool breeze from outside ruffling his hair. "Well, shit," he said. "Now I'm off dessert."

The Vancouver police were there in minutes: homicide, bomb and lab people, roping off, video-taping, shouting into radios, and taking names, pictures and prints. One of them found that the women's toilet wouldn't flush because it was clogged with small bags of marijuana, cocaine and amphetamine capsules.

With respect to those drugs, suspicion was directed at Rosie Finch, Watson's ex-moll, whom a waiter saw emerging from the toilet just after the grenade blast. But others had used it, too, and the matter was never pursued.

A few ambulances arrived, but medical aid was required for only two of the ex-defendants — one whose hand was opened up by the flying glass and who required stitches, and another who had dropped two caps of PCP before the banquet and was babbling incoherently. Others had suffered only minor cuts. Wentworth Chance wasn't hurt at all, but felt he had passed into some kind of transcendental state.

The two narcs he had seen in Archie's earlier had vanished.

The waiter who had presented the lethal little box to Brovak described its donor as male, brown-haired, middle-aged, he thought, but it was hard to tell — his moustache and beard were greying. "This is for Mr. Brovak," he'd said. "For all he's done." He'd tucked a hundred-dollar note into the waiter's sleeve and walked out.

"Somebody," Brovak informed Inspector Nordquist, "is trying to kill the great lawyers of Vancouver."

13

The Executor

The firm allowed the bomb squad to come by just before business hours the next morning to poke into the office's nooks and crannies. Inspector Nordquist also wanted to comb through Brovak's files for clues as to who might have recently taken a disfavour to him, but Brovak said, "That's a negative, Bones, old buddy."

Nordquist put a couple of people in the waiting room to keep watch for assassins and deliverers of bombs. He and Brovak then joined Max, Augustina, and Wentworth around the boardroom table of the library.

Brovak took a seat beside Wentworth, giving him an enthusiastic hug.

"As a result of Wentworth's timely warning, I was alerted to danger, and thus lost no reaction time in getting under way the process of saving maybe a couple of dozen lives. One day we'll have to seriously think about giving the kid a raise."

Max told Brovak he looked unexpectedly cheerful this morning for someone who almost had his head blown off.

The key word was almost, Brovak replied. That's why he was unexpectedly cheerful.

"Who wants to kill you?" asked the phlegmatic Nordquist.

"Lukey," said Brovak.

"Get real," said Augustina.

"Mr. soon-to-be ex—Justice Leroy Lukey. Bring him in for questioning, Bones."

"I am not about to do that."

Last night, Brovak had asked the waiter: "Was this man about five-ten, red-complexioned, puffy-faced and fleshy through the middle?"

A little shorter, the waiter thought. Then on reconsideration, yes, about that. Actually, maybe taller. Around average height anyway. Thick around the middle, yes, but maybe he was padded, because the moustache and beard, now that he thought about it, might have been false. Could have had a hairpiece as well. High voice, though it might have been a strained falsetto. Wore glasses, he thought. Raincoat for sure. Tan, or gray or some off-white tone. Only saw him for a few seconds, really.

Too busy concentrating on that hundred-dollar bill, Brovak assumed.

"Collar the judge, Bones," Brovak said.

Max said, "John, not that I want to give any credence to this ridiculous theory, but how would Lukey know you were at Archie's last night?"

"He had spies, I don't know. He's Cudlipp's bumfuck buddy. What about those two narcs in the other room? Wentworth undercovered them."

Wentworth nodded. He was still ashen, had lain rigidly awake in bed all night.

"I ran them down," said Nordquist. "They left some time before the bomber showed up."

"And what the fuck were they doing there in the first place?"

Nordquist shrugged. "They are dope squad. They were keeping tabs on a room full of dope dealers."

Who, asked Brovak, assigned them to this vital station?

"Staff-Sergeant Cudlipp," said Nordquist.

"Cudlipp," said Brovak. He smacked his forehead with his palm. "Cudlipp. Bring *him* in."

Yes, of course, thought Brovak. A victim of career frustration syndrome. Six years spent sweating the biggest case of his career, with the reward of a fixed verdict at the end. And after that cross-examination on Friday, now the laughing stock of the entire Musical Ride.

Fingered, not long ago, by the late Arthur Besterman, for some unknown piece of skulduggery.

"Why Cudlipp?" Nordquist asked.

Brovak didn't respond. He turned to Wentworth. "Remind me about a little assignment I want to give you."

"You have any realistic ideas, John?" the inspector asked.

"I've given you my main suspects. Otherwise I got nothing but friends out there."

"I think we should ask ourselves if these attempts on lawyers are linked," Nordquist said. "Besterman, Brovak... Your partner Pomeroy, he's still holed out in — what is it... Costa Rica. There was an inquiry about him from the police down there."

"What the hell for?"

"Identity check. Appears your partner is living in Mr. Twelve-Fingers Watson's house."

"This is not supposed to be public information," said Brovak.

Nordquist nodded. "I'll keep it to myself. I have many things to do. I'll stay in touch." He got up and left.

"Jesus," said Max, "we'd better move John out of target range."

"Uh-uh. I ain't leaving while I've got the attempted assassin of my own good self to catch. You trust the cops to do it? They're going to protect their own. It's Lukey and Cudlipp, I tell you. They are not above conspiring at evil-doing."

"You have this fixation, John," said Max.

Brovak uttered a grunt of dismay at their innocence, and went into his briefcase, bringing out his folders of complaints to the police commission.

"Kid, this is the assignment. You are to trace the history of this item."

Wentworth stared at the photostated note: "Call re: Sergeant E. Cudlipp July 10th. Send complaint form to Arthur P. Besterman."

"From the police commission," Brovak said. "Arthur Besterman, maybe on his own, maybe for a client, was going to make an official grievance about Cudlipp. That's why Cudlipp killed him. Oh...by the way."

He pulled from his briefcase the three thick decks of bills Watson had given him, snapped off the rubber bands and fanned the bills across the tabletop.

"Special achievement award from my twelve-fingered client. Five-oh big ones and the estate in Central America thrown in." He sat back in his chair with his hands behind his head. "This is another reason I am unexpectedly cheerful."

No one spoke for several moments.

"Listen, about that raise..." Wentworth said.

Max warned him: "Wentworth, avarice is not a quality we seek in the firm from one who may be hoping for a permanent position."

This was the first hint Wentworth had ever heard that the firm might keep him on. There was hope.

"Can I just touch them?" he said. He lovingly studied the engraving on the back of one of the smaller bills, a fifty. "Gee, I've never seen one of these before."

"This will help pay for a nice long holiday for you, John," Max said.

"John Brovak does not run from his foes."

"Take advantage, for Christ's sake," said Max. "You have a three-month hole in your calendar. The kid will look after all your shit."

Brovak looked out the window. The day was crackling cold. The mountains across Burrard Inlet were coned with ice cream. Whistler was said to have a two-hundred-and-fifty-centimeter base.

"I guess I earned a little rest and rec." Snow Valley, he decided. Aspen. Where the snow bunnies frolic.

Before court that afternoon, Wentworth went into a huddle with a crown. This prosecutor had been at the Trial and Error Society banquet and knew all about Minette Lefleur's very good defence.

Wentworth led Minette into court, told her to plead not guilty, then led the prosecutor and the judge (who had also been at the banquet) in a stately minuet, dancing around the awkward, unmentionable fact that not only a respected Supreme Court judge, but also a few other prominent citizens had co-starred with Minette in her collection of non-fiction flesh flicks.

He admitted all the facts against Minette, then argued that the houseboat, not being attached to the land, was not in the City of Vancouver as alleged, and an essential ingredient of the charge had therefore not been proved. The prosecutor had to agree there was no way around that argument, and the judge pretended to muse upon the issue of law before dismissing the charge.

Afterwards, Minette zapped him with a hot kiss and told him he could come by for one on the house. Wentworth blushingly declined, and she departed. His erection had fortunately started to subside as a genial middle-aged man drew him aside at the courtroom door.

"Rather a nice piece of work, old chap."

"Well, thanks," said Wentworth.

"Ruff," said the man. "Mr. Joe Ruff."

Wentworth took his hand from his pocket and shook Ruff's. He had seen him around, one of the local legal aid lawyers, he assumed.

"You're with Pomeroy Macarthur, I believe?"

"Their articling student."

"You can't learn from better lawyers. Top-class outfit, what? The best in town."

"And you're with…?"

"Ruff and Company. I'm Ruff and I'm the company. Well, I must toddle along." And, chuckling to himself, he walked off.

Feeling mighty self-satisfied, buoyed with the praise of a fellow practitioner, Wentworth bicycled to the offices of the police commission to commence his duties as Brovak's Sam Spade.

The receptionist had no problem identifying her writing on the note from the Besterman file. Yes, it appeared that a telephone request had been made for a blank report form — although she didn't remember the event, the names, or anything additional that might have been said by Besterman.

Wentworth then bicycled back to Gastown, past the bums huddled around the cenotaph of Victory Square, and weaved among the drunks and discarded bottles in Pigeon Park to the former offices of Arthur Besterman. A judge had ordered all of Besterman's files released to a young lawyer who had bought his practice from his estate, and Wentworth knew this lawyer from several shared courtrooms.

"Yeah, a complaint blank came in the mail after I took over. Damned if I could find a file to put it into. Besterman's secretary — I don't know where she is now — she had her own system. Erika something…Erika Anderson. You want to look through the old files?"

Only one of them drew Wentworth's interest. It was under the name of "Finch, Rosalind." A name not unknown. She had been one of the Twenty Others, one of the four women charged. Watson's ex–girlfriend.

The file contained only a copy of the indictment and legal aid forms. Apparently, just before Besterman's death last July, the Legal Services Society had appointed him to take on Rosalind Finch's defence. A notation on the front inside cover suggested he had lost this client due not to his death but for other inexplicable reasons.

The note said: "File to be closed, account rendered to Legal Aid. Check Cudlipp."

Check Cudlipp?

Check him out?

When the Monster opened last September, Rosie Finch was represented on legal aid not by the barely competent Besterman but by Wayne Buruda, a man generally acknowledged as the worst lawyer in the Western Hemisphere. But why, just before his death, had Besterman resigned from the case?

Wentworth called the Legal Services Society. "Request from A.P. Besterman to withdraw from case," was all its .ecords showed.

Besterman's secretary, Erika Anderson, had moved from her address and changed her phone number.

Later that day, Wentworth escorted John Brovak to the airport, riding low in the passenger seat of his Mercedes SL convertible. Wentworth, who loved everything about this sleek roadster, was going through this approximate mental process: okay, I'm going to the Vancouver International Airport in this wagon, and somebody is going to have to get it back to John's garage. That seems to suggest I, Wentworth Chance, will be doing so.

Brovak was smoking a Tueros corona, and ruminating between puffs. "I remember now. Besterman made a couple of court appearances for Rosie Finch. He was going to earn big wampum if he did the trial, a grand a day on legal aid for shining the seat of his pants. Okay, he must've found out Cudlipp had some kind of shuck going, and that's why he quit the case. Maybe Rosie told him something he couldn't repeat, solicitor privilege."

Their route took them past the hedge-hidden mansions of

Shaughnessy, down Granville Street, the wipers flip-flapping away a steady sprinkling rain. Bulbs were fattening on the floral trees and shrubs. Spring was creeping in upon them.

"Watson was paying her fees until last summer because they were sacking together. She got all lickey-face with one of her customers, he got pissed off, sent her to legal aid. Rosie Finch...Maybe you should track her down, talk to her." Brovak tamped a long ash from his cigar into the ashtray.

"How do I find her? Ah, do you mind if I open the window a little?"

"Talk to Buruda. He'll know where his client is." Brovak squinted through the smoke, thinking hard. "Maybe Rosie Finch told Besterman something about Cudlipp that the copper would snuff him to keep secret. Maybe Cudlipp figures *I* know this information. Which is why he tried to kill me, too."

Feeling a little dizzy, Wentworth rolled down his window a bit and drank in some fresh air.

"Where are you going, John?"

"In search of happiness. I've decided to go straight, clean out the system, and find some sweet hammer to fall in love with. I'll want you to move into my joint while I'm gone, kid, so you can be handy when I phone in for reports."

Wentworth thought: hot tub, fireplace, view of Burrard Inlet and Point Grey. But then he thought: just a minute.

"John, I don't think maybe your place is that safe."

"He's not going to go after some paltry articling student. It's me Cudlipp's after."

As the Mercedes floated over the bridge onto Sea Island and toward the terminal, Brovak flipped open the glove compartment. "All the papers are in there; the machine's yours 'til I get back."

"You mean it?"

"Flash around in it a little bit. It'll keep you in pussy."

Pussy. Basically what Wentworth knew about that topic had been gleaned from two hours of bug-eyed viewing of Minette's videos. He wondered what it would be like being kept in pussy.

The next morning, The *Vancouver Sun* ran a banner story illustrated by a photograph of a message that had been mailed to it the previous day. It was a scissor-and-paste pastiche, its odd-sized letters cut from local newspaper headlines.

It read: "Counsellers of crime, Beware the Sword of Justice. Criminal lawyers are marked for DEATH by the Executor of God." The name "Besterman" then appeared, struck through by an "X" in a red marking pencil.

The names "Pomeroy" and "Brovak" followed, not so marred.

A cut-out snippet from a page of the *New Testament* was glued to the sheet, a line from Luke 7:30, King James version: "The pharisees and lawyers rejected the counsel of God."

Then what seemed intended as a signature line in paste-up letters: "The Executor."

14

The Courting
Judge

Inspector Nordquist came by the office the next day with a photostat copy of the Executor's letter.

"Painstaking work, each letter glued on individually except for the articles and prepositions, which he cut out whole. We were able to date the editions from print on the back of the letters: last Tuesday's and the previous Saturday weekend editions of The *Sun*. He used a brand of glue we are all familiar with from school days. White linen paper, commonly available. The Bible quote is an interesting touch. From a Gideon edition, we think. Millions of those around."

Nordquist also displayed a copy of the envelope with its single, cancelled stamp. It was addressed to: "The Editor. Vancouver Sun. 2250 Granville St. Vancouver." Hand-printed block capital letters. No return address.

"Medium-weight, blue-ink ball-point pen, one of those Papermate throwaways, something like that. It's with our document examiner — sometimes even hand printing can be identified, though not, I think, in this case."

"What about the grenade?" Max asked.

Nordquist said arms experts had concluded it was a common

fragmentation type stocked by both Canadian and U.S. armies.

"And how would this Executor get hold of one of these grenades?" Max asked.

"I have no answer," said Nordquist.

"Executor," mused Augustina. "It's usually used in a legal sense — someone who administers the estate of a deceased."

Max remembered Roger Turnbull's rant. *Lawyers administer their own so-called justice, not God's.*

"Bones, can you find out what Turnbull was doing Tuesday night?"

Nordquist nodded and made a note. "Well, this letter puts a different slant on things. This may be a hoax. I *hope* it's a hoax. Or we may have a maniac on our hands."

After Nordquist left, Brovak phoned from Aspen. The story of the Executor's letter had made the local news.

"It's still Cudlipp," he said. "The letter's just a puff of smoke, and he probably mailed it himself."

"How are you doing?" Augustina asked.

"Hooperdoo."

"How's the snow?"

"Pure and cheap, but I'm weaning myself. Be back in a few weeks to solve this case."

Although a consensus of police and public held that the letter from the Executor was a hoax, the media vigorously encouraged a debate as to whether a madman was on a crusade to bring about a just society, preferably one without criminal lawyers. The Attorney General decided to take no chances. Inspector Nordquist was put in charge of C.L.E.U. — the Coordinated Law Enforcement Unit — a force of city, regional and RCMP investigators.

The Attorney General also made hurried arrangements to beef up security in the courts and to protect several lawyers defending cases of special notoriety. A chaos of adjournments and reschedulings beset the courts.

In the meantime, the Law Society of British Columbia announced a $100,000 reward for information leading to the arrest of the Executor.

But by and large the average citizen didn't seem to be losing any great amount of sleep over the threatened loss of a few lawyers and, in fact, many sardonic mutterings of sympathy were voiced for the Executor's cause.

Because Milsom's counsel, successor to the late Arthur Besterman, feared he might be successful in the Supreme Court of Canada, he quit the case. No one seemed to question why this appeal was going ahead in the first place, since Milsom — still at large — hadn't instructed it. But wherever he had evaporated to, he obviously couldn't be denied counsel in the nation's highest court.

This caused Max Macarthur concern. He would have to petition the court to press some unlucky counsel into service for Milsom.

With Brovak and Pomeroy away, the other lawyers were forced to pull extra freight, and the lights stayed on most evenings at their offices.

A few days following the near demise of John Brovak and his fellow celebrants, Mr. Justice Quentin Russell telephoned Augustina. Preoccupied with the revelations about the Executor, she wasn't prepared for the call and mentally kicked herself for her harried, fractured response to his expressions of concern. He was polite but terribly distant, and promised to call again.

More days trickled by, and Augustina began to worry that she hadn't passed whatever basic tests the judge applied in settling upon his objects of seduction.

He had seemed so…interested. What happened: someone tell him she had herpes?

They had slipped out — not too clandestinely — from Leroy Lukey's roast soon after it had collapsed in chaos. Russell did not disguise his antipathy toward his hapless brother judge and thought the episode hilarious. Lots of laughs over Spanish coffees in the lounge of a smart uptown hotel (a converted high-rise apartment that, he mentioned in passing, he happened to *own*).

Keep your legs crossed, Sophie Marx had warned her. This in reference to Mr. Justice Quentin Russell's reputation of being what the boys in the locker room (Augustina had heard) called a flashy swordsman, and what the girls called an unbridled womanizer.

But Augustina, with a spongy romantic heart beneath her thin armour of caution, was receptive to a little old-fashioned wooing and enjoyed Russell's intense stalking of her over those Spanish coffees —

the bedroom eyes, the flattering tongue, the quickness of lighter to cigarette.

He didn't insult her by asking her if she cared to join him in one of the luxurious suites of this hotel — or for that matter, the master bedroom of his mansion in the Southlands (where, he again mentioned in passing, he kept a stable of horses). Nor did he make the remotest of passes: no touching of hands, no peck on the cheek with the good night ciaos.

So what about this reputation he'd gained in the fine art of lechery?

Shamelessly, she telephoned her long-time girlfriend on Vancouver Island: Olive Klymchuk, an intimate from law school days. Several years ago she and Russell had enjoyed, as she put it, a few months of unholy bedlock.

"Enjoy it while it lasts, sweetie. Because it won't. But he's *such* a gentleman. When he ditched me he sent me twenty-four roses and a letter."

Cynical. But of course, Olive was an impossible person to live with, a fact that her doting new husband, a dermatologist, would doubtless soon learn.

Augustina pressed Olive for more inside dope.

"He's pretty."

"I can see that."

An awkward silence.

"I don't think he's what you're after, honey."

"I'm not *after* anyone. Why do you say that?"

Olive suggested a *tête-a-tête* about the subject when next they met, then changed the topic to her kidnapping case — she represented three persons charged with stealing babies and selling them to childless couples — on and on she went about it, Augustina half-listening, wondering what had made her so sour on Russell. Jealousy, no doubt.

Augustina phoned another friend to ask about him. There had been a wife, she said. In the misty past. Some story surrounded that — he'd been caught cheating on her or something.

On Friday Russell finally called her again, apologizing for the shortness of notice but asking if she cared to accompany him the next evening to a wedding reception — the daughter of one of his cherished former clients was getting married.

Augustina felt herself rebel — just a little. One day's notice for a wedding party? What if she had made plans for Saturday? She hadn't, but that wasn't the point.

When she didn't respond right away, Russell said: "There are reasons I haven't been able to invite you earlier."

He picked her up in a chauffeured limousine, a Mr. James Goodwinkle at the wheel, a tall, well-coiffed gentleman of about forty-five: white gloves, striped suit and stuffed shirt. He sniffed when Russell introduced them.

"I have been with Judge Russell for fifteen years," he announced, as if claiming precedence. A high, prissy voice. He held the doors for them, and they got under way.

"After a while he grows on you," Russell said. "I'd feel handicapped without him. Chauffeur, butler, bartender, you name it, and he also gives a hell of a massage. He's my live-in." He added, somewhat hastily, "Separate quarters, cottage in the back."

She thought: bet the butler's gay. *So* doting on the boss.

Russell told her his staff also included a housekeeper, a gardener, and a stable boy. The housekeeper did a little cooking, too, though Russell — and why should she suspect otherwise? — was also a gourmet chef.

"I'm sorry about the short notice," he said. "I had to, ah, have a talk with a woman I've been seeing."

Oh-oh, Augustina thought. The other woman.

"Dress designer. Exotic lady, very charming, but it wasn't clicking. I couldn't find my way to calling you until I felt the way was clear."

She thought: Wow, he broke a date for her.

"So whose marriage are we celebrating?"

"Lily d'Anglio. Youngest daughter of the one and only Tony."

"The gangster? But you're a *judge*."

"I won't ignore people who helped me on the way. Tony's okay."

At the Italian Community Hall, Quentin Russell seemed pleased to introduce her about, to show her off. No skulking romance this, behind the potted palms of cocktail lounges, but public and unguarded. On the dance floor, the merest touching of chest to breast, a gentle coupling of her right fingers in his left hand, a weightless hand on her waist, his legs in perfect gliding step with hers.

Urbane conversation at his table. (He was a connoisseur of period art — eighteenth century etchings — and he had a small collection of which he was fond.)

Augustina observed that everyone at the wedding party treated Russell with an almost awed respect. Some movers and shakers in the Italian community were here, Augustina observed, along with some obvious Mafia types. Russell had earned his spurs defending high-rolling mobsters, but always with as much adversarial propriety as skill, and had been a favourite of the bench in his years as counsel. That, and the fact he'd been a prominent Tory, helped boost him to the B.C. Supreme Court bench three years ago, at the age of forty-three.

"Many former clients here?" she asked, as, after a dance, they relaxed over glasses of champagne.

"Quite a few. Marvin the Mook, who used to do contracts until he quit. Got quite a scare. Almost went down on a murder conspiracy." Russell looked around. "Large Harold, who does the numbers — I think he still does them — for most of the East End. Charlie the Chunk, his muscle. And Tony, of course."

Tony d'Anglio was a wiry little man in his sixties, his mouth constantly on the move, talking, shouting, quipping. He didn't quite conjure up for Augustina an image of Marlon Brando mumbling through cotton batting.

"Eddie Cohn has all Tony's business now," said Russell. "Worked in my office years ago."

Augustina didn't notice any obvious affection in his voice when he spoke of Eddie Cohn, who was at the party, too: a serpent with his hooded, lizard eyes and skin folds on his neck. The word about Cohn was that he'd gotten too cozy with his clients. Earlier he had drawn Russell aside for what seemed to her an oddly long and serious chat. She didn't ask Russell about it; he didn't explain.

Russell was quick to light her next cigarette.

"I'm curious — why did you become a judge?"

"You mean because I have a few bucks?"

"Okay."

"Money bores me, Augustina. Forgive me — I know it sounds trite — but the law is a passion."

He seemed embarrassed. She smiled.

"Can you keep a secret?" he asked.

"Do it all the time."

"I think I'm on the short list for the Supreme Court of Canada."

"You'd want that?"

"It's the dream, isn't it? The ambition of every lawyer who gives a hoot about what he or she does. And I'm afraid you are looking at a man who is very ambitious. It's not false ambition. I know what I can do."

"You'd be good." She meant that.

But what about the divorce-in-his-past someone had mentioned to Augustina? Wouldn't it cause a little hiccup in the achievement of this ambition? She wondered if it had been messy. Would the mandarins of Ottawa see fit to select as one of the nine most powerful jurists in the land one who had, as Augustina presumed, committed the great civil crime of adultery?

What *about* this failed marriage, anyway? Augustina wondered. Were there children? If so, does he never speak of them?

"Your partner's father is also in the running. Max Mac Two."

"I know."

"Brilliant man."

"Maybe he lacks a little heart," Augustina said.

"If the implication is that I don't, thank you."

Tony d'Anglio interrupted, joining them with his legal shark Eddie Cohn at his elbow. After Russell made appropriate comments about the radiance of the bride, d'Anglio said: "I always thought you was a right guy, judge. How come you gave them guys such a heavy bit, Henderson and McCoy?" Two of d'Anglio's middlemen.

"Perhaps because they committed the error of selling the wrong kind of horse to an undercover from the Royal Mounted."

D'Anglio clapped Russell on the back, and addressed Augustina. "The guy's my fixer for ten years, and suddenly becomes Johnny Square. We got an honest judge on our hands here, what's the country comin' to? Can't trust these lawyers." He threw his arm around Eddie Cohn. "Hey, I even worry about Eddie here, I think he's got a honest streak in him somewhere."

"I try not to let it depress me," Cohn said.

D'Anglio said: "So who's the enchantress, judge? A looker."

Russell introduced them.

"Sage," d'Anglio said. "You practise with that throat almost bought it, Brovak. Hear he's a real pistol. *Arrivederci.*"

He left with his entourage.

It was long after midnight when Augustina and Russell wandered out into a moonlit night. She was tipsy, in a mood to take chances, but Russell escorted her home in his Cadillac limo (after waking James Goodwinkle, who went bright red at being caught asleep at the wheel). They lingered only a few moments at the door of her Fairview condo (there was an impeccable dry-lipped buss to her cheek), and then he departed.

Two mature adults enjoying each other's company. No expectations, of course.

Augustina decided she was prepared to forgive his bad reputation. Expert swordsman though he might be, he had obviously earned his conquests fairly, in gallant and convivial battle. He was too attractive for words.

When was he going to make his move?

The next weekend, he took her to a Vancouver Opera production of *Othello*. She wore a little thousand-dollar outfit she'd picked up last year in San Francisco, and had to admit she looked, well, smashing.

He agreed. "You look utterly magnificent," he said at her doorway.

She tried to look demur but spoiled the effect with a nervous… not a laugh: an awful giggle. Red-faced, feeling somewhat like Eliza Doolittle on her way to the ball with Professor Higgins, she took his arm and he led her to the limousine. James Goodwinkle stood like a palace guardsman by the open passenger door, barely deigning to look at her.

At the Queen Elizabeth Theatre, box seats. Russell spent more time watching her than voluptuous Desdemona. Later, over cocktails, he seemed unusually maladroit, and spilled some wine on the tablecloth. She sensed she might have this judge under a little spell. It was a kick.

At her door this time, although lips touched lips instead of cheeks, he again beat a chivalrous retreat in his big black Caddie. His restraint unsettled her. This was supposed to be a guy with only one thing on his mind. Did she not remember Olive Klymchuk boasting he had her under the sheets after the first date? Ah, but perhaps his reticence was intended as a signal to her — she was special, he was hinting. Special enough to wait for.

There was a mystery about him which tantalized her. She must talk soon to her old pal Olive — did she know some secret?

15

Mystery
Guest

Max Macarthur's identical two-and-a-half-year-olds barreled out of the door the instant he reached his front step. As he swept them up in his arms, Darrow pulled his glasses off and Clarence followed up with a thumb to an unprotected eyeball.

"Daddy can't see without those...don't!"

Too late. Darrow, testing the strength of his burly little arms, bent the metal frame of the spectacles. Clarence grabbed a handful of thinning hair and pulled.

"Yowch," said Max, as he bore them into the kitchen, redolent with Ruth's *plat du jour*, a roast of lamb in the oven.

"Thank God," said Ruth, "the late shift has arrived. I'm at my wits' end."

Ruth was an intelligent woman, a psychologist. One would think she would be smart enough to hire someone to help take the load off. But never a nanny would enter these portals, no housemaid nor servant.

As Max lifted one of the tots into piggyback position, the Velcro gave on the tot's diaper, and Max felt a sudden wetness. "I think Darrow pissed on me," he said.

"No, darling," she said, studying them closely. "Clarence pissed on you."

After dinner, Max read them some Dr. Seuss and tucked them in. Ruth had a fire going, and the two of them stretched out on the rug in front of the fireplace.

"Caroline Pomeroy dropped by," she said.

"What do you mean, she actually *showed up* here? Like, out of the void?" Caroline had been hiding behind a wall of hurt, refusing to answer calls.

"We had quite a session. Got a little weepy."

"Over what?"

"Well, Brian lied to her. He wrote her a letter claiming the thing with this woman was a one-nighter in Knot Lake. Turns out it was a four-monther in Vancouver."

"Oh, God. He was never a very good liar."

"He sends her letters. Not once does he tell her he loves her. What's with Brian, afraid he's going to lose face? He can't say he loves her because that makes her one up? I mean, they're *always* competing. And paranoid. He's always complaining Abigail Hitchins is out to get him." She mused. "Can't see what she and Caroline share, they're *so* chummy."

"So what did Caroline say?"

"Oh, she was worried about that note from the Executor with Brian's name in it. I told her not to worry, he's thousands of miles away. But she also received a letter from that ridiculous woman, Charity Slough. Told all. Requested Caroline to bless their love."

"Oh, *no.*"

"She's a twit. I mean, Brian *couldn't* have taken this hare-brain seriously."

Caroline Pomeroy spent that evening thinking about love and forgiveness. Pondering all those little questions Ruth Worobec-Macarthur had asked, the kind psychologists try to sneak by you, to entice you to *reveal.*

How stupid she had felt in front of Ruth, bathos in the front-room parlour.

On the day that Brian had almost been shot, Caroline's gynecologist had decreed her barren. That was what she'd been crying about, though she didn't admit this to Ruth; somehow she couldn't. She hadn't mentioned her sterility to anybody but Abigail Hitchins, another slosh session.

The afternoon had turned out all right, though, she had to admit. After the rainy season ended, Caroline had played with the twins — so sweet, so innocent of life's cruel jokes.

And Ruth had somehow got her laughing about Charity Slough's letter. She hadn't had so much fun in exactly three months: the sheer and utter joy of vitriol, as they shredded the silly ditz apart.

She went out to the back to consult with Howland. Her wise bird could tell her about love; he was in its grip.

One recent evening Caroline had gone out to the backyard at dawn and found Howland wooing a fellow member of the species *Otius Asio*, a shy young thing he seemed unable to coax from the forest behind the house.

Tonight, she observed, they were still at it, Howland whistling and hooting, his Juliet aloof and coy on her fir-tree balcony.

"Abigail says you have to have pride in yourself as a woman. Says I should just get rid of him."

"Hoo," said Howland.

"Whom, Howland. You know, the guy who used to hang around here. Abigail wants to issue a writ. She's pretty intense about the whole thing, doesn't think I have much backbone."

Howland delivered himself of a long, tremolo whistle, preened the feathers of his wing, then resumed gazing at her wide-eyed.

"Should I just tell Abigail to drop the damn writ on the bastard or what?"

A skeptical twitch of a feathery horn.

The female owl flew off. Howland took to the air in pursuit, but soon returned to his pear tree, dejected.

"She'll come back," Caroline said. She caught herself before adding: they always do. No. No goddamn way.

March 14

Dear firm,
    A serrated dagger of reflected moonlight stabs at me
from the Pacific horizon, as a crescent moon creeps sullenly
toward its extinction. Firebugs blink nervously on the lawn.
I write in the dance of candlelight because Puerto Próspero

has run out of kerosene for my lamps. (Add to the list: razor blades, aspirins and batteries of all kinds, not to mention Gucci purses and Venetian crystal goblets. Oh, yes, and carbon paper, very scary this, for I have no back-up copies of my last seven chapters.)

The night is busy with whistles, croaks and groans, the metal trill of crickets, and intermittent plunks like the falling of giant teardrops (which sounds are emitted by a tiny frog outside the kitchen door, telling me I am not alone in sorrow).

What, I wish to know, is the current state of disrepair of my marriage?

The phones are still down in Próspero, and I am driven to send this urgent missive fearing the office has been swallowed up by an excessively high North Pacific tide. Am I the last surviving practitioner of the fine art of letter writing?

How proceeds my action against Abigail Hitchins for alienation of affections? Why do I detect the distant odour of feet being dragged? We all, do we not, remember from law school the great cause of action under the common law which renders thieves of love liable in damages? I instruct you to sue her for all she's got right down to her little painted red claws and silicon implants.

I console myself: ah, what are my troubles compared to this planet's? The ozone is depleting, the ice caps melting, the forests burning, the deserts expanding, and the elephants and whales disappearing. How trivial the anguish of a single human being among billions too many. That is how I console myself. With the knowledge that Earth is dying anyway.

As I sit here trying to appease my sadness by contemplating the ecocide of a moribund planet, the chop-chop-chop of a helicopter intrudes. More tropical snow from the refineries of Medellin to deviate the septums of America. Via the Osa Peninsula and past my front door.

The doorstep of which was darkened not long ago by the portly form of the local captain of la Guardia Civil, one

Francisco Sierra. He said he was here to inquire about my status (all foreigners are subject to periodic immigration checks).

I made him coffee. He asked what had brought me to Costa Rica. I directed his attention to my typewriter table with pens, papers and reference books, and explained I was writing a crime novel. He clapped his hands and asked if I read P.D. James.

It turns out that Francisco Sierra — I now call him Francisco, and he calls me Brian — is not only a fervent student of the crime genre, but a little more knowledgeable about *this* mystery writer than made me comfortable.

He knew that I was staying in the house of an alleged notorious dope dealer currently on trial in Canada, and moreover seemed to know that I was associated with the law firm defending him. I was startled. How had he learned that? Simple. Having heard I was staying in the villa of the infamous Twelve-Fingers Watson, he had checked me out with the RCMP.

We broke out a couple of beer and talked for a while of the works of Sayers, Simenon, and Stout. Francisco's English is excellent; painstakingly learned so he could read the complete Conan Doyle in the original. He also loves the British cozies — Hercule Poirot is his hero. (Even looks a little like him, plump, short, quick of eye, with a well-tended moustache.) I must say he became quite animated in conversation. Me, too — I think I have been starving for the spoken word. After a couple more beer, we just rambled on about everything. He told me about his wife and three kids. I told him about Caroline.

He, too, had suffered a grievous injustice. He'd been a senior investigator in San José until he'd made the mistake of busting a heavy politician, an aide to the Minister of Security, on corruption charges. Couldn't make the charges stick, and some years ago they shunted him off to the farthest corner of Costa Rica, i.e. Puerto Próspero.

He paused before making his departure to join me in my evening sacrament, my devotions before the falling sun:

a flaming sky and clouds like fat pumpkins, Titian red. I stared at the pinprick of light until it disappeared with a soundless plop. Final fade out. No green flash. Francisco Sierra didn't see it either, and somehow this further bonded me to him.

But you want to hear how the novel progresses. Well, the ghostwriter within is still calling the shots. I often feel like a spider enmeshed in his own web, struggling, finally submissive to the demon inside, who guides his amanuensis's hapless hands across the keyboard.

Or is this neurotic behavior like over-eating, a means of dealing with stress? The pot is boiling over and I'm drowning in a frothy stew of red herrings and rabbits in the hat and well-bribed pork and suspects fattened for the kill. Whodunit? Whoknows? A third of the way through my first draft the killer not only remains on the loose but unknown. Even to the writer. I no sooner settle on one suspect to be my ultimate villain than another calls out from the weedy undergrowth of my imagination and demands the starring role.

Know where you are going, Widgeon warns. "No mystery writer may successfully embark upon a cruise across the dark waters of murder without knowing the port at which he must ultimately disembark." One plans, one outlines; one builds a skeleton on which to hang flesh (this grisly metaphor is Widgeon's own).

Mr. Widgeon lacks his usual arrogant ease when dealing with matters carnal, so he cannot assist me in that area, but I'm afraid the work-in-progress is also barren, unsexed, forsaken by the nymphs of Eros. How can I expect to write a bodice-ripping blockbuster without a healthy dose, as it were, of peripheral porn? No writhing bodies, or grunts or groans and gropes. No heaving, swelling breasts, no throbbing thighs, no rigid members seeking out the dark, sweet, sweaty recesses of intimate connection. No pining hearts here even, no teary farewells at the Casablanca airport, no drops of blood from the author's own wounded, weeping heart.

Suddenly I feel wretched. The moon has fizzled into the sea. I must abed.

Why do you not write?

Yours anxiously,
Brian.

March 14

Dear Caroline,

I have tried and failed several times to put words on paper, to express my anguish over that letter sent to you by the confused Ms. Slough (at the behest, please know, of a certain Abigail Hitchins). My wastebasket is littered with crumpled attempts to put the record straight in a form both forceful and credible, yet not acidic with the wretched, helpless anger I feel toward your lawyer for having devised yet another plot to tear asunder the already tattered rags of our marriage.

Ask her if she hyped Charity Slough to write that awful letter. She will lie, of course, but you may observe a little twitch of guilt crease her face. (Or do I kid myself? Guilt is one of the higher emotions, unfelt by the sociopathic personality.)

Are you still in the thrall of that dominatrix?

I suppose that by now, armed as you likely are with Charity's Complete History of the Transgressions of Pomeroy, you have added contemptible liar to your list of reasons to hate me. Okay, I admit I told a fib about the briefness of my acquaintance with this woman. The lie was white, intended to allay some of the hurt you felt. The truth is, this unromantic and basely physical relationship lasted exactly four months. The truth is, the series of episodes with Charity constituted my one and only marital transgression.

What is also true, and PLEASE BELIEVE ME: I was not in love with this Charity woman. And I did not tell her I was.

I may have slipped, Caroline, but I didn't fall through Alice's rabbit hole.

Anyway, I went to town on the day of your birthday, and from one of the miners I bought a nugget of pure gold, which I have asked a friendly tourist returning home to Edmonton to courier to you, along with this letter. Hope you had a happy.

I remain, contritely,
Brian.

P.S., my listings now include the Little Hermit, the Scaly-throated Leaftosser, the Three-wattled Bellbird, and the Thick-billed Euphonia. (Which sightings, I regret to inform — and believe me, I am not jousting over silly numbers — has pushed me ahead of you by, I believe, six distinct species of birds.)

Nameless (so far) are the typewriter birds — little finches that have learned to mimic the sounds of clicking keys. And the as yet unidentified night bird that repeats your name.
How is Howland?

With a charm of finches and an exaltation of larks,

I remain, hopefully,
Your husband

16

Nymph
with Satyr

Augustina invited Quentin Russell out for dinner Saturday night on his return from circuit in the Interior. He offered to pick her up, but she insisted instead upon showing up at his house — more of a chateau, really — in her three-year-old Camaro. In her anxiety to not be early, she was late.

The many-gabled greystone building stood behind a high clipped hedge and seemed to sprawl across at least an acre of lawn and rose garden. Servants' quarters, three-car garage — the pool, she guessed, was in the back — and here was Quentin Russell emerging from the doorway before her car could roll to a stop behind the limo. James Goodwinkle followed him out like a fussing mother hen, shyly averting his eyes when her skirt rode up as she stepped from her car.

A sturdy black woman hurried after Russell with his coat. "That man. Some day he's going to leave his head behind." Mrs. Collins, said Russell. The housekeeper looked his date up and down — reprovingly, thought Augustina: the brevity of hem, the brazen show of thigh. Then she winked. "Maybe he *will* lose his head."

At the restaurant, Russell showed not the least discomfort at being Augustina's guest. He sat gazing upon her as she ordered the wine, and only when she stumbled in pronouncing one of the entrées did he intercede — speaking to the waiter in faultless French, then apologizing to her for having done so. While they dined, they engaged in the morbid conjectures that so many of their profession were prone to these days: the who, why and wherefore of the Executor.

"What's the speculation in your office?" he asked.

"Oh, God, who knows? A sick joke. But everyone has their favorite suspect. Max likes Roger Turnbull. The White Angel guy? John Brovak says it's either Leroy Lukey or Sergeant Everit Cudlipp."

She expected Russell to laugh, but he said: "Cudlipp. He's infected with corruption. He's on the pad, and always has been. Maybe Brovak is onto something."

"You're not serious."

For a while Russell seemed lost in thought. Finally, he spoke: "Augustina, I want to talk to you about this. I really *need* to talk about it. I haven't been able to. It actually has something to do with the murder of Arthur Besterman. And, I guess, the attempt against John Brovak."

"Are you about to confess?" she said. "I knew it was you all along."

He smiled, but looked distracted. "Arthur Besterman, who had not the crispest of legal minds, used to consult with me quite a bit — tricky issues of law he couldn't find the answers for. I didn't mind helping him, he was a decent character. Even after I went to the bench, he'd still phone me, or come into chambers. Okay, you're familiar with that long-running drug case Brovak was doing? Cudlipp's life project?"

"Yes, the Monster."

"Up until his death last July, Besterman was acting for one of the accused."

"I'm aware — Rosalind Finch. Watson's ex-girlfriend."

"She told Besterman something in strictest confidence, which didn't stop him from repeating it to me. Anyway, he was under instructions from this Finch woman to say nothing unless…unless she disappeared or died."

"Well, God, what did she tell him?"

"Understand: Arthur said this to me in utter secrecy. Quite improperly, too, given the confidential nature of his relationship with his client. What Rosalind Finch told Besterman was this: she had been meeting secretly with Cudlipp. He offered her a hundred thousand dollars."

"The cops would spend that *much* to buy a witness?"

"Not government money. From the pockets of my old conniving friend, Tony d'Anglio. He wanted Twelve-Fingers Watson to go down. He wanted his territory, his coke markets. Cudlipp would get a handsome finder's fee from the mob if he got Rosalind to roll. She would have been the perfect Crown witness. Absolute guarantee of conviction if Rosie ultimately took the stand."

"How would she know the money was coming from the mob?"

"Cudlipp told her. He was, ah, rather close to Rosie. Besterman thought Cudlipp had been making out with her."

"But why did she tell Arthur Besterman?"

"According to him, she just wanted someone to know. In case the deal fell through, in case something happened to her. Insurance. Besterman was incensed at Cudlipp. But he was in a trap of silence. He told me he had started to write a letter of complaint to the police commission. But decided he couldn't — solicitor-client privilege. But he did confront Cudlipp personally. There was a row."

"Are you saying you think Cudlipp killed him?"

"I can only speculate. Maybe he saw his chance after Milsom was acquitted. He knew suspicion would be cast elsewhere."

"And the hand grenade, John Brovak…"

"Why not? Easier to kill a second time. He had a double motive — an act of vengeance against the lawyer who embarrassed him and won Watson's acquittal. Plus he'd get rid of Watson and most of his crew in one go, and thus earn his pay from d'Anglio. So…well, the thought struck me that maybe he — I'm not saying it's Cudlipp, I don't know — but he *could* have sent that letter to the newspaper. Very easy to blame these events on some insane self-styled Executor."

Fairly startling theory, she thought. "Do I get the impression you want this followed up?"

"This is an ugly thing to say, but I really don't wish to be involved. It's awkward, with the Supreme Court appointment looming. If there were some other way to corroborate this…if his letter to the police commission could be found…He told me he dictated it."

Their conversation came to a stop as a fellow lawyer, one Martin Wessel of the not so aromatic reputation (known in the profession by the nickname "Weasel") entered the restaurant with what Augustina could only describe to herself as a cheap bauble on his arm, a woman whose face was literally hidden under makeup. Barely twenty. Wessel was at least sixty, large and bald, although he pretended not to know that everyone knew he wore a rug.

As the maître-d' showed them a table, fortunately on the far side of the room, Wessel spotted Augustina and her date, and detoured toward them.

"How's the food?" he asked.

"Hello, Marty," said Russell, somewhat coolly. "The medallion of veal is excellent."

"And how's the company?" Wessel winked. "Hi, Augie, your partner Brovak doing okay since almost getting his head blown off? Used to think I was in a safe profession; now I wish I'd become a chiropractor."

"I think we'd all feel better if you had," said Augustina, with a smile that said she meant it.

"You going to be setting a trial date on the Doyle case, Augie, or you going to abandon? I won't claim costs."

"We'll set a trial date after my motion to order Father Doyle to answer a few more questions. Seems to me that's coming up Tuesday."

"Hey, we got a judge here. Let's call the restaurant to order and we can do it right now."

Augustina and Russell politely laughed along with him.

"Hope to be hearing from you soon, judge," Wessel said as he returned to his table.

"What was that all about?" Augustina asked. "'Hope to be hearing from you.'"

"Oh, a reserved decision I owe him. Foreclosure case. The Weasel acts for a grinch of a landlord. And what do *you* have going with him?"

She told him about her suit against the Catholic school for native boys and the infamous pederast, Father Doyle, the rector. Wessel, she said, had been stalling settlement for years.

When the bill arrived with a second serving of *café au lait* he asked if she'd care to return to his house to see his etchings.

She burst out laughing. "Your etchings!"

"My Tiepolos. I have an early reproduction of the ten plates of the Capricci."

"Of who?"

"'Nymph, with Satyr Child and Goats.' From the Spanish period of Tiepolo the Elder."

"Nymph with..." Augustina couldn't control herself, and had to wipe her eyes with her napkin. "Oh, gosh. Too much wine."

"Surely, you do not think me dishonourable for asking." He said that with a smile and fake formality.

"Well — can I say this? — you *do* have a bit of a reputation..."

Russell showed a pained expression.

"I have a friend...Olive Klymchuk."

"Yes. Dear Olive. She drove me batty."

He sipped his coffee, said nothing. Augustina felt totally awkward.

"Okay." He sighed. "Augustina, I don't hide from the fact that I'm that rare statistic: male, mid-forties, unattached. It's because I'm on the bench that I get targeted with so much gossip. Supposed to be sedate and removed from it all, don't you know. Live like a monk. Hell, I like women. I prefer to think I'm rather normal in that respect."

But what about that wife and that divorce? Augustina wanted to ask. Tell us about it.

She said, "I'd like to see those etchings."

When the bill came, he asked her if she was sure they couldn't split it.

She thanked him, but said no. She would bounce for it herself, thus ensuring that her freedom of choice would be undiluted by any sense of debt or obligation. A freedom which could come in handy later in the evening, were the etchings not to occupy their whole attention, and Russell turned into a character created by the Marquis de Sade.

The maître-d' scuttled along behind them, madam-ing and sir-ing, as they headed for the cloakroom. They waved goodbye to Martin Wessel — he had barely kept his eyes off them since he arrived — and Augustina didn't take Russell's arm until they were outside. She led him to her car in the chill of a suddenly cloudless night.

"I can't tell you how delightful a time I'm having with you," he said as she opened the passenger door for him.

"Thank you." She felt a little giddy for a moment. She turned and kissed him quickly on the lips. A *bec*, as the French say.

As she drove him to his house, she tried mentally to prepare herself for come what may.

Before one couples with a likely appointee to the Supreme Court of Canada, is it appropriate, Miss Manners, to inquire into certain aspects of his medical history? Into whether he has ever encountered any problems of, say, a viral nature?

Of course, Augustina Sage herself, on occasion, had had carnal knowledge of representatives of the other sex. A few different guys. A handful of men, really. Maybe a dozen. This was not the time to be adding up the awful toll, and anyway she had always practised safe sex. Almost always. Most of the time. It's not as if she'd had three or four abortions. Just one.

But this time, guard up. She would make no commitment beyond admiring his etchings.

It was nearly midnight when they returned to his house, and the staff had discreetly vanished. Augustina wanted to explore, to pry, to seek out the interesting ghosts of Russell's past, but she restrained herself. Ladies don't wander about their host's palaces. The front parlour he escorted her to was dominated by a massive fireplace and nicely appointed, retro-chic furniture, old world nostalgia, the room spare and uncluttered — and seemed somehow lonely, faintly echoing her nervous chatter as she reviewed the obligatory Tiepolos that adorned the walls. There they were, all right: nymph, satyr and goat.

Their history was described (rather interesting, really), and then Russell seemed, briefly, at a loss for conversation. He suggested she might like to look around the house while he built a fire and made some drinks. Den, office, solarium, a kitchen as big as her entire apartment — and that long spiralling staircase to the bedrooms on the second floor...

He caught up to her in the solarium with a couple of snifters of something VSOP, and there followed a moonlit tour of the grounds (silver sparkles in the trees) and of the back patio by the heated pool (soft swirling mists). After which, to the music of Debussy, came a crackling cedar fire, and a family album showing his wonderful parents, his siblings, and little Quentin Russell himself in short pants and a Boy Scout uniform. Cute.

And — here we go at last — the wife. The wife was gorgeous, and somehow...dignified, well-bred. A posh. Eunice was her name, Eunice of the alluring smile.

Russell's face seemed to go all rubbery as he looked at the photo.

"Your ex-wife," she said.

"Yes," he said. "She's dead."

Augustina just sat there on the couch with him, holding the album, feeling foolish, unable to think of anything to say, waiting for him to elaborate.

"Fifteen years ago." He looked from the picture to Augustina. His eyes seemed to turn dark and distant. "It was a car accident."

"Oh, my God." Augustina reached for his hand. "Were there children?"

"No."

A long, anxious pause followed that, then she tried to blunt the awkwardness with some inane prattle about time healing wounds.

"I'll talk about it with you some time. Not now. It's not easy."

"I understand."

She couldn't remember feeling more awkward. He, too, seemed apprehensive, and quickly downed his cognac. Another painful silence.

"Would you, ah, like to see my etchings again?"

She burst out laughing, a release of tension.

"God, I like that. When you laugh."

Something took over her. Body mechanisms that were unwilled and automatic. She was suddenly all over him. Her arms around his neck, her mouth open to him, her nostrils filled with him.

Zips and buttons, nibbling lips on breasts, nipples hard, hot, pause a moment for the earrings, curly fur on chest and stomach, tug at belt, blue boxer shorts, beautiful ruddy short thick prick, her hands teasing it, encircling it, his own warm, soft hands finding the truth of her, her wetness.

And softly in her ear. "I've had a vasectomy; there's a scar to prove it. But I also have condoms."

"Fuck it," she said.

17

Chance
Discovery

On Monday morning, Max Macarthur found Augustina staring dreamily out her office window. It didn't take much prying to learn her weekend had gone well.

"Quentin Russell?"

"Mm-hmm. I think he's kind of hung up on me."

"Yeah? Is it shared?"

"Sort of. A little more than sort of." She laughed at her own coyness. "Anyway, I have to tell you something else. He has a theory about the Executor. This is classified, okay?"

"All right, shoot."

She told Max about the confidences Russell had received from Arthur Besterman. About Cudlipp's secret informer Rosalind Finch, the $100,000 bribe offer from Tony d'Anglio to sink Twelve-Fingers Watson, the aborted complaint by Besterman about Cudlipp to the police commission.

Max found this hugely interesting. Rosie Finch — yes, he thought, isn't that the name of a bird, a kind of canary? She'd been Watson's lover until he dumped her. Motive to chirp? Was she still working for Cudlipp?

"Quentin didn't laugh when I told him Brovak thought Cudlipp was the Executor," Augustina said. "He kind of hinted we should look into this."

"Russell really should go to the cops with it," Max said.

"Well, I don't think he will."

"Obviously we can't," said Max.

"No, I don't think he'd appreciate that," said Augustina.

Wentworth was called in and briefed.

"I already went through Besterman's files," he said. "Didn't find any letter to the police commission. Just a blank complaint form."

"Okay," Max said, "Rosie Finch's lawyer: Buruda. He back from holidays yet?"

"I'll try him again this morning." Wayne Buruda had gone to Maui to recover after the Watson trial. He had been due back on the weekend.

"Besterman's secretary?" Max said. "Maybe he dictated that letter of complaint to her."

"Can't find her."

"Try harder," Max said. "Cancel your cases for today, pal, and get on your bike."

"I have a Mercedes."

For the last two weeks at the wheel of Brovak's 1978 Mercedes SL, Wentworth Chance had felt transformed, a young man of great charm and distinction, a member of the accelerati. He enjoyed whizzing through the city, a long plaid scarf (discovered in Brovak's closet) flapping behind him when he took the top down on rainless days. He played Mingus, Peterson and Grappelli on the fancy dashboard deck. He swished up and down the main drags of Vancouver in this car, trying to figure out the mechanics of attracting the kittens Brovak promised would be constantly mewing around a man in a Mercedes SL.

Unless a clerical error had been made on his last pay slip, Wentworth had just been given a massive three-hundred-and-fifty-dollar-a-month increase in his salary. So he not only had a fast car but enough bucks to buy gas — and he also had a pad with a view and a hot tub. So where were the girls?

He realized: you have to *meet* someone first. You can't just pull up to a bus stop and ask a woman if she wants a ride to work...Or can you? How do people do these things, anyway?

Wentworth had been considered somewhat of a strange kid in the town where he grew up, intellectual with his owlish glasses and sort of...bookwormy. A wonk, they'd called him, a grunt. He'd had a couple of adolescent zits and tits experiences with the postmistress's daughter ("I don't go all the way"), but generally speaking, meeting strange women was as easy for Wentworth as making encounters with extraterrestrial humanoids.

Every evening at nine, at the end of his late shift at the coal mine, Wentworth would pick up the Mercedes from Brovak's reserved garage space, drive down Robson Street, up Davie, over to Fourth, back down Broadway, wondering if he should just park somewhere, stroll casually into a bar...yeah, and take the chance of some goon slashing the ragtop and yanking out about a thousand dollars worth of stereo.

So he would just drive for about an hour. He'd get back to Brovak's eyrie at about ten or eleven p.m. and climb into the hot tub on the deck outside, looking down the slope of Hollyburn Mountain to the great city spread below him, two million people, half of them women.

On working days, Wentworth would drown his loneliness in non-stop labours. During the week after Brovak's departure, he averaged about a trial-and-a-half a day — bylaws, traffic citations, Youth Court. But today, all trials cancelled, he would be working as the law firm's flatfoot.

He first went to Buruda's office, a hole in the wall in an old building near Chinatown. His office door was locked — Buruda seemed to employ no secretary — and a note on it suggested he try Pop's Coffee Shop.

Wentworth found the Great Buruda in this café, freshly tanned, labouring over the morning paper's crossword.

He inquired as to the whereabouts of Rosie Finch. Rosie, said Buruda, had mentioned something to him after the trial about "flying south."

"Where?"

"Seayar," he said. "I dunno, never heard of it. Thailand? Anyway, some place hot with lotsa drugs. I imply from what she hinted is she's on a business trip with her ex."

"Watson."

"Yeah. Anyway, she's already made ankles outta town and I've closed the file and sent in the bill. A hundred and two thousand bucks from Legal Aid, it ain't enough for a hundred and two days of Leroy Lukey. I had to go to Hawaii to chill out."

Had Rosie ever talked about Cudlipp?

Nope.

Flying off somewhere with Watson on a big drug deal. Seayar? Wentworth would look it up in an atlas. Good luck, Watson, he thought: all through those hundred and two days Rosalind Finch had been a rotten apple in the barrel. Primed to bring Watson down (along with nineteen others) with a guest appearance as a surprise witness at the end of the Crown's case. Assuming she was still working for Cudlipp (and Tony d'Anglio), the RCMP would be laying in wait for him on his return from far-off Seayar.

Cudlipp couldn't have cared less about that stay of proceedings. He had always had Watson in the bag.

Wentworth had phoned every E. Anderson in the book in his luckless pursuit of Erika Anderson, the former secretary of Besterman. Finally this morning, out of desperation, he phoned through a list of secretarial agencies. He scored a goal. She was Mrs. Erika Penholder now, newly married, and working as a legal temp.

He rang her up.

Erika Penholder could not recall Besterman making any complaints against Sergeant Cudlipp; in fact she had been off sick for a few days before her boss's death.

But she agreed to meet Wentworth in her former place of employment. Just as another long search through Besterman's files seemed about to prove fruitless, she found, in a drawer of her former desk, a few scattered cassettes with Besterman's dictation.

"He used to leave them here for me to transcribe," she said.

Wentworth asked to borrow them, and he took them to the office and listened for several minutes: inconsequential letters to clients and prosecutors. But finally, this one:

"Letter to the RCMP police commission. Ah, Erika, do this one in rough, I want to look it over. Let's see, ah, Dear sirs, re Staff-Sergeant Everit Cudlipp, and then start off, Please find enclosed herewith a form of complaint of, ah, with respect to the above-named officer in connection with certain acts perpetrated by the same which resulted in a, ah, an interference in the administration of justice and the... violation of a solicitor-client relationship.

"The complaint involves, ah, tampering, cross that out, certain improper approaches made by the above-named Cudlipp to a client of mine on legal aid, one Rosalind Finch, and a promised payment of currency in the amount of one hundred thousand dollars and, ah, a promise made to her that she could avail herself of the witness protection program for giving Crown evidence at the forthcoming trial in the case of Regina versus Watson et al. Miss Finch has informed me she is interested in accepting these offers. I therefore declined to act for her further.

"And as well, she advised me that the said Sergeant Cudlipp is involved in...a certain matter which could lead to criminal charges, involving an underworld bribe to Cudlipp...No. Delete that last sentence, Erika. Continue: When confronted by the undersigned as to these matters, the said Sergeant Cudlipp said, let's see, uh, open quotes, 'If you gum up my case, I'll make porridge out of your face,' close quotes."

Pregnant pause. An excited Wentworth thought: here was the proof of Cudlipp's complicity.

"Uh, Erika, put a hold on this letter — I just thought, maybe I can't repeat what Rosalind told me...I don't think this is going to work. Uh, okay, I want you to send out a bill on that hit-and-run, Billingshaft, or whatever his name..."

Wentworth listened to the rest of the tape, the last dictations of Arthur Besterman. Nothing more of interest.

As his secretary transcribed the tape, Wentworth felt a niggle of worry about what Wayne Buruda had told him. Rosie going off with Watson. On a big drug deal.

Hadn't Brovak said something about Watson going down to Costa Rica to sign the papers for that property?

Seayar. C.R.

Costa Rica. Of course.

Now the niggle of worry began to take shape and grow.

Max and Augustina were having lunch at Au Sauterne, and Wentworth jogged anxiously to their table with the transcript of Besterman's unfinished letter to the police commission.

He waited until they read it.

"Wow," Max said. "But it's not something you could take to a jury. The hearsay of the dead is usually kind of inadmissible."

Wentworth told them his fears: Finch the fink was on her way to Costa Rica with Watson, who was being fattened for the kill. Pomeroy was in danger of being dragged into some scam, perhaps involving that Costa Rican property. Which Pomeroy, Macarthur and Co. was in the process of taking title to.

They returned to the office. The international operator in Costa Rica told them all phone lines to Puerto Próspero were still down.

"Howland, this is Wentworth," Caroline said.

The owl didn't acknowledge the lowly articling student, but merely buried his head in his shoulders.

"And that's Howland's wife, Olga."

The female screech owl, in the nesting box, winked at Wentworth.

"Wentworth will be looking after you while I'm gone. Only a few days. I'm off to protect the Marbled Murrelets."

"Marbled Murrelet," said Wentworth. "Sounds like some kind of Victorian furniture."

"Wentworth, they're little diving birds and they're *threatened*. The logging companies are chomping up all their nests. Okay, you guys, remember to keep your feathers preened, and be good parents to your eggs."

She led Wentworth back to the house. "Just feed them once in the evening. Chicken heads and rabbit guts are in the fridge."

Wentworth made a throwing-up face.

Caroline just laughed. "God, I feel good about this. Getting active: it's a tonic."

"An illegal blockade, um, I don't know, Mrs. Pomeroy. They could arrest you."

In the house, as Caroline packed, she showed Wentworth the gold nugget from Brian.

"Might make a nice ring," she said, "maybe for his nose, the kind that bulls have."

18

The Pretend Lawyer

As Max was leaving the Provincial Court, downhearted after losing a hit and run, wondering why he hadn't kept his babbling, incoherent client off the stand, he saw Joe Ruff outside the Cordova Street entrance: suit vest buttoned over his pot belly, briefcase in hand, looking like a real lawyer — an expensive one at that. Max remembered vaguely a promise to consult with Ruff about one of his plethora of cock-eyed cases, something about a suit in damages against a small claims judge.

Max tried an end run, but Joe Ruff spotted him.

"Oh, Max, old boy — can you spare half a minute?"

Half a minute, Max feared, could expand agonizingly into half an hour — the man rambled endlessly when you gave him a chance — but politeness demanded he at least acknowledge him, and Max slowed from his brisk pace to allow Ruff to catch up.

"I have a meeting, Joe, but what's half a minute more?"

"I say, that Executor chap has me worried. No one's safe, what?"

Max refrained from assuring Ruff he was an unlikely target of the Executor's fury.

Ruff dug into his briefcase and drew out some documents. "Rather suspect I must have got someone's goat." He seemed proud of that. "One would think the government might have other things to do while a killer is running amok."

A petition and an affidavit, Max observed. The Attorney General of British Columbia versus Joseph Ruff.

"They seek to bar me from, quote, 'instituting any legal proceedings in any court in the province.' Well, what do you think of that? Preposterous, what?"

The affidavit complained of Ruff's twenty-three law suits, all current, almost all against judges, government clerks and inspectors. Ruff, alleged the Attorney General, was "clogging" the court system with "unnecessary, scandalous, frivolous and vexatious" proceedings.

"Thought you'd get a rise out of this," Ruff said. "With your strong civil rights beliefs."

Max continued to read. Avoid committing yourself to anything here, he told himself.

"Absolute outrage, what? Barring a citizen from the courts."

"Yes," said Max. "It looks like that's what they're trying to do."

"We can't let them get away with this, can we?"

Max didn't like the "we." But the civil libertarian in him took exception to this attempt to deny a citizen access to the courts, even the troublesome Joe Ruff, all his vexatious suits notwithstanding.

"The hearing is set for next week. Of course I could handle it myself, but I rather thought this is the sort of thing a bloke like you would get incensed about. Given your reputation as a fighter for people's fundamental rights."

Max stifled a groan. "Okay, Joe, come on down to the office this afternoon, we'll see if we can't get you some help."

"Knew I could count on you, old boy."

When already burdened and faced with the prospect of taking on another unwanted task, the lawyers of Pomeroy Macarthur traditionally passed the puck to an open winger, and on his return to the office, Max Macarthur, knowing that Augustina Sage had a hole in her calendar next week, sidled up to her in the coffee room, where she was standing, bent over a newspaper and its latest scarehead about the Executor: "Will He Strike Again?"

Max gave her a friendly hug from behind.

This had the wrong effect: she screamed.

"Jeez, pass the Valium."

"I almost jumped out of my skin. Don't *do* that."

Max poured himself a coffee, and affected a chatty tone.

"Poor old Joe Ruff. Hear what they're going to do to him?"

"Give him an honourary doctor of laws?"

"Gag order. They want to bar him from the courts."

"Gee, well, I have to get back to the pits, chambers hearing this afternoon."

Max barred the door.

"Augie, Augie, I just can't fit him in."

"I have to do battle with Martin Wessel today. I'm in court until three."

"Well, gosh, that's damn fine of you. I'll tell him to wait." He extended Ruff's petition and affidavit. She didn't take it.

"Max, I know you like that pompous fop, especially because he's always polishing your apple, but I honestly find him to be the most utterly boring human being on the planet, and two seconds in a courtroom with him, let alone my office, will drive me starkers. No. I won't do it."

"Just *see* him. Listen, this guy actually has money, an inheritance or something. Simply tell him you have to charge a normal fee. *I* can't do that."

"Why?"

"Well, he and I have this little game, where we pretend he's a real lawyer...professional courtesy. He'll be hurt if I charge him. You don't know him as well."

"Thank God." She stood there with her arms folded, still declining to take the papers.

"Charter of Rights. Section Fifteen, subsection one, 'every individual has the right to equal benefit of the law without discrimination.' It's a doddle, a snap. I've got a whole brief on the law, all the cases; you don't have to look up a thing."

"Aw, Max..."

"Please, Augustina. The guy's nuts but he means well. And goddammit, there's a principle here."

She took the papers. "If I'm not too bagged at the end of the day, I'll see him."

Augustina returned to her office and reviewed her motion for the afternoon. She would be seeking an order from a chambers judge that would hopefully allow her to put a stop to Martin Wessel's blatant objections to her discovery of Father Doyle.

At two o'clock she arrived at the heavily-guarded bastion that was the Vancouver courthouse, and, looking at the posted docket, was aghast to learn that her hearing was on the list for the courtroom of Mr. Justice Quentin Russell. Whom, it must be said, Augustina knew only too intimately. Wessel, of course, had seen them together Saturday evening.

It would not be drawing on fantasy to foresee Martin Wessel making a hullabaloo in court today. Augustina could just hear him: "I suggest Your Lordship might want to consider declaring yourself incompetent to preside over this case in view of the fact you spent the weekend having carnal knowledge of my learned friend."

But having such knowledge gently, Mr. Wessel, with whispers and kisses, much parrying before the delicate thrust of this swordsman. She'd never been loved with such courtesy.

She had enjoyed the novelty of being something more than a blow-up plastic doll to her bed partner. The judge *could* have been a little more…um, passionate, but…

Small complaint.

Also, he had nightmares. He had tossed and mumbled and moaned in the middle of the night. Once she had awakened to the repeated phrase, "I'm sorry, I'm sorry," but this stopped as soon as she nestled him against her breasts. Beneath his surface equanimity, was he haunted by some old and terrible memory? Lovely Eunice, she suspected, who died at the wheel of her car.

Yesterday he failed to phone. That made her nervous. This was getting serious: pull in the reins.

At five minutes to ten, she hauled herself into Russell's courtroom, and saw that the Weasel was already there.

"Let's get the show on the road," he said, beaming.

"You *want* to go ahead?" Was she hearing things? Wessel was the master of delay. Two years of it so far. He had the perfect excuse to seek another one.

"Why not? Just 'cause you guys got something going? It's a positive in my favour. He's gonna bust his ass to be fair to me."

Wessel gave her a cunning look that unsettled her.

"You been balling him?"

"Go to hell."

When chambers was called to order, Quentin Russell came in, sat, looked at them, and sighed.

"I want to know if either of you think I shouldn't preside."

"No, I'm happy," Wessel said.

"I think it should be put on record that I've been seeing Ms. Sage socially," said the judge.

"As long as you haven't been talking about my case. That's the only thing. Course, that'd be grounds for an appeal court."

Although Wessel was a knave, he was no fool. Augustina felt dismay.

"What does counsel for the plaintiffs have to say?"

Was he telling her: do the right thing? She sighed. "M'lord, I think we should find another court."

"Aw, gee," said Wessel, "you know, I happened to check with the Registrar in case something like this came up, and looks like all the other judges are booked. With this psycho running around bombing our brethren it's caused a lot of courts to shut down."

"M'lord," said Augustina, "Mr. Wessel has managed to get this application adjourned three times in two months."

"Well, as usual, I'm the bad guy. So let's just go ahead right now. Long as you can guarantee you weren't talking about the case when you were seeing each other socially."

"Well, Ms. Sage, maybe we are going to have to adjourn this thing one more time."

"Well, that's up to her, I guess."

She gritted her teeth. "May this application be adjourned one week, m'lord?"

Wessel leafed through his diary. "No…that's next Tuesday, 'fraid I'm full up, let's see…I got a spot here in a couple months if a trial falls through…pretty chancy, though."

They finally pinned him down to a day three weeks hence. Before court recessed, Russell silently mouthed to Augustina: "Call you tonight."

"Real honourable guy," said Wessel as he followed her out of the court.

"Marty, ever think you may be on the Executor's list, too? Maybe he's got it in for the defender of Father Doyle." She wished she hadn't said that, but the man got to her.

"Naw, they'll have the Executor in the rubber room by the time we get to court. Case'll drag on for another ten years. Your clients will be all grown up with nice healthy families. Public's going to forget all about poor old Father Doyle."

In the barristers' lounge, she watched Wessel yakking it up with his partner Eddie Cohn. The two shysters probably had some illicit business going — not unlikely: Cohn was mobbed up with Tony d'Anglio.

Every time she saw the two men together they looked as though they were conspiring. They'd practised together for a dozen years — many crooked stews had they jointly concocted in their kitchen.

Cohn was robed today; he had been retained for almost a year on a contract case that was now getting under way. The contract involved the icing of an informer, and the contractor was one of d'Anglio's gorillas.

Cohn laughed at something Wessel said, then turned to look at her. Some ribald jest had been made, she supposed, at her expense.

She returned to the office in a black mood, not lightened by the fact that Joe Ruff was sitting in the waiting room with enough files to fill a truck. She decided she was suffering a bad case of PMS, and retreated toward her office to try to think of some excuse for him. At the library door, she spotted Wentworth Chance standing on the bookshelf ladder and gave him her most alluring smile. Wentworth had a thing for her, she knew that, a little twist-around-her-finger thing. She felt mean taking advantage, but what was the alternative? Joe Ruff.

"Wentworth, I'm going to give you the biggest break of your career."

He peered over his half-moon glasses at her. He had heard similar refrains before. "Break, yeah. Give me a break. I'm not human, I can only do everything."

"*Huge* civil rights case. Fellow being barred from the courts by the A.G."

As he descended, she passed Ruff's papers to him.

"He's in the waiting room. Mr. Joe Ruff."

"Ruff...I met a Mr. Joe Ruff."

"Hard to miss him." She blinked prettily at him.

"Augie, I'm just buried — "

She gave him a buss on the cheek and fled.

The kiss burned sweet for a few minutes as he puzzled over the petition and affidavit.

Ruff, Wentworth thought, that strange lawyer who was always in court but never in action. The one who had congratulated him after his big houseboat win. Why were they barring a lawyer from the courts? This was a serious matter, not some two-bit claim you hand off blithely to the articling student.

But they *had* given him that raise. Living as he was in Brovakian luxury, bombing around town in a Mercedes sportster, it was as if he were a *real* lawyer now, worthy of representing a more distinguished clientele. But Joe Ruff, a member of the bar?

Maybe this was a different Ruff. Wentworth peered around the partition behind the receptionist's desk and saw the Ruff he'd met, a tall portly man sitting with his thumbs in his vest pockets, a metre-high pile of files on the floor beside him.

Wentworth used Pomeroy's vacant office for this important client, an office impressive in size, Robert Bateman prints peering from between the tendrils of vines growing over the brick walls, a small forest of potted plants. Pomeroy's personal reforestation project.

Ruff sat primly on a chair as Wentworth nervously settled himself under the branches of a potted tree behind the desk.

"I'm afraid Augustina Sage is a little tied up," he said.

"Oh. I was rather expecting to meet with my old chum Max."

Wentworth got the picture. The ball had been passed around the infield. Tinkers to Evers to Chance.

"I think they want you to start off with me," he said, "so I can collect the facts."

"Spot on. I've seen you in action, Mr. Chance. You have the right stuff. I want this to go directly to the Supreme Court of Canada."

Wentworth laughed at this sally, but Ruff continued to look serious.

"We'll just bypass the local courts, what, and go right to the top." He pulled a thick writing pad from a file. "I have some ideas. What do you think of a writ of prohibition with certiorari in aid?"

"I really don't think there's jurisdiction in the Supreme Court... uh, how long have you been practising, Joe?"

"Well, of course, I don't hold a current practising certificate, so I'm...a bit of a para-legal."

"You don't have a licence to practise law?"

"I can't say really…I was in law school once, but they said it wasn't necessary for me to take a degree." He chuckled. "I already knew more than the tutors."

"I see." Wentworth began to suspect Augustina of playing a practical joke on him. This guy was a bit eccentric.

"Father was a lawyer, what? Dead now. Grew up with it, don't you know. Three brothers and a sister in the calling, too."

"Why are you not seeking help from them?"

"Oh, they…" He waved a hand, dismissing them. "We're not really that close. I have funds, old chap. That's why I have chosen the best. Pomeroy, Macarthur and Company."

"I guess you better start from the top, Joe."

"Right-o. I brought along a few scraps of paper to start with."

Wentworth looked at Joe Ruff's huge collection of files with trepidation.

Max Macarthur had found himself saddened by the fact that as a result of Wentworth's inquiries, suspicion was now attached to Sergeant Cudlipp. He carried no candle for the man, but he had his heart set on Turnbull as his choice for the Executor.

Lars Nordquist didn't bat an eye when Max briefed him about Cudlipp in the C.L.E.U. offices, on the top floor of an anonymous downtown office building. Eighteen detectives were serving under him here, of whom several — Max was nervous about this — had been drawn from the federal force, the very RCMP which employed Mr. Cudlipp.

"He may be on the pad to Tony d'Anglio," Nordquist said. "He may be bent as kingdom come. But Everit Cudlipp…our Executor?"

He read through Besterman's last dictated letter again.

"I know Cudlipp. I don't see him doing this. He's lazy and unimaginative."

"I still vote for Roger Turnbull."

"Build me a case."

19

The Case of
the Puzzling Purse

Max fell far behind in his work during the hectic days following the all-too-real bomb scare at Archie's Steak House, and began taking work home in the evenings — to his sprawling, stolid 1920s home in upper-Yuppie Kitsilano, not far from English Bay.

While Ruth instructed the twins in the mysteries of Duplo on the living room floor, Max showered after his daily ten miles, then squirreled himself into his den, put on his headphones and listened to O.D. Milsom's gruesome confessions to murder.

"I walked into the bedroom and she was, ah, listening to some record with her eyes closed, there on the bed, and she didn't have a chance to scream or nothing before she was dead." Victim number three.

The voice of Lars Nordquist: "How did you break in there, Mr. Milsom?"

"I followed her home the night before, from a bar, and I saw where she got the key from her mailbox."

The over-cooperative O.D. Milsom, an unblushing torrent of guilt. He had given them everything, calmly, with an empty dispassion. Max thought it odd that he had vented so freely: there was an almost hypnotic quality to his rambling answers. Probably he was psychotic, but of course Besterman had not had the wherewithal to work up a mental defence.

He had incinerated his bloodied clothes, and claimed to have lost his murder weapon, a hunting knife.

And as for motive: he didn't know why he did it. Only one psychiatrist had examined him, a Crown shrink who questioned him for a cursory hour and a half, and opined, as he was hired to do, that Milsom was a sociopathic misogynist but legally sane, simple-minded but not retarded.

Nothing much more was known of Milsom than that he was a forty-seven-year-old loner who'd moved out here from Toronto several years ago and entered a common-law relationship with a woman living in the east end. She'd kicked him out after enduring three years of his silent staring at the boob tube. After the trial, he apparently bought a bus ticket back to Toronto. Odd, thought Max, that there was no blotter on this man, no hint of previous violent behavior.

"Okay, in this woman's apartment, the basement suite, what was the music she was listening to?"

"A record by...I don't know music. The Beatles? And it was going round and round, and then it was the end of the record and the needle just kept scratching back and forth, and I didn't touch it, and then I just went out — "

"Just a sec', here. Do you remember any of the songs that were playing?"

"No, but I saw an album cover, it was called *Make It Bleed*. I remember that. A big birthday cake or something on the cover."

Let It Bleed. Not the Beatles but the Stones. Otherwise, he was accurate: the police on arrival saw the record still turning, saw the album cover sitting on the amplifier. From another woman's basement suite, he had remembered a pair of love-birds in a cage. These were untainted corroborations of murder, proof of a killer's candor.

Despite its built-in offers of truth, the confession hinted of something worrisome and unsatisfying. Unaccountable slips of memory. Always this over-eagerness on the part of Milsom to please, to be believed.

He turned off the tape as Ruth came in. "Max, there are a couple of...strange gentlemen at the door."

Max found Roger Turnbull and Jack Calico, his bodyguard and chief helpmate, standing on the porch.

"And how is Max tonight?"

"Turnbull, I'm busy."

"Hard work, no play, keeps the bill collectors at bay. Couldn't reach you at your office, so, hey, thought you wouldn't mind if I popped in for a sec."

"This had better be important."

"Thought we could put our noodles together over this business of Milsom's lawyer quitting. That going to cause any hitches?"

"Before you gentlemen leave, tell me what you were doing at midnight on Tuesday, March 2nd. When the grenade went off."

"Grenade?" Turnbull kept his smile. "Say again?"

"'Beware of the Sword of Justice.' Sort of thing you might write."

Turnbull's response seemed stagey, rehearsed. "Max, Max, goodness gracious. Now where does that come from? No, I see my job as a street sweeper, a vacuum cleaner of filth. Where the garbage gets dumped after the courts finish isn't my concern, and I don't hold any grudges to lawyers who work in the garbage dump; I'll be blunt, people like you and your partners. Or like Arthur Besterman for that matter." He smiled piously.

"What's the answer to my question?"

"When your partner and his friends were almost being blown up I was in another part of the city. I was with Mr. Calico here and a small squadron working the Kingsway area."

The ogre Calico nodded his agreement.

"We collared a snatch-and-grab thief and there was a heck of a scene around that. The police have interviewed the witnesses. I told this to Inspector Nordquist. Now I hope it wasn't *you*, Max, who asked him to call on me."

"What time did this episode occur?"

"I logged it in at 11:15."

"The grenade was delivered at midnight."

"Max, Max, this is simply crazy."

Max closed and locked the door, and heard him shouting: "Hey, I thought we were on the same side of this case! I only called on you to help. What's this attitude problem you have about me?"

Through the window he saw they weren't budging. He glanced

over to Ruth and the kids, playing and laughing on the rug. Finally, Turnbull and Calico left the porch. Max watched them until they got into their VW van and drove off. He walked back to his den.

"Keep all the doors locked," he said to Ruth. "It's that asshole, Turnbull."

Returning to his desk, he picked up a dog-eared transcript of the Milsom trial, and opened it to Besterman's cross examination of Turnbull. He pictured him on the stand, over-eager, preening to the press and browning to the judge.

"Q: You followed the accused from this bar?"

"A: Well, of course. I was very worried about the young lady he had targeted — "

"THE COURT: Just answer the question, witness."

"A: Sorry, your lordship."

"Q: And you pounced on him?"

"A: I took him around the neck, sir, in a full nelson. There was no violence."

"Q: And you said, 'You have claimed your last victim, Milsom. You are under arrest.'"

"A: Citizen's arrest, yes."

You have claimed your last victim. How pompous, thought Max. Why didn't Besterman question him about this scripted line?

"Q: And he said?"

"A: Nothing. At first."

"Q: That's when you threatened him?"

"A: I told him…yes, I threatened him, I guess. I wanted quick answers, before he had a chance to make up some story."

"Q: You said…?"

"A: Ah, I said, 'Talk fast, or I'll cut your nuts off.' Pardon my French, your lordship. And he said, 'I did it. I killed them girls. I had to.' And I had one of my squadron immediately phone the police. Mr. Calico, he went right to the bar, and phoned from there."

"Q: And how long did the police take to get there?"

"A: Oh, they came right away."

"Q: And did you make other threats before they came?"

"A: Absolutely not. I had what I wanted. I held onto him, and he just kept repeating, 'I did it, I'm sorry, I couldn't help it,' things like that. And I didn't say a single other word to him, sir."

Why did Max doubt that? Did the voluble Mr. Turnbull really ask no further questions while he had an eagerly confessing Milsom at his mercy?

There seemed to Max to be something almost…contrived about this arrest — or at least Turnbull's account of it. Odd that he had managed so easily to put the collar on Milsom. How had he found himself in the very pub that Milsom was haunting that night? Of the several hundred bars in Greater Vancouver, how had he made a bull's-eye?

Max turned to the evidence of the young woman whom Milsom had followed from the pub — and from whose clutches Turnbull had saved her. Stephanie Bresciani, a lab assistant at Vancouver General.

Her evidence was brief: she had been enjoying a few whiskey sours with two girlfriends. At ten o'clock, she left the bar for the parking lot, and was unlocking her car door when she heard a brief scuffle nearby. She turned, startled, to find three gentlemen in white berets subduing — with little real effort — the man later identified as O.D. Milsom. While Turnbull continued to hold Milsom, Jack Calico and the third Angel returned her to the safety of the bar, and sat her at a table until the police came.

"They seemed to take a century," Bresciani testified.

How odd of her to say this, thought Max. A prowl car was there two minutes after Calico's call was logged at the police station. Two minutes wasn't a century. But the woman was obviously flustered, and time stretches when one has nearly been murdered. Yet… how negligent of Besterman not to have followed this up.

The next morning he visited Vancouver General Hospital. It took fifteen minutes of wandering through its maze of corridors before he found Stephanie Bresciani in a small coffee lounge near her laboratory.

She was a plain woman of twenty, pleasant and forthright. She said she was awfully worried about that terrible Milsom. How could they ever have let him go?

"Ms. Bresciani, is there anything you can remember that you didn't mention to the police? Because you thought it not important…or embarrassing or dumb?"

Bresciani frowned. "Well, you know, there was one thing."

Max smiled hopefully. "Yes?"

"When those White Angels there were taking me back inside, I saw Mr. Turnbull start to search the creepy guy, Milsom."

Turnbull had testified to that, as well: his frisking of Milsom, going into pockets, looking for that missing knife. Coming out with a wallet bearing Milsom's few scraps of i.d., a bus token and a five-dollar bill. No Visa or American Express gold cards.

"I thought it was, you know, a little weird? — Milsom was holding a kind of change purse."

"Excuse. A what?"

"Like a little ladies' purse." She pulled her own from her bag. "You know? The kind that snaps shut? With your keys and coins and shit? I was being really *pushed*, you know, back into the pub, and I didn't get to see it very good, but I saw Mr. Turnbull take it off of him."

Max recalled nothing in the reports about a change purse. He was mystified.

"You didn't mention this to anyone before?"

"Well, no, it slipped my mind. You know? I mean, they come at you with all these *questions*, and of course you've just been scared out of your tree."

"When did you remember this purse?"

"Couple of weeks before the trial. It just came back to me. You know? Like, I'm washing up from the lab, and, hey, O.D. Milsom had a *change purse.*"

"Why didn't you tell the prosecutor? Mr. Lukey." The lately unlucky Mr. Justice Lukey. The Milsom trial had been his last appearance as counsel before his elevation to the bench and, more recent, sudden descent from it.

"Oh, I did," said Stephanie Bresciani. "I did tell Mr. Lukey. He told me not to bother mentioning it in court. He said it would only complicate matters."

Max tried not to look astonished.

"I wouldn't have lied, you know? If somebody asked me. But no one asked me. I guess it wasn't that important."

Max thought: if Turnbull had seized this exotic item of non-evidence from Milsom, why had he been so eloquently silent about it in his testimony? Leroy Lukey: had he been up to his old habit of withholding evidence? Why would a change purse complicate matters?

"One more thing. You testified that it took the police a century to get there."

"Well, it was at least ten or fifteen minutes. Like, Mr. Calico and this other guy sat me down and told me to stay calm, and he — Calico — went to the bar to phone. The police didn't come right away, and Mr. Calico left again, and then got on the phone again. *Then* the police came."

"And all this time Mr. Turnbull was outside with Milsom? Alone with him?"

"Well, I guess so."

Ten or fifteen minutes — a strange disparity in the evidence. Turnbull had testified the first patrol car "came right away." Why would he lie? And why hadn't the police responded to Calico's earlier call? If, indeed, he'd made it.

"Don't talk to anyone about this, okay?" he said.

Max didn't phone ahead to Leroy Lukey, hoping to catch him unready with lies or excuses. He'd heard his wife had gone to live with relatives after learning he'd been boffing a hooker, but he wasn't alone today in his sprawling brick house in upper-crust Shaughnessy. Max saw an extra car in his driveway.

Lukey came to his door looking as if he was bottoming out from a two-week binge. He didn't invite Max in, just stared at him malevolently as he made his inquiries.

"There *was* no goddamn change purse. The girl had been drinking, she was confused. Nobody else saw the purse. Turnbull didn't know anything about it, no one did."

"You didn't disclose this evidence, Leroy."

He flared. "Bullshit. What evidence? Minor crap like that just confuses juries. Anyway, I have better things to do than palaver with you. Another fucking Macarthur trying to jump all over my ass." This complaint, Max knew, had to do with his father, the Chief Justice, who, furious about the Minette Lefleur fiasco, was demanding Lukey give up his robes to avoid an unseemly public inquiry into his amorous misdoings.

Max looked sorrowfully upon the wreckage that was the former Mr. Justice Lukey. As he was about to take his leave, he spied Leroy's long-time fishing buddy, Sergeant Everit Cudlipp, zipping his fly as he exited a bathroom down the hall.

20

Untrue
Confessions

Odd twosome, thought Max, as he jogged down the street to visit his mom. His parents were neighbours a block away.

"A change purse," Lars Nordquist said. "This is important?"

"I don't know," Max said. Voices droned in the background. One C.L.E.U. officer was talking to a munitions expert about hand grenades; another was compiling a list of recent graduates from the Riverview mental hospital.

"Bones, if Milsom was going to kill Stephanie, why no knife?"

The parking lot had been searched stem to stern; the bar, too, in case he had accidentally dropped it there. In Milsom's statement to the police, he seemed confused, rambling about having disposed of his hunting knife a few days earlier: somewhere, he wasn't sure. He "wanted to kill" Stephanie Bresciani, but couldn't explain how he intended to do it.

"It was pretty well lit out there, Lars. This wasn't his usual m.o. I don't know...hasn't this guy got *any* kind of history?"

"Three murders is some kind of history. Otherwise his sheet is blank."

Max looked at a copy of his record. "So what's this?"

"Etobicoke, Ont.," it read. "Arson. d.n.p." August 12, 1979.

"D.n.p.," Max said. "Did not proceed. Why?"

Nordquist shrugged.

Max returned to his office to make some calls to the police in Ontario, and located a detective who had been a junior officer on the arson case. He remembered vaguely that a derelict was picked up hanging around the razed warehouse, and questioned. But the real arsonist had been arrested later, the owner of the well-insured building.

Milsom's lawyer in Toronto, a Mr. Frederick Robbin, was retired but sounded hale on the long-distance line.

"Milsom...don't remember the name, but I do recollect the man. Barely smart enough to find his way to the bathroom. When the police arrested him I guess their hearts soared because he promptly broke down and admitted to this conflagration. Didn't do it, though. Said he did, but he didn't."

"Please elaborate, Mr. Robbin."

"Well, I went to this poor people's hostel and talked to some folks who said he'd been in there that whole night of the fire. Milsom's story started changing, and we realized we had some kind of weird bird on our hands. He hadn't much of a claim to fame, poor Mr. Milsom. He so wanted to be noticed in life."

Max heard alarms going off all over the place.

But no...Milsom, as they say in the gangster movies, knew too much. The love-birds, the Stones album...

"There was this psychologist told us he was suffering from some sort of...notoriety syndrome, or something."

What was her name? Dr. Siskin, that was it.

Max learned that Dr. Mabel F. Siskin was currently a professor at the University of North Carolina. He phoned her.

"I recall looking up several references in the literature to what I suppose could be called a notoriety-seeking neurosis. A rather odd form of grandeur delusion. Typically, these persons are attention-seekers; they hunger for a fame of any sort. Which means they are usually pretty inadequate in themselves."

"Tend to be loners?"

"Yes, but not always of their own wish. They don't quite fit into the neighbourhood, if you know what I mean. They might exhibit some odd personality characteristics which cause people to avoid them."

"And what else?"

"Well, this is interesting. I remember reading that they're quite susceptible. By that I mean easily persuaded to a belief — even as to an unlikely matter. Put a person like this in the presence of a detective trained to elicit confessions, and he's liable to admit to anything."

Max wondered: had Turnbull, continually poking and prying into police investigations, learned the inside information about the victims? The love-birds and the Rolling Stones record, those hooks the police had baited for the questioning of suspects? And had he then, somehow, somewhere...bumped into Milsom, persuaded him he was the killer, coached him, drugged him...what? That change purse...

Maybe it was this easy: in the nearly fifteen minutes that had transpired between Turnbull nabbing Milsom and the arrival of the police, Turnbull had talked to him about the Rolling Stones and love-birds. Turnbull needed time to coach Milsom, so Calico stalled making that call to the police. But how could the simple-minded Milsom have got these facts straight on the re-telling?

A pale afternoon light misted through low, sullen clouds as Max jogged through skid road on this third day of spring. Beggars were about and the drunks were already staggering from bar to bar. Prowl cars cruised by. At The Corner, as it was called, Hastings and Columbia, the heroin crossroads, the dealers weren't dealing: two of Turnbull's White Angels were on nearby foot patrol.

Turnbull. Milsom. Notoriety neurosis. What were the possibilities here?

Theory One. Milsom was a serial killer who also happened to suffer from this neurosis.

Theory Two. Milsom, a compulsive confessor of crimes, was induced into admitting to the three murders. By someone who knew of his propensity for making false confession. That someone perhaps being a grandstander who announced bravely to the world that he was going to track down this murderer. A person whose ravenous ego needed a big feed of glory.

But then who was the real killer? The murders had ceased with Milsom's arrest, during his eight months' imprisonment, awaiting trial...

Theory Three. Turnbull murdered those women. In a despicable, psychopathic attempt to win credit and gain fame as the hero who collared a multiple killer.

How unlikely, really.

But then…having gone to such devious, brain-sick efforts to achieve a place in the sun, wouldn't it be in keeping with the man's personality to have reacted with violent retribution against the lawyer who reversed the tables on him by winning that acquittal? And after bumping Arthur Besterman, to have continued on in a berserk vendetta against other criminal lawyers?

Max puffed up Hastings Street, to the Strathcona low-cost housing complex. Milsom's former common-law wife lived here with her two pre-adolescent girls. Throughout, they had insisted he wasn't a killer.

Mrs. Jucovics had lived with Milsom for three eventless years until she decided to just stop feeding him — he could never keep a job. She was a harried divorcée who toiled daily at a meat-grinder in a whole-sale sausage outlet.

She didn't seem to find it odd that a lawyer wearing a jogging suit was at the door of her boxy-looking suite.

"He didn't murder them women," she insisted.

"Why do you think that?" Max asked.

It just wasn't in him, she said. He was strange, yes, and hard to get to know. But he had never so much as raised his voice to the children.

Her two girls spoke to similar effect. During his three years as a live-in layabout, Milsom had regularly cared for them while she was at work.

After Mrs. Jucovics evicted Milsom, he'd taken a room in a house a few blocks away. Max went over to talk to the landlady. Didn't get to know him real good, she said. Went about his own business, whatever *that* was. Real quiet. But it's the quiet ones who are dangerous, isn't it?

The next morning, he found Turnbull, without appointment, in the waiting room.

"And how is Max today?" Turnbull asked.

"Absolutely boffo. And you?"

"A-number-one," Turnbull said cheerily. All was forgotten, Max's insults and accusations.

Max decided not to kick him out of the office this time. There might be ways to gain his confidence.

"Max, I'm about to shoot some business your way." He drew closer and spoke with a hushed voice. "One of the boys kind of…mishandled a pimp. Poor old Jack Calico. It's urgent: bail hearing's tomorrow."

Mr. Calico, it turned out, had hauled the alleged pimp from a Cadillac, and in response to some sass had broken the man's jaw, two of his rib bones and ruptured his spleen. He was charged with aggravated assault, fourteen years maximum.

Calico looked at Max warily when they brought him from the cells into the small, stark waiting room. He was right out of a haunted castle: bald, eyes sunk deep into their sockets.

"I guess I flipped out," he said. "But here was this black pimp, and he had a white girl in that car, she couldn't of been fourteen."

"Do you have a record?" Max asked.

"Yeah, some minor stuff. Couple assaults and like that. Before I found the truth, though. You know, with the White Angels."

"Tell me about these assaults."

"Little shoving match one time. Guy lost a couple of teeth, that's all."

"What else?"

"Aw, just dinky things, like, you know, I broke some kneecaps once."

"With what?"

"Um, I think a hammer."

"You do time?"

"Couple years." He shrugged. "And then I got parole."

"Work record?"

"I been, you know, donating my time. Street work."

"How do you suppose I'm going to get you out on bail?"

"Roger says you have to do it."

"Why does he want you out so bad?"

He shrugged again.

This man had assisted in Milsom's arrest. Had he been in league with Turnbull to set him up? What did he remember of a change purse?

"It's going to help a lot if we can tell the courts about some of your good deeds, Jack."

"Well, I been doin' lots of them. Catching muggers and stuff."

"Muggers are a dime a dozen. What about the Milsom case?"

"Well, uh, really not s'posed to talk about that one."

"Why?"

"Uh, well, I better talk to Roger on this."

When nothing else seemed to be forthcoming, Max told him to speak to no one else, then cancelled his afternoon clients and sped down to the C.L.E.U. offices.

He told Nordquist that Milsom was a congenital claimer of crimes he did not commit, then related the blackest of his theories: the leader of the White Angels, alone or in concert with his underlings, had not only murdered Arthur Besterman out of resentment over tarnished glory, but the three young women, too, in a warped seeking of that glory.

Nordquist showed about as much expression as a stone Buddha. "And what is the course of action?"

Max told him about the charge against Jack Calico.

The odd reluctance on Calico's part not to talk about Milsom had piqued Max's curiosity. Though bound in ethics not to recount his client's words to Nordquist, he said, "I am going to try to, ah, tap my source. Which means laying it on a bit. Keeping him out of Turnbull's clutches."

"Max, I thought you were hired to *prosecute* O.D. Milsom."

It was confusing. Somehow Max had gotten into the old, bad habit of defending.

Jennifer Tann, the Vancouver Regional Crown, looked at them askance. "You want this cretin out on *bail*?"

Nordquist smiled his dour smile. "We want to play with him for a while. Bait."

"There'll have to be some stiff terms."

"I have some in mind," Max said.

Turnbull was waiting for Max at the courtroom door.

"Your Mr. Calico is playing cute. I want you to tell him he'd better not hold anything back from me. Lawyers have something in common with the Lord, Roger — you can't keep secrets from them."

Turnbull crinkled his nose, as if finding the analogy offensive. "I'll explain it to him. Soon as you get him out." He put a confiding arm on Max's shoulder. "Max, I have to talk to him."

"Why?"

"He's not too swift upstairs. You might confuse him. He trusts me."

"Okay, I want you to sit here. Nice and close." He positioned Turnbull in a seat near the prisoner's dock.

When Calico was brought into court, Max leaned toward him, speaking solemnly. "Roger is going to tell you something, and I want you to listen very carefully."

Calico nodded.

Max motioned to Turnbull to approach them. "Tell him."

"Ah, yes," said Turnbull. "Okay, you have to cooperate with Mr. Macarthur here. Tell him everything."

"Everything?"

"Yes…and I'll talk to you more later."

Max picked up Turnbull's signal, a warning to be circumspect. He hoped the somewhat dimmer brain of Calico might not have received this message.

"If you've finished your brainstorming over there, Mr. Macarthur," said the judge, "perhaps you might give me some reason why this gentleman should be allowed out walking what we happily once regarded as the safe streets of Vancouver."

"Because he saved a sixteen-year-old girl from being forced into a life of prostitution," Max said.

Max told the judge his instructions were that Calico simply over-reacted to seeing what he thought was a knife in the complainant's hand. Also, he was a much-changed man from the past. Mostly for Turnbull's benefit, he made a speech about Calico finding the Right Path.

But Jennifer Tann recited several other recent incidents of violence involving the White Angels. She was adamantly opposed to bail on any terms unless the accused was ordered not to associate with them.

Max, also for Turnbull's benefit, made a show of complaining about this, but the judge caught his message that he would not find that condition impossible to live with.

Calico was ordered released on ten thousand dollars, no deposit, one surety; the conditions being that he report twice-weekly to the police department and not associate with any member of the White Angels.

"I have to talk to him," Turnbull said as he signed as surety in the bail clerk's office.

"Yes, we'll discuss it. Meet me in my office." He pointed him toward the exit door.

With Turnbull temporarily out of his hair, he had Calico brought out to sign the papers, then quickly led him out a side door to a waiting taxi.

"That was real slick," said Calico.

"If we handle this right, we're going to make a hero out of you, Jack."

"A hero." He seemed to like the sound of the word.

Max had reserved a room for him at a small mid-priced hotel in the West End. He guessed Nordquist would have people watching the room. Probably covering all the hotel's exits.

"This is okay, I guess," said Calico, looking around, checking the view of busy Robson Street.

"Roger says nothing's too good. Only thing is, you can't phone to thank him, just one contact with him means he goes to jail, too. And the cops are sure to have the phone tapped." He believed, though, that Nordquist was too straight a cop to bug a lawyer and a client.

"Later I'll bring up toothbrush, shaving kit, some clothes, a few books. You read books?"

"Oh, yeah. Read one years ago."

Max viewed the menu of pay movies. "'Marcie Goes to Vegas.' Well, you can have some nice clean fun with that."

"Haven't seen one of them things in three years. Roger don't like it."

"How about a drink?"

"I haven't had alcohol neither for three years."

"Roger won't know." When Max opened a beer for himself, Calico relented and accepted one, too.

Max loosened him up with some questions intended to make him feel important: drawing from him tales of brave arrests of various bad people on the streets.

But when he casually turned the topic to O.D. Milsom, Calico balked.

"Roger wants you to tell your side. Nothing will get repeated."

"You talked to him."

"He and I don't have secrets. We're very close."

Calico seemed skeptical. "What did he tell you?"

Max took a chance. "Everything. He explained about the change purse."

Calico relaxed.

"Yeah, well…Yeah, okay, I was in the bar, like, where this Milsom was."

"Yes, I gathered." Max fetched another couple of cans of Heineken from the self-serve bar. "Yes? Continue?"

"I was supposed to set him up, eh?"

Max didn't react. "Yes, go on."

"Roger tell you what the plan was?"

"Please, Jack. I have to hear it in your words."

"Well, like, I'm s'posed to watch and when a girl leaves the bar alone — don't matter, any girl will do — I'm s'posed to give Milsom this little ladies' change purse and to tell him that a girl just left and he forgot it at her table, and so, like, he'll follow her out."

"Yes, and you did this?"

"Yeah, and this girl leaves, and I go over to Milsom with the purse, and he gets up quick — there was no one saw us talking or nothing — and he goes out after her, and Roger and me go out after him."

"Retreat a bit." Max kept his voice steady. "This was Roger's plan, to get Milsom to follow that woman out of the bar."

"Yeah, 'cause we had to get him dead to rights. Roger wants to make it look good, see, nothing wrong with that."

"Yes, of course. You already knew he was the killer, right?"

"Roger sure knew. He divined it, eh? Roger has these powers nobody else has. He's kinda subliminal. And also, we already had Milsom's confession."

"That's what I understand. Now, how did that come about?"

"Roger, like a few days earlier, Milsom started talking with him in a bar and said he'd done these murders."

"He said this to Roger."

"Yeah, so here's this guy braggin' to a stranger about being a murderer, can you believe it? Course, Roger needed something harder, 'cause I think Milsom was pretty drunk at the time."

Max's palms were sweating.

"By the way, whatever happened to that change purse?"

"I dunno."

"How is it no one ever found a knife on Milsom that night?"

"That didn't make none of us happy. Roger said after, we should of set him up with one."

"This is really going to help. You could come out of this with a medal, Jack. So, ah, why don't we order lunch, crack open another, and then go over it again in detail?"

Max could hardly still the excitement as he brought out a small tape recorder from his briefcase. Somehow he would have to roll him, persuade him to testify against Turnbull. But how? Calico worshipped prostrate at the man's feet.

Ruth was at day-care picking up the kids when Max returned home after spending all day with his excellent new client.

Jack Calico had been somewhat shy about having his words recorded on the micro-cassette machine. But he had repeated everything, even adding more. The reason for Calico's delay in calling the police: Turnbull had told him to stall "while he got Milsom to confess." To prompt him, more likely, with Turnbull's inside information about the Rolling Stones album and the love-birds.

When he had asked him as an aside what Turnbull was doing the night after the Milsom acquittal — when Besterman was killed — he had become nervous, and Max had dropped the matter.

The phone rang. Max made no effort to pick it up. From the answering machine: "Max...ah, are you there?"

A pause.

"It's me again. Hey, Max, I really have to talk to Calico. Telephone contact isn't against the law, is it?" A strained chuckle. "Can't you just leave his number with me?... Are you there?..."

Max heard the line disconnect.

The next morning, Saturday, as Max was pounced awake by Clarence and Darrow, he heard the alarums of a persistent robin outside his window announcing that spring was in full bloom. It was a week after the solstice, and the sun was strong, pumping hard. Life was bursting forth in the park across the street, the maples sending yellow tassels, the chestnuts in sudden leaf, a Japanese plum tree in pink bloom, daffodils winking.

Great day for a run.

He was puffing when he got to C.L.E.U.

He told Nordquist: "I had a long and useful talk with Mr. Calico."

"Off the record, what did he say?"

"I can't."

"Not much good to us, is it? Let me hazard a theory. Milsom, we know, suffers from a hunger for the spotlight. In his room were found some newspaper clippings about the murders. These were famous cases, and a man charged with them could be famous, too. Say that in the course of some idle conversation he told someone he was the serial killer the police were looking for. That someone told Roger Turnbull. Turnbull set him up."

Max listened to the normally taciturn inspector with growing respect — he was almost dead on.

"What can we offer him to go public?" Nordquist said.

"What have you got?"

"Witness protection, a couple of thousand a month."

Max thought Calico's price for betrayal would be higher. But he assumed he had a price. Perhaps the hundred-thousand-dollar reward for the Executor?

21

Family Man

Though Eddie Cohn enjoyed the company of gangsters and toiled an honest nine-to-five for them, he didn't take his work home. He was a family man who enjoyed his leisure like anyone else. He barbecued steaks on the patio like anyone else. He watched TV after dinner like anyone else. He lived better than most, though, in a grand house on half-an-acre in Beach Grove, the mortgage for which he had recently paid off. He had one Persian cat and one German Shepherd and one wife and one twenty-year-old stay-at-home ne'er-do-well son on drugs and one anemic teen-aged daughter with acne and a Walkman. He had a normal family like anyone else.

He protected this family as best he could from possible contagions from his legal practice, which was an almost full-time job with the mob, doing d'Anglio's paper and his defence work. At 55, after nearly three decades in the courts, he was good at it, though he would never ascend to the reputation of d'Anglio's former lawyer, Quentin Russell.

Cohn had been retained to defend one of d'Anglio's enforcers on a charge of assassinating what was known in the business as a chirp, a betrayer who had been d'Anglio's masseur. (Machine pistol, blood on the massage table.) The trial almost didn't get off the ground. With the courts in confusion, the Crown wanted to adjourn, but Cohn knew he had a win in the bag if he didn't wait around. The main Crown witness, the massage parlour manager, had been paid off. Cohn didn't want to miss this opportunity for a quick acquittal.

That came on Friday, March 26. The massage parlour manager was arrested for perjury, but the judge had to grit his teeth and tell the jury to acquit the hit man.

Cohn was thought to have bribed the witness himself — soft clothes officers had seen the manager make two visits to Cohn's office before the trial. The case attracted some untoward publicity ("Witness Bribed, Crown Complains"), but Cohn refused protection. He wasn't afraid: the person who wrote "Criminal lawyers are marked for death" was obviously a jokester. Anyway, Cohn didn't believe a run-of-the-mill gangland hit would whet the appetite of any self-proclaimed Executor.

And he definitely didn't want a police car sitting out in front of his house all day and all night. He worried about what the neighbours would think.

Early on the evening of his victory, he was seen enjoying a few drinks, not overdoing it, with his partner Martin Wessel, and that apparently led to an invitation for Wessel to join him at Cohn's home for dinner to continue the celebration.

It was a pleasant night, not too cold to hang around the patio and throw some steaks on the propane barbecue. Cohn was in high spirits as he entertained Wessel out back of the house. It was dark by then, just past eight-thirty. As Cohn was sharpening his steak knife, he asked Wessel to run inside to grab a couple of beers from the fridge. While in the kitchen doing so, Wessel heard, as he later told the police, a soft cry and a grunt from Cohn and thought his host had either cut himself or burned the steaks. Then came a kind of crash and a clatter, the thump of a large, falling object.

Mrs. Cohn and her daughter, in the living room watching television — the son was apparently toking up in his bedroom — also heard the crash. They ran outside and saw Wessel, an open bottle of Löwenbräu in each hand, staring down in horror at the body of Eddie Cohn, lying across the toppled barbecue. His throat had been sliced from ear to ear by his own steak knife.

+ + +

On the following Tuesday, the Sun published a second cut-and-paste letter from the Executor: "Scum of the sewars. More shall die." Another passage from the King James version of the New Testament, Luke 11:46, was glued onto the page: "Woe unto ye lawyers! for ye lade men with burdens too grievous to be borne." The name "Cohn" then appeared in large headline letters, two intersecting lines slashed through it by a red felt marker, an "X".

Saturday, March 27

Dear partners,

A confession: I have just committed the egregious crime of cheating the reader.

An hour ago I put a sleazy lawyer on ice, a character whom I have been pregnant with for months, and whom I gave birth to after several hours' labour, then slew with a smile — I kissed the asshole off with a Smith and Wesson .32.

The problem is: what to do with the body? The eyes of this body are open and staring at me. "Why me?" it asks. "I know you've always despised me, but why now, why here, in the middle of your book? Why, all of a sudden, me?"

Yes, my former friend, you seem blithely, flippantly inserted there, a throwaway, a bone tossed to the hungry readers to keep them at bay.

"Remember that the modern mystery reader — those who worship the great Dame Agatha must sigh at this — thirsts for blood," Mr. Widgeon cynically observes. "Around page 150 he will feel deprived and forsaken if the author does not trundle out another corpse."

But Alexis Huggins, we hardly knew you. Can one just throw in some crooked floozy from the blue, and blip her off and flick the droplets of blood from one's hands? This murder seems contrived, convenient.

The inexplicable death of Ms. Huggins has put me in a stall. I examine the night sky for inspiration: a powerful, pulling moon has just shouldered up over the eastern hills.

Brittle starlight. The big dipper sitting up there at its kwonky tropical angle, the blackness of the night spilling from it, and beyond the milky mass of the galaxy.

I feel very small and hollow and alone, a speck, a microcosmic mote, a blackhead on the backside of God.

From a distance I can hear a chattering of Róbelos, a babbling of babies. Leticia's laughter, like chimes.

A lack of love, I fear, is beginning to sour my creative processes. Oh, yes, I have known physical love, at least one sweaty scene that had my fingers slipping from the keys. But romantic love, that direful blinding light of passion that burns between man and woman: am I afraid of it? Afraid to write about it because I fear it? Is love like the green flash at sunset: I am blind to it? Do only lovers see it?

I'll never be a writer. I lack soul.

I will try to mail this before I slit my wrists.

Yours posthumously,
Brian.

Monday, March 29

Dear office,

Alas, my muse, that fickle goddess, has flounced out the door and out of my life. Who can blame her? I have been churlish company, demanding, sarcastic, lousy in bed, constantly complaining about her poverty of new ideas. I finally snapped at her, and she packed her bags, blew me a kiss, and fluttered off on fairy wings.

For the last two days I have been sitting here staring blankly out into the steaming green jungle: I am brain-dead, unable to compose paragraph, sentence or word. Every hour or so, the fingers go to the keyboard, and little brown foxes and lazy dogs cavort there briefly, and then I stop. And I hear only the typewriter birds clicking, like echoes, from the mango tree.

Somehow I must find a way to pull the cords of my

book together, to tie a knot. Mr. Widgeon demands a tummy-filling sense of completion. No loose ends of spaghetti left on your dish.

And in what you have wrought, he asks, is there intrigue, is there tension? "The writer must endeavor to end each chapter with a gut-churning, page-turning moment of high suspense. Nudge your fickle reader into the next chapter before he escapes from your literary clutches, turns off the bedside lamp, rolls over, and enfolds himself in the arms of Morpheus."

(The prose of Widgeon's own mysteries — he claims to have written twenty-three cozies — is somewhat turgid and over-dressed, as in the quoted passage. His novels I have read seem like retreads, all set in some mythical town in the south of England, starring the same Meerschaum-smoking Inspector Grodgins and his straight man, the bumble-footed Constable Marchmont. But Widgeon knows the rules: the murderer is always the last person you'd expect.)

I must try to break the block, dynamite the dam like the Kitswuk Five, save the spawning streams of my novel.

Wow.

I just felt a short, violent shuddering of the earth, a random shrug by God, maybe about a four-point-fiver. It's the second earthquake this week. *Tremblors* hit often here, perched as we are over half-a-dozen fault lines on this bubbling section of the planet's skin.

No aftershocks. All again is placid in paradise.

I have a visitor — it is Captain Francisco Sierra with a bottle of guaro.

To be continued…

March 29, later.

Francisco has just left. I am in a much-improved state of mind.

I poured my heart out to him: my doubts about my book, the sudden withering of my creativity. He said: read me the first chapter.

I read him several chapters and he was most encouraging, though he caught some pomposities and trite phrases from the had-I-but-known school of writing (Widgeon damns such usage). As to my block, he told me he'd read an article by, I think, the great Raymond Chandler, whose advice to the stalled writer is to send someone through a door with a gun in his hand. We laughed; already I was feeling much better.

Before he departed, I mentioned that I had seen a lot of police today in Puerto Próspero. He said the OIJota are in town: the O.I.J. are akin to the FBI. He warned me to be careful for the next few days. Obviously there is going to be some kind of action.

Anyway I feel like my springs have been refreshed.

March 30, the wee hours

Exhausted, I am finally putting both note pad and author to bed. The dam did burst, an explosion of ideas in the night, new directions found, pages of scribbled notes. My head is buzzing, and I have seen — in my mind, at least — love's green flash. But I must kill again, and am racked with guilt.

B.

22

Tropical Snow

March 31

Dear office,

I am quickly to the keyboard following my trip to the river. The first thing one must do is record one's observations, for later it is often necessary to refresh one's memory from notes before giving evidence. At whose trial will I give this evidence? My own, I fear.

I solemnly swear, so help me God, to the following:

Léo Róbelo had promised to lead me to some river pools, and thinking these might be waters of inspiration, I set this morning aside for the trek.

Still weak from my travails of the day before (scenes of gunshots, death, lust, and yes, the twang of Cupid's mighty bow) I rose before the sun. In the cool of the dawn, I followed Léo and three of his brothers as they hacked their way over the brow of a hill and down toward the river bank, under high-branching trees stingy with their light.

When Mrs. Róbelo came by with some *gallo pinto* for breakfast, we took a break. We would not have looked up

had we not heard the bark of a tribe of cara blanca monkeys
and heard them swishing through the branches. Above us we
espied a great cuboid white object in the branches of a tree.
Bound in rope and covered with some kind of manila cloth,
this pendulous ominous cargo of suspect goods hung from
a branch around which its parachute lines had caught and
twisted.

Elementary logic suggests it was jettisoned from one of
the helicopters whirling around here last night. Looks like it
weighs a few hundred pounds. At current street prices, not
including provincial sales tax and GST, I fear we are looking
at several-million-dollars worth of nose powder hanging
from this tree.

You will have to appreciate my dilemma. A circumstantial case can be made against me, as tenant of these
grounds, of being an aider and abetter in the transport of
drugs. The OIJota were gathered in force in Próspero.
Looking for someone to bust.

So I told the kids to hurry to Puerto Próspero and fetch
Captain Francisco Sierra. And to tell him exactly what we
had been up to.

While they were gone, I prowled through the house looking for hidden stashes (and between me and Señora Róbelo
we have done this many times, coming up only with a few
roaches of the inanimate kind).

Finish this later. Visitors. Four-wheel in driveway. Two
short nervous official-looking men, sunglasses, white shirts.
Gun coming out. Shouting at me to

March 31

Dear citizens of the free world,

I sent Léo on an errand for pen and pencil and a *ham-
burguesa*, and he has just returned. I don't know what to
think of my situation. They have not taken my wallet or my
money, my belt or my shoestrings. I am as is. After several
minutes of close questioning ("Why, Señor Brian Pomeroy,

you tell thees Róbelo boys to make trail right to whar ees beeg bale of cocaine?") the OIJ commander seemed to grow bored with my explanations and just threw me into the Puerto Próspero jail, or what passes for a jail in Próspero, since the real jail burned down three years ago and has never been replaced.

I am, in fact, in the yard behind the Rural Guard station. The police office is a converted former warehouse, a large zinc-walled shed which abuts the street. Until a few minutes ago it was the centre of much activity, cars pulling up, dis-gorging people — a fence blocks my view of most of that — conferences taking place within. And I am absolutely sure that one of those muffled voices was speaking in English, and I believe I heard the words, "You can bet he's one of them" — something like that — as faces with Miami Vice sunglasses peered at me from a small window.

I didn't see the Yank, but I am not surprised that some American cop is here. The D.E.A. spreads its tentacles everywhere.

Suddenly there was another flurry of activity, a bustle of four-wheel drives and automatic weapons. I could see them speeding off on the road south toward Watson's finca, and now there is no obstacle to my freedom but Pedro the guard, and he is dozing in the shade of a tree. It would be nothing for me and my fellow outmates (the town drunk and Carlos the Peep) to storm and overwhelm him. I could then easily Tarzan my way through the jungle and seek refuge in the nearest Canadian embassy.

Where is Captain Francisco Sierra, I want to know. A shrug was the response I got from Pedro before he fell asleep; he is not the kind of guy you would want to guard the crown jewels. But I guess he knows I have no means of escaping: the next bus out of town leaves at eight p.m.

The only (now former) lawyer in Puerto Próspero was recently arrested over a complicated land fraud, so I will try to call some hot shot from San José. Under Costa Rican law, I have the right to a phone call: this the OIJ grandly con-ceded. But my right to make a phone call is compromised

somewhat (or you would have heard from me before this,
collect and at length) by the fact the telephone system is still
non functus here in Próspero.

My main concern right now is not about the prospect of
spending twenty years improving my Spanish behind Costa
Rican bars, but for my goddamned manuscript, which I left,
in a confused, escorted hurry, in a drawer of my desk. It
provides not only some proof of my innocent role as a writer
but also happens to be my only copy.

Please phone Caroline as soon as possible and tell her
not to worry about my incarceration. Make sure she under-
stands I do not blame her...

Ah-hah! Here comes my saviour, Capitan Sierra.
Until later,

Yours nervously,
Franz Kafka.

Time: Wednesday, the thirty-first day of March, seven o'clock
in the evening. Buenas tardes, Señors y Señoras.

This is an oral postscript to my letter which I am dictating into a tape recorder that Francisco Sierra lent me.

I am, I suppose, under a form of house arrest. Matters
are still confused but a ray of hope glimmers from yon
distant moon, full and glaring as she rises from across the
gulf. I am on the back stoop of Francisco's little frame
house and have just dined with his wife Maria and his
children, who are now in the living room. Captain Sierra
has kindly asked me not to try to leave the premises, and I
have complied.

The house sits on stilts over the water's edge and affords
a pretty prospect of Golfo Dulce, the wharves, and the lights
of the fishing boats rocking on gentle waves. Night's dark
curtain has abruptly fallen — after another brilliant but
green flashless sunset. But the light of the moon is strong.

Thanks to the good offices of Francisco Sierra, I am no
longer a prime suspect, especially since he has talked to Léo

Róbelo and confirmed that cutting that trail was his idea, and that I had, in an act of telling innocence, ordered him to fetch the police.

The OIJota would have held me in the jail were it not for Francisco's firm defiance of them. I am his informer, he informed them. Francisco ordered me to calm my fears. Though he was apologetic about the fact he had no spare room, I might enjoy an evening on the very hammock on which I now lie.

He would return later, and we could talk about the masters of the locked-room mystery over a glass of guaro. Indeed, why not take the bottle of guaro out to the back porch with me? Enjoy a few mellow moments with this portable tape recorder, reciting into it my various denials of guilt, while he cleans up some loose ends at the scene of the crime. He would ensure my manuscript was preserved.

I have the impression they have staked out the house. The loose ends Francisco was talking about are probably the owners of the cocaine — friends of Twelve-Fingers Watson? Surely it could not be Watson himself, whose trial in Vancouver is continuing through all eternity. The intruders may be a gang who thought the property was deserted.

The first glass of guaro has left a slightly raw feeling in the gut, but has begun to heat the body and calm the nerves. The second glass goes down better. It is not all that bad.

If I swivel my head to one side, I can see the pretty little square in front of the church, with its wooden benches and whitewashed tree trunks, young couples strolling hand in hand. I hear the plunkings of a guitar from somewhere. It all seems unreal, too gentle, too normal, too placid, too ominous.

Hi again. H-I-G-H. I think I have had too much guaro, so my senses may be clouded, but I could almost swear I just saw, getting off the night bus from Piedras Blancas, the person of my most horrible imagim…imaginings.

Well, I guess my vision is skewed with drink. But there is a street lamp right at the corner where the buses stop.

Quite a few passengers got off, Ticos mostly, and a few packers and trekkers out here to catch a last glimpse of the dying wilderness. One of them was lugging a fairly large suitcase. She didn't seem to be equipped for extensive overnight camping. Knee-high boots and pink hair and scarlet lips: not the typical *bon ton* of downtown Próspero.

I would have sworn on any witness stand that person was Abigail Hitchins.

But of course this woman has been a lot on my mind, and with the help of a little guaro (okay, half the bottle) it may not have been hard to conjure up her noble image. Her apparition had the same rapacious look, the same arrogant stride. Tall, like her, with thrusting hooters. The Tico men were staring at her: I guess there are some who would call Abigail's type attractive.

Anyway, she disappeared from my view, and I haven't seen Abigail's doppelgänger since.

Who else will I see with my next glass of guaro? Elvis Presley? Bugs Bunny? The Channel Two weatherman?

Me again. It's nine o'clock and I just saw Caroline's face in the reflected moonlight of the bay…It's gotta be the guaro.

Caroline. Again. She winks. A green twinkle of a forgiving eye. The green flash of sunset that I long to see.

A twinkle, a wink, and to her sad green absent eyes, I drink.

It's okay, folks, it's just the guaro.

It helps if you realize you are not crazy, only a little tiddled. Okay, guys, turn this thing off. The rest is for Caroline. You are to place this tape directly into her hands. It must not be routed via Abigail Hitchins.

Hum-de-dum.

I told you peeping Toms to turn this off. Give the tape to my wife.

Okay?

I pause as you glance at one another with guilt in your eyes. Do we snoop and sneak, or is our morbid curiosity overwhelmed by our sense of honour?

That's better.

Hi, Caroline. It's me.

Doubtless by now you have heard about the piggle… pickle I am in. Very dill. But appropriate, since I am myself a little pickled this night. I believe it is the first time I have, uh, let myself go since the day of the Kitswuk Five trial, when I tarried over too many cognacs in Au Sauterne and returned to my loving home to find both dinner and you burnt to a crisp.

Squiffed as I am, with all defences down, I am about to embark upon a monumentous journey into truth. I am weak and I have sinned (from the pews: "Hallelujah, brother"). But I shall be cleansed by confession, and you will decide, upon hearing my mea culpa, if you want to assist in the rebuilding of our marriage or cast the bloody mess aside and throw the blighter into the eternal flames of lonely perdition.

Truth: I was seeing Charity Slough almost every week. For instance, that night I said we had to cancel the Macarthurs because I had to spend some time in the library, and you were so forgiving…

"I understand, darling," she said, giving him a peck on the cheek. "Your work comes first."

Our hero lurched in shame from the doorway and drove off to Charity Slough's that night.

But most times it was during the afternoon, when, for instance, a trial suddenly aborted, and anyway, you don't want to hear…She bored me stupid, Caroline; she's as empty as a soap bubble, and I swear on the grave of my mother that I decided, long, long before Knot Lake, to end the affair, and I was telling her so in clear and unmital…unmitigated language when I almost got snuffed.

Okay, that's Slough, that's the story. Finito.

Okay.

This is hard. I'm going to tell you the truth. No more lies. I wanna clear the decks here.

There was another. Before her. The bar convention in Banff, um, a prosecutor from Calgary who told me she loved her husband but what the hell. And I mention that not because you found an earring in my jacket pocket when I got back and I lied and said I found it on the street, but because I am wiping the slate.

There were also a couple of petting sessions with Charlene Thomas, you remember she used to do our office books, but that was a non-thing, really, once we maybe went a little too far, and we never ever again.

Okay, well, this leads me to a final and most regrettable intiggle...entanglement...Couple of years ago, she and I were both involved in that abortion reference, and there isn't much to do in Ottawa and we were stuck there for a couple of weeks, and I think she got a little hung up on me, and there was a lot of diffigul...hardship over that, and it kind of continued for a while in Vancouver, and I had to tell her my heart was pledged to a different pawn shop, and there was some weeping and wailing and gnashing of teeth over some assurances of undying affection, that sort of thing, and an *alleged*, and I emphasize that word, *alleged* vague sort of suggestion she thought I made that you and I might break up and she and I would sort of, um, shack together...And knowing her as you do, she doesn't parade her hurt in public, but we had, I guess you could call it, a disastrous falling out...a scene in her apartment, a kind of blow-off that literally involved vows of vengeance and shit like that.

Abigail Hitchins will never tell you about all this dark history, our *affaire de coeur* was all kept secret because around this time she was in a kind of mess with her first marriage, suits and counter-suits flying off in all directions, and if *her* adultery was found out, her case is out the window, and he was sorta rich, and then after the divorce she just boomeranged into another marriage which went into meltdown, too, and I know she's always blamed me for the psychological muddle she's in, sort of having discarded her into the swamp of eternal matelessness, and it's like, boy, who let the wasps loose every time I see her in court or when you're not around, but of course when you're around she's sweeter than candy floss, and with just about as much substance.

She has a minor role in my book. Or had. A ball-biting feminist lawyer. I painted her in my favourite clashing, *fauviste* colours, but I'm worried I, uh, overdid it. Hard to portray her without straining the reader's credulity... credulity. Gonna have to lighten up on her in the next draft before I blast her away again. Maybe the knife this time.

I am haunted by her, Caroline. I even see her image stalking the broken sidewalks of Puerto Próspero. I swear I just saw her getting off a bus carrying a suitcase with that ugly punk hairdo she's affecting these days.

Or does guaro have hallucinic...hallucinogenic properties? I am beginning to think it definitely has locomotive inhibiling...inhibiting powers as I slop it onto my hands while trying to juggle bottle and glass and this tape recorder mike here.

That hiccuppy sound you just heard is a hiccup.

Oops, there it goes again.

Anyway, I detrained my rail of thought. Where was I?

Oops, pardon me.

Abigail Hitchins. In fiction if not in life, she will be paid off appropely...appropriately. Ah, yes, the writer as God.

'Scuse. We'll pause now for a short message from our sponsor who has gone off to have a cold clink...dink of water. This is Brian Pomegranate reporting from on location in a hammock in Puerto Hiccup. Next up, the sports and weather.

23

Disorder in the Courts

The death of Eddie Cohn spread panic through lawyers' ranks. Several major trials were adjourned — and a couple of accused murderers were granted bail because of these delays. Legal aid lawyers sought danger pay, and talked about a strike, and the government was forced to raise the tariffs to lure counsel back to their trials, to keep the justice system functioning. The Law Society's reward for the capture of the Executor was raised to two hundred thousand dollars.

Martin Wessel managed to get his face prominently displayed in the papers ("Cops Question Cohn's Partner") and the morning tabloid published a rather unsavoury profile of him, the story speculating about mob connections and repeating the two-year-old allegations against his client Father Doyle. Augustina regarded this as helpful; it enhanced the prospects of a biased jury.

Almost reluctantly, Lars Nordquist and his squad quickly ruled out Wessel. Though he was at first too ill to be questioned, he didn't seem to be faking his palpitations, fainting spells or grey pallor. Nor could he have mailed the letter from the Executor — he was in hospital all the next day recovering from shock.

Moreover, no blood was found on his hands or the sleeves of his clean white shirt and tan blazer, where a knifer from behind would likely have had it smeared.

Police scientists had reconstructed the scene: the killer had been hiding in the detached garage, several yards away, waiting for Wessel to disappear. Presumably the assailant brought his own weapon, but when his chance came, he simply picked up the knife that Cohn had honed to a razor's edge, jerked his head back, and sliced his larynx open almost to the spinal cord.

He was clearly right-handed — the cut went left to right. On the knife — which was found discarded at the scene — no prints came up but Cohn's, so the attacker had worn gloves. Plus, Cohn's teeth had clenched upon and bitten off a strand of leather: expensive deerskin, said the hair and fibre lab.

Because so much of the back yard was tiled, police didn't find foot impressions. Presumably the killer had a vehicle, though none of the neighbours had seen or heard one.

Methodically, the police began to dig into Eddie Cohn's affairs for a suspect with motive — of which there could have been many — and interviewed the few clients and business associates who were prepared to talk. His partner Wessel knew of no former client with a grudge.

The police did not perform these inquiries into motive with much fervour. It didn't seem a fruitful quest. Clearly a psychotic was on a crusade to cleanse the justice system of criminal lawyers.

The crude message mailed to the newspaper indeed seemed to suggest an unhinged mind; but the quick, clean, though gruesome operation at the Cohn household (and the rather more theatrical attempt on John Brovak's life) hinted of a more complex personality, someone with means and skill and strength and imagination.

Various experts of the mind erected structures often contradictory: the Executor was sick and compulsive; he was keen-witted, cocky, enjoying a high-risk game of catch-me-if-you-can. Psychiatrists agreed on one thing: he suffered from either a hatred or a fear of lawyers.

Because the Executor chose his victims so selectively, the good burghers of Vancouver suffered little unease. In the beer parlours, among the black-hearted and the cynical, some merriment was even had. Lawyer jokes were told to loud guffaws. (How can you tell when a lawyer is lying? His lips are moving.)

Roger Turnbull claimed to have been with the boys, watching *Terminator 2* on video, the night of Cohn's murder.

Everit Cudlipp was known to have been off duty that Friday night, but otherwise his whereabouts were unknown. He was divorced and single, given to eating out alone most evenings, and was often seen at Archie's Steak House, the site of the grenade blast. The detectives were surreptitious in their inquiries — they did not want Cudlipp to know he was a target. Following the weekend of Cohn's murder he had flown to Central America. All Nordquist knew about this sudden trip — through an RCMP conduit — was that Cudlipp was serving as a foreign adviser on a drug investigation.

The envelope containing the note from the Executor was compared with the one sent after the attempt on John Brovak: a single stamp, same type of standard manila envelope, block capital letters in blue ball-point pen. A handwriting analyst concluded that the author of each was the same person. The writer was believed to be right-handed.

The lawyers of Pomeroy Macarthur — the remnants of that firm — soldiered on in various states of paranoia in the days following Cohn's demise. Max continued to try to work Calico and to avoid Turnbull. Wentworth continued to feed the owls and struggle through Joe Ruff's papers and transcripts. Brovak continued not to call in — no one knew where he was, maybe up some mountain without radio reception.

Eddie Cohn's funeral took place on an appropriately sombre last day of March at the Beth Israel Temple on Oak Street. Augustina went on behalf of the office, esquired by Quentin Russell.

After the ceremony, as Augustina tried to escape for a smoke, she and Russell were accosted by Martin Wessel, much perturbed about the publicity surrounding him.

"Jeez, I'm a fucking celebrity already. Pal of Eddie Cohn, mouthpiece for the mob. And I get my mug on page three again this week, along with the pederast priest. Next thing you know I'm gonna get targeted by that loony Executor guy."

"Very nervous fellow," said Russell.

Augustina led Russell outside. Tony d'Anglio, who had dropped in briefly to pay his respects, joined them.

"This is gettin' excessive. The guy's whacked too many lawyers.

One or two, maybe, he wants to get the point across, but he shoves over my personal lip he's gone too far." He said all this in a light tone, and Augustina thought he didn't seem the least concerned.

"Miss Sage, you wanna do me a favour, put me in touch with that shooter in your office, Brovak. I may wanna throw some action his way."

"He's working for the other guys, Mr. d'Anglio." Twelve-Fingers Watson, Augustina meant, the competitor d'Anglio had sought to remove through his machinations with Cudlipp.

"Well, maybe the other guys ain't gonna be needing his services much longer."

She looked straight into his unwavering eyes and guessed he was letting her know that *he* knew Watson's career might soon be over.

"Why don't you go with Cohn's partner, Martin Wessel?" she said, and couldn't understand why she asked that; she had him on her mind.

"Yeah, he'd kill to have me as a client." He winked. "Okay, I'm thinking of using him for the day-to-day stuff. But in court I wanna guy with testicles. Hope to see you at the next funeral. 'Cause if I do, at least it won't be yours or mine." He drove off with a few of his boys in a fat Chrysler.

Augustina saw that several uninvited guests were working the parking lot — police officers noting the licence numbers. Talking with Inspector Nordquist were two brown suits with briefcases, strangers to her. As she and Russell passed by, they heard one of them speak with a New England twang.

When she returned to the office, Augustina found among her messages a call marked urgent from her friend Olive Klymchuk in Victoria, former bed partner of Mr. Justice Quentin Russell. They had talked about getting together for some gossip about the judge, but never quite found the time.

But the call was about business: "You want to act for the Jaegers, honeybun?"

"You have to be kidding," Augustina said.

She heard the proposal out. Three persons were accused of running a cross-border black market in kidnapped babies — six had been abducted in all, from supermarket shopping carts and from playgrounds. Olive had been acting for the three accused since their arrests nine months ago: a disturbed young woman from a good Vancouver Island family and Mr. and Mrs. Jaeger, a couple running an underground adoption agency in Los Angeles.

The publicity of the arrests convinced two of the six sets of illegal parents to turn themselves in to California police. The two purloined toddlers were returned to their rightful parents, and the joyful celebrations were captured by the TV networks. Four tots remained missing, however, their keepers fearful of coming forward. An extradition hearing had concluded; Mr. and Mrs. Jaeger were to be flown this weekend under escort to Victoria. Olive had decided they needed separate counsel.

Augustina listened to Olive's proposal with a distinct lack of ease. Yes, the case could mean lots of ink — that opiate of the legal profession — and the trial would normally be one to die for. On the other hand, thought Augustina, these days it was a case you *could* die for.

"Olive, I'm just not doing much criminal work these days."

"Not important. You can stand on your head and spit gumballs in court and you're not going to get them off. There's money." The kidnappers, Olive said, had charged $75,000 per baby.

"Olive, I just returned from Eddie Cohn's funeral. I'm a little on edge."

"Well, I'm afraid Eddie's death doesn't rank very high on my personal tragedy list. I'm sorry for his family, but I can't cry real tears. I knew the guy. Articled for him, remember? Real hands-on relationship. His hands on me. Hey, don't worry about this Executor. I told you, we have as much chance of getting these people off as we have of flying to Jupiter. And just because the, ah, alleged conspirators are dead meat doesn't mean we have to cop them out. We pick up about a hundred thou each, get our faces in front of the cameras a few times — come on, we're ladies, honey, the Executor doesn't kill *ladies.*"

Olive was never the most ladylike of women when it came to getting her face in front of cameras.

"Somehow I'm not reassured."

"Don't be a chickenshit, Augie."

"When's arraignment?" she asked.

"This Monday morning. No one's wasting any time here, Crown's tuning up the steamroller for this baby... ah, this trial. Come on,

Augie, do it. They're really a couple of scum artists, so you won't lose any sleep."

"Scum artists, right. Olive, two of my partners almost got killed, and they were defending *reputable* people: dambusters and drug importers."

"This is a *loser*, sweetie, you can't get killed when you lose: that's the rule, and my honest feeling is this guy, the Executor, plays by the rules."

Augustina uttered a cynical laugh. But what the hell, she thought, it would be fun to work with Olive — she was a good lawyer, though perhaps marginally ethical. And the trial could probably be delayed for a year or more.

"Okay. I'll hop a flight Monday morning."

"How're you making out with Mr. Justice Casanova?" The tone was snide. Ego problem, Augustina decided.

"You have a problem over my seeing him?"

"No, but you do."

"Why?"

"I found, dear heart, that he tended to get a little lazy in the sack."

"Oh, that must have been terrible for you."

"You snip." But she laughed. "Seriously, I want to talk to you about this guy. Don't get in too deep."

By now, Max Macarthur was ruefully playing an ever more unfamiliar role, a kind of cop: he seemed to have been unofficially seconded to Nordquist's team. When Max dropped by C.L.E.U. that day he received introductions to a Mr. Donoghue and a Mr. Hochmier. FBI agents. They showed him, from the file spread upon the desk, a colour photograph of a young man with brilliant blue eyes and crooked teeth.

"Am I supposed to recognize him?" Max said.

"Doubt that you could," said Donoghue. "This is him before. We'd don't have a shot of him after."

He awaited an explanation.

"The picture was taken sixteen years ago. He had his face done after that. His name is Hughie Lupo. Or was, he's using a flag. He's our number one."

This was too cryptic for Max. "Number one what?"

"On our wanted list. Killed two agents in Philadelphia." Donoghue had the most deadpan look he had ever seen on a still-breathing person. Was he human or was he android?

"What's this about, Lars?"

"Our friends think the Cohn killing fits a pattern. The agents were…an undercover team?"

"Working interstate racketeering," said the other suit, Hochmier. "Hughie Lupo was the target. He's Calabrian Mafia, the N'Dragheta. A collector."

"Also their number one button man," said Donoghue. "Somehow he made the two agents. One of them was stabbed in her sleep. The other had his throat cut from behind." Mirthlessly, he drew an index finger across his throat from ear to ear.

"*Exactly* like your Eddie Cohn," said Hochmier. "From behind, left ear to right ear. Like they teach in commando training. He did service in Saigon, taking out unworthies, infiltrators from the other side. Regular Rambo."

"What would Hughie Lupo be doing in Vancouver?" Max asked.

"We think the Calabrians put him in a safe house after his face surgery," Hochmeir said. "Could be here. Could be anywhere. He's never been sighted."

"That's all you have?" he said. "A similar pattern?"

"He blew up a barber shop one time with a U.S. army grenade," said Donoghue. "Same type of device your Executor used in that restaurant. Lupo went AWOL after stealing a bunch of 'em."

"Anything else?"

"He's a bit of a kinko, a wild card," said Hochmier. "We do have his prints."

"What do you think, Max?" Nordquist asked.

"The N'Dragheta doesn't work Vancouver. This is Tony d'Anglio's territory."

"They all go to bed together," said Donoghue.

"Sounds unlikely," Max said. "Unless he's also crazy in the head, and hates lawyers."

"Just thought we'd open some lines here," Donoghue said. He added: "We want him real bad. We want to fry him."

24

Famous
Lost Words

April 1

Dear Non-Communicators,

The surface of the softly-rolling Golfo Dulce is unbroken,
furrowed only by the bow of the Alonzo B., where — on this
Day of the Fool — I sit with pen and notepad, legs dangling
over the water as I try to clear my tormented head in a gentle
wash of wind.

The Alonzo B. reeks of former fish. A converted seiner,
she now ferries people between Próspero and Golfito, the old
banana port across the bay, where I am being slowly borne.
There, a functioning phone system can be found. Possibly
contact can be made with that far-off fairyland, mystical
Vancouver, which, like Atlantis, may have descended into the
sea. Rendered nearly mute by the most head-splitting hangover in human memory, I will also find a fax machine and
get these notes to you.

Okay, John, light up a big fat Corona. Here's the whole
grisly tale.

Little did I know Foul Death was afoot...

No, let me do this chronologically. Where did I leave off last night? Not sure. (Some event from the night is tugging at my mind…I can't bring it into focus.)

Start with the dreams. All night I lurched drunkenly from plot to plot, stories that didn't interlock, myself their confused protagonist, nightmares, guaro-mares, a dagger glinting in the lamplight; the hero lawyer — the author himself — lying in a pool of blood; pages of number fifteen bond cast by an arm into the air and falling like leaves into the sea.

At about ten o'clock I awoke to the thrum and throb of wild drums and cymbals from deep within my head. Heroically, I stifled the ralph response, and turned my bleary eyes and saw Francisco writing in a notebook in longhand. He looked drawn, sleepless. I made an ungainly escape from the hammock and knocked over the empty guaro bottle. Last night's paint remover, which I'd been chain-drinking.

Francisco told me there'd been a death at my house.

I stood there uncomprehending. I tried to clear my head under the pulsing, cold stream of his outdoor shower. I looked at the shrimp boats cleaving the flat waters of the Golfo Dulce and listened to the metallic squeaks and bugles of the Great-Tailed Grackles patrolling the mud flats below.

Then I asked Francisco if I had heard him right. I had.

His account: the SWATs roust the place just after midnight, along with Francisco and the foreign adviser I spoke of yesterday. He is none other than — hold your breath — Everit Cudlipp of our very own redcoats. The perps are Twelve-Fingers Watson and his gang. Eleven males, three females packing cocaine into suitcases with false linings — the parachuted cargo the police had been watching.

They are told to hug the walls — all but Rosalind Finch, whom Cudlipp cuts from the herd. Actually puts an arm around her (more on this farcical relationship later). Knowing Cudlipp, he just has to give Watson a dig. He says he's had Rosie in his pocket all along and that she "really fucked you over good, pal."

Grief, anger, who knows, but the cops hadn't fanned

Watson yet, and he comes away from the wall holding a small gun. To be blunt and not pretty, Cudlipp fires three rounds into his chest.

Controversy surrounds this death. Francisco didn't have a good view but he was pretty sure Watson hadn't raised his gun. But the OIJ Commandante claims Watson was turning that gun on Finch. Cudlipp has been asked to stay in Puerto Próspero until a coroner files a report.

A further complication: Francisco told me some legal papers were found on the person of Mr. Watson showing his property is being conveyed into my personal name. Also, a letter from his San José lawyer asking me to stop by to complete the transaction. Brovak, you illiterate swine, what the hell is going on up there?

Thankfully, Francisco has convinced the OIJ Commandante I am a highly trusted fink. I thanked him, told him he was an ace buddy. He had a final, regrettable announcement. He hadn't found my novel. He thought somebody might have removed it.

I waited several seconds for him to cry out, "April Fool!" and then got sick. Five minutes of the technicolor yawn. Horrors: has my manuscript been removed with the evidence, destroyed, scattered upon the sea as in my nightmare?

Francisco was unable to offer a lift to the finca, so I leaped aboard his older boy's bicycle. Astride it, with its tinsel and streamers, its wide handlebars, its orange tires set in green plastic spokes, I felt like a refugee from a circus, but I didn't care who laughed. I was in a frenzy.

When I arrived at the house I found a police photographer there and another cop packing up his tools. They seemed content to ignore me as I rushed to my desk.

My manuscript truly was gone.

I searched everywhere. The officers knew nothing. Maybe it was among the exhibits held at the station.

The wheels of my bicycle turning like propellers, I sprinted back to Próspero wreathed in swirling clouds of gloom. The OIJ guys at the police station remembered searching my desk, finding nothing of interest.

Cudlipp — he might know. I found him in Horvath's Bar, at a table by a window, staring out at the gnarl of mangrove. A nearly empty beer chaser was beside his nearly empty shot glass.

Horvath, a long horse's testicle protruding between thigh and tattered shorts, was seated by the bar and glancing at Cudlipp's glass from time to time to see if it needed topping. I ordered an Imperial, joined his table and asked him if he needed a lawyer.

Cudlipp looked at me blankly through crimson-hued eyes — possibly he had never seen me outside a suit or legal gown. I guess I looked pretty scruffy — I hadn't shaved in several weeks.

Cudlipp, who was half in the bag, finally did a make on me, and went on some kind of tirade about being trapped in a fuckin' banana republic. I told him the jails aren't too bad once you get used to the lice.

He launched into a furious defence of himself: Watson had been about to drop Rosie Finch; that gun was coming up; he had witnesses. Maybe not my buddy, Captain Sierra, but half the SWAT team. Then he started coming on with the subtle threats. Yesterday a shit-load of blow arrives on my newly deeded land. Brovak, he is up to his ears. (I detected a slight note of reproval when he mentioned your name, John.)

Selfishly motivated, I decided to seek out his good side, and offered my counsel. But no, he hadn't seen them search the house; he hadn't seen any manuscript. I should check with the Commandante in Golfito, where he is questioning the smugglers.

Dispirited, I asked him what had happened to the Watson trial. Does no one ever write to you? he asked. (Okay, he didn't, but he was nonetheless shocked at my ignorance.)

No, I hadn't heard about Brovak slagging Leroy Lukey last month over some business about a hooker, and getting the charges dropped. No, I hadn't heard that a crazy called the Executor had tried to blow you up, Brovak. Or that Eddie

Cohn got his throat slit Friday night. I could have been in Oz.

And now I hear *my* name was in one of those letters from this Executor. I am marked for death, but who gives a shit, right? Thanks for not writing. I didn't want to know.

Cut. Back to the bar. Roll 'em. Rosalind Finch enters, all yawny and fresh from a nap, and proceeds onto Cudlipp's lap, whereupon occurs a series of obscene pecks and pinches. Camera holds on this playfulness. Cut to Lance Valentine (played by Brian Pomeroy) throwing up. Cut to

CUDDLES: They had a strange dame with them I figured was the official taster.

ROSIE: Naw, she's clean.

CUDDLES: Clean? She had a fuckin' spoon up her nose when we came in.

Exterior shot of Pomeroy walking from Horvath's Bar into a slap of heat from the tropical sun. We can tell he feels ill, confused, as he stumbles down to the ferry dock.

And that's the movie of the week, folks, from on location above the abyssal depths of Golfo Dulce, whose sweet deep waters beckon this poor strutting player with inviting eyes of green…

Holy shit.

I just remembered.

Caroline. The tape.

The day's events so unnerved me I forgot about it. Left it behind at Francisco Sierra's house. Oh, woe, I think I put it into an envelope last night and addressed it.

An incredibly messy outpouring to my wife, dictated last night when snockered. The whole sordid…

I am making a connection.

Abigail, the apparition of my drunken evening…the strange dame, the knockout…Watson's official taster?

Yes, yes, *indeed*. It would have been just like her to show up at my doorstep with those divorce papers, and God had served her deservingly well if she had walked into a wasp's nest.

On this Day of the Fool, have the fates decreed that someone other than I shall play that dubious role?

We are chugging now into a small inlet. Golfito's ram-
shackle buildings come into view, strung like a funky charm
bracelet along the shore under the forested cliffs. Near the
dock, a working telephone...

25

The Hitchins Post

Checking his watch, Max burst into the office, panting. "Damn, I'm half a minute off." He headed for the steam room.

"Slow down, Max," his secretary said, grabbing at his track suit. "Brian phoned from Costa Rica, wanted to talk to you. Emergency, he said."

Emergency. Max had a sinking feeling.

"He leave a number?"

"He said he was at a pay phone and couldn't wait. He sounded really rattled. He left a message." She gave Max a cassette tape. "Hope you can decode it."

Max plugged the cassette into the stenocord machine.

Brian's first words, which seemed to be embellished with profanity, were drowned in the roar of a passing engine, muffler-less, and when he could make him out, the phrases came in staccato gasps.

"...Can't hang around, where the hell is everybody, what's going on, Cudlipp threatened to hang some kind of beef on me, did we buy Watson's finca or what, is it part of the fee? There's been a hell of a foofera here, half a ton of coke, the house got busted, and Everit Cudlipp dropped Twelve-Fingers Watson with a .32 police special, dropped him dead, the fucker. Brovak, that grenade, and Eddie Cohn, and this Executor guy…am I really on his hit list? Listen, I'm okay. If I sound a little frazzled that's because I'm a little frazzled. Fax coming shortly, gotta see the cops, I think Abigail Hitchins's ass got busted, over and out."

Silence but for the hissing tape.

Max tried to make sense of this mishmash. Abigail *Hitchins?* Was he cracking up again? He said Cudlipp…killed Watson?

He phoned Nordquist at C.L.E.U., who called back a few minutes later with the word from RCMP headquarters: Cudlipp had indeed shot Twelve-Fingers Watson — apparently in self-defence.

He had earned his reward from Tony d'Anglio to eliminate the competition.

In the dark stifling police station, Brian Pomeroy found the Commandante questioning one of the dope dealers.

"Do you have an Abigail Hitchins?" Brian asked.

The Commandante lowered his mirror glasses, smiled, and waved Brian into a small inner office. He said, "You mean the wan with the beeg maracas?"

Brian nodded.

"She geeve some kind of story about coming to visit you. She is *muy, muy…*" He searched for the word. "Annoyancing."

Brian smiled. He hadn't meant to. But suddenly he was enjoying the first warm feeling of the day.

"But she is only wan who is say anyt'ing. Thees guy, they all shot op." These guys, they all shut up. "So maybe she is *diferente* kind of feesh in the net. Were you expecting thees lady?"

Brian thought about this. All he had to do was tell the truth, destroy her alibi. One can get into trouble by lying, personal experience attests, so he was tempted to say he'd never met her in his life. Instead, he winked.

The Commandante's knowing man-to-man grin said he got the point — thees lady with the beeg maracas was his main squeeze.

"Commandante," said Brian, "your visiting Canadian officer is in a lot of trouble. I think this makes you all look bad. I can help out."

Brian composed dozens of opening lines in his mind for Abigail, mostly relating to the fact it was April Fool's Day, but when the

Commandante passed her in and closed the door, he was rendered mute by her smiling sang-froid. Odd how untainted physically she seemed from her experience. Lipstick as red as the hibiscus that bloomed in his yard. Fresh-painted nails even, long like cat's claws. A filmy sun dress through which could be seen the fulsome outlines of her breasts, the dark daubs of her nipples.

Abigail looked him over dubiously, his torn T-shirt and ragged shorts, a pair of sun-blackened legs emerging from them thin as poles, a scraggly blond beard, a head of hair that had not known a pair of scissors for more than three months hanging lank over his shoulders.

"Brian. You look like hell."

The sweetness of her smile denied him the triumph he felt entitled to enjoy.

"Treating you okay?"

"Can't complain."

She reached into her bag and withdrew a petition for divorce and an order for service *ex juris* and handed them to him. "I take it you won't be contesting."

Brian felt a sudden stiffness of limb, tried to order himself to be calm, but feared she had observed a trembling of hand. He heard his own ghostly voice. "Caroline is serious."

"I begged her to reconsider."

Brian lost all control. "You foul, lying, ball-busting vulture, you're trying to…to…" Brian's shrill voice cracked and went silent.

"You seem on edge. You *haven't* been looking after yourself."

Brian reassembled himself. He was free. *She* was in jail.

"What did you do with my manuscript?"

Abigail smiled demurely.

"I *know* you were snooping around. You came in through the door next to my desk. You were looking for evidence, right? Confessions of guilt. I could smell your goddamn *perfume!*"

He grabbed her bag, looked in. Not there.

"Didn't see it," she said.

"I should leave you here to rot. I guess this is what happens when you stick your nose into other people's cocaine."

"Oh, I explained everything. I was only *pretending* or they would have killed me."

"What's the true version?"

Unruffled, serene, she told a story of taking a taxi to the villa, blundering into the nest of smugglers. Fortunately for Abigail — no mean connoisseur of Peruvian snow — one of them turned out to be her own personal dealer. To prove she posed no threat she accepted a little taste. Just as the police broke the doors down.

"Tell it to the judge. When you get to trial in about two years."

A long moment passed, a Mexican standoff, eyeball to eyeball. Summoning all the strength within him, Brian didn't blink until he saw her mask begin ever-so-slightly to disassemble: a tiny crease, a frown of worry.

"What kind of drug laws do they have in this country?"

"Zero tolerance. No bail."

"But they can be bought."

"In a normal situation, maybe. But this is a high profile case. Guy got killed by a foreign cop."

As she thought this over, her toughness of composure continued to trickle away. Brian, earlier behind on points, was now winning rounds.

"Might be something I can do to help."

"How?"

"I'm connected."

Brian suddenly saw something helpless in her eyes, and then her face went slack. "Please, do something." She burst into tears. "Shit, I'm scared," she sobbed. "I hate doing this in front of you. I *hate* it."

Between choking sobs, she offered a plea in mitigation that Brian listened to in astonishment: "Brian, you're so dumb. It was all a joke between Caroline and me. We were just trying to scare you out of your pants. We weren't *serious.*"

"You want me to believe that?"

"I *love* Caroline, goddammit, like a sister, I wouldn't hurt her. She wants you back, and she never wanted you to go in the first place. How the *hell* did I get into this mess?"

"I don't trust these crocodile tears."

"*Ask* her, you cluck. Phone her up and *ask* her."

Brian had to think hard about that. His heart began to race. Maybe Abigail was suffering a rare burst of uncontrolled veracity.

"Well, goddammit, how *can* you help me?" she pleaded.

"The manuscript."

"I have it in my cell. I tried to save it for you. Anything could have happened; that place could have been blown up."

Brian's spirits soared. She was lying, of course, about saving it for him, but inadvertently had done so anyway. He felt a brief spasm of affection for her.

"I've been reading it, Brian." She smiled through damp eyes. "It's…I hate to say this, I absolutely can't bear pumping up your ego, but the book isn't bad." She sighed. "I really wanted it to be crap."

Brian Pomeroy knew her too well, he knew she was working him, trying to oil her way out of trouble. But there's a kind of bullshit that goes right to the heart. Praise of one's art, however hypocritical, has an uplifting effect on the listener.

He took Abigail's elbow and led her to a chair. She went limply, unresisting.

"I understand you told the Commandante that Watson hadn't raised his gun before Cudlipp shot him."

"Yes."

It is not ethical to advise a client to alter a statement or to lie. The proper practice is to suggest that one might, on reflection, reconsider an earlier, less helpful version of the facts.

"Think hard, now," Brian said. "Did you tell the Commandante the truth?"

"I've got Abigail Hitchins in tow here, released to *my fucking custody*! I foiled her plot to blow my mind if it's not blown already. Did you get the Max, fax?"

The distant voice of Max Macarthur: "Jesus, twenty pages of hieroglyphics. Did you get mine?"

"Yeah. Gotta go, ferry's leaving in two minutes. Have to try Caroline again."

Exhausted by his rapid-fire speech into the coin telephone, Brian made one more try to reach Caroline; he must confirm, if he can, that the divorce action had merely been a coarse practical joke to keep him tied to the Hitchins post. No one home but her answering machine. The secretary in the English Department said she was away for spring break.

The ferry was loading and the engine chugging, so he returned to his prisoner. She was standing near the dock in that filmy, low-cut sundress, attracting many looks, men striving to see her silhouetted in the flat, last rays of the sun, to see if in addition to not wearing a bra she was also not wearing panties. She was pretending to ignore them.

"Why do they *stare*?"

"They're in awe of you. Come on, or you'll be staying here overnight."

And that wasn't allowed. The terms of release were that Abigail remain in Brian's custody until the coroner took her evidence. Having done her part in exonerating Cudlipp, she would likely face no charges and be free to go.

Now if only he could recover and destroy that tape he had dictated, that inane explosion of honesty about past affairs. About Abigail. Just how drunk had he been last night? Leaving it at the home of Francisco Sierra in an envelope sealed and stamped…he had addressed it to the office, hadn't he?

A dozen people swarmed aboard the launch with them, a few of them Prósperonians he knew on a nodding basis. They couldn't keep their eyes off the painted woman with him, and he hoped they would not think she was his whore. But he had more than intimated that to the Commandante, and doubtless the word had spread through the community.

She took his arm. "I want them to think I'm with you."

"You are — unfortunately — with me."

"Yes, but in a cruder sense." She moved closer to him. "I really *adore* the way they gawk at me. Put your arm around me." He did so, tentatively. For the galleries, she gave him a radiant smile. "Don't assume I'm enjoying the closeness of all your agitated male-sweat."

He could smell her, too, something synthetic, musky. He felt her heat against him, and an acute discomfort in his loins. He remembered a time with her long ago, also on a boat, a savage bout of love-making on the deck of her ex-husband's forty-foot sloop, part of her loot from that first marriage.

At six-thirty the sun wearied of this confusing day, and set behind distant hills, spilling butter over the ripples of the Golfo Dulce. No green flash.

In Puerto Próspero, while Abigail collected her suitcase from Hotel El

Grande, Brian stopped at Francisco Sierra's house. But only his wife Maria was home.

"Wanted to ask if you saw a fairly bulky envelope I left here."

"Francisco, he mail it for you. He say it's what an ace buddy does."

In an abysmal funk, Brian fetched Abigail and led her home.

"Where are the light switches?" Abigail asked.

"I don't have power."

"Well, it's *dark*. This place gives me the whim-whams."

Brian lit a candle. He saw her pale, frowning countenance.

"So how do you heat your shower?"

"I don't."

"How long am I sentenced to be here?"

"The coroner is coming tomorrow. There's a plane out of Golfito the next day."

"I need a drink," she said. "Would you mind awfully?"

He fixed both of them a screwdriver, found the fridge had not run out of propane: ice in the trays.

"Ice," she said. "All hope for survival is not lost."

It was a while before he dared ask the question.

"How is she?"

"She's coming out of it just fine, my dear. Getting active in eco-politics, womaning the barricades, saving little birds. It's good. She'll meet some new faces."

Brian tore the divorce petition up, letting the scraps fall into his waste basket. She just watched.

"This better have been a joke, Abigail. If you lied to me I'll kill you."

"Ooh, just as you did in the book. I hope I didn't encourage you too much; it needs a lot of work. Some of the characters are a little overdone. Alexis Huggins, for instance, you prick."

"She's only a bit player."

"Is that why she suffered such a blood-curdling death? You must think I'm some kind of twit."

"The divorce was your idea, wasn't it? You've been trying to think of ways to get me ever since..." He stalled, reminded himself he had planned to avoid this.

"Since what? Can't you say it? Ever since you stopped fucking me? Ever since you lurched out of my life?"

He mustn't let her wig him this way.

"You can have the bedroom, I'm going to sleep out here under the stars." He brought out a foamy and began stringing up a mosquito net. His mind was on that cassette tape. Two weeks, on average, the mail takes to travel to Vancouver. Two weeks, he had to get back to intercept it…

A creak on the step outside made Abigail jump. "What's that?"

"Probably a little Róbelo."

"What's a Róbelo? Are they dangerous?"

It was the señora and Leticia, their arms filled with babies. The excuse was to collect his laundry, but he knew they had probably heard the strained, raised voices and were curious.

Abigail listened, uncomprehending, as Brian apologized for the confusion of the night before, explained that everything was all right now; he had a guest for a couple of nights.

Leticia, in her faded, patched dress, watched him throw up the extra bed, then coolly turned her eyes towards Abigail, the gaudy, zizzy city woman in her war paint, then followed her mother out.

Abigail said: "So that is the alluring Leticia whose higher education you intend to underwrite. How noble."

"Caroline showed you all my letters, too?" He felt invaded.

"Of course. We share all — except one little thing."

She said that as if she was prepared to hold their ancient affair over him, like a sword, a weapon of blackmail.

"Don't have a cow, I will keep our dirty little secret. You just keep your fucking marriage vows."

"You can't stop nosing into our private world, can you?"

"Frankly I never thought you were the right person for her."

"And who is?"

"Maybe a handsome Greenpeacenik."

"*Who?*"

"Terrance? Is that the name she mentioned? Oh, it's probably nothing."

God, Abigail could do it to him. A lying Iago to his innocent Othello. Now he was assailed by jealous thoughts. Caroline had gone off somewhere for spring break. With whom? whispered the green-eyed monster within.

He sat down to his typewriter and placed a sheet in the roll.

"You must get awfully tense writing those sex scenes. What's it been now? Three-and-a-half months?"

He tried to ignore this.

Abigail watched him for a while, a long, cool study. Then she lit herself a candle and dragged her suitcase to the bedroom.

Abigail's manner was more civil the next day, in fact convivial. She avoided topics that wounded, and even got him chuckling with the blow-by-blow story of Judge Lukey on candid camera at the bar banquet. She even made breakfast, fried bananas and a spicy omelette.

When they stood from the table, she took his hand. "Let's not fight, hey?"

In the afternoon, she changed into a bikini, put her sunglasses on, slimed herself, then stretched out in a deck chair. After a while she took her top off.

Brian watched her rub sun block onto her breasts. *What's it been now?* she had teased. *Three-and-a-half months?* He felt a nauseating hunger for her.

"Wish you'd cover up," he said.

"You've seen them before."

"Anyone could come down the road."

"Men bare their breasts *quite* legally. Do my shoulders, that's a darling."

She handed him the lotion and when he touched her skin he felt prickles. When she turned suddenly to reach for her coffee her tit brushed against his stomach.

She smiled at him, her lips slightly parted.

"Sorry."

Brian was hugely uncomfortable. He feared her sudden openness, her friendliness: did she wish to taunt him into some dangerous episode? He could smell her, all sunscreen and estrogen, he could almost taste her.

He escaped, went to the back of the house to the outdoor shower, and stripped. He felt the cold water stream over him, felt the tremblings ease.

✣ ✣ ✣

A police jeep pulled up to the gate toward evening. Its occupants, the OIJota Commandante, Everit Cudlipp, his girlfriend Rosie Finch, and an older man Brian assumed must be the coroner. He went down to the road to greet them, to give Abigail a chance to scramble into some clothes.

"I owe you, counsellor," Cudlipp said, "Hear I got you to thank for this. We got a plane back tomorrow if everything comes out okay. Rosie and me."

He gave Rosie a squeeze. She smiled and melted a little into him. What was Brian a witness to here? Could this be that ethereal rapture which he had so tenaciously sought for his novel? Was even Cudlipp capable of love?

As he led his visitors into the house, Abigail swung gaily from the bedroom in a silk wraparound. He watched as this hard-core feminist chameleon began flirting with everyone.

No, she told the coroner, she wasn't under the influence of drugs the other night. Watson was dangerously high on narcotics and had a gun trained on her; to win him over she claimed she was a drug user, though she abhorred the taking of drugs.

While this questioning was going on, Cudlipp said, "A beer would go down," and Brian fetched cans of Pilsen for the staff-sergeant and Rosie Finch.

"Hope she lays it on thick. Rosie here backed me up to the hilt, eh, babe? Told the coroner Watson threatened to kill her once."

"You saved my life, Cuddie." She hugged him.

"Any time, buttercup." Cuddie. Buttercup. Brian could just see it. Mr. and Mrs. Cuddie.

Cudlipp shook his head. "Thing like this happens in Canada, nobody bats an eye. This is a real backward little country, full of dumb little laws and fucking lawyers just like back home."

Full of fucking lawyers just like back home. The phrase had a chilling ring to it. Another lawyer-bashing cop.

After taking Abigail's statement, the coroner shook hands with Cudlipp and told him he was free to catch his plane the next day unless he wished to stay on and enjoy the scenery of Costa Rica.

"I already enjoyed it," said Cudlipp, staring at the sunset.

"Did you see that?" asked Rosie.

"Yeah," said Cudlipp. "I'll be fucked."

Brian saw their eyes were on the horizon. He had missed the setting of the sun. "What did you see?"

"A green flash," said Rosie.

The flash that lovers see. It ruined Brian's evening. He couldn't write; he stared into the darkness until Abigail, tiring of his silence, went to bed.

At an uncertain hour that night as Brian lay in his makeshift kip, awake and tense, another earthquake rumbled through the jungle, shaking the rafters and sending Abigail yelling naked from her bed to his.

"My God, that terrified me."

"They happen all the time."

"Hold me," she said.

Brian didn't move. He felt another bump, an after-tremor.

Her voice was soft. "It's still there, isn't it? Admit it, Brian. That's why there's so much anger."

Her hand went to the swelling protuberance in the sheet, stroked it. "I won't tell Caroline." She moved her lips toward his. "Sleep with me tonight," she said softly.

Brian looked into her eyes, which were close, probing, hungry.

"I'd burn in hell first," he said.

She withdrew her hand, stood, and stalked off. "I lied to you, by the way. Your book is total dreck."

26

Popping
the Question

At nine o'clock Friday night Augustina jumped when her phone rang, an odd reaction given that she had been sitting by it all evening waiting for her lover's promised call. She would punish him. With coolness.

"Hello," she said, too pleasantly.

"I intended to make contact when the fog lifts and I can see my way clear to flying out of here. But it's not looking good."

"You're at an *airport*?"

"No, the courthouse."

Augustina laughed, *much* too politely.

"You sound a little peeved at me."

"Not at all."

"Listen, I did want to get together tonight, but I'm writing some reasons for Monday and I want to clear the weekend for you. The judgment is so far making no sense whatsoever. I don't know whether I'm creating a precedent that will open the floodgates to sin for all eternity. What I'm saying is, I'm going to be here until midnight."

"In your chambers."

"No less a prisoner than any man I have sentenced."

"I'll bring up a bottle of wine at midnight."

"Call me just before you come, I'll clear it with security."

Augustina arrived in Russell's chambers just after midnight to find he hadn't yet finished his judgment. Tie askew, sleeves rolled up, he was struggling over sheets of paper, writing in longhand. Spread across his wide desk were casebooks and statutes. She caught a musty smell, maybe from the books, or from him, the pungent odour of brain work.

"Two minutes more," he said. "Then I can put Anvil Engineering versus Saanich to bed."

"Don't let me distract you," she said.

She wiggled her bum onto the top of his desk, busied herself with bottle and corkscrew, poured two glasses of wine, and lit a Player's Light.

Russell scribbled and grumbled. "Zoning bylaw — is it valid? Who knows? So what you do is bury yourself under a pile of obscure precedent. Everything I write is being scrutinized these days by the people in Ottawa. They want fuzzy thinkers. If I make my judgments too lucid and coherent, I won't get the job."

"You really want to move to Ottawa?"

He looked up. "I don't have to be out there all the time. In fact, I can spend about six months of the year right here. If you'd like."

"If *I'd* like?"

"I had better finish this." But he didn't; he kept staring at her. "It's down to a couple of finalists: Max Mac Two and me."

"How do you know?"

"Friends in high places." He leaned back in his chair, hands clasped behind his head. "Darling, I have run twice for Parliament. I carefully picked my ridings, mind you, to avert any chance of winning. I've been policy chairman for the Conservative Party. The P.M. and I used to get drunk together. I know stories about him that would make your hair stand on end. I *advise* the Justice Minister; I've been her campaign manager. That, in short, is why I'm on the short list. It really hasn't much to do, frankly, with my exceptional brilliance as a legal thinker."

"So modest."

"I am suspect, however, in some quarters. Because I'm unmarried. Might be a closet faggot, you know, embarrass the courts."

"I'll testify for you."

"You can do better than that."

"What?"

"Marry me."

He might as well have been ordering Kentucky Fried Chicken.

"I'll be with you in a moment," he said, and returned to his judgment, scribbling, checking the wording of a sub-paragraph of a sub-clause of a local bylaw.

She sat there with her mind a buzzing blank, and quickly puffed her cigarette to the filter. An ash dropped onto Russell's judgment. "Sorry."

He looked at it, brushed it off, returned to his labours.

Augustina tried to bring analytical powers to bear on the situation. Had she heard him correctly? If so, was this a proposal? And is there an appropriate response to be made to it?

"Done." He dotted his last page with a period, and when he looked up from what he had wrought, he observed her staring at him, frowning. She handed him a glass of wine.

"I am desperately in love with you, Augustina."

She looked into his eyes and felt their pull. She leaned across to him and kissed him. Her tongue went into his mouth like a burning fuse, and he ignited.

He was suddenly peeling off her clothes, throwing them helter-skelter about the room. With one wide sweep of his arm, Russell sent everything off the desk: books, ashtray, pens and pencils, his written reasons in Anvil versus Saanich, and he brought Augustina beneath him, startled but willing, and made love to her on the desktop with a raw intensity.

Augustina had an orgasm after three minutes and was reaching for another when Russell exploded within her. She thought: My God, the judge may be a lamb in his own bedroom, but he's a lion in the courthouse. He had never made love to her like this before, so fast and hungry.

He lay, finally, limply atop her. "I really don't know what got into me."

"Must have been a hell of a judgment." She was still hot with passion, felt herself trembling beneath him.

"I don't know how much my, ah, feelings for you are shared."

She mumbled incoherently.

"I feel magic, Augustina, electric. That's banal, I'm sorry, I can't think of how to tell you how much I...Augustina, I'm really feeling clumsy right now, with words, and I'm struggling to ask you...I mean, I don't want you to answer right away..." He seemed suddenly aware that they were in naked connection on top of his desk, and he raised himself on his elbows. "My God, you can't be too comfortable." He laughed. "This isn't the most decorous situation in which to propose, is it?"

"Well, you're not exactly on bended knee."

They both began to laugh, she a little hysterically. Slowly, they disconnected, and took turns in his washroom. After, they had another glass of wine, and Augustina chained one cigarette from another; she was still woozy, unsure, embarrassed. He seemed in even worse condition, unable to construct a sentence.

Finally: "Some proposal. I honestly didn't mean it that way. Blurted it out of fear I wouldn't get the courage later...I wasn't really planning, I mean..."

"You're being incoherent, darling," she said, and kissed him. He *was* uncomfortable — she found that somehow charming. "Quentin, marrying me *won't* get you appointed to the Supreme Court of Canada. If they check me out, they'll find I'm one quarter Cree, I've picketed the legislature, had an abortion, and smoked pot in the privacy of my home. You'll be ruined."

He waved away her protestations. "You don't have to give up your career. In fact, I want you to keep it. You don't have to move to bloody Ottawa; I'll fly back here on weekends..."

She put a finger to his lips. "I don't know...I have to think."

"I've blown this. I feel devastated."

"It's just too sudden; I'm confused."

Not long ago she had been brooding: thirty-five, a spinster without expectations. No nice men out there. And suddenly Mr. Perfect rides over the horizon. Why was she hesitating?

"Would you like to come over and see my etchings?" he asked.

At his house, Augustina was weak-kneed, her mind a jumble. Russell wandered about, hanging up coats, turning on lights, tending the bar, then went to the den to check his answering machine for messages.

She heard the voices of his callers indistinctly. "I'm waiting," said a male voice. Then a squeak, as if Russell had pushed fast forward. *I'm waiting.* A voice somehow familiar. Then an older woman's voice, chirpy and confident — his mother?

Yes, it turned out.

"She's 75, perkier than a pup," he said, returning, putting on some chamber music.

"Who's waiting?" Augustina asked. "And for what?"

"Oh, that's...nothing."

He seemed suddenly to lack for conversation, and Augustina guessed he was hugely embarrassed about his awkward proposal. He was like a large uncomfortable kid.

"I just got a very big case," she said. "The Jaegers? The baby-nappers?"

"You're doing *that*?" He seemed unduly shocked.

"Yes, with Olive Klymchuk. I heard you rather abruptly tossed her out of your life." Her tone was teasing.

"I had to. To preserve my sanity." But Russell looked grim, distracted. "Augustina, this kidnap case...it's risky, isn't it? What with that maniac running around..."

"I'll be damned if I'm going to let some self-styled Executor send me running like a coward from the courts." She spoke braver than she felt. "Anyway, the case is a loser."

"I *don't* like it. I absolutely *don't* like it."

"I'm going to do it, Quentin."

He sighed. "You'll be a couple of days in Victoria?"

"I think so."

"I'll fix you up at the Topaz. It's close to the courts."

He owned the Topaz, probably Victoria's most elite hostelry, often used by visiting mucks: politicians, lawyers.

"I am going to make bloody sure there is ample security."

"So protective."

She struggled with what she wanted to say.

"I do love you." Admitting this, to him and to herself, had a strange effect on her. She began to weep.

27

The Kundalinga
Method

Wentworth Chance spent much of that week wading through Joe Ruff's turgid soup of paperwork, seeking examples of non-frivolous suits. The man had a habit of suing for the slightest slight, had learned just enough law to drive a public servant to madness. Injudicious judges, recalcitrant court clerks, peckish officers of officialdom, all were put to the whip of his many writs.

An animal licensing officer who refused to take "any proceedings or actions whatsoever" about the neighbour's dog. A municipal clerk who "did commit the grievous tort of slander" by calling Ruff an obnoxious pest. A justice of the peace "who did conspire to deny justice" by refusing to issue witness subpoenas.

On Saturday evening, after fourteen straight hours of perusing Joe Ruff's files, Wentworth felt like a zombie, his mind a slovenly mess of facts, laws, and rules of court. You have the right stuff, Joe Ruff had said. Yeah, stuff *you*, Mr. Ruff.

Wentworth, however, a firm idealist, was of the view Ruff was being wronged. The fellow just happened to be one of life's minor annoyances, a tiny pebble in the hiking boot of the judicial system. The price you pay for democracy.

Wentworth was determined to win this if it killed him.

It was seven o'clock and the groans and hisses issuing from his stomach insisted on being responded to, but he had by now cleaned Brovak's cupboards bare.

He walked outside, wondering where to get a cheap meal.

A starry night; the winds had whipped the clouds away. April. April is for lovers. But despite Brovak's assurances Wentworth would enjoy enhanced sexual appeal when behind the wheel of a Mercedes SL, that vehicle had not added flesh and bones to any of his erotic fantasies. Maybe he should take Minette Lefleur up on her offer of a freebie. Seek therapy to overcome his tormenting shyness.

He remembered that a health food bar had just opened in the New Age Awareness Center: maybe he could get them to load up on the sprouts and sunflower seeds. He wandered in past a notice announcing that Swami Krishnavich was leading a seminar tonight on multi-sensual energy linkage, and he heard moans and erotically-rhythmic grunts from one of the rooms as he made his way to the small eating area: a few bar stools and tables.

At one of them, a haunted-looking young woman was seated: about twenty, a tall, Titian beauty. Long shiny hair falling over her eyes as she concentrated over a heavily bound note pad, maybe her journal. She looked up at him and her eyes were deep, pulling, haunted. She went back to her writing.

Wentworth ordered a soya burger with everything on it. Waiting for it, he slowly turned his head to take in the young woman again. So beautiful and so sad.

She caught him staring at her, and this time didn't look away. "How do you spell 'disconsolable'?"

"Maybe you mean 'disconsolate.' Or 'inconsolable.'"

"Oh. Maybe that's the word. Yeah, right."

"With an 'a' in the 'able.'"

She went back to work.

You're welcome, Wentworth said under his breath. No one else was in the restaurant area, though a few men with cropped hair and saffron gowns were standing outside a door in intense conversation. He was jolted by the sound of a shrieking woman, a primal scream, demons being exorcised somewhere in this building.

After a while, he turned to her again. "Hope it's not the story of your life."

"It is, in a manner of speaking." She scrutinized him. "Life as fiction, you know? I'm a poet, really. But I can't spell worth a hoot. I've never seen you in here before. Are you doing the energy linkage?"

"No, I'm a lawyer." That seemed not quite responsive, but ignited her interest. When his soya burger arrived, as did some soup for her, she asked him to join her.

"I'm taking kundalinga yoga," she said. "It's supposed to open up your centre so your energy flows out?"

It seemed a question, though Wentworth didn't know how to answer it. There was a sexy, breathless quality to her, which — in combination with the rounded, braless tits he observed pressing against her shirt — caused a hunger to stir in Wentworth's nether regions.

"What *are* you writing?"

"A novel about a woman scorned."

Vajeeta, it turns out, was her name. A spiritual name, newly adopted.

"I have a lawyer character in it?" she said. "Maybe you could help me with him."

"Uh-huh. Sure."

"He's a tragical figure. He's in a prison of his own making? He wants to be free, but he's a coward. He hides by working too much."

"Well, the law is a cruel mistress."

She wrote that down.

Wentworth wasn't much help to her in plumbing the obscure depths of a lawyer's psyche, but she was attentive and eager. At the end of their meal, as they walked from the New Age Awareness Centre into a misting rain, he gained the courage to ask, "Uh, do you want to do anything?" Maybe, he thought, he should have paid for her soup.

I have a '78 Mercedes. We could drive around for a while, and you could tell me why you look so sad, and I could invite you up to my pad and help you with your book. What are your feelings about hot tubs?

"Where do you work?" she asked.

Wentworth pointed to the brass plaque on the nearby door. Pomeroy, Macarthur, Brovak and Sage. "My name's not on there. Yet."

When she turned to him after studying the plaque, her smile was bright. "Upstairs? Here?"

"I'm actually a student-at-law. But I've only got three months to go, and I get the big 'C', the certificate to practise."

She took his arm. "Well, what do *you* want to do?" she said.

Wentworth was too stunned to move. He felt the merest hint of a plump left breast near his lower right biceps.

He asked her if she'd like to go for a drive.

When he escorted her to the car, Vajeeta said, "Oh, what a cuspy machine," a sexy voice that made Wentworth's knees tremble.

They drove to Stanley Park, the green but not untrammeled wilderness at the First Narrows, a thousand acres of tree, beach, cliff, lake, and jogging trails on a peninsula jutting between English Bay and Burrard Inlet. Wentworth took the long way around, by Brockton Point. Vajeeta searched through the tapes, found something loud and electronic.

"Do you defend cases in court?"

"All the time."

A nightcap, perhaps? I have this spot overlooking the city. Actually, from the hot tub on the deck there, you can see all the way to the airport.

"Where do you live?" she asked.

"I have a heck of a view. Do you want to see it?"

She said that would be great.

He took the approach to Lion's Gate Bridge, and fed the Mercedes smoothly into the two lines of traffic going north, cars bound homeward to the upwardly mobile North Shore suburbs.

"We can have a nightcap."

"Sure, or whatever," she said. He darted a look at her. She was smiling at him, lips parted. "What's your sign?"

"Taurus." When he added, foolishly, "The bull," he blushed.

"Artistic, egotistic, sensualistic. I'm on the cusp of Taurus? This could spell trouble."

"Spell trouble?"

"Okay, T-R-U-B-L-E."

Wentworth laughed a little too giddily.

"Because I know what our love signs are?"

Wentworth almost missed the Upper Level Highway.

To the sounds of thumping guitars, Wentworth opened the engine up on the Upper Levels, and prayed that his erection would subside before he had to emerge standing from the car.

At the Twenty-first Street interchange, he left the freeway and switch-backed up Hollyburn Mountain.

"I like lawyers," she said. "I went out with one once."

Condoms. Does John keep his condoms in one of those bathroom drawers?

When she saw the house, she said: "Cosmic view."

How do you put them on?

As he set the scene for seduction, starting a Presto-Log fire, putting some music on, Wentworth Chance wore a false face of insouciance. But he was anxious, horny, confused, wondering how to do this. One mistaken signal, one wrong move, and these days a guy can get hauled up on a date rape beef. *I know what our love signs are. I like lawyers.* These were the verbal clues that hinted she might not be intending to prefer charges.

He took his glass of Brovak's private reserve port to the window where Vajeeta was now standing, the front window overlooking the covered hot tub sunk into the deck. She was not a consumer of alcohol: a fruit juicer. Wentworth had counted on a little substance abuse tonight: how do you spell uninhibited?

"Do you own this place?"

Wentworth couldn't lie. "One of my bosses is on a skiing holiday. I'm house-sitting for him."

"I thought something like that. You don't look like you've been around long enough."

Wentworth felt deflated, but she looked winsomely at him, and smiled.

"Are you good?" she asked.

At what? In bed? Good as opposed to evil?

"A good lawyer?"

"I, ah…I won the MacKenzie Prize in evidence."

"Wow."

Wentworth went wobble-kneed. The "wow" was like a long kiss; it issued from plump, pouting lips.

"It's so splendorous," said Vajeeta, looking out, "the lights."

Look down. Beneath the window. That is a hot tub.

"What's that down there?"

"Oh…a hot tub."

"Boy, you must really suffer here."

"Like to try it out? I, uh, can't promise to find you a bathing suit."

"Don't be silly."

A few minutes later, Wentworth, in the pulsing water up to his neck, watched the long, bare right leg of Vajeeta test the water with her toes.

"Ooh, hot, hot."

Wentworth watched as one leg, then the other, slipped into the water, knee, thigh, cunt, tummy, tit.

She floated toward him, her teeth shining, sharklike. "'And I, too, I am become like the flowing river.' That's from a poem I wrote, there's a rhyming couplet at the end, aquatic and erotic? I don't know why I have this strange thing about lawyers." She giggled.

Her arm brushed his rampant cock. "Oh-oh," she said. She came closer. "I warned you — we're on the cusp."

A few minutes later Wentworth was supine on the cedar decking, arching, convulsively exploding, as Vajeeta's strong fingers pulled him powerfully into her mouth. He was deflowered that night in the many exciting ways of kundalinga yoga.

The next morning Max showed up at Jack Calico's hotel, intending to tell him he'd arranged a deal. If Calico agreed to sign an affidavit about his brave role in the apprehension of O.D. Milsom, the court would dismiss his aggravated assault charge.

Max found Calico's door slightly ajar, and walked in without knocking. Only Lars Nordquist was there. He had a set of small screwdrivers and was fiddling with the clock radio. Max was puzzled at first.

"Where's Calico?" He saw Nordquist slip a small metallic item into his pocket. "Bones, is that a bug?"

"You didn't see it," he said.

"Christ, Lars."

"Sorry, Max, I'm under a ton of pressure to solve this thing."

"So you heard everything he told me."

"You're not going to turn me in."

Max slumped into an armchair. "So what happened?"

"The premises were not under faultless surveillance, Max. The RCMP member on this floor saw him get into the elevator. He made radio contact with the member in the lobby. Which officer observed that the elevator did not come to a stop in the lobby, but proceeded to the third parking level. We did not have a member at the third parking level."

"Aw, shit," was all Max could say.

"I'm sorry, but you know our resources are taxed."

Members, thought Max, A good word for them. This was a disaster. Jack Calico, his set-up man for Turnbull, had somehow lost faith with him.

He had been milking him gently all week, but Calico had gradually stopped delivering; a suspicion as to Max's motives seemed to be glimmering in the dank recesses of his brain. Max felt like a clown; he had made a grievous mistake in his handling of Calico, hinting he might qualify for that two-hundred-thousand-dollar reward for helping uncover the Executor. At the mention of murdered lawyers he had suddenly zippered up.

This had made Max wonder: were Turnbull and Calico — and maybe others in an inside group of the Angels — running a paramilitary death squad? Under cover of a cartoon character who sends letters to newspapers?

"Did Calico phone anyone?"

"I'm afraid so. Yesterday. From a coin machine on the ground floor. Non-traceable."

"So Turnbull picked him up."

"It would seem so. By the time our people made it to the garage exit, three cars had gone through, and the fare collector couldn't remember a single darn person in any of them."

"I guess he's been debriefed by now. Turnbull is going to smell something very stinky about what I've been doing."

Max hadn't heard from him since the night Eddie Cohn's throat was slit. Turnbull had the usual alibi for that Friday night: in the barracks with the Angels watching the good guys waste the bad guys on the little screen.

"We don't have anything from Calico we can use in court, Bones."

"Turnbull may not appreciate the legal nuances. He is going to be worried that the cat is crawling from the bag. We'll surveil him openly — a warrant for Calico's arrest will justify making a few visits. Maybe Turnbull will get panicky."

The barracks of the White Angels weren't extravagant, comprising the lower two floors of a cheap hotel on Powell Street. Here seven male Angels lived full-time, the other volunteers commuting to Turnbull's briefing room for their assignments.

Roger Turnbull was there with a group of them when Max and Nordquist walked in. Turnbull didn't seem fazed.

"And how is Inspector Nordquist?" he asked. "Ah, and Max Macarthur." Pointedly, he ignored them for a moment, returned to his perusal of a city map which was spread on a table. "Andy, Jorgy, I want you to do the Main and Kingsway area, we've had complaints about a pushy panhandler." To Nordquist: "Had quite a few calls recently, people upset about a lack of policing. But you've been busy with other things."

"Where is Jack Calico?" Max asked.

"Has he gone missing?"

Nordquist showed him the arrest warrant.

"This is for Calico?" said Turnbull. "The silly ass, he skipped bail. Does that mean I owe ten thousand dollars? Well, maybe I'll earn it back by nabbing the Executor." His voice seemed stilted, the words rehearsed. "We're hot on his trail. The public don't think you guys can pull it off." He turned back to his maps. "We've got work to do. You can wait outside. I'm sure Mr. Calico will be wandering by."

"I thought we might have a talk," Nordquist said.

"I don't like all this harassment, gentlemen. I'm *not* the Executor. I'm disappointed in you, too, Max. Thought I retained you to help Mr. Calico, and here you are working against him with the police."

He refused to say anything more, and Max and Nordquist left.

C.L.E.U. posted a surveillance van on the street outside. Calico never came by that day.

28

The Dealership

Augustina spent a nearly idyllic weekend with Quentin at Harrison Hot Springs. He had ordered her to enjoy herself, and not to think about his proposal of marriage. But of course, that was all Augustina thought of.

Walks in the forest, forays on a rented outboard, wine and candle-light, a big moon above the lake at night, secret hand-holding in the steaming pools. People smiled at them, at the stars in their eyes.

On Monday morning, her heart pulsing, her head full of Quentin Russell, she flew to Vancouver Island, to Victoria, the capital of British Columbia, a tourist stop: much fake Tudor, some real Victoriana, a strived-for English air.

Augustina was met at the float plane dock by three persons dressed in business suits, led by a Mr. Lucius Ponsonby, who intro-duced himself as president of Securi-Corps Services Ltd. "We're your watchers," he said. "We're armed, of course, but we'll try not to be obtrusive."

"Where did you come from?"

"We do the security work for Judge Russell's hotels; for eleven years we've been doing this, very valued client and a truly wonderful gentleman."

They escorted her to the Topaz, an ivy-clad, six-storey building, old, carefully restored. It was surrounded by flower gardens, daffodils and hyacinths and the early buds of roses. The hotel manager mewed and clucked over her, and said he hoped she would enjoy her stay in the Princess Victoria Suite. He and Ponsonby escorted her to the second floor, to one of two large, adjoining suites. Augustina's contained a large living-room and a bedroom with a canopied bed, velvet curtains, and a wide balcony overlooking the pretty inner harbour.

Ponsonby poked around, peered into closets and under the bed, checked to ensure the door to the adjoining suite was locked. He made Augustina nervous. "Can't be too cautious; I understand you're the judge's *very* special guest."

Atop a writing desk were a laptop computer, a printer, a combination fax-copier and a carton of Player's Light — all compliments of Mr. Justice Russell. These were arrayed in the shade of a bouquet that probably earned his neighbourhood florist enough to retire on.

She found Olive Klymchuk waiting for her in the dining salon. She was Augustina's age, blonde, petite, dimpled and full of snap. They greeted with a hug and a buss, and ordered breakfast.

Talking non-stop, Olive gave her a procedural briefing. The three baby-snatchers would be arraigned this morning; the Crown wanted to set aside an entire month for the preliminary hearing; Crown prosecutor would meet with them this afternoon for a disclosure hearing.

Augustina wasn't focusing on this; she looked to be in a distant world, not quite smiling — beatific.

"Are you okay?" Olive asked. "You look zoned out."

Augustina seemed to regain consciousness. "Oh, yeah, I'm fine."

"I gave instructions to the doorman. If a guy says he's the Executor, don't let him in."

"I'm not even thinking about that."

A long pause as Olive watched Augustina fidget with one cigarette, while another was hanging unlit between her lips.

"Okay, what kind of shit is going down here?"

"He proposed."

"Omigod." Three fast syllables.

"I would have dropped my socks if I had them on. He says he's frantically in love with me."

"Do you believe him?"

Augustina resented the sardonic tone. "I think he gave credible evidence."

"I am noticing something here that disturbs me. Something mushy and maudlin in those starstruck eyes."

"I'm in love. For the first time."

"That's what you said the *last* time."

Augustina thought: how could her friend be so blasé? Not blasé, *negative.*

"Well, did you give him an answer?"

"Not yet."

"Thank God."

"Thank God, why?"

"I think it's…" Olive searched for the word. "Dangerous."

"Good. I live for danger."

"I'll talk to you about it, but this isn't the time or place." They were becoming quite loud.

"Is this all just jilted pride?" said Augustina.

"I don't give a shit about pride!"

Other customers were starting to stare at them. Augustina chained another cigarette.

Olive said softly, "I *do* give a shit about you. I'm sorry, baby, but marrying Quentin Russell is a cheesy idea, I mean it. He's a recidivist Don Juan. He's not the one. I don't want to talk about it now. We have guilty clients to defend."

Augustina was not blind. Olive, a fierce competitor, had settled for second best, a dermatologist, a zit doctor, bald and stodgy, as she recalled from the wedding. Well-to-do, but not wealthy — and Olive rather *liked* money.

The hell with Olive and her attitude. Up yours, Olive, I'm marrying him.

Suddenly, that decided, she underwent a powerful mood swing; she felt bold, strong, a bird on the wing to the top of the world. The answer is yes, m'lord. To have and to hold. Until death do us part.

The adrenaline of love gave Augustina power, and she had never felt more clever in court than on this day. She made a row when she learned her client Mr. Jaeger had had one of his eyes blackened by a fellow prisoner in the wagon en route to the courthouse.

Her shocked tones seemed to unnerve the prosecutor, a bumptious young man named Buddy Svabo. He tried to make light of the problem, but his jesting only made a loud clong. The provincial court judge decided to make a play for the gallery — reporters' pens were working furiously — and sternly lectured the sheriffs who'd been responsible for prisoner safety.

Olive could only watch in astonishment as Augustina, glowing and confident, bewitched cantakerous old Judge Enber. She had him lapping from her bowl.

Others in the gallery were not so enraptured with her. Young mothers and fathers. Faces creased with pain and anger. Four children still missing.

Augustina then asked that the case be put over one day while arrangements for her clients' safety were made. The judge agreed. Tomorrow the accused would make their election for mode of trial: not Enber, who was a mean old hack known locally as Father Time, but a high court judge.

In the interview room of the courthouse lockup, Augustina had no trouble persuading the grateful Mr. Jaeger to sign a check for a $50,000 retainer. The Jaegers were scared — the Crown had gone vigorously on record demanding life sentences for all three defendants. And chances were ninety-nine to one that that's exactly what they'd get.

"I want this clear," she said. "You are to talk to no one but me."

"Ma'am," said Jaeger, "we have always kept our traps shut."

She gave them some vague words of encouragement, the tranquilizer of false hope. "We will see what the prosecutor has. It may not be so bad." But she wasn't fooling herself.

Still propelled by her euphoria, she joined Olive and prosecutor Buddy Svabo in a hearing room. As he brought out his files for them to peruse — nothing to hide, ladies, they're dead and buried — Augustina nigged at him a little too much, got under his skin about how he had died standing up this morning with his attempt at humour.

"Why, you supercilious…You think I give a freaking hoot if some guy hammered Jaeger out? Probably had kids. I got *five* kids, you don't think I didn't live in sheer bloody terror? I'm going to guarantee they never see the outside of a concrete cage for the rest of their lives. They should get the freaking *rope!*"

He panted for a while when it was all over. The guy was somewhat marginal, Augustina decided, and a little over-awed with his responsibility.

Svabo plunked some massive transcripts in front of them. "And I got a little rope. And a lot more wire. Phone taps — better than a confession. They're toast." He grinned malevolently. "No deals, ladies, no deals. Cop 'em out if you want to save some time. But I got all the time in the world…and they'll be getting even more.

"No deals," Svabo kept repeating, like a mantra. "No deals for the dealership."

Augustina and Olive walked out with a pile of wiretap transcripts, loaded them into the arms of the two security guards, and returned to the Hotel Topaz. Ponsonby and his two Securi-Corps guards preceded the lawyers into Augustina's suite, did a walk-through, and said they'd be downstairs watching for anyone suspicious.

Augustina and Olive ordered up tea and wine, and sprawled over Augustina's king-sized bed with volumes of transcript. Every once in a while one of them would groan or yike. There was enough evidence against their clients to choke a hippopotamus.

The three defendants had spoken often on the telephone, using a chilling but obvious code — babies were "products" or "goods;" parents were "original manufacturers;" baby customers were "markets;" the kidnappers themselves ran a "dealership" in merchandise never specified.

Augustina soon wearied of the task of finding something salvageable in the transcripts, and began staring out the window.

Olive looked up at her. "You're somewhere in the ether again." So far this afternoon — and it was nearing five o'clock — neither of them had brought up the disruptive topic of Quentin Russell.

Augustina suddenly felt an odd, empty distress — she had to hear his voice, needed a reality check.

She went into another room and called him. As she was describing her interesting day and prosecutor Buddy Svabo's no-deals-for-the-dealership dirge, Russell interrupted: "But you can make almost any deal you want."

That was all he said, but comprehension suddenly bathed Augustina in an incandescent light.

"I'll call you later," she said.

She hung up and hurried back to Olive, who was getting into her coat, looking impatient.

"Sit down. I have a monstrous, horrible, evil idea."

"Yeah?"

"Our clients know where the four missing babies are?"

"Mine doesn't. Your two might."

"Of course they do."

It dawned now, also, on Olive Klymchuk. They had nothing to lose.

There could be a deal for the dealership. But it would have to be done fast, before the four pairs of illegal parents were tracked down. The missing babies were the lawyers' dreadful collateral.

At the courthouse, they went straight to the cells to talk to their clients. Augustina told them they deserved life, but if they were smart they could do better. Maybe five to seven years. Parole after a third of that.

"That's if we know where the products were placed," said Mr. Jaeger.

Products — how offensive. Augustina simply said, "That's right."

"I may have an idea where they are."

Augustina and Olive continued on to the office of Buddy Svabo. The strategy: Augustina Sage would play nice cop to Olive Klymchuk's mean cop. Olive would beat Svabo up and Augustina would apply the bandages and mesmerize him within her powerful aura of love.

"How does eighteen months sound?" Olive said. A little *too* brusque, Augustina thought.

"Excuse me while I die laughing."

"Buddy," Augustina said, "between us, we might be able to help some of those parents."

"Those monsters are getting freaking *life*! No judge is going to give them two seconds less!"

"I guess we should see the judge in chambers," Olive said.

"What for?"

"Buddy, I don't think you're hearing us very clearly," Augustina said softly. "I'm saying it's possible we can reunite four kids with four families."

"And I'm saying we're prepared to make that point in open court," Olive added.

Svabo looked exasperated. "I'm not following this…" But then his expression slowly changed. "Why…you scumbags." He couldn't find words. "You…you…dirty blackmailing vipers. You want to trade those babies for an eighteen-month slap on the ass…" He shouted: "Goldarn it, there's going to be no freaking deal!"

"I can't believe this of you, Buddy," said Augustina. "You could really come out of this looking very good. A year and a half isn't that much if no harm was done in the end."

"No *deals!*"

Olive shrugged, and turned for the door. "I guess we'll just have to explain your position to the media as best we can. Let's see the judge."

"Wait!" Colour had slowly begun to creep back into Svabo's face. Augustina could see he was beginning to work through the implications. "Let me get this straight. They know where the four kids are."

"And they'd be willing to give the names of the illegal parents," Augustina said. "So that's a few more notches on the old rifle barrel, Buddy. We'll make you look good; we'll say you worked it out with us — heck, your idea."

That was one of the most clever parts of their plan: not just to butter him up, but also to avoid the attentions of the Executor. Make it look like a victory for the Crown.

"This is blackmail," said Svabo.

Augustina spoke softly: "Can we work it out?"

"Just for a laugh, I'm going to call the assistant deputy." The Assistant Deputy Attorney General, the senior criminal law officer of the province. "He won't go for this in a billion years. Eighteen months — give me a break."

"We want to do it today," said Olive.

"Right *now*?"

"Right now. Today or the deal is off."

Svabo went into an inner office and when he returned after about fifteen minutes, he looked subdued, and Augustina thought this a good sign. He cleared his throat. "They're talking it over. It's going to the Attorney himself." The attorney general was an elected official, and Augustina knew that in the end it would be a political decision. "They want time. A couple of days."

"Today or never," Olive said, biting the bullet. "It's unfair to wait. Some of those kids have already forgotten their real parents."

Svabo glowered at them for a time, and suddenly said, "Seven years. It's the *absolute* bottom line."

Augustina didn't alter her benign expression, but suddenly she felt very relaxed. The assistant deputy had given a green light: they were plea-bargaining.

"No way," said Olive.

But Augustina was more conciliatory. "Okay, maybe there's a little room for give and take. Not much, Buddy. I'll ask my people if they can handle…say, two years."

"Absolutely out of the question," said Svabo.

They played him like a furious fish, Olive impatient and negative, Augustina soothing and hopeful. When Olive finally announced she was ready to walk out if Svabo wasn't prepared to accept their final, non-negotiable offer of two-and-a-half years, Svabo went into the back room to make another call, muttering to himself.

He was gone a long time. Augustina feared the fish had slipped the hook. "Olive, you shouldn't have backed us into a corner. I thought we agreed to go five."

"This is poker, honey. He knows we've got the case ace."

When he returned, he said: "I don't believe these guys. They'll take three."

Olive didn't bat an eye. "You've got us against the wall…okay, Augustina?"

"Done."

"The Attorney wants to make some kind of political event of it," Svabo said. "But you've got to give us time to sort this out. We need to take statements from your clients, we have to locate those kids. A few days."

Olive looked at Augustina, who nodded. "It's Tuesday," she said. "Let's give them to Thursday."

"But we take their pleas today," Svabo said. "And if they sing the right song — and I mean *full* cooperation — you've got your three years." He shook his head, weary, defeated. "One year to parole. Then the Jaegers get deported. It's like giving the freaking bastards a medal."

"Let's get the judge on side," said Olive.

In Judge Enber's chambers were also a clerk, a court reporter and her recording machine. The judge was grumpy.

"I don't like these meetings out of court," he said. "This is officially on the record; everything's being taken down."

"We want to talk about sentence," Augustina said.

"Okay, stop right here. If there's any kind of plea bargain being discussed, I don't want to hear it. I thought there was going to be a preliminary hearing."

"No, judge," Augustina said. "We want to take a plea in front of you. Mr. Svabo is going to tell you the state seeks a maximum of three years..."

"No. Stop right there."

She ignored him. "In return for such a sentence, the accused will disclose where the missing children are."

"I *don't* want to *hear*..." Enber grew red in the face, and began delivering a hectoring speech. "Young lady, I don't take instructions about sentence from anybody. I have a great pride in the independence of the judiciary, and if you plead these bastards in front of me, you're going to have to go some far, far distance to persuade me not to give them the limit."

"Judge," said Olive calmly, "if the court is not prepared to pass a sentence of three years top, the defendants have instructed us they will decline their offer of cooperation."

For a moment, Judge Enber seemed on the verge of cardiac arrest. "*Who* do you think you are, young lady!"

"Our clients have instructed us to inform the media this offer has been made," Olive said, not missing a beat. "We thought you should be apprised of that."

Before Enber could respond, Augustina said, "If all goes well, judge, we can have those kids in their own beds in a day or two." She put a hand on Svabo's arm. "It's cleared with the Attorney General, isn't it, Buddy?"

"The Attorney says do it, judge," said Svabo sourly.

For several moments chambers was still.

"I see," said the judge. "Well, the accused will expect quite a tongue-lashing from this court."

The two lawyers had an hour alone with their clients after that. RCMP interrogators waited until an FBI team flew up from Seattle, then they all crowded into an interview room at the courthouse. There followed two hours of bean-spilling by the defendants. All parties were sworn to secrecy regarding the proceedings while warrants were issued in the U.S. for the four pairs of baby purchasers.

In the afternoon, the three accused entered their guilty pleas before Judge Enber, who adjourned the case until Thursday. He wished time to consider, he announced, the penalties he would impose upon the filthy trash who had admitted to this unspeakably evil crime. This brief speech elicited a murmur of approval from the sold-out gallery.

Quietly jubilant, Augustina and Olive parted ways, and their two watchers escorted Augustina to a chartered float plane for her return to Vancouver.

"Don't do anything until we talk, okay?" said Olive.

"Anything?"

"Like saying yes to Quentin Russell."

Their day too filled, they hadn't got around to having that little meaningful chat. Augustina had stubbornly avoided the topic, no longer interested in Olive's sour views.

29

The Case
of the Passionate Poet

Corn flakes were all over the pantry floor, and since Clarence was stomping on them, Max decided he was the prime suspect. He gave him a whisk broom and a dustpan, and showed him how to sweep. Clarence shook his head and pointed to Darrow. "*He* did it."

"Two sons and already one's an informer," Max grumbled. "The other will be a cop."

"Darling, get the phone," said Ruth, who was busy at the stove. Max lugged both boys into the living room. It was Caroline Pomeroy.

"Hi, where are you?" Max plumped into an easy chair.

"At home, but I'm on my way back to the bush."

"Are you all right?"

"Fine. I'm thriving."

Darrow vaulted from the back of the chair onto his stomach, a twenty-five-pound projectile. Max gasped.

"Are *you* all right?" Caroline said.

"I've been jumped by a mugger, and his accomplice is strangling me with a telephone cord."

"They'll make great lawyers. Ruth there?"

Max fetched her, and cleaned up the flakes. On her return to the kitchen, she said, "Wow, she's in great shape. Hundred per cent better.

She's been scooting off to the Nahanee Valley every break she gets, and as soon as her term ends next week, she's going to move permanently into a tent until the loggers leave."

"Choo, choo, over your head," said Darrow, running his train engine over the bare area of Max's scalp.

"She mentioned a man named Terrance a couple of times. 'Terrance and I do this,' 'Terrance and I do that.' I didn't ask who *he* was."

"What did she say about Abigail?"

"Well, she definitely did not instruct her to go down there with a divorce petition."

Max wondered: had it been an excuse to fan the flames of the old fire? One splifflicated afternoon at Au Sauterne, Brian had disclosed all, then, repenting, had begged him to keep quiet counsel. Loyally, Max hadn't mentioned *l'affair Abigail* even to Ruth.

It was late in the day, and Wentworth Chance couldn't wait for his trial to end. He wanted to escape his irritating client, a denturist who beyond all reasonable doubt had falsified his Goods and Services Tax return. The case was a loser, it would break his string.

But the judge also hated taxes, and though he convicted the denturist, he suspended payment of the minimum fine for ten years. Wentworth's client gave him a two-hundred-dollar tip and told him not to report it to his bosses. Wentworth would never dream of doing a thing like that, but he was pleased with himself; you really had to count this as a win — five straight now.

About equal to the number of John Brovak's condoms expended during the last few evenings' long and rapturous ordeals.

Walking back from the Provincial Court, he avoided the office and picked up the Mercedes. The stack of files on his desk would be dealt with in due course; Vajeeta was waiting.

Another cheap date, wheat germ and orange juice.

Followed by carnal bliss in the hot tub. Aquatic rhymes with erotic. Also neurotic, which maybe she was, a little.

This passionate poet had taught him things he hadn't imagined in even his wettest fantasies. Hitherto undiscovered erogenous zones had been revealed. The tongue, he learned, could be a weapon of exceptional cruelty. Fellatio — he had read widely about it, but words could not convey.

After a battle with the going-home traffic he found his way to the eastern end of Chinatown, where Vajeeta lived in one of the area's ornate frame houses converted to suites. The door to hers was open, and her voice called him in.

Mandalas everywhere. A massive chart of the zodiac on one wall. She was at a desk, writing in longhand.

"Is 'heartbreak' two words or one?"

"Depends on whether it's totally broken, I guess."

She stood up and kissed him.

"You're so *zenny*. I should put that in a poem."

"How's the novel doing?"

"Okay. This guy's married but he's in love with another, who's sort of a person of the soul, mystical, and he's this linear kind of thinker? You know, like lawyers are, all strung out and wrapped tight, like *you* sometimes, you're afraid to go deep? And to save himself from this uncaring woman — she's all surface? — he has to take a journey into himself, to the centre. And this is where the heroine comes in; she leads him to an understanding of himself and to love."

She was wearing some kind of sarong, the left hip bare. One tug, Wentworth thought, it falls to her feet, and quickly they are writhing on the floor.

"Hey, that sounds like a really good story," he said.

ᐟ   "Yes, and at the end she takes him through, we call it, dynamic meditation? Where you have to whirl around fast like this…" And she began turning on her toes like a top. "And scream out, hoo, hoo, hoo!"

Wentworth remembered there were owls to be fed. Yet another in a series of tasks set to test the skills of last year's grand moot winner at the UBC law school.

"And anyway, I need some insight into this man. Like I'm not sure I know exactly how lawyers think? He fears to make a decision about his life, and it starts off he's running away from everything, off to some funny little tropical country I call Lugumbria."

"Could be a bestseller. Look, I've got to feed some owls — want to come?"

"Feed some owls. I'm into different experiences."

Vajeeta put away her pen and paper and went to her tiny bedroom to change clothes. Wentworth poked around, opening the cover of a huge scrapbook that lay on her desk. Pasted to each page: newspaper stories of recent dramatic trials. Here indeed was a story about Brian Pomeroy's successful defence of the Kitswuk Five. A few pages later, the news report of the hand grenade that almost blew up John Brovak (not to mention Wentworth himself and twenty-plus others). And here, Max Macarthur's successful appeal of the Milsom acquittal. But there were many newspaper stories about other lawyers, too, and their court cases, mostly murder trials.

Vajeeta reappeared, and caught him looking at the scrapbook.

"Like I said, I'm kind of fascinated by lawyers."

On the way to the North Shore, Wentworth thought about this fascination. Maybe she was a kind of groupie. Rock stars and hockey players have groupies, why not lawyers?

He told her he had been in that restaurant, Archie's, not three feet from the live grenade before Brovak tossed it out the window.

"Oh, my heavens," she said, staring at him oddly. "I read about it — that stuff scares me. You must have used up a lot of karma."

And the house they were going to was owned by Brian Pomeroy, the guy who won that Kitswuk Five trial.

"Kitswuk Five?"

"That dam that got dynamited; it's in your scrapbook. He was shot at after the trial…You've been following this stuff about the Executor?"

"Yes, but I don't like to talk about it. It gives me goose pimples. Is he a good lawyer?"

"Who?"

"Mr. Brian Pomeroy."

"The best."

The owls were waiting in their pear tree, one of them nesting, frowning at him from inside the door of its attractive, gabled birdhouse, the other looking down upon him even more sombrely from a branch. The owl on the branch took sudden flight, swooping over Vajeeta, forcing her to duck.

"I don't think it likes me," she said, scurrying toward the house. The owl returned to its perch.

Wentworth retrieved a key from under the back-door rug, and led Vajeeta into the kitchen, where he brought some raw chicken bits and strips from the refrigerator.

"Yuck," said Vajeeta.

"Yeah, well, they're not vegetarian."

"I don't like them. I don't like things that hunt and kill."

Outside, he fed the owls — carefully, but they seemed not to mind him as they did Vajeeta. Maybe owls just don't get along with some people.

Vajeeta stayed in the house, and when Wentworth returned to the kitchen he found she'd wandered off somewhere in the darkness.

She wasn't in the living room. He went upstairs, where he saw a light on.

Vajeeta was in the master bedroom, reading what looked like Caroline's personal correspondence, a letter, an air-mail envelope beside it. Wentworth saw the Costa Rican stamps. Wentworth was about to rebuke her, but saw to his confusion she was teary-eyed.

She put the letter down and began taking off her clothes.

"This is where I want to do it," she said.

April 7

Dear Max,

This comes as an addendum to our telephone conversation of last week. I had to come here to Golfito to courier this, but I am glad I did, for it was an excuse to put Abigail on a plane. I must wait a couple of hours for the next boat to Próspero, and the notes I am now assembling over coffee in a harbourside bar will be on the next flight north.

I write them because I did not dare mention over an open line certain instructions I must give you to detain, arrest and place in solitary confinement any letter or packet addressed to the office which has Costa Rican stamps on it and enough bulk to contain an audio cassette.

Max, you are the one person I most trust in the world, my friend through all mortality, and immortality, too, if it turns out the atheists have been lying to us. You, Max Macarthur, the unutterably trustworthy friend aforesaid, must incinerate the evidence.

I would perform the task myself, but I've run into a problem here, preventing me from quickly returning. The OIJota seized my passport while searching the house, and it

is somewhere in their offices in San José. Although Francisco
Sierra has lent his good offices to the task of retrieving it,
local officialdom works slowly, and another week may pass
before I see it again — and then I have to fart around with
Immigration because my visa has expired.

So it is up to you. Your task will be to intercept it
immediately. Let no one hear it, not even your wife. I did
not explain to you how sticky will be the wicket if this tape
surfaces in the wrong hands. Bluntly, it is in the nature of a
full-blown confession to Caroline of all past sins. Including
one particularly lurid and ugly series of physical comings
together the circumstances of which I once confided to you.

You are the Keeper of My Secrets, Max, my guru, my
protector. Insofar as a healthily heterosexual person can
actually love a person of the same sex, I do love you. I will
do all your shit cases for a year. I will never again complain
about your leaving wet towels in the coffee room. I will not
make short-person jokes.

BURN the tape. It must not be carelessly thrown out
with the office trash where curious fingers might retrieve it.
However distasteful the thought is to me of releasing noxious
plastic fumes into the atmosphere, this tape must be burned
to the crispness of bacon fried on high heat for five hours.

The subject of that dotty confession, Abigail Hitchins,
has by now boarded the plane after nearly a week of sun'n'-
surf. I feared for a while she was going to hang on forever,
stuck to me as with Magic Glue, a kind of Siamese-Twinlike
growth coming out of my patoot.

I am going to be blunt with you, Max, so you will know
how imperative is the work I have charged you with. Abigail
came on to me like a freight train while I was in a weakened
state.

She tried to rape me.

Manfully, as it were, I repelled her, and I'm afraid I left
her twisting slowly in the wind. She bears a fierce enmity
toward me. I fear what she may do out of vengeance.

I should have left her in her cell. Had I but known...I'll
try to get up there before she does more damage.

To other, less critical matters:

I thank you for your detailed report about what the sweet fuck is going on up there. I needed to know — I've been drowning in a sea of questions.

Now I am drowning in an ocean of conjecture.

Turnbull. Does there lurk beneath the smarm a stone-cold psycho? That fellow the FBI were inquiring about, the Ramboid ex-Green Beret with the face job — I wouldn't exclude him. Maybe he exchanged his green beret for a white one — anyone think of that? And all that stuff about Cudlipp getting mobbed up with Tony d'Anglio, and this being found out by Arthur Besterman throws oil on the fires of suspicion. Cuddie has returned to Vancouver with his buttercup, by the way.

How life mimics art. I have to tell you that these events in Vancouver often echo those I have imagined and prosed. I have a Besterman, as you know, and a Lukey and of course a Brovak and a Macarthur and a Sage, and yes, even a Pomeroy. All handles have been changed, of course. You, Max, are Bruce McGillicuddy IV, a rich fop at first glance, a Scarlet Pimpernel dallying in the law, but on closer study a man of principle, stubbornly loyal to his friend the much-misunderstood Lance Valentine, the bird-watching eco-lawyer.

Brovak is Carl "The Animal" Hlinka. There is an earnest student, Marcus Strange. Augustina is Hillary Queen. After Ellery Queen, of course.

(By the way, I am frankly disturbed that Augustina has put herself at risk by taking on those babynappers. And tell her to be careful with Quentin Russell. He's a stand-up guy, but Augustina has this habit of going overboard, and I don't want to come back to some bleak, weepy scene where she's threatening to jump off the Burrard Street Bridge.)

Somehow, I have a suspicion that the recent events up there and down here are related. The shooting of Watson by the Canuck cop with the knee-jerk reaction. The drugs. Abigail? There's some hidden connection.

I am as much at a loss as to who your Executor might be

as I am to the identity of the black hat of my own unsolved mystery tale, though I can tell you who he is not. There is a certain class of suspects I am admonished to disregard: the servant class. Widgeon says the butler mustn't do it. Unveiling the valet, the gardener or the cook as the culprit is regarded as a cheap shot.

Also still vexing me, by the way, is the identity of the ultimate hero. I would *like* it to be Lance Valentine, but fear he may not be in the right place at the right time. Hillary Queen has earned a toss at the ring, as has Bruce McGillicuddy IV, that noble guy.

Who shall solve this crime? Where is my Hercule Poirot? "We examine. We search. *Pouf! Voyons!*" Where is my monocled Philo Vance, my bookish Peter Wimsey?

I must now take another victim. Alexis Huggins was small potatoes. The stakes must be raised. The victim must be someone I know and care for, and must die a suitably horrible death.

Shock the reader, says Widgeon. Massage a vein and jab him with a hit of anger, make him lust for vengeance.

Kill whom you love.

How? Baseball bat, rope, rifle, bomb, what cruelty haven't I committed yet? I tried it yesterday with poison. Too gentle a way to go into that good night.

Instead I took up a knife. So armed, I began to compose a scene of terror, and it repelled me to the point that I had to lie down and comfort a queasy stomach. It is going to be the hardest chapter.

My writing reflects my current disturbed state.

Destroy the tape. Destroy this letter.

Your friend,
Lance Valentine.

30

Phantom
of the Courtroom

When the FBI raided the homes of four couples in California, they found all four kidnapped toddlers — too young to comprehend the tumult surrounding them — in excellent physical health.

The Attorney General of British Columbia took much personal credit for the operation, and announced he would personally escort the deliriously happy parents on a government charter to their children. On their return, a gala welcome was planned which the premier himself would attend.

Augustina Sage was pleased to know the government was taking the glory. Let them *have* the credit. Musn't permit the Executor to get the wrong idea.

On Thursday, Judge Enber would be sentencing her clients to a laughable three years of penance. Although all parties had given their undertaking to remain silent about the plea bargain, she had, of course, let slip the word to Quentin.

She hadn't been able to spend any time with him during the week — he had flown to Ottawa to consult, as he explained on a long-distance line, with some rainmakers in the Department of Justice, including his old friend the minister. Calling in his political debts.

The weekend coming up was Easter. Augustina would be happy to

get the Jaeger case behind her, to spend the holidays in the tranquil-
izing arms of her lover. Four days ago he had popped the question;
she would pop her answer on Sunday.

Augustina was picked up Wednesday night by James Goodwinkle,
Russell's butler-cum-chauffeur. With him was Lucius Ponsonby, the
head of Securi-Corps, and three of his watchers.

"We are beefing up for you," he said.

"I really would rather be alone."

"It's what Judge Russell wants."

He was wringing his hands. He was really *too* obsequious. She got
into the back of the limousine and smiled and waved and shut the
door on Ponsonby. He joined the watchers in another vehicle, and followed the limo to the Tsawwassen ferry terminal.

Goodwinkle slid open the glass compartment with a gloved
hand, and surprised her by actually *smiling*. Nice straight teeth,
but they looked like dentures. "He's a nervous twiddler, that fellow
Ponsonby. I'm at your service until whenever you want to take
the ferry back home. I won't let anyone bother you." He closed the
window again.

He had read her mind. Too many watchers, it was out of Orwell.

James Goodwinkle had obviously resigned himself to her relationship with his boss. Not such a bad guy after all. A little in the
closet, though, rare in this age of liberation. Sophie Marx, her mentor
and best friend, was proudly, loudly lesbian. Anyway, being the legal-
ized, limousined life partner of Quentin Russell wasn't a bad way to
travel. She must keep her head on straight. Delicate discussions must
be undertaken. She would keep her name, would not submerge her
identity. His possible appointment in Ottawa would also be an
issue...

A recidivist Don Juan, Olive had said. Well, Augustina was too
confident of herself to fret about that. But tomorrow, for sure, she'd
talk with Olive.

In the morning, brushing her teeth, she observed through the bathroom window of the Princess Victoria Suite that it was a graceful, soft
spring day, leaves and tendrils poking their noses from tree branches.
She opened the window and breathed it in, the potion of spring,
of love.

Croissants and coffee and morning newspapers arrived along with another huge bouquet: Easter daffodils. The Hotel Topaz concierge — her personal busboy — scuttled out bowing and scraping as the phone rang.

It was Russell: he had just returned to Vancouver, and he sounded concerned. "Well, it looks like the, ah, excrement has hit the fan."

"What do you mean?"

"You haven't seen the newspaper?"

She looked at the bold headline in *The Province*:

**Babynappers to Be
Free in One Year?**

"Oh, Jesus."

"They're making it look like quite a victory for the defence. Some clever reporter got hold of a transcript of that meeting you had with the judge in chambers Tuesday."

Of course — Judge Enber had imprudently insisted those proceedings were a matter of public record. The press had simply bought a transcript. It was all here, verbatim, defence counsel coercing the judge into the three years. And it looked very bad in print:

"The transcript reports Klymchuk as telling the judge: 'Our clients have instructed us to inform the media this offer has been made.'"

"I think you should stay in the hotel tonight," Russell said. "I'll fly over tomorrow."

Augustina continued to read the story with sinking heart. "God, I come out of this looking like a con artist. Is this going to mean you'll stop loving me?"

"I'm afraid so."

"I figured you were shallow."

A few minutes later, the phone rang again. "This is the Executor. Can I make an appointment to see you?"

"Olive, where are you?"

"Downstairs. Let's get this over with. There's press outside, security people all over, and I think they want to drive us to jail in a Brinks truck."

They used the limousine instead, directing Goodwinkle from the hotel's parking garage to a side door of the courthouse. Sheriff's officers pushed a path for them through the reporters gathered at the courtroom door.

"Miss Sage! Miss Klymchuk! A lot of people are going to think three years is pretty cheap for...Miss Sage!"

The lawyers escaped into the sanctity of the courtroom. There, a gloomy Buddy Svabo was seated at the counsel table, reduced in rank: beside him was the assistant deputy.

"Ah, yes," said Olive. "They brought in the spin controller."

"Well, ladies," said the deputy, "Looks like you get all the kudos. The minister is nonplussed at that story in *The Province*. He was doing a radio interview last night about how he personally negotiated the return of the kids when someone shoved the front-page proofs in front of him. Makes certain people look like fools, and I don't mean you two. You guys did a socko job."

One person he might have meant who looked like a fool: Judge Enber. ("I take great pride in the independence of the judiciary," he had huffed before being given his orders.) As court was called into session, the judge went briskly to his post and glared at the three prisoners with such venom that Augustina thought for a moment he was going to break ranks.

"You three monsters," he scritched, "have seen fit to perpetrate in the most callous way one of the foulest deeds condemned by our laws. Were it in my power...Never mind. I sentence you each to three years in the penitentiary."

Silence. Then someone in the gallery hooted. Another hissed.

Judge Enber, furious with embarrassment, turned to look at Augustina and Olive. He then swivelled abruptly, rose and departed.

As Augustina gathered up her briefcase she could hear low, sullen conversation in the galleries, the rumblings of unhappy citizenry. Before she could leave, Joe Ruff marched toward her. He was smiling, and he held out his hand.

"I say, you really put the knife to their throats."

She shook his hand: damp, soft. "Thank you, Joe."

Knife to their throats — an awful way to put it, she thought. A couple of days ago this man had been in their offices, a client sloughed off to Wentworth Chance. What was he doing over here in Victoria?

As if he read her mind, Ruff said: "On my way to serve some documents upon Her Majesty, thought I'd stop off and catch you at work, what?"

"Well, there wasn't much work to catch."

"Can't fool an old courtroom hand, my dear, all of it was done behind the scenes. Your partners will be proud of you." He bowed slightly, and took his leave.

"Who was *that*?" asked Olive, as they headed to the corridor.

"Phantom of the courtroom."

In the hall there was no escape from the reporters who encircled Augustina and Olive within a ring of note pads.

"Miss Sage, Miss Klymchuk, how do you feel about this?"

"Justice was done," said Augustina.

"Parole in a year. How big a victory do you consider this?"

"A big victory for the parents," said Olive.

"What do you say to charges that you blackmailed the crown?"

"Well, that's a pretty harsh word to use," said Augustina.

"How do you feel about making that kind of plea bargain?" another reporter said. "In exchange for babies."

Olive got hot: "We reunited those families!"

"If they were charging $75,000 a baby, how much of that was your fee?" They were ganging up now, a wolf pack.

"No goddamn comment," said Olive, and the two lawyers battled their way out of the unfriendly encirclement and fled down the hall to where their escorts were waiting.

"Up theirs," said Olive. "We scored the coup of the century."

As Ponsonby and two of his watchers joined them in the back of the Cadillac, Olive opened Goodwinkle's window: "The Topaz, my good man." She handed the cellular phone to Ponsonby. "Call ahead for a table for two and champagne."

"I'd have given them life," said one of the watchers.

Augustina and Olive were being ostentatiously gay in the restaurant, ordering eighty-dollar bottles of Dom Perignon — the best, said Olive, because dear old Quentin *wanted* them to have the best.

Their hilarity was made more manic by their continual evocation of the spectre of the Executor. Would he attempt to come tonight in their sleep? Would he shoot or bomb or bludgeon? Or employ a more original device, piranhas in the bathtub, belladonna in the *soup du jour*. Ponsonby was the Executor, no, it's Goodwinkle, wrong, the maître-d', no, one of those three Japanese businessmen.

"Joe Ruff," said Augustina.

Olive looked up from her menu and they watched Ruff seat himself at a far table with a comfortable grunt, and tuck the corner of his napkin into his pants. Joe Ruff, the play-acting lawyer.

"Is that his name?" Olive said. "Your phantom of the courtroom?"

"He must be staying here," said Augustina. "Well, he's *not* the Executor. He *loves* lawyers." But she thought of that thin, hard-to-find line between love and hate.

"It's always the person you least suspect," said Olive. "How about the guy who's going to be patrolling your floor tonight?"

"No, I have it," said Augustina. "The hotel concierge. He'll bring the gun hidden in the next bouquet. Lilies this time. He has a *key*."

In the course of all of this they utterly terrified themselves, and Augustina made Olive promise to spend the night in her suite.

"That's great," said Olive. "I brought some dope. We'll get real down and *paranoid*."

As they reached another crescendo of mirth, Joe Ruff smiled over at them, making a victory "V" with his fingers.

In Augustina's room, squatting on the big bed, they drank more champagne and smoked a hash spliff — Player's Light and shavings from a chocolate-dark block Olive said came from Amsterdam by way of a client. Strong, buzzy stuff, the fumes so pungent Augustina had to open the balcony door. She hoped the watcher out in the hall lacked an acute sense of smell.

Their giggles eventually subsided into a silence which became uncomfortable for Augustina, a little oppressive. There was something in the way now. Something that had to be dealt with.

"Okay," she said, "honestly, tell me what's wrong with him."

Olive sighed, rolled onto her back, stared at the ceiling in silence.

"He isn't nauseatingly sexist," Augustina said, "and he's not too bad to look at over your first cup of coffee. Well, okay, we can't have kids."

"Why?"

"Vasectomy."

"That's new. Guess he decided to stop playing Vatican roulette. Shoot blanks, you don't get sued for child support." A stifling silence followed that, then Olive said: "You want to know, he's still all gummed up over his wife."

"Bullshit."

"Eunice. She was rich, you know, pulp and timber money. A swank from a mucky-muck family."

"She died *fifteen* years ago."

"He has nightmares."

"You can hardly blame him. It was terrible."

"Thinks he's somehow responsible," Olive said.

"They had a fight. She left in a blinding rage, and drove over a cliff. Of course he thinks he's responsible."

"'I killed her.' That's what he used to say in his sleep. That's when I used to wake him up."

"Oh, shit, Olive, he's just a man with deep feelings. He *loved* her. She was incredibly attractive."

"She's in the way. She blocks the view."

"I can handle it." Augustina turned thoughtful. "Was it suicide, Olive, do you think?"

"Suicide or anger. Or both maybe. He won't talk about it, will he?"

Augustina didn't answer. It was true, though. The wife was hallowed ground; he wouldn't let her enter.

"There's more, Augie…I don't know, a kind of faint smell of disrepute. Maybe it's all those old dealings with Tony d'Anglio and the mob. Maybe some stuff rubbed off on him."

"For Christ's sake, Olive, you think they don't check out somebody they're considering for the Supreme Court of Canada? It's between him and the Chief Justice of B.C. Being engaged isn't going to hurt his chances, by the way."

"Oh, *that's* why he proposed. Sure, they want 'em tied to the home and free from temptation. He's got it in the bag anyway. He's linguistically correct; Max Mac Two doesn't speak French."

"Olive, you haven't made out a very convincing case. What else is there?"

Olive just sighed. Augustina pushed past her and reached for the telephone and dialed out.

Augustina brightened to Quentin's voice: a weary, "Darling, it's almost midnight."

"I know. You asleep?"

"I rather suspect I'm not."

Augustina giggled.

"You sound very merry," he said.

"Very marry me...whoops, I'm blasted. Olive's staying the night with me."

"Not in the same bed."

"Well, yes, if you don't mind. It's kind of scary."

"But you belong to another."

"I'm getting all the dirt on you."

A silence followed that. "Let me speak to her."

Olive seemed startled to have the phone passed to her. "Hullo, Quentin," she said. "Miss me?"

She laughed at something he said. "Sure, I'd love to change places. You sleep with Augustina and I'll be a rich judge."

Olive then listened in silence, and Augustina watched her expression slowly change, turn serious, as if she were hearing something she didn't like. Then she said: "Augie and I don't keep secrets."

Her voice was decidedly frosty; Augustina was uneasy.

After another short speech from Russell, Olive said: "Quentin, nothing personal, but I don't want you to hurt her. If it's simply a career move —"

"You bitch!" Augustina quickly grabbed the phone. "Quentin, she didn't mean that, that was awful, I'm incredibly embarrassed and totally pissed off —"

He interrupted in a sombre voice. "It's okay. I'll fly over tomorrow —"

She in turn interrupted him. "No, it's *not* okay. I'm not feeling very merry any more, and...Goddammit, yes, yes, I'm saying yes, I'll marry you. Goodbye. I love you."

She hung up and looked at Olive with hostile eyes.

They didn't talk for a long time after that. While Olive was in the washroom, Augustina, loaded on champagne and hashish and irritation, checked all the doors and windows, made sure the dead bolt was turned and locked, then climbed into the canopied bed that she now regretted Olive was sharing.

Quentin had said she almost drove him bonkers; Augustina could see why. How brazen of her to say that to him. There was a mean streak in Olive — she *was* jealous. Wanted him for his money, probably, the mercenary hen.

But maybe she should have waited for a more lucid moment to

give him her answer. Stoned and in a swivet: it wasn't the way she'd planned it.

After Olive joined her in the bed they turned the lights out. They lay there silently, their backs to each other and as far away from one another as they could get. Augustina's head was whirring.

Olive's voice was quiet, distant. "Augustina, there's one more thing."

"Please, I don't want to hear."

"He *was* into something crooked."

Augustina turned and got up on an elbow, peered toward Olive in the darkness. She could see the whites of her eyes staring back at her.

"I'm waiting," Augustina said primly.

"I pried. I used to stay over in the manse. I found some cancelled cheques. Payments to a numbered account in the Bahamas. Fifty, sixty thousand dollars."

"Investors move their money around."

"I think he's being blackmailed for something. I asked him about it. He got defensive, of course."

"You had no business!"

"That's what he thought. I got the roses the next weekend."

"I don't think I will ever forgive you for tonight."

"There's something in his past, Augie. Something black."

"Give me evidence!"

What the hell had got *into* Olive? Augustina wondered. Mysterious numbered accounts. Blackmail. Preposterous.

Olive groaned and snuggled into her pillow. It was a while before either of them descended into the abyss of sleep.

Augustina awoke to the quiet nagging of her bladder. She was dehydrated, her throat raw.

For a moment she couldn't locate herself. Strange room, strange bed, another body in it, snoring.

We are in the Princess Victoria Suite of the Topaz Hotel. We have been celebrating. I am about to have a hangover. I have to go to the jane.

The sky outside was still pitch dark. A pale line of street light squeezed in through a gap in the curtains, and with its aid, without switching on the bedside lamp, she crept from the bed to the bathroom door. Inside, she decided she couldn't face the prospect of a fluorescent light, and fumbled along the wide, tiled counter with its French soaps and colognes until she found a glass. She filled it with water, and slowly drank it down.

Following which, she drew her pajama bottoms down and sat on the loo, feeling the tension release from her bladder, the waste waters of an engine running at high torque for too many days.

The bathroom door was ajar, and from behind it she heard a scraping noise. It wasn't Olive — she was snoring.

Now a soft click. It seemed to come from the living room.

A different, softer sound, a padding of feet?

Augustina was fighting hysteria. It was the hashish, still burping in her head, summoning up a ridiculous nightmare.

Her pee dried up. She didn't flush.

She stood, pulled herself together, peeked through the doorway.

A man.

A man hovering beside the bed. Beside slumbering Olive. Both arms raised. Something in his hands. A gleam of steel.

Augustina screamed. Wildly, with the unbridled voice of blind, sheer terror.

He turned, startled, a flattened, stockinged face, black rollneck, black-gloved hands on a knife handle.

She stumbled, dizzy, fighting hysteria, and her pajama bottoms, still untied, fluttered to her knees, catching her around the ankles as she tried to step back into the bathroom, as she flailed wildly for the doorknob. She couldn't distinguish her own screams from Olive's, and now Olive was scrambling from the bed, the man still standing, arm upraised, but looking at Augustina, then turning and pursuing Olive to the front door of the suite.

And then Augustina was in the bathroom. She knew the door locked, somehow it locked, but her numbed hands couldn't find the brass latch, and then they did and just then she heard a sickening series of thuds.

And then a scraping and a scrambling. She smashed the bathroom window with a vase and screamed. And then she saw the man one more time. He was on the balcony, grabbing for a vine, looking at her: his flattened, stockinged face, his bloodied knife clenched in his teeth.

31

Bad
Friday

That Good Friday morning Wentworth Chance slept until he was rocked rudely awake just before ten o'clock by a top-twenty hit on the radio alarm. He turned the sound down, wiggled in the sheets, and wondered if he could steal another hour. He had needed his sack duty, and had caught up — a full twelve hours. Sweet Vajeeta had gone off to "retool" her consciousness, an Easter weekend retreat at the New Age camp up on Cortes Island — advanced kundalinga methods under the direction of Master Choh Chuk Yo.

Wentworth would be spending most of the weekend in the office, sinking ever deeper into the sucking swamp of unread files, unwritten letters, unresearched opinions. He had only so much time. He could spend it with Vajeeta or with the *res gesta* exception to the hearsay rule, but not with both.

He opted for Vajeeta. She had been an almost nightly occurrence, voraciously demanding of his time, his attention, his body, demanding until all hours.

He didn't mind these demands. He was in a state of…not quite love, he guessed, but something similar. Something to do with his being a Taurus, and with her being on the cusp. This was the first truly spiritual person he had known — wild, naked, free, unfettered by society's false and rigid boundaries. She had a philosophy that seemed sexually liberal, to say the least: renouncing the world was wrong; it meant denying your physical body and its pleasures. People attained their spirituality through physical love, through a holistic seeking of one's centre.

She chattered a lot, too, about preternatural phenomena. His rational mind rejected these, and though his views went unvoiced, she said she could read what was in his head, and it was too bad he couldn't think fourth-dimensionally — it's so typical of lawyers? And isn't the law really an artificial man-made mind game?

She had this repugnance to the law, it seemed, yet a fascination for its practitioners.

While lying there daydreaming about the holistic seeking of Vajeeta's centre, and wondering if he should be seeking enlightenment instead of a full-time career in the Pomeroy Macarthur sweatshop, he faintly heard the radio newscaster say something about the latest grisly murder of a criminal lawyer. "More, just after this."

Wentworth turned up the sound and waited rigidly while an announcer told him all about the bargains in Car City. And then he heard the news from Victoria.

His mind reeling, he dressed, stumbled out the bedroom door and down the stairs, aiming for the kitchen, knowing he needed a zap of coffee, that's what he needed, the newspaper should be here, no, it wouldn't be in the papers yet…

He froze. There was a body in the living room, sprawled on the couch.

Startled, he uttered a terrified whoop.

Brovak opened one eye. "What's up, kid?"

"I expect this will be very hard," said Lars Nordquist, "but I want you to recreate the scene. It will never be fresher in your memory than now. By acting it out for us, you might recall details that would otherwise slip away forever."

Augustina was still in shock, felt as if she were floating. "Yes. I'll try…" Words faded, words died.

It was 10:15 a.m. They were in the hallway outside the Princess Victoria Suite of the Hotel Topaz. Max had just arrived on the harbour-to-harbour flight. Russell and Nordquist had flown over on a charter many hours earlier. Olive Klymchuk's husband, the dermatologist, was there, pacing, white-faced, in shock. Lucius Ponsonby, the president of Securi-Corps, was standing by the elevator, looking scared.

In the suite, the i.d. team was cleaning up, putting away cameras, forceps, cotton swabs, Benzedrine reagent, vacuum sweepers. They worked in almost utter silence; there came not, issuing from this room, the usual cynical and often ribald conversation of men and women inured to scenes of physical violence. This murder had been a most ghastly affair: a violent struggle, three deep and unerring knife thrusts into the heart.

Olive's body had long ago been taken to the autopsy room in Victoria General, where a team of pathologists was examining it, taking their tissue samples, their fingernail scrapings. From the latter, said the chief pathologist in preliminary report, a possible rich ore site. Olive's nails had pierced the roll-neck sweater: strands of cotton, skin, hair, even a trace of blood — though probably not enough to yield a DNA print.

The guard who had been on patrol in the hall outside had heard screams and scuffling at 4:07 a.m. Courageously, she hadn't waited for back-up, but by the time she squeezed into the room — Olive's corpse partially blocked the door — the assailant had disappeared, over the balcony, down the vines, and onto the ground.

The police also, this time, had evidence in the form of the living witness whom the guard had found hiding in terror in the bathroom. Not much of a witness, it is true, for Augustina's description lacked detail and precision — not surprising given the trauma, the darkness, the stockinged face of the murderer. About average height and somehow...portly.

"Okay," said Nordquist, "let's put you back by the bathroom door. You're looking at the bed."

The bed was stripped by now; blankets and sheets had been bundled off to the lab. She remembered a shadowy portrait of a man standing above this bed, a dark photograph that will never go away, tattooed into her brain.

"She was...on her back, snoring a little...She awoke when I screamed, she...Oh, God."

"It's okay," said Nordquist.

Augustina braced herself against the door frame. Russell took her hand to steady her.

He had been the first one she phoned. At home, his voice fuzzy with sleep, he had begun to laugh before quickly realizing this was not some black joke. Two hours later, six-thirty, at the dawn, he was at her side, overcoat over pajamas, wild-haired, wild-eyed. She had thrown herself into his arms, crying then, weeping for the first time.

Calmly, she told herself. Slowly. Bravely. "He turned toward me with that knife, and Olive tried to run, and he...he turned away and went after Olive, because she was trying to get to the front door, I guess, and I..."

"Okay, just try to relax."

"I'm sorry, I am trying to do this. I know it's important."

"Get her some water." Russell snapped his fingers at Ponsonby, who scurried for a glass.

"I'm all right."

"Let's take a break," said Russell. He lifted a tumbler of water to her lips, holding her by the shoulders.

"I want to finish this and go," she said.

"You didn't see him attack Miss Klymchuk," said Nordquist.

"I saw him leap toward her. That's all, and I was in the bathroom, and...I saw him outside the window, he kind of vaulted from the balcony onto the ground. He rolled, like an acrobat."

"No vocal sounds from him at any point."

"If he was talking, I didn't hear him. How could not the entire floor have heard us screaming?"

"There was no one else staying on that floor, Augustina," Nordquist said.

"Those were my orders," said Ponsonby. "Second floor was off limits."

Russell looked at Ponsonby, who in turn made a tight face, as if to say, What a horrible thing.

"How did he get in, Bones?" asked Max.

"I could use a little jolt of coffee," said Nordquist.

They filed into the adjoining Princess Elizabeth Suite where a large urn and cups and saucers were set on a table. Nordquist sat everyone down.

"Okay, let me set the scene for you. We thought at first the assailant might have gained entry to the hotel by climbing through a window on the ground floor. But the outside perimeter of the hotel was under floodlights, and Ponsonby had four people out there, one at each corner of the building. No signs of surreptitious entry. So our perpetrator came in some other way."

"How?" Max asked.

"He may have come to the hotel earlier. He may have taken a room. We are making inquiries of all the guests — forty-three registered, plus Ponsonby's staff, and who knows how many additionals there might have been. Unfortunately some of the guests have checked out, and others are continuing to do so. That is regrettable, but we cannot detain *everyone* for questioning. Especially with the upper echelon clientele here: professionals, lawyers, judges. I have someone at the desk advising everyone that they will be personally visited.

"The culprit could also have been a restaurant guest. Or come in with members of the Toastmasters Club which met last evening in the Duchess of York salon, hiding somewhere until the late hours. The elevators were being watched, so were the stairways. The guard posted on the second floor would have had a view of both the fire escape exit — which in any event was locked from the hallway side — *and* the elevators *and* the door to the Princess Victoria Suite.

"So we believe that at some undetermined time this individual took an elevator to the third floor — or he could have been a guest on that floor. We found a hallway window open there, almost directly above her suite. We presume he crawled down the vines to Augustina's balcony."

"Don't know how he wouldn't have been seen," said Ponsonby.

Nordquist answered that: "The outside floodlights were directed too low." He turned to Augustina. "One of your balcony doors was found unlocked, wide open, with no signs of having been jimmied."

"I…was sure I closed it." But had she? The door they had opened to air out the suite?

"It locks automatically when you shut it, Augustina." Nordquist seemed to read her mind: "We found a little hashish in Miss Klymchuk's bag. It doesn't have to be mentioned in the reports, but…"

"It's okay, Bones, we were a little stoned."

"I see. Okay, he left as he came, out the same window, over the balcony, scrambling down it along the vines and leaping — literally — into the tulips. A soft plot of ground. But he stirred things up so badly we don't even have a boot impression. Anyway, the security people outside saw him run toward the alley. He vaulted over an extremely high fence. They heard a car engine, then a squeal of tires. It was all very fast."

"Sounds like we're dealing with a psychopathic Batman," Max said.

There was a long silence, a clinking of cups, the sounds of throats swallowing.

"How long have you provided security for our hotel system, Mr. Ponsonby?" Russell asked.

"Eleven years. Without a ruffle." He added: "Before this."

"You call *this* a ruffle?" Russell's voice took on a sharp edge. "I'm putting the word out. You're through." He began advancing on Ponsonby. "I'll sue, I'll see you bankrupted!"

"Easy," said Nordquist, restraining him.

Augustina rushed to the bathroom and proceeded to be sick there. People were falling apart. Olive's husband was making a horrible snuffling sound.

"What do you think, Bones?" said Max. "Jack Calico? And maybe Turnbull waiting for him in the car."

"Perhaps," said Nordquist. "Calico hasn't surfaced. I have someone checking on Turnbull's recent doings."

"And what about Cudlipp?" said Max.

"He hasn't reported in to front office. We know he flew back from Costa Rica to Vancouver four days ago, we have him and that young woman — Miss Finch — booked on an incoming Continental Airlines flight via Dallas. He picked up his car in the airport lot — we're assuming that: it's not there now, and it was there last week. He hasn't returned home. I don't know why Cudlipp...I'm lost for motive."

"Well, there's another glaring possibility, isn't there," said Max, "if we're talking about a Batman."

Nordquist nodded. "Hughie Lupo." He explained to the others: "Ex-commando, button man for the N'Dragheta. FBI were asking about him. Killed one of their agents by slicing his throat. Like Eddie Cohn. Stabbed another in her sleep. Like...well, almost like last night."

"Why would he be in Canada?" said Russell.

Nordquist shrugged. "He's a professional rubber, maybe he's working for someone here. I'd better get in touch with those characters from the FBI."

It was half an hour later that Augustina remembered Joe Ruff. She was lying on the bed in the Princess Elizabeth suite, a wet cloth over her forehead, relating her movements of the night before for the umpteenth time with yet another interrogator.

He asked: "During dinner — anyone you see in the restaurant remotely suspicious?"

It came back — how she and Olive had been silly and giggly, seeing the Executor in different clothes. The maître-d', the Japanese businessmen…Joe Ruff. Who had congratulated her in the courtroom. *I say, you really put the knife to their throats.* Joe Ruff, who with one hand was spooning soup and with the other making a "V" at her with index and middle finger.

"The phantom of the courtroom," she said.

They called Nordquist over.

"Why Joe Ruff?"

"I don't know. He gives me a creepy feeling." She told him about their brief *tête-a-tête* outside court. But then wondered if her theory wasn't too preposterous. "No. The man was Ruff's size, maybe, his shape, but he's hardly athletic. He can barely walk. He *waddles.*"

Ruff's room, they learned, was on the sixth floor. It was empty of all signs of its occupant except for some damp towels. No blood on them, no traces of it in the tub. No one had seen him leave, but there had been much confusion during the early hours — police, reporters, staff, guests, gawkers.

They checked with the desk and discovered that Joe Ruff had used the hotel's Quick-Check system, leaving his key in an envelope, depositing it in a special slot. Exactly when he had done this was not known. The desk clerk hadn't thought there was much unusual about it: Mr. Ruff was a frequent guest and kept a running account.

Nordquist arranged for Max, Augustina and Russell to fly back across Georgia Strait in the RCMP LongRanger helicopter, which would take them into Burrard Inlet near the Gastown offices. Just before they left, Max was paged for a phone call.

"Happy Easter."

"John. When did you get in?"

"Late last night. How's Augie?"

"Shaky."

"I can't believe this…"

"No one wants to."

"You got a description or anything of the whack who did it?"

"Average height, athletic. Could be a lot of people."

"Including Everit Cudlipp." Brovak exploded. "Where is he? Why has nobody put the sleeve on him yet? I'm taking personal charge of this investigation, someone's covering Cudlipp's ass —"

"He disappeared. He arrived back, then vanished."

"Yeah, stopping over to collect his swag from Tony d'Anglio, stabbing people to death en route, and he's gone for good now, off to fuckin' Brazil. It was Augustina he wanted, he wants to murder everyone in the whole Jesus firm…why didn't anybody try to contact me about how d'Anglio was gonna iron him off with a bribe…never mind, it's time we got our act together, we're going after this guy, I get pissed off when he kills my friends and fellow workers. Get your asses back to the office, it's gonna be action central, let's get pumped. Let's *do* something, Bones is too slow, he's too fuckin' *methodical*, we gotta form our own vigilante group and I say fuck due process, let's just nail the pig."

"Calm down."

"I mean business."

32

Deathless
Prose

Friday, April 9

Dear Office,

Horrible wim-wams came upon me while I composed
my last chapter, a Norman Bates scene, death in the
swirlpool bath (a stiletto, bubbles of blood, the naked,
ravaged body of Hillary Queen).

But I had grown too fond of my passionate, reckless
Hillary.

I immediately erased her scars, scribbled life back into
her bones and took a stab at a different sacrificial lamb: the
skinny bespectacled student Marcus Strange. But the knife
stopped six inches from his heart. Marcus had done no one
evil.

Yeah, it's not so easy to kill whom you love. Why can I
only do in the unworthy?

I am now working at trying to compose not my book but
myself. I need a break. I remain trapped down here, without
passport, so I'm going to take a holiday in the jungle. I have
been denying to myself how stressful were the events of last

week — my concentration was much disturbed by the sultry emanations of Abigail Hitchins, not to mention the clanking of Twelve-Finger Watson's chains.

Today I bought cheaply from an unhappy camper a state-of-the-art tent. The vendor had come from Corcovado Park footsore, burned purple, and covered with tics — until then the closest he'd ever been to the wilderness was *World of Nature* on the idiot box. Now Lance Valentine is about to practise his survival skills in the Corcovado.

Francisco assures me he will secure my passport by the time I get back, and then I'll be taking the next flight north to cobble my marriage together.

By the way, the phone company has finally emerged from hibernation, and lines are being restrung to Puerto Próspero. I will phone you when I get back from the Corcovado — though I seem only to get horrible news from Vancouver which works its way like an insidious leech into my plot. More and more my book begins to reflect real events and less and less does it seem to be drawn from imagination.

In any event the time has arrived for reflection. Widgeon speaks of the need to pause and assess before those final excruciating moments when the mask of innocence is swept from the culprit's face. Trot out the suspects one by one, put them on the scales, examine their psyches for flaws, collate the evidence, then tell them to get dressed and we'll be in touch.

Who will be guilty, who will go free? Who will break down under the lash of an accuser's tongue? Who will stumble from the climax, nervous and sweating, safely into the sheltering arms of the denouement?

The writer should also be asking himself: Are the clues properly in place? May all red herrings be safely released from the nets? Has the reader been given fair opportunity to match wits with the writer, to solve the mystery?

The crime must be solved, Widgeon maintains, by natural, deductive means. "No seances, ouija boards or crystal gazing dare enhance your concluding pages."

We had a long session on the weekend, Francisco ("Call me Frank") Sierra and I, jawboning about the art of the final revelation. Frank has read the entire script and his concern is that I may be pointing too obvious a finger at some of my felons. Isn't it always someone you don't suspect? he asked. Ah, quite true, I said, but knowing this, the reader will suspect someone he doesn't suspect and will be fooled into not suspecting someone he *should* suspect.

Upon rereading, I suspect this is not crystalline clear. (It may be difficult for you non-creative souls to comprehend the labyrinthine processes of a mystery writer's mind.)

Nobody is above suspicion. That includes me. Lance Valentine.

Almost as interesting to Frank as my mystery story is its alter ego in Vancouver. I have given him the whole poop as transmitted to me by you, Max, and, mystery buff that he is, he craves more. Send me a packet of information, and perhaps between us, Frank and I will solve the case.

Has anyone talked to Caroline yet? I am accepting Lady Macbeth's word that my wife wants to reunite. If Caroline's not in town, beat the bushes for her — according to Abigail she's been going off to Vancouver Island spiking trees or some goddamn thing.

And who is Terrance?

Abigail poked a tiny wiggly worm of suspicion into my ear just before she left, and I feel it munching toward my heart. Terrance. Some kind of eco-hero of Caroline's to whom she has allegedly been cozying up. "That's all I know," said Abigail. "I'm sure it's nothing to worry your little heart about." Is she just doing a head job on me? Is Terrance merely a construct of her twisted mind?

Totally farcical idea that Caroline would be unfaithful. I refuse to fall victim to such Abigamesmanship.

I want one of you to run Caroline to ground and tell her I am returning to fall into her arms.

("He wants to meet with you."

Caroline shook her head. "My duty is to these trees." And she turned her face wistfully away, and looked into the vastness of the forest, from which emerged, muscles rippling, Terrance...)

Wrong story.

Maybe it's better if she comes down here — and brings my good binoculars. A birders' honeymoon. Away from Terrance and the Executor.

Well, I am going to get a good jump on her first. I intend to arm myself for a week within the Corcovado: camera, film, dried bananas, and *The Birds of Central America*. Nearly three hundred species of birds flit and flut about the place. (I'm ahead of Caroline by two dozen listings now.) And the time to go is before the rains begin.

By candlelight in the night of the jungle I will work out some way to end it all. Not me, my book.

(By the way, Max, you remember that innocent little task I set you? I take it that by now you have executed it. As in, immolated it.)

Yours,
Brian P.

When Max returned to the office on Good Friday afternoon, John Brovak met him in the library, where Wentworth Chance had been bringing him up to speed on the latest doings of the Executor.

"How's Augustina and where is she?" Brovak asked.

"Gone off to Quentin Russell's in his luxomobile. A cruiser is following them out there, and it's going to stick around. Augustina's tough, she'll get strong again. How was your holiday?"

"The tits. I'm in great shape, no broken ankles, cleaned up my act, avoided all illicit snow, only used the cheap stuff, H_2O. When the snow started to melt in Aspen, I found a fresh supply in New fucking Zealand. I spent twenty K. I almost fell in love a few times but they didn't look so good in the morning. I was happy as shit until today."

They brought him up to date on the attack at the Topaz. Brovak reflected, then said: "I got the whole grind from the kid here about Cudlipp. Tony d'Anglio paid him to ice Watson, to get rid of the competition altogether. I was only a secondary target of that grenade. D'Anglio is on my suspect list, he's in there like Cudlipp's asshole buddy. Okay, take notes, kid."

He licked a long Garcia y Vega corona and fired it up. Max found Brovak's cigar almost as oppressive as his energy, but he was exhausted and willing to let him take over.

"But maybe I'm too fixated, let's broaden the focus. So there's this number two possibility: Roger Turnbull and this Calico Jesus freak who just mysteriously disappeared. That exhaust the known possibilities before we get into the twilight zone stuff?"

Max said: "Add Joe Ruff."

"Ruff? You got to be making jest."

Max related Augustina's sightings of Ruff in Victoria.

"You know he carries on about how he thinks our firm is just the cat's ass," Max said. "Always thought there was something kinky about how much he loves us."

"He's a mental case," said Wentworth.

"Okay, kid," said Brovak, "you're assigned to the Ruff file. Progress report in three days."

"Does the office cover me for insurance if he kills me?"

"One more possibility," Max said. "A couple of Uncle Sams were up here asking about a hit man named Hughie Lupo. A cop-killer." He told Brovak about the FBI's number one, the Mafia hit man.

"Okay," Brovak said, "throw this guy in the pot with the others, and let's start cutting this thing up."

For the balance of the afternoon and into the evening, the three of them did so: were there other links between the murderees other than that they were lawyers? Some shared client or acquaintance? Was it significant that three of the targets had been lawyers of this very firm? Was there a form of motive that had been overlooked? Or was this, after all, the work of Nordquist's favourite perp, the psycho?

O.D. Milsom, someone mentioned — he was still on the loose, was he a possibility? Conked his lawyer for getting him off when he hungered to be convicted. "Too much of a tard," said Brovak.

What if the killer was far more clever than they thought? He could have worn padding in the Topaz. He was obviously in disguise when he spoke to the waiter at Archie's Steak House. Beard, moustache, that falsetto voice…

Maybe a woman. A big strong woman. That's crazy. But perhaps a brilliant mind here. A gamester, a master of the ruse. The misspellings, "sewars" for "sewers," "counsellers" of crime. Were these errors intentional? "Executor" — had he meant "Executioner"?

After the meeting, Wentworth contemplated the long haul over Lion's Gate Bridge and up into the North Shore mountains. Woe, the Mercedes had been returned to its rightful owner. As had the hot tub and the view of Burrard Inlet. Homeless now, for he had given up his one-room-shared-bath to live in Brovak's eyrie, he had wheedled a house-sitting job from Caroline Pomeroy until her return from the Nahanee wars.

Astride his old steed, the Outback 310 twenty-one-speed mountain bike, Wentworth chugged off to feed the owls.

He was exhausted after the long meeting; he had covered thirty pages of foolscap with his energetic scribbles. He thought there was some kicker in the recounting of all the names, theories, and clues. Something passed over too quickly, the significance overlooked, a carelessly discarded thread that would tie these murders together.

He was shaken by this latest death. The bomb that nearly killed him at the steak house had been gulped down, swallowed, digested. This one would live within him.

Now his bosses had blithely assigned him to marshall the case against Joe Ruff. They were asking a lot, he felt, of a fellow who, so far, hasn't been invited to stay with the firm. What were the perils he was facing if Ruff indeed turned out to be a demonic assassin of vigorous young counsel such as himself? But the thought of this mild-mannered paper pusher attacking someone with a gun, knife, bomb or baseball bat seemed too ludicrous to consider...

On the other hand, what if?

33

Mew
and Shivers

Wentworth spent the next two days dictating his notes into a tape recorder, and had just about wrapped up late Sunday when Vajeeta phoned him at the office.

"How was the retreat?" he asked. "The, ah, kundalinga thing you were at."

"Cuspy. I left early. I learned some transformative ways from Master Yo."

She hinted she would like to try them on him.

Wentworth pedalled out to the east end of Chinatown, to her rickety rooming house.

She said she was enjoying a moment of inspiration — would he please wait around until it subsided?

Vajeeta returned to her desk and resumed scribbling in her notebook. Wentworth stood there uncomfortable as the soft, melting, all-knowing eyes of Sri Yogananda watched him from a poster on the wall.

He broke eye contact, then noticed the weekend newspapers on her desk, their headlines shouting Olive Klymchuk's murder. Would she clip these and put them in her scrapbook? Odd, given her fascination with lawyers, how she never talked about this recent spate of deaths. Always nimbly changed the subject.

"How do you spell counsellor?"

"I should buy you a dictionary. Two 'l's and an 'o'."

She closed her notebook. "I am into a scene where their spirits merge? Into one, into the spinning void of Eros. At the end, he will come back, transformed, and he will rip the mask from his face, the mask of laws he has been hiding behind. But it will be too late. For he will remember he has killed her."

"Who?"

"His wife. In the end, he will go to jail, but evermore he will be free within."

She approached him with a smile. She licked his neck and gave him a hickey. "Vampire," she said, "rhymes with desire and, um, funeral pyre."

The next morning, in an exhausted state after a night of kundalinga, Wentworth got his chance to do his Sam-spadework when Ruff called the office.

"They have been coming to the door," he said.

"Who?"

"The state, old chap."

"The state?"

"Under the ruse of making police inquiries about that terrible murder in Victoria, the government is seeking entry onto my property. I rather pride myself on my good citizenship, and I have already talked to them once on the telephone and answered all their questions, but now they are becoming...vexatious, what? I shall have to take out a writ."

"I think you should avoid any rows," Wentworth said.

"We have had one. I shut the door on one of these impertinent clerks and ordered him off my land."

"Why? What happened?"

"The unspeakable, sordid implication made was that I, Joseph Ruff, know more about this killing than I let on. I say, I was totally flummoxed. Then it dawned on me: they seek to put me in fear. They want to stop my cage-rattling."

In any event, an officer was threatening to come by again this afternoon, and Ruff wanted his attorney present.

Wentworth pedaled over to Joe Ruff's address in upper bourgeois Kerrisdale.

He found his house by a heavily-treed gully in a neighbourhood uncommonly respectable even for Kerrisdale: large homes and tall trees on big lots. Joe Ruff lived in one of those solid, two-storey, heavily-timbered buildings they made many years ago, when wood was cheap. A lot of room for a bachelor, Wentworth thought.

He could see several curious neighbours pretending to potter about in their front-yard flower beds. A cruiser was at the curb, near the driveway to Ruff's garage. A detective was leaning against the open passenger door, smoking, looking thoughtful.

As Ruff emerged from the house to greet him, Wentworth shouted at the officer: "Look, I want you to stay off Mr. Ruff's property. You don't have a warrant and you're embarrassing a respectable citizen in his own neighbourhood."

The detective glared at him as he got into his car.

Inside, Ruff shook Wentworth's hand vigorously, and they watched from a foyer window as the policeman drove away.

"It's the only way to deal with them," said Wentworth.

Two fat orange tabbies came purring up to his feet.

"Mew and Shivers," said Ruff. "I don't need a dog. My name is Ruff, after all." He tried to scare the cats by barking at them. "Ruff! Ruff!"

This character simply couldn't be a murderer, thought Wentworth.

"You will have some tea?"

Ruff quickly ushered him into a library adjoining the entrance foyer. It was lined with law books and manuals: a complete practitioner's library. These books must have cost a fortune, Wentworth thought. But Ruff apparently could afford it — he lived comfortably: his furnishings were expensive, some antiques.

Ruff told him to take the comfortable settee, and left to brew the tea.

Wentworth waited until his footsteps faded, then rose from his chair — the two cats pursuing in his step — to make closer examination of an oak *secrétaire* in the corner. On it was an IBM Selectric, inserted into which was a blank sheet with a carbon-backed copy. Wentworth recalled that everything had been neatly typed in Ruff's files: all those petulant letters to officialdom, and his legal pleadings, all peppered with misspellings.

Texts lay open on the desk — not legal texts, but writing manuals, a Thesaurus…and a book called *Famous Unsolved Murders*. Bookends held other references. Prominent was the Holy Bible. Beside it, a slim volume of one of Shakespeare's plays, *Henry VI, Part Two*.

Wentworth pulled it out and opened it at a bookmarked page: a line of prose was circled with a red marking pencil: "The first thing we do, let's kill all the lawyers." He blinked several times, then quickly replaced the book. Shivers and Mew purred around his ankles. No sounds of a kettle boiling yet.

Wentworth could find no pages of wit or wisdom from this man's typewriter lying about. He tried the drawers. In one he found a stack of Ruff's embossed letterhead and the usual stationery supplies: ballpoint pens, erasers, stamps, stapler, glue, a small pair of scissors. The other drawers were locked.

He bent to the wastebasket, which was filled with litter, including dozens of pages of wasted carbon. He quickly grabbed a couple of these pages and stuffed them into his jacket pocket.

"Orange Pekoe or Darjeeling?" said Ruff, reentering the library.

Wentworth was still bending low at the waist but he kept his wits, pretended to be crouching to pick up — which one was this, Mew or Shivers?

"I love cats," he said. He turned to find Ruff staring at him as he caressed the cat.

"Pekoe or Darjeeling, old fellow."

"Either is fine, Joe."

Ruff was frowning. "Perhaps we will be more comfortable in the parlour, what?"

Wentworth set the animal down and guiltily followed him down a hall to a large room plushly furnished around a large fireplace, and his client returned to his kettle.

Kill all the lawyers. A red marking pencil. *Exactly* the same type of writing utensil used by the Executor to mark his "X"s.

Interrupting his meditations, Joe Ruff wheeled in a tea service on a trolley, with scones and English marmalade.

He was in an effusive mood. "I intend to let your employers know how well you handled matters. I say, have they asked you to stay on after articles?"

"Uh, no, not quite."

"Their bad luck if you don't make the team. I see a future, Mr. Chance, a future."

Instead of steering directly toward the Olive Klymchuk murder, Wentworth spread on the lard about how he was heavily researching the Attorney General versus Ruff.

That set his client off on discursive tangents about his rights as a supposedly free citizen, about his many gripes against the system. Wentworth thought it would never end, but Ruff finally got back to business. He wanted to know if Wentworth thought an injunction against these harassing police was a good idea.

Wentworth said he'd have to know all the facts.

His client became animated: he was aghast at insinuations he was hiding something.

He had been in Victoria to serve a witness subpoena on the Superintendent of Motor Vehicles (the validity of a parking summons was at issue). He dropped in to watch the kidnap case, exchanged a few pleasant words with Miss Sage. He saw them at dinner. He turned in at ten p.m. and slept through to seven. There was a literal melee at the front desk in the morning, so because he had a scheduled HeliJet flight, he used the Quick Check service. It was not until later that day he discovered that Olive Klymchuk had been murdered.

"I was utterly dismayed. That unfortunate young woman. Only saw her in action once. Abrasive, I thought, but effective. Ours has become a dangerous business, Wentworth, what? Well, this fuss has put a dent in the day, and I have affairs to tend to. I'd much prefer to spend my time with a bright chap like yourself, and debate the intricacies of the law, but one of my, ah, clients, is about to arrive."

One of his *clients*? Wentworth followed him to the door.

"An injunction," Ruff said, "restrictive in form. That's the ticket, what? We'll sue the blighters, Mr. Chance. It will be most enjoyable working with you."

The "client" was coming up the flagstone walk as Wentworth departed. A hefty young man with gorilla arms and grim, blank eyes that refused to meet Wentworth's. The guy exuded a kind of uncomfortable aura, vaguely evil.

Wentworth vaulted onto his Outback, bounced over the curb to the street and checked his pocket. Two rumpled sheets of carbon paper, surely they could be read by experts. *Famous Unsolved Murders.* Scissors, glue, ballpoint pen, red marking pencil, everything had been there. Spooky.

The next day, Wentworth turned over the two pages of carbon paper to Max, who in turn handed them to Nordquist. They had each been used at least a dozen times. The document examiners said they couldn't guarantee much, and it might take them several days.

"What are my chances for a warrant to shake Ruff's house?" Nordquist asked.

"Weak," Max said.

The inspector tried anyway, with an affidavit reciting Ruff's possession of the Bible, the book *Famous Unsolved Murders*, the red-marked quote from Shakespeare, the scissors, stamps and glue. But he flubbed it, got referred upstairs by the Justice of the Peace, and was turned down by a judge.

Max and Nordquist met later at C.L.E.U. with Hochmeir, the FBI agent, who had driven up from Seattle after receiving a brief on the Klymchuk murder.

"No prints?" he said.

"Never took his gloves off," said Nordquist.

"How do you know — you check anyway?"

"Of course."

The question had implied laxness. Max could tell the inspector felt affronted.

"She scratched him pretty badly through his shirt," Nordquist said.

"Get any of his blood? Enough to do a DNA print?"

"No. We tried. We have some Type A blood on her hands, but it could be Miss Klymchuk's. She's type A."

"So is Hughie Lupo."

"So is half the population."

"You boys need any, ah, extra help on this case?"

Max caught the intimation: these foreign amateurs might not be counted on to do the job of collaring the FBI's number one.

"Thanks," said Nordquist. "If there's anything we need, we'll call."

"If it's Lupo, you'll pass him down to us?"

"He'll be dealt with by our courts."

"Trouble is," said Hochmeir, "you good folks don't have the death penalty." That elicited no response. He stood to go. "He's a smart one, Hughie Lupo. Couple of years in college before he joined the Special Forces. That's where he earned his advanced degree in murder. He's quirky. He's a brilliant actor. And he's capital D dangerous."

Soon after they saw Hochmeir to the door, Nordquist received an urgent message to attend at the Vancouver Post Office.

Two teams of C.L.E.U. and postal investigators had spent all Easter Weekend in the Victoria and Vancouver Post offices. No letters-to-the-editor from the Executor were discovered. But this morning an alert mail sorter had found what it seemed they were looking for: ball-point block printing, addressed to the morning tabloid, the *Province*. No return address.

When Max arrived an i.d. person had just finished dusting the envelope. No prints.

"From a bag in west Point Grey," said a postal inspector. "Mailed some time before eleven-forty hours this morning."

Nordquist's document examiner held it gingerly by a corner, slit one end open, and pulled out a folded piece of paper.

Max could barely see it over Nordquist's shoulder: paste-up newspaper letters, a couple of red slashes.

"Oh, God," Nordquist said, and his shoulders sagged.

Max leaned forward and focused on the letter. Two Bible quotes: "Think not that I am come to destroy the law." "The law is good, if a man use it lawfully." Then: "Klymchuk X-ecuted." The "X" was hand-drawn — two bright red, intersecting slashes. And there was another red 'X.' The note continued: "Wessel X-ecuted. As Ordered by God."

Martin "the Weasel" Wessel?

"Check his office," Nordquist said to one of his investigators. "And his house."

The document examiner bent close to the paper, lightly touched the red cross-marks, put her nose to them. "Fingernail polish," she said.

It wasn't until mid-afternoon that Wessel's body was found, already starting to grow ripe, beneath the cliffs of Wreck Beach below the campus of the University of British Columbia. The beach is a haunt of nude sunbathers, one of whom spotted the corpse wedged between a rock and a tree.

He had last been seen alive at about 8:45 p.m. on Thursday, the eve of Klymchuk's murder, when he kissed his girlfriend good night at her apartment door in the West End. The woman — the same one Augustina had seen Wessel esquiring to dinner — said that an hour earlier he had made a phone call but she got only the gist of it: something about his getting together with someone. He consumed three tall rye-and-gingers during the evening. They dined on Salisbury steaks. When he left, he seemed "up," though earlier he had been brooding about how it wasn't safe to walk the streets these days.

She had expected to see him the next day — he had talked vaguely about "celebrating" that evening — but when he didn't show or call she was miffed and went out on her own — dressed to kill, as she unthinkingly put it. No word from Wessel through the rest of the weekend, either, but she said sometimes the guy was like that, wouldn't call for days. Maybe he'd gone off sailing for all she knew.

He shelled out on their dates. That, assumed the police, was the basis of their relationship.

His secretary had spent the long weekend in Seattle, and returned to work Tuesday morning to observe that Wessel, usually an early starter, was not there, and it appeared he hadn't been in since Thursday. When he didn't show up for his 11 a.m. with Father Doyle, she began making phone calls, to his home, his girlfriend, and was about to call the police when they arrived at her office door.

Wessel hadn't many other friends to make inquiries of. He had been known to be close to only his late partner, Eddie Cohn. He had no family.

Investigators dispatched to the apparent scene of the crime observed the condition of the corpse's clothing and the scraped clay surface of the slope above him, and deduced he had fallen some distance, perhaps a hundred feet from the top of the Point Grey cliffs. There, his Saab 900 was found deserted, but with the keys in the ignition.

In his sports jacket were found a wallet with several hundred dollars in it and, crumpled in his pocket litter, a note on a small sheet of lined paper. In block pencilled letters, one word: "Midnight," followed by the initial "E." Police puzzled over that. A midnight meeting?

The body was moved by helicopter to the city morgue, where pathologists looked in vain for exterior wounds other than the scrapes and bangs suffered in the fall. No defensive marks. Most signs of rigor mortis had disappeared and the body had begun to bloat, so death had likely occurred at least three days earlier. Thursday night, it was assumed, probably about midnight of the eve of Good Friday.

This was confirmed when they opened him up: stomach contents consisted of undigested Salisbury steaks. He hadn't had a meal since leaving his girlfriend's that evening, and even there, he hadn't eaten anything with curry, though the pathologist detected the smell of curry powder.

The doctor was intrigued by the macabre fixed grin upon his face, a kind of *risus sardonicus*.

The toxicologist later told Nordquist he'd found enough strychnine in him to kill a bull.

34

To Marry
a Mystery

During the weekend, Augustina left Russell's manse only once, an Easter Monday brunch with her ex-partner Sophie Marx, to show off her ring, a stone as big as a hazelnut. She was chauffered to this brunch date by James Goodwinkle. Russell had told him he must carry a pistol while with Augustina, and his manservant was now packing a piece in a shoulder harness, constantly adjusting it, uncomfortable with it.

He didn't seem like he'd be much help in a crisis.

The staff, brought back from their weekend holidays, tried to keep Augustina's mind occupied: Mrs. Collins, the housekeeper, with her friendly nattering. And when she went out walking on the grounds, the gardener with his earthy homilies. She took a few riding lessons from the stable boy. She went through three packs a day, spent a lot of time in the pool and in front of the TV, but never quite escaped from the Topaz Hotel.

On Tuesday, after absorbing the news of Martin Wessel's death, Augustina chain-smoked for a couple of hours trying to work out her confusions. Wessel had been murdered about midnight last Thursday, Klymchuk five hours later. How could this killer of lawyers have moved so quickly from Vancouver to Victoria in the small hours of that night? The overnight ferry, probably. It was the long weekend: extra sailings, extra flights.

When Quentin Russell returned home from court late Tuesday, he was fidgety, seemed distracted, and unwilling to talk about Wessel. He sat for most of the evening in front of the television, watching a Toronto Blue Jays game — the season had just begun. He was a nut for baseball, a Jays fanatic. Boring, but Augustina could live with it.

That night, asleep, he broke into a sweat, and his nightmare awoke them both.

"What were you dreaming?"

He didn't say. He lay there in silence, and when his eyes turned to her, she saw they were hollow and damp.

Much on her mind now was that disquieting conversation she had had with Olive before they fell asleep on the eve of her death. The last conversation she or anyone had ever enjoyed with Olive Klymchuk.

I think he's into something crooked. Maybe he's being blackmailed for something.

Mysterious cheques to a numbered account in the Bahamas.

And she remembered Wessel's curious words to Quentin in that restaurant: *Hope to be hearing from you soon, judge.*

On the following day, she escaped from watchful Goodwinkle for a few hours, flying over to Victoria for Olive's funeral, returning late that afternoon. At seven-thirty Russell called to say he was besieged by paperwork and would be another hour and would she warm the oven.

Augustina turned the oven on, then made sure Mrs. Collins was gone for the day and that Goodwinkle was outside — as he was, in gloves and coveralls, polishing his boss's antique Peugot.

She hated the idea of snooping, but was experiencing qualms about marrying a mystery. She walked into Russell's den. Some opened letters sat on the desk blotter. Nothing of consequence, a few bills. A letter from his stockbroker. It advised him not to sell certain industrial shares on a plummeting market but if he insisted, the transaction could be complete within the following week.

Why was he hurriedly selling off these shares? In debt? She again wondered about those big payments Olive had mentioned. But his chequebook was locked away.

As she stood there musing she saw a little red light gazing solemnly at her from the answering machine. And she flashed on a call Quentin had played from this machine — when was that — a couple of weeks ago? *I'm waiting*, said that oddly familiar voice, before Quentin had put the tape on fast forward.

She rewound the tape, replayed it, heard Quentin's mother. She backed up the tape a little more. After some buzzing and clicking:

"I'm waiting. We have limited patience, my old friend." That was all.

A kind of weary twang to the voice. A weary…weasel-like twang. Yes, the late Martin Wessel.

She returned to the front parlour and chain-smoked and channel-surfed on the television and wondered what her fiancé's reaction would be if she asked him about what the hell was going on. Would he send her two dozen roses and a nice letter?

When Russell returned at eight-thirty, he was grinning — a changed man. He jauntily kissed her and fetched a bottle of Mumm's.

"I'm in," he said. The cork popped, sailed past his nose. She took the extended glass and gulped it down.

"I thought you might have wished to toast me with some of that." She held out the glass for more, watched it bubble and fizz.

"You are frowning. Augustina, I'm *in*. Just got a call from the minister. Top secret, your ears only: they're going to announce my appointment next week. Goddammit, dig down, at least come up with a smile."

"Did it help — us getting engaged?"

"What's wrong, darling?"

"I'm sorry. It's wonderful. Congratulations. It's your dream."

"I note a lack of keenness in your voice. Again, Augustina, what's wrong?"

"What dealings did you have with Martin Wessel?"

"Dealings with…" His grin vanished. He went pale, then tried to be jocular. "Why, has someone accused me of secret meetings with him in men's rooms? Oh-oh, there goes the Supreme Court."

Russell tossed down his own glass of champagne.

Augustina slowly lit a cigarette, filled her lungs with smoke, blew it out in a stream.

"Was he hustling you for something?"

"What's in that cigarette besides tobacco?"

"Just tell me. Olive had a theory you were being blackmailed."

Silence but for the ticking clock on the mantle.

"What else did Olive tell you?"

"Just that she saw some big cancelled cheques to a numbered account. What's going on, Quentin?"

"Excuse me. I think I need to shower."

Augustina stood rigidly in front of a flickering TV set while Russell went upstairs. To shower — or to compose himself? To think of some lie? She was in a state of high tension.

He returned shiny, clean, wet-haired, wearing pressed slacks and shirt. Augustina had a terrible image: a man who has just washed the blood off, the evidence. He clicked off the television, and stood facing her. And suddenly looked helpless.

"I *am* being blackmailed. Or I was."

The announcement gently reverberated around the room.

He seemed to age in front of Augustina; creases furrowed his face.

"I was debating with myself about when to tell you, but decided to wait until we were married. I know that's unfair, but I didn't want to give you a chance to change your mind. Now you may do so if you wish." He was distant, detached, his speech mannerly.

"For God's sake, Quentin, I'm not going to call the emergency hot line. How bad is it?"

"Ugly. I suppose I had a motive to kill him."

She had lifted her glass of champagne, but now paused before bringing it to her lips.

"There's no strychnine in it," Russell said.

She took a sip, eyeing him over the rim of the glass.

"I've never told you how I made my money, Augustina. I think you know my parents were poor; I didn't inherit it. When I was young, I was a little reckless and a lot ambitious. I wanted to show all those folks on Commercial Drive that Quentin Russell could make it big."

She nodded and waited for more. "Sit down," he said. "Make yourself comfortable."

She sat but wasn't comfortable.

"In 1978 I bought forty acres in Ladner on speculation. It was zoned rural but I knew there was a mall going in nearby. I sought to have it upzoned to commercial. I wouldn't dream of being my own client in an application like that, and normally I would have hired an honest municipal lawyer. But Martin Wessel approached me. He said that for the right kind of fee, he could get me my rezoning. It was that blunt. By fee, he meant bribe. Two hundred thousand dollars. Part of it he would pocket, part would go to a crooked alderman crony of his. He wasn't so specific, of course."

Russell lost his composure, slumped to the arm of an easy chair.

"How stupid I was!" He mimicked his own voice: "'I won't be a party to anything nefarious, Martin.' I can hear myself, all the false sincerity. Oh, he said, wouldn't dream of involving me in anything remotely improper. Anyway, I retained Wessel, paid him off, and they rezoned."

Russell shook his head. Augustina felt his sadness, her own relief. It wasn't the crime of the century. "Technically, you didn't do anything illegal."

"Morally I did. If he were to have put it on the street, I'd have been ruined. I turned the property over for thirty times what it cost me."

"And since then you've paid for it again."

"And paid. And paid." His smile was bitter. "He started hitting me up after I was named to the bench. A little to start with. Then more when he realized he could keep squeezing the tit. I'm mortgaged tighter than the Reichmann brothers. I'm going to have to sell stock. I'm going to have to sell the Tiepolos, the Riccis, the entire collection. The last payment was to have been ten million dollars."

"The...last payment?"

"That's what Wessel was bugging me for. I told him there'd be no more. If he tried to ruin me, I was going to drag him down with me."

"And you were going to pay him this ten million?"

"I was assembling it just before he died." His eyes didn't waver from hers. "With what you know you could call the police."

"Where did I put the phone?" she said.

He tried to smile. "I only have Goodwinkle to say where I was Thursday night. I sent the rest of the staff home for the weekend."

"You have another witness," she said. "I phoned you just before midnight."

"Great. My butler and my fiancée...Are you still my fiancée?"

"Yes. But you should have told me, Quentin. I want no secrets."

"Do you intend to keep this one?"

"I'm embarrassed that you ask."

✛ ✛ ✛

Unable to come to terms with preparing dinner — Russell still refused to let Augustina loose in his kitchen — he asked Goodwinkle to order a pizza, and they waited on the terrace by the pool, where Russell kept one distracted eye on the twelve-inch set there, another ball game. When Goodwinkle came out with the pizza, John Brovak was following.

The butler announced him icily. "I'm sorry, I asked him to wait at the front door." Augustina could tell Brovak had been brusque with him.

Brovak gave Augustina a buss, hugged her. "You okay, babe?"

"I'm alive. Barely."

"Just in time, I see," Brovak said, looking at the pizza box. "Eat-a-Pizza-Pie. Best in town. One of Tony the Angle's front-door operations, isn't it, Quent?"

"They say he runs a book behind the pizza ovens, and the vans collect the bets on weekends. Quite a system. Have a piece."

"You get the foreman's job at last, Quent?" Brovak asked. "The gig with the Supremes?"

Russell glanced at Goodwinkle, still hovering nearby. "Ah, no, nothing formal has come down the pipe yet from Ottawa. It's all right, James, thank you."

Brovak held a slice of pizza inquiringly to Goodwinkle, who coldly demurred, turned on his heels, and left.

Brovak saw that Russell was into a Jays game. "Stewart throwing tonight?"

"Seems to have his good stuff going."

"Don't want to interrupt it, but the reason I came calling, judge, is I want you to set me up an audience with the maker of this here pizza."

"I don't think it would be wise for me to call him. But I think you know where to reach him. He'd be delighted to see you."

"Mr. d'Anglio wants to retain you, John," Augustina said.

Brovak studied the view through the window, the bluffs of Point Grey. "Guess we're only a short hop from where they found the Weasel. Strychnine. Jesus. What happens is it hits your breathing centre. Twitchings, convulsions, then suddenly you think you're okay, and they come again, only worse. Then you wait in dread for the next one. You kick off from exhaustion finally."

"John, for Christ's sake," Augustina said.

"Hey, sorry." He sucked up a strand of cheese. "Anyway, I'm think-ing maybe we have a blackmail situation here."

Brovak saw Russell turn white. It couldn't be the game — the Jays were ahead, and Alomar had just stolen second.

"What do you think, judge?" Brovak asked. "Hey, is something wrong? You look a little anemic."

Russell seemed to take some time to formulate a thought. "Yes, blackmail. Perhaps Cudlipp…There was that note found in Wessel's pocket."

"Right on," said Brovak. "'Midnight.' Initial 'E.' 'E' for Everit. The Cud set up a meet in their usual place, maybe a noisy bar, and bought Wessel a double rum and strychnine. Cohn and the Weasel were threatening to turn Cudlipp in unless he pieced them off with a share of the bribe d'Anglio gave him for taking out Twelve-Fingers Watson."

Joe Carter lifted one out with two men on. With that, Russell's colour seemed to come back. He seemed more relaxed. "Maybe it wasn't blackmail at all. If the deal was brokered by Eddie Cohn, maybe he tried to swindle Cudlipp out of the *whole* three hundred thousand."

Brovak was excited. "Hey, judge, that's it. The firm of Cohn and Wessel tried to earn extra vigorish. Cudlipp — it computes — arranged a meeting with the Weasel Friday night at which final account would be rendered. Jeez, he's not smart enough on his own…Leroy. Yeah, Lukey'd be the mastermind, his bumfuck fishing buddy."

"Somehow I really doubt that, John," Russell said.

"You don't get it. Lukey and Cudlipp are the number one and two prime suspects in my near-death experience. They invented the fuck-ing Executor so Cudlipp could hide behind the same shield when he killed two other lawyers."

"They had no reason to murder Olive Klymchuk," Russell said.

Brovak turned to Augustina. "You got any theories, Augie? Anyone else with a motive for Wessel?"

"No, I don't…No."

Brovak saw them exchange a look. He finished his pizza. He watched the mists curl from the heated pool. "You mind?" He started stripping off.

✛ ✛ ✛

Brovak discovered it was easy enough to reach d'Anglio: one phone call to an office near the stock exchange, where d'Anglio washed most of his money. D'Anglio invited him to the Friday meet at the Cloverdale Raceway.

Brovak found d'Anglio and a few of his sidewinders at a long table in the clubhouse, surrounded by women and drinks. He gave Brovak an energetic wave.

"I got a proposition," d'Anglio said. "We'll take a walk about it."

Brovak followed d'Anglio out. They left the grandstand area, strolled towards the paddocks.

"I got a animal here is gonna surprise," d'Anglio said. "Sam Slick in the fifth. He'll come in at four, five to one at the gun. Put down a big nickel to place."

Brovak watched as a couple of buggy drivers loosened up their horses around the curve to the far straightaway. "You've got another animal out there who's maybe gonna surprise."

"Who might that be?"

"Horse named Cudlipp."

D'Anglio gave him a searching look.

"I'm asking in confidence, where is he?"

"I don't know. Maybe he earned hisself a holiday."

"You pay him to ice Twelve-Fingers Watson?"

D'Anglio looked hurt. "John, this is not the way I play, whatever you've heard. It is not good business. In fact it was a tragedy I lament, and I have extended myself to those he left behind."

This was true. Brovak knew d'Anglio had hired some of Watson's crew; from others he bought their networks.

"But you paid off Cudlipp to set up Watson for a fall."

"*That* is business. Free enterprise."

"The deal was middled by Eddie Cohn, right? What was it, half down, and half on delivery?"

"You ask too many questions, John." D'Anglio gave Brovak a pat on the arm, forgiving him for his presumptuous manners. "As you know, I just lost my mouth. Tried to bring in Wessel from the bullpen, he got bombed in the late innings. The word is you're a right person. You don't give a fuck for nothin' is what they say, and I think that's a fine attitude."

"Life is dear."

"I'll protect you."

"Yeah, like Cohn?"

"Believe me, John, I offered him. This was a great loss. If I knew who did it, I'd send one of the friends with a message."

D'Anglio could be bulling him. But Brovak wondered if he shouldn't give him the benefit of the doubt. Knives and poison: it *wasn't* the way d'Anglio worked. You want a guy taken down, one of the friends calmly blows him away with a heater. He wondered if Tony knew anything about the Mafia assassin Hughie Lupo. Maybe it was too early to ask.

"You want some free legal advice, Tony? Watch your back."

"You think Cudlipp?"

"Yeah."

D'Anglio smiled. "I will make inquiries. Twenty large in advance, that's just for the right to have your phone number in case of emergency."

Brovak watched as the pacers began to line up for the third race. Sam Slick in the fifth, he thought. He smiled at d'Anglio. He pulled a cheap El Ropo from his pocket. D'Anglio brought a Cuban corona from his.

"Try this," d'Anglio said.

Brovak lit it up. Had to be a thirty-dollar cigar. "So hire me."

35

Lightning Bolt

FAX TO: firm of Valentine, McGillicuddy, Hlinka, and
        Queen.

Quick note. Phones are in, Frank Sierra now has a fax.
He is about to drive me to the northern gates of the
Corcovado, the beginning of the trail to Los Patos. I have
instructed him he may intercept the brief of evidence that
I asked you to send by air courier. Fax him any additional
material.

Francisco is pulling up. I must gather my tent and my
fart sack and head out to the wilds.

Pura vida,
Brian.

P.S. Fax me some information on this Terrance. Sounds like a
real lout.

✝ ✝ ✝

April Something

Dear Office,

   Lightning has struck on the banks of the Rio Claro.

   Let me set the scene. This morning I was awakened by the cacophonous alarm of the primal forest at dawn. I rolled lazily out of my tent and attended the Rio Claro for my morning ablutions and took a swim in the pool it formed beneath the almond trees. Clouds had bullied up to great height in the west, a red sky in the morning to make the forest blush.

   I was sliding naked on my back, gently kicking across the surface toward the high, thin chute of water coming from a ledge above, when there came a sharp clap of thunder, and when I turned my eyes again to the western sky, I saw a thunderbolt.

   I knew who my murderer was.

   Like Archimedes I sprung from my bath and sped to my tent and this notepad.

   (Okay, so the lightning bolt wasn't *exactly* coincidental with my inspiration — in fact it's just started thundering now. But what the hell, I'm a writer.)

   Anyway, inspiration struck me like an orgasm (or what I think I remember as an orgasm). The culprit, of course, turned out to be someone I didn't suspect.

   Now I am burning to end my idyll and run my idea by Francisco. To the east, another day's march, is the end of the trail.

Brian.

Max could see that Nordquist, who was working sixteen hours a day, was showing cracks. Ever-immaculate, he had begun to arrive on the job unshaven. He showed a curtness ever more bold to the politicians and the press.

His nonperformance was blamed for the criminal court system, already in near shambles, falling into total disarray after the recent deaths: an anarchy of no-shows in court, the few lawyers who wandered in often hung over, having drunk their fears away the night before. Calendars were backed up for five years.

Word was that the Attorney General might move Nordquist aside for a heavyweight from RCMP Special X, the Mounted's elite crime unit.

Max felt that one of the clear signals of the slow tilting of Nordquist's balance was his decision to bring in a couple of clairvoyants. One had been recommended by the FBI, a bell-shaped woman from Arkansas named Mrs. Sawyer. The other was a young man from rural Quebec who had apparently — a couple of times — led police to the remains of missing persons.

They were shown the scenes of the crimes, photos of the suspects.

Mrs. Sawyer had a curious vision — fish hooks hanging from a wall, a row of brightly-coloured lures. The man from Quebec couldn't get rid of an image of a kind of "*sorcière*," a witch, her nails painted bright crimson.

Max thought all this was bogus, but Nordquist took careful notes.

Word of Caroline Pomeroy's arrest reached the office on Saturday, but it wasn't until the next morning that Wentworth was able to arrange a charter to the little town of Weeping Willow River, where his boss's wife — along with fourteen other Nahanee protesters — was being held in the RCMP lockup.

The sergeant in charge was stiff and humourless as he described to Wentworth how Caroline had frisbeed his hat into a ravine. They never did find his hat, and she was charged with assaulting a police officer. She and the other arrestees were also charged with obstructing a logging road.

There were no interview facilities in this small detachment, so Wentworth was shown into a cell holding Caroline and several of her female comrades. Down the hall, from another cell, a long-haired man was leading a chant: "Na-ha-nee! Na-ha-nee! Save the trees of the Na-ha-nee!"

Caroline was grinning. She seemed…happy.

"Hi, there, Wentworth. How are my owls?"

"Um, just fine. Keep swooping at my girlfriend, though."

"Girlfriend?"

"Vajeeta. She's a kind of…spiritual person. Uh, look, it's Sunday, and the courts aren't open and there won't be a judge here until tomorrow for bail."

"Bail? Oh, don't bother."

"Well, look, I'm sure if you promise not to return to the block-ade — "

"Nope."

"Gee whiz, don't say that, Caroline. Max told me I have to bring you back. Um, John Brovak is on his way to Costa Rica to fetch Brian, he's apparently out on some jungle trek…"

"Free the Nahanee Fifteen. Free the Nahanee Fifteen."

"Who is that guy chanting?"

"Oh, that's Terrance. He's a total ecomaniac. Actually, getting arrested was a relief. Didn't know if I could keep running from him. He almost treed me yesterday." She leaned toward Wentworth. "I think he's a little stuck on me."

Wentworth pulled a thick envelope from his briefcase. "Oh, this came in the mail, um, from Costa Rica."

Caroline looked at Brian's oddly scrawled handwriting. Made out to Pomeroy and Company at her *house* address.

Early Tuesday, Ottawa officially announced Quentin Russell's appointment to the Supreme Court of Canada. Max immediately called his father in his chambers. Max Mac Two seemed to be taking it with a stiff upper lip.

"Can't quarrel with it. Quentin's young enough to make Chief, though I might have, too."

Chief Justice of Canada: his father's long-held ambition, the crowning achievement of a heritage of Macarthurs on the bench. A goal now thwarted.

After Max rang off, he decided he'd had enough of clanging phones, complaining clients, and rebelling secretaries, and closed up shop for the day. He would visit his mother, who might be feeling blue. And it was time to start training for the annual May Day Marathon.

He donned his track suit and began a lope through the streets of Vancouver. He had run the May Day for each of the last nine years, and had once come tenth. This year's goal: make the top five.

Legs, lungs, heart and a clear, unworried head were the required physical components of a long-distance runner. If one's mind is busy with Turnbulls and Calicos and Ruffs and Lupos, one uses up a lot of energy.

He floated down Beatty Street, past the teflon dome of the city's huge white elephant, B.C. Place Stadium, past the old Expo grounds, over the Cambie Bridge, through a clutter of fancy condos. Calico: where had he disappeared to? What was Turnbull's game?

Up the hills of Fairview, steep and mean, down tree-flowered Cambie, up Little Mountain for a full-compass view of Vancouver. Joe Ruff — what secret was he keeping locked in the drawers of his *secrétaire?* Those carbons had been sent to a lab in Ottawa for deciphering.

He checked his watch. Damn, minutes off the pace he'd set for himself. Clear the head. West into Shaughnessy, the bastion of the rich. Home of Chief Justice and Mrs. Macarthur. Lukey lived nearby, too. He and Cudlipp…was there anything to Brovak's theory? Well, Max would spin past there, see if Cudlipp's car was out front.

A Channel Eight news van swept past him, barreled around a corner onto Connaught Drive. As Max jogged past Lukey's house he saw no cars in the driveway, but a block down he was startled to see two more TV news vans and a clutter of other press-mobiles.

Parked in front of 57 Connaught Drive. His parents' house. Max sprinted.

Neighbours were standing on porches, staring. The Channel Eight crew was lugging a camera down the lane behind the Macarthur residence, a formidable brick fortress on a third of an acre. As Max trotted up the driveway he heard voices from the back. It sounded as if someone were orating.

In the alley, a melee of reporters and men in white berets. Max could hear but not see Roger Turnbull in the middle of this, apparently giving a press conference.

Muriel Macarthur and her maid were standing on her back porch, staring at this scene with looks of utter confusion.

"Mom, what the heck is going on here?"

"Max…I don't know. They just all…suddenly showed up."

Max could hear Turnbull's resonant voice: "My people intend to guard this thing until the cops decide to show up."

"Stay in the house, Mom." Max raced across the back lawn to a low cypress hedge. The White Angels were clustered around a bin where the Macarthurs kept their garbage cans.

"This anonymous caller," said a reporter, "he was male?"

"The voice was disguised. I think it was a lady, and she was trying to talk like a man. I suspect a female associate of the perpetrator who couldn't live with her guilty knowledge. I think she'll call us again; she obviously doesn't trust our boys in blue. Ah, this must be them, finally."

Max could hear sirens.

"Just give me those exact words again?" another reporter said.

Turnbull consulted a note pad. "'I'm calling about the Executor. You will find all you need at 57 Connaught Drive. Look in the garbage cans at the back.'"

"When did this call come in, Mr. Turnbull?"

"Ten forty-seven hours was the call, sir, forty-five minutes ago."

Evidence was being destroyed in the course of this royal ring-dang-do, Max saw. People were everywhere, poking around, smudging things, trampling footprints. This was the house in which he'd been raised, this the alley where he'd played dirt hockey as a kid. It was a sacrilege.

He strode out the back gate. "Turnbull, what the hell is this?"

"Can I believe? Is that Mr. Max Macarthur out of uniform?"

A fully harnessed car swooped into the alley, and a male and female constable warily emerged from it.

Turnbull spoke triumphantly: "Take a gander in here, officers. You, too, Max, since you're now basically a cop."

Basically a cop. The asshole.

More sirens. Max peered into one of the garbage cans, its lid off. Within was a copy of the Bible, a pair of shears, some scissored pages from newspapers. He sucked in his breath.

Lars Nordquist and a team from C.L.E.U. now poured into the lane. As officers set up a ribbon cordon and cleared the area, Nordquist looked into the can, then drew Max aside.

"That son of a bitch. He called the press, *then* me. Who tipped him? A woman, he said."

"He said."

By now, the other White Angels had been shunted behind the lines. An i.d. team dusted for prints, snapped photographs, and checked for boot impressions while Turnbull talked into a reporter's tape machine.

"If this leads to our Executor, I'll be claiming the reward. I believe the Law Society has just raised it to three hundred thousand dollars. Only happy to relieve the rich lawyers' club of some of their filthy lucre."

The material in the garbage was gingerly removed, item by item. In addition to the shears and several cut-up sheets of the Vancouver *Province* was a container of glue. The Gideon Bible was tattered, verses cut from it. A little screw-cap bottle of red nail polish was discovered.

The evidence technician doing the probing suddenly took a step back.

"Hand grenade," he said. "Pin's in. Get the bomb squad."

Everyone scattered.

At the crime lab, Nordquist and Max hovered about the forensic experts as they worked through the day. Results came in quickly. The individual letters stuck to the Executor's last note made perfect match with letters missing from the shredded newspaper found in the garbage. The Bible snippets glued to all three of his notes had clearly been cut from the Gideon edition found there. The grenade was the same type of army fragmentation device that exploded at Archie's Steak house. The nail polish was of a shade called "Crimson Flush," the same tint the Executor had used to mark the X's on his last letter.

"Doesn't make sense," Max said. "Why *there*? In my folks' goddamn *garbage*?"

Nordquist shrugged.

"It would be just like Turnbull to try to embarrass my family. Hates the court system, picks on the house of the chief justice. Yeah, I bet he planted all that shit there. That telephone tip was phony. He's the Executor, Bones."

Tuesday, April 20

Dear Office Fax Machine,

    I came in from the Corcovado only an hour ago, ranting to Frank about my lightning flash of inspiration, but found

him totally engrossed in the long report you guys couriered.
He showed me the police photos: a rogue's gallery of dead
lawyers. When I looked at them I almost flipped.

Besterman's body in the parking lot. Okay. The aftermath
of the grenade blast at Archie's Restaurant. Okay, I knew
about that. And Eddie Cohn astraddle a propane barbecue.
Then I saw the frozen, smiling face of Martin Wessel.

And then Olive Klymchuk…And *nearly*, dear God,
Augustina. What monstrous evils were wrought as I lay on
the banks of the Rio Claro.

And then Frank gave me your fax about Caroline assaulting a cop and refusing bail.

I'm spinning. And why does all this happen just as I'm
about to finish my book?

Frank Sierra has my passport and he's going to help me
pack, but I may have problems — looks like all flights north
are booked with tourists fleeing the rains.

(Max, did you intercept that tape?)

B.

36

Killer
Bees

A shadow fell over Augustina's romance-of-a-lifetime after her fiancé's disclosure of his long-ago misdeed with Martin Wessel — not a capital crime, a blind eye turned to Wessel's act of bribing an alderman. That he'd been so stupid as to expose himself to blackmail finally showed a flaw in him, that's all. But it had been unfair of Quentin not to trust her with this secret. She hadn't liked snooping around, cross-examining the truth from him.

That visit from John Brovak — with the misread hints about blackmail — had really rattled Quentin, but he hadn't raised the subject again to her. When he wasn't watching his beloved Blue Jays, he was working feverishly in his den on reserved decisions, clearing the decks for a busy spring calendar in the Supreme Court — he was to be sworn in this Friday in Ottawa. When Augustina begged off flying there with him to the ceremony, he looked at her in amazement.

"Quentin, I just can't face it." She explained: the terrors of a smoke-banned reception at Government House, all those smiling mannequins from Parliament Hill. Dinner with his Conservative cronies and their snobby spouses.

"That's selfish," he said sharply.

"I'm not going to be put on show in front of a bunch of gossipy, winking political ladder-climbers."

"You'll meet the P.M."

"God preserve me from *that*."

But in the end he swallowed his ire, and she decided she wasn't going to let their little spat sour their relationship. She was in love; love was all.

Brian stuck his loyal old Underwood on a shelf, promising silently he would soon return to it. As he collected his bags and clothes, he noticed Francisco Sierra looking pensive. Thousands of miles away, in fact. Somewhere in downtown Vancouver? Frank hadn't said much on the ride over, and once again was reading that twelve-page account of the many misdeeds of his favourite criminal, the Executor.

A tousled head poked into the bedroom.

"*Señor Brian, venga*."

The six-year-old, Gabriela. She came in and pulled Brian's pant leg. "*Venga. Venga*."

Brian and Francisco followed the scampering child down to the road and up to the Róbelo house at the mouth of the river. Señora Róbelo ushered them quickly in.

There, on a thin mattress on the swept dirt floor lay none other a personage than John Brovak. Leticia Róbelo was cradling his head, one side of which was blown up like a balloon, and squeezing aloe juice upon his wounds. He was staring up at her with an expression of considerable confusion.

He slowly turned away from her to squint at Brian, silhouetted by the sun in the doorway, stunned and silent.

"That you, Brian? Jeez, you look like something out of a zoo. Throw this man into the car wash. I came down to bring you back, Augustina nearly got snuffed; Caroline's been charged with illegal tree-hugging —"

"I heard."

"I got two plane tickets back for tomorrow. Only I decided not to use mine just yet. I'm not sure what's going on here, but I think I want to stick around a while. I'm feeling kind of…I don't know — weird."

When Brovak's eyes turned again to Leticia, Brian saw that they seemed to have turned into a kind of soft, melting wax. Leticia's own eyes were dark and simmering as he studied her wounded guest. Brian was suddenly apprehensive. He stammered out an introduction of Francisco, then asked what the hell happened.

Brovak recounted arriving by plane and taxi from San José, and finding Brian gone. Out for a stroll on the trail to the river, he had stumbled into a nest of bees, and they'd pursued him toward the pools — where Leticia was bathing at the shore.

"I saw this brown-skinned gossamer-winged fairy standing there, and these bees were coming, and I mean, man, killer bees, and I just picked her up and carried her into the deepest pool I could find. She didn't get stung once. I almost got killed."

Leticia confirmed this with a nod. She said brightly, "I t'eenk he save my life." Then she studied his swollen face again, and laughed. "Normal, he ees handsome, or no?"

"Normal, he..." Brian didn't know what to say. "He's not normal. Look, John..."

"I mean, can it happen just like that?"

"Can what happen?"

"Listen, man, galaxies collided."

Brian wanted to believe Brovak was ill. Sunstroke? Bee venom — they say it can make people hallucinate. How would he ward off Leticia's future defilement by Carl (The Animal) Hlinka? He felt powerless in the face of their electric emanations.

Brovak drew Leticia closer. "I'm going to Mass with her Sunday."

"Mass? *You*?"

"Yeah, I found God. He sent His most beautiful angel to save me from a life of dissolution."

Brian saw Señora Róbelo doing the dishes in the other room. Smiling, apparently *happy* to see her daughter in the arms of this dangerous man. And the kids who surrounded him seemed to think he was a stitch.

"You're whacked out of your mind, Brovak."

More whispers and caresses. Leticia's gentle laughter. Brain looked down upon this scene with a grisly fascination. Had love once again visited Finca Pomeroy in all its abominable glory?

He turned to Francisco, who had been watching all this with wry amusement.

"Frank, you have some leave saved up," Brian said. "Want to come to Vancouver? Your ticket is paid for."

On Wednesday morning, two RCMP officers and a dog were called out to the Sturgeon River Bible Camp in the eastern Fraser Valley to investigate a report of a man seen bolting from the cookhouse with a bowl of potato salad. The camp had opened for the season the previous day, and forty boys and girls were out there during the April school break. Their counsellors were alarmed.

The intruder had been hanging around for a while: a Baptist minister showed the officers broken locks on doors to a dormitory and the cookhouse. One of the bunks had been slept in.

The dog master let the German shepherd sniff for a while at a sock the man had left behind, under his bunk. Then the dog anxiously pulled them over a stretch of lawn and into a grove of cedars. It wasn't long before they found Jack Calico sitting under a hollow beneath the trunk of an ancient tree. He had a blanket, a roll of toilet paper, the empty bowl of potato salad, and nothing else but his clothes, less one sock.

Calico was taken in handcuffs to the camp office. One of the constables ran a make on him, then called C.L.E.U.

"He wants to speak to the minister alone," said the officer.

Lars Nordquist thought that over. "Let him."

The two constables called for backup from their detachment, and waited while Calico, at the far end of the room, continued to speak in a low voice to the clergyman.

It was an hour later that a helicopter with Max and Nordquist and a couple of his senior people fluttered to the ground at the Bible camp amid a crowd of cheering children.

A sergeant from nearby Chilliwack had taken command, and he drew Nordquist and Max aside.

"He's still talking to that preacher," he said. "Kind of broke down a couple of times."

Max thought: how clever of Nordquist to let Calico talk to the minister, who didn't really enjoy any privilege at law; he could be subpoenaed.

Woops, he thought, just a minute now, I'm this guy's *lawyer*. He suddenly realized he was into a shameless conflict of interest. Working for the state, obsessed with these murders of lawyers, he had his roles confused.

Calico looked up with red-rimmed eyes as they entered. "He says I should tell you everything."

Max said: "I'm afraid I can't be your lawyer any more, Jack, but I... well, I have to advise you to say nothing."

Nordquist gave him an annoyed look.

"No," said Calico. "I want to talk." He lowered his head, then looked up at Max. "Mr. Macarthur, you mentioned a reward."

In the windowless dungeons of the CBC building, Max and Nordquist marched to a studio door where a light was flashing. Nordquist knocked, and a harried-looking TV news producer quickly slipped out.

"Nordquist, homicide. We understand Mr. Roger Turnbull is here."

The producer led them into the studio. Turnbull was in front of a painted backdrop of the Vancouver skyline, adjusting his tie and practising smiles for the camera. A makeup artist was applying some final touches of powder.

"We're on air in forty seconds," the producer said in a low voice. "It's going live to the East, so please, *please*, give me a break here, don't — "

Nordquist held up a hand to quieten him. "We'll wait until it's over."

"Bless you." He returned to the set. Nordquist and Max remained out of Turnbull's view, and watched a monitor.

They heard the sound engineer: "Give me a couple of words, Mr. Turnbull."

"I am thankful for whatever small service —"

"Good —"

"I'm doing for my country —"

"Good, that's enough."

"That sound all right?"

"Perfect. Fifteen seconds."

Turnbull hurriedly glanced at some cards, and stuck them in his pocket, then turned on his high beams and directed them toward the camera, live to the East.

The woman interviewing him switched on a manicured smile. "Well, Mr. Turnbull, looks like you're in the news again —"

"Major break in the Executor case, yes. Found the goodies in the Chief Justice's garbage."

"This isn't the first time you've played a prominent role —"

Turnbull eagerly cut her off again. "You're talking about the Milsom case, Monica. Yep, I collared that bloody killer."

"Well, nothing's been finally settled in the courts, but —"

"And I'm going to nab the Executor, too, and I want to say I'm thankful for whatever small service I'm doing for my country."

Max couldn't help smiling: it was classic Turnbull.

Monica's smile had become tight. "This person who called you, did you tape —"

"No, we can't afford all that fancy equipment."

"Could you describe the voice — it was a woman?"

"Definitely. Now, it was deep for a woman, but I'm pretty good at voices. And I want to take this opportunity to plead to her on this great national network: call me, my dear. Please don't be afraid."

"What exactly did she say —"

"Let me add this: if you're out there, young lady, I want to tell you an entire half of the reward is yours. And hopefully all you other good people in TV Land will find it in your hearts to make up the difference by giving to our great crusade to rid our nation of vermin."

Arms were waving anxiously from the control room.

"Thank you, Mr. Turnbull."

"Yes, I…is that it?"

The producer strode up to him. "Thanks, that was great. Now we'll just get you out of this." He unclipped the mike from his suit jacket collar.

Turnbull looked stunned. "I had a little more to say."

The producer urged his guest from the studio, and at the door Turnbull almost stepped on Nordquist's toes. He took the officer's elbow in a friendly grasp.

"And how is the inspector today?"

Nordquist looked down coldly at Turnbull's hand on his arm. "Mr. Turnbull, you're under arrest for the murder of Arthur Besterman."

"I'm sorry?" Turnbull, still with his hand on Nordquist's elbow, looked uncomprehending at him.

Nordquist told him his rights.

Nordquist's ace interrogator couldn't get anything out of Turnbull in the C.L.E.U. interview room: he remained sullen and silent. Nordquist decided to leave him on simmer until Calico was brought in to sign his statement, now typed and ready.

In this statement, Calico alleged Turnbull had disappeared on the evening of Milsom's acquittal last July, still in a fury. Calico, who shared a dorm room with Turnbull, awakened when he returned, though he pretended to remain asleep. Turnbull had blood on his jeans and his brown leather jacket.

The evidence was circumstantial, a bare-bones case. Motive, opportunity, apparent blood, and Turnbull's own lie about having been in the barracks all night.

They hadn't promised Calico anything. Nordquist had considered withdrawing the pimp assault and putting him under witness protection, but in the end Max advised against that. He wasn't as trusting as Nordquist of Calico's vows of repentance.

Turnbull hadn't been told Calico was now on the premises — or even that he'd emerged from hiding. While Nordquist remained closeted with Calico, filling in gaps and crossing t's, Turnbull twice came out to use the phone, and finally turned to Max in exasperation.

"How do I find a lawyer? They're all out of the office or sick."

"There's never one around when you need one, Roger."

For another hour, even after the video camera and the tape machine were removed from the room at his insistence, Turnbull refused to chat with his interrogator about anything more relevant than the pleasant spring weather.

"This guy is physically incapable of keeping his mouth shut," Max told Nordquist. "Let's have a go."

Nordquist dismissed his man and he and Max entered the interrogation room to find Turnbull pacing.

"Have a chair," Nordquist said.

Turnbull looked coldly at them, didn't sit.

"Want a light refreshment, coffee, anything?"

Turnbull shook his head.

"Don't you think you want to tell us your side of the story?"

Turnbull finally spoke. "Who told the other side?"

Max thought: they hadn't got far keeping him in the dark. The time to confront him was now, before he could reflect. Nordquist instinctively knew that, too.

"Jack Calico," he said.

Turnbull didn't seem surprised. "And what did he have to say for himself?"

Nordquist quietly related the allegations by Calico.

"That's it?" Turnbull said.

"Okay, I've been fair. Now it's your turn."

Turnbull took a chair, straddled it backwards, and for a long time pondered a desk calendar in front of him, as if trying to figure out why this was such a bad day in his life.

Then he made what Max thought was one of his more stagey speeches: "I'm just thunderstruck. I protect him and he turns on me like a snake. He told the story backwards, fellas. *I* woke up in the dorm when *he* came back from killing Besterman. *I* saw blood on *his* clothes that night. Splashed all over his shirt front. I was horrified…horrified. Why oh why did I agree to protect him? This is my reward."

"I wonder if you'd care to run that by me again, Roger," said Nordquist.

"You heard all I have to say."

After a few desultory attempts to get Turnbull to open up again, they returned to the coffee room, where Calico was being pampered with soft drinks and cinnamon rolls. When he learned of his mentor's accusations, he fell into an ill humour such as Max had never seen overcome this firm believer. He ranted. He wept. He blasphemed.

"After Milsom's trial ended, Roger said he was going to get that bleeping lawyer, that's what he said. Only he used another word, not bleeping. And then the next morning he told everyone in the barracks to say he'd been there all night in case the cops came. But I was the only one seen him come back that night, the others were asleep. He had blood all over him, on his hands. He had a shower first thing, and I saw him burn them clothes in the oil barrel out back."

After being confronted with this, Turnbull again took some time to think.

"It's b.s., if you'll pardon my French. Can he come up with one witness? Don't let yourselves be taken in by that dim-witted back-slider. I've *never* raised a finger in anger to anyone, and God's my witness. Now, this is becoming a joke. I've got nothing more to say." But after a further pause, he added: "He must've used a baseball bat on Besterman, he always had one in his car. Little League, with his kids from Sunday school."

"You see any bat that day?" Nordquist asked.

"You have my evidence."

They shuttled back to Calico.

"Well, yeah, I had all sorts of baseball junk, like it was July, but he…he's trying to make stuff up. And, ah, okay, I didn't say this but Roger must've got some blood on his car seat, 'cause I saw him washing it the next morning."

"Anyone else see that?"

"No, sir."

They were about to leave him when he added in a voice so low they almost missed it: "Now I think about it, Turnbull could've killed them three girls, too."

"Why, Jack?" said Max.

"Because he went off somewhere each of them nights. By hisself."

"Anything else? Blood, a knife?"

"Well, um, I can't remember nothing like that."

En route to the interrogation room again, Nordquist said: "That opens it up."

"Let's keep feeding Roger," said Max.

Turnbull's display of disbelief at Calico's latest accusation was worthy, Max decided, of an Oscar.

"Those young girls? How dare he! He's desperate, now he's expanding the field. It's obvious what he's doing."

"Appreciate it if you'd tell us about this change purse thing, Roger," said Nordquist.

Again Turnbull thought awhile. "I have nothing to add until I see a lawyer. I have witnesses for each of the evenings those poor girls were killed. Ask my people."

Nordquist had remained in contact with officers taking statements at the Angels' barracks. Alibis for both Turnbull and Calico were starting to leak; some White Angels had become disillusioned with their leaders.

As Max had surmised, Turnbull seemed incapable of holding his own counsel — though his evidence came reluctantly, quick sound bites between many thoughtful pauses. He and Nordquist continued to whipsaw the two suspects, who in turn kept trying to build the case against each other. But as the day wore on Max realized they were beginning to scrape the bottom of the barrel: irrelevant details, uncorroborated. Much useless invective.

One or the other of them, they were satisfied, had surely killed Besterman — but what about the murders of the other lawyers?

"I wouldn't put it past poor Jack to have killed them," said Turnbull. "But that's all I'm going to say."

"Now I think about it," said Calico, "maybe he wasn't in the barracks any of them times a lawyer got killed."

Max didn't like this "now I think about it" business. Calico seemed too anxious to please, to agree with anything that would guard his ass and expose Turnbull's.

By afternoon, Calico seemed to become more downcast, sensing he was losing to the quicker-witted Turnbull. Nordquist and Max couldn't find many holes in either story, or ways to confirm them.

"Maybe each of them is telling half the truth," Nordquist said. "Maybe they killed Besterman together. And everyone else to boot. So we charge them both. Let a jury sort it out."

Max wondered: what would be the result of that? Could Turnbull blow enough smoke to win an acquittal?

37

The Case
of the Red-faced Cormorant ·

Wentworth Chance stayed on in Weeping Willow River in a state of near-panic: Caroline had been amiable, even spirited, when he had first come calling. But she'd become a seething cauldron of mute anger shortly after he'd brought her that cassette player.

There was an awful scene in court when he tried to appear for her. "You get back and look after the bloody owls!" she had shouted, a remark which seemed to make the judge confused. The other fourteen protesters had joined her in denouncing the conditional offer of bail, and Terrance had made a speech about the civil rights of trees. They would sign no peace bonds forbidding their return to the Nahanee.

Wentworth called Max for help, and was told it was on its way. Abigail Hitchins would make Caroline see reason.

On Wednesday morning, when Abigail came into the interview room, Caroline remained seated with her arms folded, her face black, her eyes a green blaze. Abigail was about to kiss her, hug her, but reacted uncertainly, and merely took her hand. Caroline withdrew it.

"This is ridiculous, Caroline. They *want* to give you bail. All you have to say is you won't go back out there."

Caroline could have been looking at someone's unrecycled waste. "What are you doing here?"

"Representing you. I'm not going to leave you at the mercy of that confused pubescent out there — imagine your husband's office sending the student. The trial will take *months* to get off the ground. Or if you want, I'll plead you guilty, and you can get a slap on the rump and go home."

Caroline slowly got to her feet.

"You sneaking, double-timing, two-faced cheap whore, you snake, you slut…"

Wentworth could hear the tirade from the RCMP offices, where he was awaiting the result of Abigail's promised reasoned approach to this stubborn client. Through the next few minutes, until the sergeant went to Abigail's rescue, Wentworth heard a thesaurus of uncivil words. Abigail was finally led out white and shaking.

She walked past Wentworth without looking at him, proceeded outside to her rented car, and sent the gravel flying as she gunned it.

Wentworth stayed on fretfully in Weeping Willow River, torn between his duty to Caroline and his duty to her owls. He was in court Thursday when she and her comrades were trooped in from the lockup. The judge said he wasn't pleased to see them.

"I told you all you could go. This jail does not have the facility to keep you, nor the manpower because of all the kerfuffle with this Executor. Now get smart, sign the papers, and trot off to your comfortable Yuppie homes in Vancouver."

"We will not sign peace bonds when we are at war," said Terrance.

"Mrs. Pomeroy," said the judge, "I know your husband. What does he think of this?"

"He can go screw himself," Caroline said.

Brian Pomeroy walked into court as if on cue, legs striding, long hair flapping. He'd shaved his beard, but was still in jeans.

"Appearing for the defendant Pomeroy," he said.

Caroline seemed to take a moment to recognize him. "Oh, no, you aren't."

Brian looked at her, shocked at this response. "Yes, I *am*."

"Just a minute," said the judge, but Brian interrupted him.

"I'm acting for her if she likes it or not. And for everyone else — "

"You're not saying a word for me!" Caroline shouted.

"Madam," said the judge, "calm down. Mr. Pomeroy, I'll hear you as a friend of the court."

"Just release them on their promise to appear, your honour. So what if they go back to the Nahanee? It's the end of the world? There are another twenty people out there today anyway."

"Madam prosecutor?" said the judge.

"I'm about ready to go along with anything."

"Well, you folks want to be martyrs, and I won't let you," said the judge. "Okay, everyone can go on their promise to appear here in two weeks. I'm adjourning this court."

Brian grabbed the prosecutor before she could leave the room. "What's this assaulting a policeman? She assaulted a *cap*, not a cop. Drop the charge, let's get real."

"If it'll help save your marriage..." She shrugged. "I think you're deep in doodoo, Mr. Pomeroy."

He turned to Wentworth. "What's *eating* Caroline?" he said. "She's still *that* pissed off at me?"

"Apparently something to do with Abigail Hitchins, a tape you sent..."

Brian blew air out slowly as he watched the prisoners being released, and said in a soft, tortured voice: "Okay, mother-sticker, this is a fuck-up."

Francisco Sierra had felt awkward about accepting Brian's gift of a passage to Canada, fearing he would be in the way: the Pomeroys had problems to work out. But Brian — before retrieving his car and racing off to defend his wife — had arranged suitable accommodation away from the scene of any marital carnage, the comfortable guest room in the home of Max and Ruth Macarthur.

Francisco had a week of unspent holidays saved up, so he'd jumped at the chance to journey to Vancouver, where foul murder haunts the streets. Also, he had always wanted to see the snow: the far north, the land of the reindeer and the polar bear. All his life he had wanted to jump into a big pile of snow, a snowdrift they called them. He had never seen the real thing.

He had brought his camera, thinking he would bring home pictures of a winter wonderland, but alas: green grass where snow should have lain. The city was tidy beyond belief, and seemed to move at a hectic pace. Laid back, Brian had described Vancouver. Maybe Francisco didn't understand this term laid back.

Yesterday, Max Macarthur had driven him to the various sites of the assassinations. Francisco liked this brisk, amiable lawyer, who in turn seemed to enjoy the company of the courtly, rotund Latin gentleman, with his understated sense of humour. Touring about with Max, he felt like a...kickback? Sidekick, that was the word. Constable Marchmont to his Inspector Grodgins. Watson to his Holmes.

How Francisco longed to return to the fray. Stuck down there in Puerto Próspero, jailing drunken gold miners instead of international jewel thieves, with another fifteen years before that paltry pension kicked in, how he hungered for the tasty meat of a great crime to be solved. As a career move it had been a mistake to investigate that oily vendor of favours, the aide to the Minister of Security: Francisco had sniffed too closely at the Minister himself, and the perdition of Puerto Próspero was his reward. But one has to live with one's choices.

After a sumptuous repast and some hide and seek with the playful twins, he and his hosts had gabbed late into the night about the challenging case that was so dear to Francisco's heart.

Matters were rushing to a quick conclusion, Francisco realized: all that evidence found in the garbage can behind house of Max's father, the judge. How odd. And the Besterman issue was now resolved — apparently — with both Turnbull and Calico charged with his murder. Take your pick. Max believed the two men were behind the other murders, too. But Francisco wasn't sure about the Turnbull-Calico theory. Too pat.

Cudlipp? He was still — what was the saying? On the lam. He was the only member of this cast of desperados Francisco had met. A twisted policeman...no, the expression was different: bent. Was he in league with someone? Perhaps on hire. And what about this Joe Ruff fellow? And that police assassin, Hughie Lupo...

He would have bet his last *centimo* the murders were linked by a common motive. The police had hired psychics and soothsayers. They should hire *him*. The Hercule Poirot of Costa Rica.

✢ ✢ ✢

Brian had rescued Caroline from prison; he had saved her from a criminal record; he had freed the Nahanee Fifteen; the valley was still closed to logging. Damn it, he had done great things within the day. Not a whisper of gratitude from his reluctant kidnappee.

Though Caroline hadn't jumped from the Honda, her face remained set in a mask of relentless disapproval as she journeyed toward the sea with her abductor. She had offered few words along the way: "This isn't the way to Vancouver." "I don't know where you think you're taking me." "Watch the road."

Brian had decided upon a romantic setting: what could be more pacifying to the bruised heart than the vastness of the Pacific itself? The slush of waves beneath bare feet, mists pouring across the distant breaking rollers, the tortured beauty of windswept pines upon the rocky capes of Barkley Sound.

Here, near the town of Bamfield, the hills of Vancouver Island rose from the sea, and one could sense infinity beyond the curve of the earth. Here, Brian would argue the cause of the most difficult client he'd ever defended, himself. Here he would woo his wife and attempt to steal back her heart.

He stopped at a store, then negotiated the rental of an isolated cabin on the beach: cozy, with a fireplace and a balcony, cedar shakes weathered to the colour of silver. She refused to budge from the car, and Brian just carried on, gathering wood, starting a fire, sprinkling almonds on a pan-fried sole, and keeping the cabin door open in mute invitation to his wife. He had left the keys in the ignition; she could escape any time. But Brian heard no sound of engine.

As he sank a bottle of Chardonnay into a sink filled with ice cubes, she came to the door.

"Where are my bags?"

Brian felt his hopes wither.

She went to her rucksack, which he had placed just inside the door, and pulled out her binoculars and her Leica. "Probably only a Double-crested," she said.

He followed her to the door, and watched her clamber over the driftwood logs to the beach where, on a reef, perched a cormorant, drying its feathers, wings spread scarecrow-like, its long neck bowed. He watched Caroline line the bird up with her telephoto lens, and was surprised to see her take at least six shots. Finally, the bird wheeled into the air. Caroline watched it skim off across the bay, then turned and walked toward the cabin.

She sat on the steps and took her shoes off, and emptied them of sand.

"I don't think one's ever been sighted this far from the Aleutians."

"One what?"

"Red-faced Cormorant."

In the cabin, she replaced her camera and brought out her old copy of *Birds of Canada*, and studied it. "Yep. Too bad you didn't bring your camera."

She still wouldn't look at him, but scrutinized the simmering lemon sole on the propane stove, the artichoke salad, the bottle of wine. Then she quietly unpacked her bags. "You want the cot out here — or the bedroom?"

Brian took her bags into the bedroom. He took a deep breath and returned. "Caroline, I'd like to start again. No lies."

"Maybe I'd rather have the lies. The truth stinks."

He saw she was waiting for a response. He had vowed not to argue with her.

"Abigail told me you came on to her in Costa Rica," she said.

"She was just yanking you, for God's sake. I almost had to beat her off with a stick. And what about this Terrance she said you were schmoozing around with?"

"She said I was…how could you have been such a fool ever to get involved with that rattlesnake?"

"Judge thyself. You haven't figured her out, have you? She's probably *bi*, for Christ's sake. Hot for you."

"Oh, bullshit."

"Well, she was definitely using you to get at me." *Don't argue.* "Caroline, give me credit. Drunk or not I had the guts to bare everything." He realized, too late, that was an inappropriate verb. But the effect on Caroline was to produce a smile — a wry smile, to be sure, but the first he had seen all day.

"I suspect you had second thoughts about that tape."

"No way." He paused. "Okay, maybe a little third or fourth thought."

"No more lies, Brian."

"No more lies. And nothing like that will ever happen again. I swear." He spoke fiercely now: "Caroline, I love you deeply and without reservation. I want back in your life, and I want to raise a family."

Caroline looked at him sadly, and for a long while said nothing. "I can't have a family. I'm sterile, Brian."

Donnie Brown ultimately wasn't able to live with his secret and during a break between classes on Friday, April 23, he timidly entered the counsellor's office at the Knot Lake Secondary School.

Head bowed and staring down at his runners, he said: "I helped almost kill that lawyer at the lookout last December."

"What lawyer?"

"Um...I think his name is Mr. Pomeroy. Anyway, I was wondering...if you could break it to my dad."

His dad was a corporal in the RCMP detachment.

"I'm not the Executor, and neither is Punky Wilwich."

Donnie Brown and Punky Wilwich were both sixteen years old, and the counsellor knew them to be good boys, not difficult, though still partaking in the adolescent rites of mischief.

"'Cause of it, I can't sleep."

The counsellor put an arm around the anxious boy. Corporal Brown was a tough old soldier. This wasn't going to be easy.

"What happened?"

Donnie took a deep breath. "Well, we had the old Dodge that Punky's father lets him use, and Mr. Wilwich's hunting rifle was in the trunk, and it was just after school...um, and we had a couple of beers, maybe, each, and we went out to cruise around, not planning anything. And there was this car at the lookout, and a guy and a girl were kissing, and it looked like she was going down on him. It was a joke, Punky was gonna fire in the air as we were driving off, but I kind of jostled his arm."

The counsellor phoned Corporal Brown, who angrily sped up to the school and arrested his son.

Though the morning was bright, the lazy northern sun seemed to put little effort into the task of warming Francisco's body. Yet people were walking the streets in T-shirts, in *shorts*, barely dressed. Such hardiness.

Max led him up Water Street, past a steam clock which hooted the time and sang a tune. Francisco stopped to take a picture. A vista opened of a cruise ship beside a strange building with sails on it. Francisco stopped to take a picture.

"We shouldn't dawdle, Frank."

Always in a hurry, these Canadians. In Costa Rica, *mañana* is the busiest day of the year. Here there is no *mañana*. He decided it must be the weather. Canadians had to hurry up to stay warm.

He could see the snow-capped mountains across the inlet. There would be people up there with skis and dog sleds. He would like to throw a snowball. Icicles, that is something else he yearned to see. And the utter perfection of a single snowflake.

They walked by several large banks — how odd, they didn't have any lineups. He stopped to take a picture. No sign of the Executor stalking these clean streets.

Max took him into one of the tall, menacing towers of the downtown area and up a swift elevator. Here, in the C.L.E.U. offices, they were met by a doleful-looking man introduced to him as Inspector Nordquist.

Francisco looked around: computers, laser machines, printers spewing out graphs, high technology.

"Ever see one of these, captain?" Nordquist showed him a printout, a parade of little gray ovals. "DNA print. This one's from a specimen of Olive Klymchuk's blood."

"Ah, yes, I have read about this new science. As good as fingerprints."

"Useful in case we find any bloodied clothing in possession of one of our suspects."

"A wonderful…how do you say, innovation in the art of detection." What happened to old-fashioned foot-slogging and brain sweat, Francisco wondered. Hercule Poirot never had to employ such tools.

"Been able to loosen Turnbull up any more?" Max asked.

Nordquist shook his head. "He has a pretty good lawyer now. A.R. Beauchamp."

"When he's off the sauce, he's the best lawyer in the world."

"So I don't think it'll be easy to make him on these other murders. Unless we do a deal with Calico. But *he's* not talking any more either. Beauchamp got *him* a lawyer. Always lawyers getting in the way, eh, captain?"

"Always, inspector. But everyone is certain this Roger Turnbull is the Executor?"

"Frank has some doubts," Max said.

"Who do you think it is?" Nordquist asked him.

"One perhaps whom we least suspect."

This wasn't immediately clarified. Nordquist answered the phone — a call from Corporal Brown of the Knot Lake RCMP. Nordquist put it on speaker, and they listened to the officer's painful recounting of his son's misdoings last December.

"The other boy has confirmed this?" Nordquist asked.

"Yes, sir. They are both in custody. Charged with reckless use of a firearm."

"I'm sorry about your son, corporal, but don't you think you should take him home? They're both juveniles, no one's going to give them jail terms."

"Thank you, sir."

After hanging up, he said: "Well, well. Looks like we can close one more file. Simplifies things."

"But there is one complication," said Francisco.

"What's that?" Max was still digesting the call from Knot Lake, wasn't focusing.

"The first letter which the Executor mailed."

Francisco drew his attention to a blown-up reproduction on the wall. "Here under where it says 'Criminal lawyers are marked for death,' we observe three names: Besterman, Pomeroy and Brovak. The Executor for some reason sought to take credit for the attempt on Brian's life."

"Right," said Max. "Well, obviously Turnbull did it to move us off track."

"Turnbull, perhaps," said Francisco. "Or someone else with a motive for this false claim. We must seek that motive." *We* must seek that motive. How insolent of him. He was an outsider, he must be careful not to cause ill feelings.

"You have a theory?" Nordquist asked.

"Olive Klymchuk was murdered in Victoria at about four a.m. on a Friday. Martin Wessel was poisoned in Vancouver several hours earlier. Is it easy to move so quickly between these cities, one of which is on an island? And enter the Topaz Hotel without being seen? Clearly, we seek…you seek two murderers, one who enjoys violence, the other, subtler means. The mastermind and the henchman. There is one person who has not been much discussed. A judge named Leroy Lukey."

Nordquist turned his doleful eyes to Francisco, and raised one quizzical eyebrow. "Lukey? Where do you come up with that?"

Francisco shrugged, looked a little embarrassed. "A literary hunch. I understand this Judge Lukey is a frustrated, angry man, whose career is in ruins. Who does he blame for this?"

"John Brovak," Max said.

"In part, but also your father, no? A powerful man who seeks to have Lukey dismissed from his high office."

Francisco saw — as they say in novels — the lights go on in Max's eyes.

"He lives just down the street from Dad. He knew my father was on the short list for the Supreme Court. And is this your theory? — he kind of…dropped that pile of shit in his back yard to embarrass him, maybe to tilt the scales against him."

"And is not Lukey associated with one of the other suspects?" Francisco said. "He and Everit Cudlipp are ace buddies, no? The mastermind and the henchman slaking their anger at the system by killing its practisers…practitioners. And perhaps this officer hides at the house of Judge Lukey. You might, ah, wish to look into that."

38

The Satanic
Key

Nordquist knew an undercover van in front of Lukey's house would immediately be spotted by Cudlipp — if he was there — so he sent a woman into the neighbourhood with a petition to preserve the Stanley Park Zoo.

As this detective was getting short shrift from some animal rights people residing across the street from Lukey's house, she saw a young woman walk from it and turn down the sidewalk. The undercover officer stayed a distance behind her until the young woman entered a variety store on Granville Street.

The description the officer later gave Nordquist matched that of Rosie Finch.

Nordquist decided he shouldn't bell the cat just yet. He hadn't much admissible evidence against Cudlipp, even upon a charge of accepting corrupt favours. Why was Francisco Sierra so drawn toward this theory that Lukey and Cudlipp were the perps they sought? A literary hunch, Captain Sierra had said. Whatever that meant.

Wentworth Chance could see the big, sombre eyes of the owl nestlings staring back at him from the door of their birdhouse. From the nearby perch, Olga scolded and whistled at Howland, who was gulping his food, chicken innards. Olga wasn't into the dead stuff like her lazy husband — she liked to hunt the varmints Wentworth attracted by scattering bran flakes about the back yard.

Wentworth had formed a bond with these owls, would miss them when Caroline returned, with or without Brian, from wherever they'd gone. No calls from either of them. Wentworth had his orders: he was the owlkeeper, and must continue to live here until the regular shift arrived.

And after? Well, there was Brovak's pad again for a few days maybe. Who knows, maybe the great Brovo would never come back from Costa Rica. "He saw the green flash," Brian had grumpily advised. This seemed an enigmatic metaphor for love. Brovak? Love? No one was safe.

Vajeeta had also offered to put him up. But she was getting spookier all the time, had taken up witchery, was reading a book about black magic: *The Craft*. A pentangle, a five-pointed star, hung on a chain in the deep, sweet cleft between her breasts. She was given to dusting her face with white powder and painting her lips and nails a brilliant crimson. She talked about starting a coven. "It would be a gas. You can be a witch, too."

This transformation had occurred immediately upon the finishing of her novel. She had sent it off to a publisher in Toronto, was sure it was going to be a worldwide success.

Wentworth went back into the house to wash his hands. Vajeeta was at the kitchen table, totally absorbed in the newspaper: the story of the two teen-aged boys who had admitted to their dangerous practical joke in Knot Lake. Wentworth couldn't understand why Vajeeta was poring so industriously over it — she'd read it ten times at least.

Accompanying the article was a picture of Brian Pomeroy — an old file shot, Brian speaking to the Sierra Club. And beneath that, a sidebar — Brian's surprise appearance in Weeping Willow River to defend his wife.

"I'd like some scissors," Vajeeta said. Her lips licked flames at him from a ghost-like face.

"Vajeeta, I think we should get you home."

"Tonight I stay."

"The Pomeroys could return any time."

"I want to meet them."

She spent much of that evening staring out a window at the owls. "They foretell death," she said. "Couriers of Lillith, goddess of death. It's in this book."

She continued to study her text, *The Craft*, and kept Wentworth up late practising chants: "Gorgo, Mormo, gods of the darkened way, hear me."

In bed that night she took the pentangle from around her neck and hung it over his erect penis. "This becomes the Satanic key, it unlocks evil. Enter me."

On Saturday morning a weary Wentworth rose without waking his lustful sorceress — he assumed she would ultimately make her own way home, by broom if necessary. He arrived at the office late, surprised to see that the waiting room was full: four squirming, busy children and an older, smiling woman nursing a baby with a bottle. All dressed up as if they were going to church. Whose clients were these? Some convoluted family law problem he feared would be dumped on him. Joe Ruff was there, too, without appointment.

Wentworth had been engaging in orgiastic Satanic rites when he should have been preparing for Monday: the hearing to ban Ruff forever from the courtrooms of British Columbia.

Evidence had newly come to light that thrust Ruff more squarely under the spotlight of suspicion. Fifteen years ago he had been bounced from UBC law school after failing to pass first year on a second try. Letters from Ruff had been found on file there, paranoid rambles about a "cabal" of lawyers conspiring to deny him entry into their holy ranks. Ruff was nuttier than a filbert, but somehow…sly. The police were now working on a theory that two killers were at large. Was Ruff the brains? And his accomplice that young ape with the deadened eyes, his so-called client?

"Ah, Wentworth, just dropped by to ask about the Attorney General versus me. We are scheduled to don battle garb on Monday, what?"

"Um, yes. But I think our best strategy is to adjourn it one more time."

"Delay is the game, yes, brilliant, excellent. We'll make the rotters pay roundly for this one, what?"

"Sure. Um, Joe, that client who came to see you when I was at your house. Odd-looking, ah, chap…"

"Curtis?" Ruff tapped a finger at his temple. "Not all there, old boy, not all there. I render him professional services. Valued client, many years."

Not all there. Wentworth would follow this up.

Ruff trotted out the door, and Wentworth went to the coffee room to fuel up for the day. There he was startled to see John Brovak, who had once again shown up unexpectedly, this time entertaining a perky, dark-skinned young woman.

"Kid, I want you to meet my fiancée, Leticia."

Leticia stuck out her hand. "*Mucho gusto*, keed."

"Um, yeah," said Wentworth. "*Mucho gusto* to you, too."

"I been up all night arguing with some shitsticks...excuse, some jerks from Immigration who don't know doodley-whoop about the law...Never mind. Those are just a fraction of the kids out there, by the way, Señora Róbelo's two youngest plus her dear departed sister's three little ones; the bigger kids stayed home to watch the farm."

Max came in to refill his cup, staring in wonderment at Brovak and Leticia, still hand in hand.

"Never thought he was capable of loving anything," he mumbled to Wentworth. "Except his dick."

Leticia, who had good ears, was perplexed. "Who is thees deek?"

Max went red. "Uh, oh, a joke. I meant he's in love with, um, what he sees in the mirror."

Leticia laughed. "Ah, *claro*. I 'ave to compete with hees deek."

Wentworth barely suppressed a guffaw, and Max nervously cut the conversation short. "Can you guys join us?"

Brovak, scowling at Max, pulled himself away from Leticia and he and Wentworth followed Max to the library where sat a solemn Francisco Sierra.

"We found out where Cudlipp's hiding," Max said. "At Leroy Lukey's house. His buttercup is there, too."

Brovak slapped his forehead. "Why didn't *I* think of that? When I said Lukey, everyone scoffed. Lukey and Cudlipp, I said, working in tandem to get back at the system that fucked them. What a dumb idea, everyone said. So what's the next step? How do we infiltrate this circle jerk? Tell me how this development came about."

"Frank had a flash about Lukey," Max said.

"Finally a comrade," said Brovak. "I was getting lonely."

"It seems unlikely they were working alone," Francisco said. "We thought you could help us locate a third party."

"We've been doing some heavy thinking," Max said. "Frank and I."

"Yeah, well, keep me in the dark."

"How close can you get to Tony d'Anglio?"

"Why?"

"Hoping he can give us a tip."

"Tony is not a rat and he doesn't really dig those who are."

"Are there not ways he can be persuaded?" Francisco said.

"Yeah, we could kidnap his mother and shove splints up her fingernails. Listen, you guys are asking the impossi..." He stopped in mid-stream. "What's today? Saturday, right? Sports action weekend."

It was a misty, moody evening when Brian and Caroline returned to their home in North Vancouver. The mountains still shone brightly in the dying sun, but fingers of fog were slipping through their lower slopes, curling around the trees and hedges, hiding the neighbours' houses.

Brian's heart was pounding with hope. Let's give it a try, she had said. This morning, while standing on the beach, she had let him take her hand. He had felt as if he were on his first real date, nervous, thrilled, wondering what the next step was, how does one steal a kiss?

"Okay," she said. "A life of unparalleled domestic bliss begins. It had better not be *too* boring."

Brian could see a dim yellow glow through the living room window, and wondered what its source was. Then when he unlocked the front door he caught a whiff of incense, pungent, unpleasant. As he held the door open for Caroline, he heard a woman's chanting voice, a voice he recognized, a voice that sent the fear of the Lord through him: "Belial, Moloch, Mammon, Beelzebub — come, you princes of hell."

"My God, who are you?" Caroline said, standing at the living room door. "And *what* are you doing?"

"I am summoning the dark spirits," said Charity Slough.

Brian was in shell shock as he stared at her: in the middle of the room, kneeling before two burning black candles dripping wax onto the glass-topped table, squinting at a book, apparently trying to follow its instructions.

"They don't want to come, I guess," she said, standing, turning to them. "But *you're* here. Hello, lovely people."

"You are…Wentworth's friend?" Caroline cast at Brian what she intended as a look of shared puzzlement. She saw he was pale, his mouth working, like a fish out of water.

"You must be Caroline," said Charity.

Caroline forced a smile. "Yes — and this is Brian."

"We've met," Charity said.

"You have?" Caroline looked at her husband, immobile, an ice sculpture. "Are you ill or something?"

"No, I…no."

"But we met in a different world," said Charity.

Caroline was lost. "A different…"

"A world of dreams." She added brightly: "We all inhabit different worlds?"

"Yes, of course," said Caroline. "I'm not sure which one we're in right now, frankly. It's…Vageena, isn't it?"

"Vajeeta. But that was a different me. I am now another."

"And who are you now?" Caroline asked.

"My name is Lillith."

"Good," said Caroline. "Well, ah, would you like a drink?" Under her voice, to Brian: "We don't have any blood, do we?"

"Are you happy together?" Lillith asked.

"Delirious," said Caroline.

"I can tell." She knelt and extinguished the incense and blew out the candles. "Poof. Out, out, brief candle. That's from Shakespeare?"

"'Life's but a walking shadow,'" said Caroline.

"Isn't it, though?" said Lillith as she began putting her spirit-summoning equipment into her shoulder bag. "I must go."

"Yes, well, maybe Brian can give you a lift."

"No. You must be alone. Together. Forever."

They watched her float past them and out the door.

"My God," said Caroline. "Have you ever encountered anything like that?"

No lies, Brian told himself. "No, never."

39

Cereal
Killer

The chaplain of the Winnipeg Salvation Army wondered how long a sermon he could get away with this morning. Last Sunday there had been mutterings among the destitute: he had harried them with so many godly injunctions that their porridge had gotten cold. Fifteen minutes wouldn't kill them, he decided.

He watched his volunteers ladeling steaming oatmeal into the latecomers' bowls. These, the tardy ones, tended to reek of last night's drink, but he had a fairly good house today. There was hope for that big, bearded fellow sitting over there, not touching spoon to bowl, patiently awaiting the sermon. Always attentive to the word. He had been coming in regularly for the last two weeks. From Vancouver, someone said.

The chaplain stopped at his table and said: "Done your good deed for today?"

"No, but I want to," said O.D. Milsom.

"Been looking for work?"

"No one will hire me."

"Oh, come now."

"They would if they knew I was famous."

"Famous?" The chaplain sighed. This gentleman, alas, was minus a gear or two. "And what great deed have you done?"

Milsom leaned to the chaplain's ear. "I killed them lawyers in Vancouver."

When Brovak began to explain to Señora Róbelo how to use the washing machine, he realized he wasn't sure what button did what. He always had a hired woman come in. Anyway, he said, a door-to-door diaper service was available. This was beyond Señora Róbelo's comprehension; she laughed at the absurdity of it.

Electric stove, dishwasher, coffee maker — she was determined to master all these things. Brovak had an urgent date with Tony d'Anglio on this Sunday morning, so he called the Pomeroys. Brian said he and Caroline would drive over and help integrate Brovak's new family into the ways of the mechanized world.

"So how's your sex life?" Brovak asked.

"Working on it."

"I guess you heard it wasn't the Executor who tried to shove you."

"Yeah, disappointing."

"You been filled in?"

"Wentworth came by."

"Okay, I'm gonna see if I can smoke d'Anglio out according to plan. Where we meeting tonight?"

"Max says the office."

"Naw, tell him Russell's. He's got a heated pool, a billiard table, and probably a case of Glenlivet behind the bar. I want to show Leticia what it's like to be really poor."

Though the day promised to be warm, the mists of the early morning had not lifted. Leticia's tropical wardrobe offered her little protection, so Brovak put her into his wine cardigan, which hung to her knees like a dress. With the sleeves rolled up, she looked okay in it, he thought, actually a little smart. Tomorrow, a shopping spree.

In the Mercedes, she held her breath as he sped over the suspension bridge and into skyscraper city. He reached for her hand and she flashed a smile. He felt that odd sensation again: the body dissolving, limbs becoming rubber.

He found a place behind one of the delivery vans in back of Eat-a-Pizza-Pie. This was one of d'Anglio's more upright businesses — though the vans couriered as much lettuce as pizza. The capo was in the betting shop in the back, and several of his scruffier-looking goombahs were lounging about.

Charlie the Chunk, one of Russell's biggest and ugliest hoods, looked at Leticia with pupils that seemed like pinpricks. Cocaine eyes, thought Brovak.

"Chewy," the Chunk drawled. "Table grade."

D'Anglio was old-country courteous, though, and kissed Leticia's hand.

"Nice. Nice. My new mouth has a taste for the finest and I'm not talking just cigars. Why I called you, one of my drivers got pulled over on a speeding beef. Traffic dick found a roll in her purse could sink a ship, three hundred thousand slabs and change. My whole weekend action."

Brovak looked at him with an expression of serene innocence. He had been calmly waiting for d'Anglio's call.

"This party got busted happens to be my niece-in-law, and without a lawyer she won't be able to find words to express how she came by this sum. I'd appreciate if you'd speak to the cops before they steal it all."

"Let's take a walk about it," Brovak said.

D'Anglio said he was sorry, but he'd prefer if Leticia didn't accompany them. "Cut her a hot slice," he told one of the friends, and escorted Brovak out and into the vacant lot next door.

"The smoking room," said d'Anglio, offering Brovak a cigar. "Some of the guys complain. Not loud, you understand."

Brovak bit off the end, and spat it against the brick wall. "Tony, let's say I do get your swag back — it's not going to be easy, but let's say I do-"

D'Anglio cut in. "Your hog is twenty per cent. These are the winnings and losings of some honest citizens of Vancouver, John, most of it ain't really mine. But I'll have to make up."

"Assuming I pull off this feat, Tony, I have to ask you: can you do me a favour? And I won't charge you a cent."

"If it's in the realm of human possibility, John, I will do you this favour. Who is the unfortunate bastard?"

"I just want information."

"Now that is a thing I maybe ain't able to do. There is a tradition of silence. *Omerta.*"

"This is about the guy who's zapping the lawyers, Tony. He killed two of your eagles. *I* was a target. How does a businessman make an honest living without a lawyer?"

"Okay, I am in sympathy about this Executor thing. I'll listen but I won't commit. What's the requested information?"

"What do you know about Hughie Lupo?"

D'Anglio hadn't lit his cigar yet. He rolled it between his fingers contemplatively.

"Come on, Tony, this is beyond *omerta*." Brovak struck a wooden match on the brick wall and held it for d'Anglio. "Hughie Lupo. He killed two federales in Philadelphia. Fifteen years ago. Changed his i.d. The FBI want to piss in his grave. If he turns out to be the Executor, I'll join them."

D'Anglio pondered. Finally: "As I think about this, I am thinking maybe there are two kinds of *omerta*, there is big *omerta* and little *omerta*. Big *omerta* is the vow. Little *omerta* is the stuff you overhear, matters that can be shared in comfort with one's good friend and lawyer. Also, it would be nice to have the three hundred dimes back. Not to mention the niece-in-law who I'd like to see her butt kicked around the block."

"I can maybe work a deal, Tony. Give me a little teaser, that's all I want."

D'Anglio blew a giant smoke ring, watched it float past Brovak's ear. His decision made, d'Anglio drew closer to him and spoke in a low voice.

"Okay, John, you understand: fifteen years ago I was just a little schmoe in this business, ran a few shops with adult explicit material. But you hear scraps, and it seems that a certain friend to whom an old favour was owed, a Calabrian friend from Cleveland, approached the late chairman of our board, asking could he instill into our local community in a unobtrusive way a fellow citizen of his."

"Hughie Lupo."

"You are not hearing *me* say this name."

"*Capeesh*."

"So you have your teaser."

"One minor little thing more. Is he still in town?"

"You gonna get back my scratch not to mention my niece?"

"You got a lock on it."

"I hear he's in the area. I ain't seen him, but if I did, I don't even know what he looks like. Coulda had a sex change, for all I know."

"Answer me just one little diddly thing extra. Anyone around here know who he is?"

"Eddie Cohn once kinda slipped a hint he knew. But Eddie ain't gonna be much help, is he?"

He blew another ring, looked innocently at a sky from which the last wisps of mist had disappeared. "Looks like it's settlin' in for another gorgeous spell of weather."

"Yeah, it's going to be a righteous day." Brovak dinched his cigar against the wall, two sparking, intersecting strokes, an X.

D'Anglio stayed outside to finish his smoke while Brovak returned to the bookie room. There, he saw Charlie the Chunk kneeling beside Leticia's knees, too close. He was holding a saucer, and had just cut two rails of coke with a razor blade. Leticia was shaking her head timidly.

As the Chunk offered her a straw, Brovak kicked the saucer out of his hands, and it sailed against the wall and smashed.

The Chunk slowly rose from his knees. With one hand, he brushed the cocaine dust from his Harris tweed sports jacket. The other hand held the razor blade between thumb and index finger. He studied Brovak's face with a scowl, as if wondering where to start his cut.

"Keep it in, Charlie," warned Large Harold, d'Anglio's numbers boss. "Don't fuck with Charlie the Chunk, Mr. Brovak."

"I wouldn't dream of it," Brovak said.

As Charlie slowly lowered the razor, Brovak grabbed his wrist and twisted, then threw Charlie head first into the drywall, smashing a skull-sized hole in it. He pulled him back, spun him around, and pinned him by the upper arms to the wall.

"You come near her again with that crap I'll cave your head in."

Charlie only heard this dimly.

Brovak dropped off five fully loaded Eat-a-Pizza pies at the C.L.E.U. offices, where he conferred with Max, Francisco and Nordquist. The inspector called the gambling squad, who released the niece-in-law and the money.

The day was still young. Brovak went off to collect his skis.

"What's next on your agenda, Frank?" Max asked.

"Now I would like to talk to Miss Augustina Sage. I have some confusion about the murder in the Topaz hotel."

"Give him all the help he wants," said Nordquist.

None of his staff knew what Francisco Sierra was doing here. As the detectives did justice to the pizzas, they kept looking oddly at Francisco. It was assumed Bones had brought him in as some kind of foreign expert.

"Anyone heard yet when Milsom's being flown in?" a detective asked.

"Tomorrow morning," said Nordquist.

"So what are we going to do with him?"

"We'll have a psychiatrist look at him," Nordquist said. "I don't think we can hold him forever."

"Hey," said another officer, "he confessed to being the Executor, didn't he?"

"Yeah," someone said, "and he shot President Kennedy, too."

Everyone laughed but Francisco, who was staring from the window at the snow-topped mountains. Max had promised to take him up the Skylift this afternoon. John Brovak had offered him a ski lesson. Snow, glorious snow.

Caroline had a most agreeable time at John Brovak's, playing house with Señora Róbelo and the kids — and with Brian, whom she could see they adored.

They had loaded up at a toy store on the way, and Brian seemed as absorbed in all the squeakies and rollers and pop-ups as the three little wobblers, two of whom were still in diapers. Brian played with the kids while Caroline instructed Señora Róbelo as to the wonders and the workings of the first world.

She was a fast learner, and quickly shooed Caroline from the kitchen and started preparing *arroz con camarones* for everyone.

Caroline walked around picking up — this bachelor palace needed a spring cleaning — then went out to the deck to help Brian direct traffic. He had brought all five kids outside: it was a lovely warm day, a day that swept the mind clean like a broom, brushed away memories of the winter blahs: her own, inner spring cleaning.

Last night, after that creature from the netherworld left —

Vajeeta, now Lillith — Brian hadn't been able to relax. He said he had a queasy stomach. "Must be the water," he told her. "I'm not used to the chemicals."

She had taken him to the back yard to introduce him to Olga and the triplets, and that had repaired his spirits. Then he began one of his favourite rhetorical conversations with Howland:

"Whodunit, Howland?"

"Hoo."

"Hoo who?"

Howland had just crooned evasively.

They hadn't made love last night. She was willing, but sensed he was scared, not ready.

Tonight? But he has a meeting with his partners, and God knows how long that will last.

Caroline knelt and handed six-year-old Gabriela the ragamuffin doll she had dropped. Shyly, wordlessly, she accepted it.

Brian squatted between them. "*Gabriela, dice a Carolina: gracias, Señora.* In English. Come on, you remember."

"Goo mor-ning, Señora Carolina."

"Goo mor-ning," echoed the three-year-old, a winsome boy with big, knowing eyes.

Very sly of Brian, she thought, to tell Brovak to bring up the three motherless kids. He'd known all along she couldn't have children. Abigail had told him, he'd admitted that.

We will bring them up bilingually, Caroline decided. And she must teach them French, too, if they're going to be Canadian. Brian's Spanish was pretty good but *she* had taken a year at the Sorbonne.

40

Locked Room
Murder

Francisco watched the long black Cadillac of Mr. Justice Russell quietly purr toward the curb in front of the C.L.E.U. building. He had never been in a limousine. And later today he was going to learn how to ski on top of snow. What tales he would have for Maria and the kids.

James Goodwinkle nodded to them as he primly stepped from the car. "Mr. Macarthur, good morning. And to you, sir." Very correct, Francisco observed, not some flighty *mariposa*. He saw him tug at a leather strap beneath his suit jacket. The man didn't carry a gun well.

Francisco and Max eased themselves in across from Augustina, who was on the backward-facing seat. Another of Brian's characters come to life: the chic and sultry Augustina Sage, captivator of judges.

With his gloved hand, Goodwinkle wiped any unsightly smudges they had marred his car with, and returned to the vehicle's controls. Augustina slid open the window behind him. "Home, James." She shut the window. "He's like American Express, can't go anywhere without him." She took Francisco's hand, smiled at him. "You're Captain Sierra."

"Augustina's beau is in Ottawa," Max said. "I wanted you to meet him."

"I hope I will have that pleasure."

As they drove toward southwest Vancouver, Max regaled her with the drama of cupid's armed raid against Brovak and Leticia Róbelo.

Then Max said: "By the way, Brovak told me he was over to see you and Quentin."

"Yeah, he took all his clothes off and jumped in the pool, and after, when James brought him a towel, he said, 'I hear you give good massage.' Goodwinkle used to work in a rub parlour or something; he won't do me, though, reserves his fingers for the judge. 'I don't touch anyone else,' he told John. Brovak said, 'I bet you touch yourself.' Poor James."

Max said: "John thought something a little strange was going on between you and Russell."

Francisco saw the humour slowly drain from Augustina's face. He picked up on the awkward silence as she slowly, somewhat elaborately, lit a cigarette.

"What do you mean?"

"Quentin turned awfully white when John mentioned something about blackmail. You and he were exchanging secret looks."

"I can't imagine what John thought was going on."

"Forgive me," said Francisco, "but was Judge Russell acquainted with any of the victims?"

Augustina spoke rapidly. "Oh, sure, he knows all the criminal lawyers, it's like a club. Eddie Cohn worked in his office a long time ago."

"Martin Wessel's partner."

"Yes, that's right."

As Augustina settled her guests in the front parlour, she herself felt very *unsettled*. During his visit last week, John Brovak — a blunderbuss, but with keen courtroom instincts — had tuned into the guilty vibrations between her and Russell. But she daren't share with anyone Quentin's dark secret.

Russell had phoned her earlier today. He had seemed buoyed up, the ceremony over, the last hand clasped, the last cheek bussed. He wouldn't be coming home for a while — he had to read several thick factums of law; the spring sitting was due to commence, a big constitutional reference.

Mrs. Collins brought out a tray with a coffee service. "Okay," Augustina said, "you have some questions, Francisco."

He commenced a calm interrogation about the night of Olive Klymchuk's murder, about the sightings of Joe Ruff, the nature of the security, the layout of the Princess Victoria suite. He handled her in a deferential way that she found almost soothing.

"You believe you closed the balcony door that night before going to bed?"

"I guess I didn't. He couldn't get in any other way. That door locks automatically when you shut it."

"Yet you *think* you shut it."

"I've been asked so many times I don't really know."

Francisco pursed his lips and frowned. "Perhaps this is the classic case of the locked-room murder. The theory is, as I understand, that the killer crawled from a third floor window to your balcony with the aid of some vines. But the pictures I saw do not suggest these vines were disturbed. Have you ever considered that he could have been in the room all along?"

"Their watcher did a complete check," Augustina said.

"This watcher was on your floor before you arrived there?"

Augustina tried to remember. "No…she escorted us up. Then stayed near the elevator."

"And, from the photographs, I note there is a door that seems to lead somewhere. Would that be to the adjoining suite?"

"It was always locked when I was there. But yes, the two suites could be connected — for receptions, that sort of thing."

Augustina heard a throat being discreetly cleared behind her, and turned and saw Goodwinkle in coveralls at the door leading to the garage. "Will there by anything? I have work outside." More compulsive washing and polishing of vehicles, she assumed.

"Any calls while I was out?"

"A Mr. Schwartz. His number's by the phone."

She knew she should recognize this name, but it didn't ring the right bell. "Thank you, James."

He bowed and left.

"By the way," said Max, "Frank has a theory about one of our favourite judges."

"That's ridiculous," Augustina said abruptly. "He was in this very house that night. I called him."

Francisco cocked his head at her with a look that suggested he might like clarification.

Augustina was flustered by her knee-jerk utterance. "I mean, if that's who you're talking about."

"I'm thinking of the judge named Leroy Lukey," said Francisco.

The blush that ruddied Augustina's cheeks did not escape Francisco's detection. He took a sip of the insipid beverage the locals called coffee, then said: "Augustina, you will forgive me, but why did you think we were referring to your friend Judge Russell?"

"How silly." She cleared her throat. "I can't imagine *what* I was thinking." She was totally flustered. Should she confide in Max about that rezoning bribe to Wessel? Suspicions can become coloured, blown out of shape.

"Um, Francisco, do you mind if we take a break? I have to make a phone call."

Francisco rose and put his coat on. "The body tires sitting. I will go out and stretch it." He ambled out.

Augustina studied the number the butler had scribbled down: long distance, Victoria.

"The zit doctor," she said.

"Who?" said Max.

"Not Mr. Schwartz, *Dr.* Schwartz." The dermatologist, Olive's grieving widower. Olive had kept her name after the marriage. Augustina hadn't talked to him more than twice in her life — at the wedding, at the funeral.

Schwartz seemed to be waiting by the phone. "I don't know who else to talk to…"

Augustina hoped she was up to a hand-holding session. The man had been badly out of shape at the funeral.

"It's about a bank account I found in Olive's name. Well, not her name. A small company she controlled. It's very large, nearly a million dollars."

Though it was still sunny, the day had mysteriously cooled, and Francisco noticed a haze in the air, a light fog drifting in from the sea. Out here in front of the house, spraying the Cadillac with a hose, was James Goodwinkle in wet coveralls and rubber gloves.

"Weatherman says we may be in for an inversion," said Goodwinkle.

"An inversion?"

"Well, sometimes you get ground clouds around here. Stays sunny upstairs about fifty feet, but gets dark and foggy at sea level."

Francisco nodded. "I understand you live on this estate."

Goodwinkle pointed to a stone cabin behind some rose bushes. "Fifteen years in my home sweet home."

Francisco, glancing down, saw that Goodwinkle's gun and shoulder harness were lying on the driveway beside him.

"That is careless," said Francisco, pointing to the gun. "You could step on it. It is loaded?"

"I'm not used to it. The judge wanted me to carry it."

Francisco gingerly picked up the gun, a revolver, and snapped open the cylinder. Fully loaded. Shiny, polished Colt Cobra .38. It looked never to have been fired.

"I am surprised the judge would let someone untrained be in possession of this."

"I told him he should hire an expert to guard her."

Francisco handed him the gun and the harness. Goodwinkle turned off the hose and tossed a sponge into a small pail, which he carried to the garage. He returned wearing a fresh pair of coveralls and leather gloves and carrying cans of car wax and chrome polish and a chamois.

"How long have you been in the judge's service?"

"Fifteen years. I do everything for him."

"I hear you are an excellent masseur."

"His Lordship enjoys it."

How proudly he said that, thought Francisco, how reverential his tone when he spoke of his employer. Perhaps there was more to this relationship than originally met the eye. An ambitious judge, so anxious to show off a new wife: was he hiding a secret — in the closet, so to speak? A secret that had enriched one who shared it?

Goodwinkle was now shining the car with long, fluid strokes: strong hands that massaged not just cars but their owner.

Francisco took a stroll about the mist-laden grounds: a fountain, a goldfish pond, neatly-clipped hedges. A fortune must be spent daily managing this estate. The excesses of the rich. He realized he had no idea how Russell had made his money — hadn't someone told him he started off poor?

Francisco wandered into the garage: an antique Peugot and a third car, a Buick. He observed that, again carelessly, Goodwinkle had left his gun and harness here, hanging from a hook along with the wet apparel he had changed from. He was tempted to commit a minor, temporary theft. Hercule Poirot would do it.

Francisco and Max spent another two hours with Augustina, a probing question-answer session. Afterwards Goodwinkle drove them back to C.L.E.U., where he dropped Max off. He then took Francisco across Lion's Gate and up to the mountains for his first ski lesson. Fog was spreading through the city, but soon they were above it, in the opulent heights of the North Shore.

"It'll be real warm up top," Goodwinkle said. "Seventy degrees or more."

Goodwinkle let him off at the Skyride, where Brovak and Leticia were waiting. Swooping up the mountain in the gondola, Francisco held his breath. Spreading below was a panorama of forest and ocean, dense fog stalking across the city, only the top storeys of the taller buildings showing now, a busy, buried civilization.

"Main runs are closed, Francisco," said Brovak, "but we'll try you out on the bunny hill."

They were transported into a blinding white world.

As Francisco walked from the upper station, he stepped onto the hard-packed surface. It made a crunch. He took three more steps and suddenly his legs went out from under him, and he slid down a slight decline on his bottom. What an absurd spectacle he made — but it was fun. Sitting there, he picked up a handful of this frozen cotton and compressed it into a ball. He threw it at a tree and it fluffed apart.

Incredible.

Brovak and Leticia helped him to his feet, laughing with him, and led him to the ski rental office.

41

Parlour
Game

Augustina parted the drapes covering the leaded-glass windows and
looked into thick grey jelly. Still daylight, but she could barely make
out Nordquist coming up the stairs followed by Brovak and Leticia,
with Francisco Sierra between them, wearing his best suit. He would
have looked more distinguished were he not hopping on one leg. His
companions were helping him stay aloft.

As they rang the chimes, she walked briskly from the front
parlour and intercepted Goodwinkle, coming from the kitchen, in
shirt sleeves. No gun — she had ordered him not to carry it in the
house.

"I'll get it," Augustina said, and with a gentle steer turned him
around. "You help Mrs. Collins." The housekeeper had volunteered
to stay late to make hors d'ouevres.

As she ushered these guests inside, she looked down at
Francisco's very fat right ankle. "What did you do to yourself?"

"Only a sprain," said Francisco.

"I guess I was showing off, hot-dogging when I should have been
watching him," Brovak said. "I tried to catch him."

"I have a place for you by the fire, Captain." Augustina led them
back into the front parlour where a fire of alder and fir glowed hot.

She laid out some cushions in front of the fireplace, a hassock for his leg. "You want to keep it raised for the swelling."

Francisco hobbled to his station. His ankle was very painful. Maria, his wife, would surely give him a lecture about his *bravo* efforts to ski. Poles flailing, skis crossed, he had performed a majestic pirouette when he'd let go of the T-bar, and hadn't been able to find the brakes.

Snow is not always so soft. Snow is something that has to be mastered.

He lay on his back and put his leg up. The other chairs were arranged nearby, all close enough to catch the heat of the fire.

Augustina went to the built-in bar, in an alcove opposite the front windows. "Something hot for you, Francisco? Everybody name your poison. So to speak."

The room was dimly lit, but the fire made it glow with a mellow, dancing light. Francisco saw, on the wall facing him, the valuable etchings, the Tiepolos. Nymph with Satyr Child and Goats. Above the mantle, riding trophies. Oak wainscotting, stained glass above the windows and the main door leading to the hallway.

Ah, yes, thought Francisco, this wonderful mansion offered a classic setting for a fine murder, the strangled body found in the dumbwaiter, and later…Inspector Grodgins puffing on his Meerschaum pipe, pointing at the disinherited nephew: "You killed Mrs. McGillicuddy, with her panty hose in the pantry."

Unfortunately, the author of tonight's mystery play had not been able to assemble the entire cast of suspects for his grand finale. How delightful it would have been to build up to that tense moment, the suspects neatly arrayed before him, and point the finger as the curtain falls.

Everyone was seated now except Nordquist, who strolled about, examining things. Memorizing the room, thought Francisco, as policemen must always do.

But it would be Francisco's show, Nordquist had told him.

He wanted to do it the Poirot way. Climax and dénouement in the grand style.

Goodwinkle came out solemnly with a tray of crackers and cheese, and passed it among the guests. He looked affronted at seeing Augustina behind the bar.

"Miss Sage, I always do that."

"I'm perfectly capable."

He laid the tray down and looked pleadingly upon the others. "She makes me feel useless."

The chimes rang again, and Augustina yielded up the bar to him. "Make up a hot toddy for Francisco, okay? Ask the others what they want."

She returned to the door: Max Macarthur, with Wentworth Chance in tow.

"Are we late?" Max said. "It's thicker than goulash out there." He had driven from home at half the speed limit, stopping off to pick up Wentworth.

"What's supposed to be going on here?" said Wentworth in a low voice. He had no idea: he had spent the whole day in a fruitless search for an affordable apartment.

Last night — after Caroline had gone to bed — Wentworth had had a hectic conversation with Brian Pomeroy which began when he innocently suggested he would probably shack up for a while at Vajeeta's place. "You will not do that," Brian had said in a tone that threatened fierce retribution.

This woman had turned out to have been conning him, a little. In one of her former lives she'd been his boss's surreptitious girlfriend, one Charity Slough — if *that* was her real name. Brian had threatened to plant Wentworth in an anthill if he ever divulged that name to Caroline. His career with Pomeroy Macarthur would be abruptly terminated if he did not stop seeing her. If he cooperated, he might be able to contemplate an offer to stay with this firm.

No problem. A deal. Wentworth was actually relieved to be able to break off with her.

Max and Wentworth sat down on the sofa while Goodwinkle toured about with a tray of drinks.

Francisco's quiet voice seemed to rise mystically from the floor.

"May I now begin to relate my theory?" Francisco paused and the room babble dimmed, then died. "Let us retrace our steps briefly to last July. The death of Arthur P. Besterman. That death is solved. Let us quickly bury him. Mr. Turnbull and Mr. Calico will pay the price of the law for the pleasure of their vengeance."

"We hope," said Nordquist. He was at the windows now, had

drawn the drapes slightly open, and was looking into the opaque greyness outside.

"Mr. Besterman was not murdered by the Executor, but his death planted a seed. The attempt on Brian Pomeroy five months later — an accident as we now know — caused the seed to grow. These two events inspired a plot to kill others."

He pondered for some seconds, and Wentworth finally asked, "You mean all the other murders were planned?"

"Let me keep my thoughts in order, Wentworth, or I may lose sight of the beaten path. Very well. Besterman, Pomeroy — two attempts on lawyers. The opportunity seemed too good to be true. Each had won fame — perhaps that is not the word — for defending unpopular persons. The speculation that a crazy person was on a vendetta against defenders of criminals added gristle to the mill."

Was that the right expression? Francisco paused to sip his toddy, and with a grimace stretched his wounded leg.

Goodwinkle had scuttled off, and now returned with Mrs. Collins, helping her roll out a trolley with coffee, fruit, and a pot of caviar. The eggs of a bottom-feeding fish, thought Francisco, conjuring up the filthy harbour in Próspero. He would taste a tiny bit, so he could tell Maria.

He continued: "The Executor then quickly decided to take advantage of the victory John Brovak won for his drug clients. The charges were withdrawn on a Monday, and the grenade was delivered the following night.

"This trick with a grenade, by the way — a gift box, with the pin fixed to the lid — was used by F.W. Weathers in *The Calcutta Connection*. But with a sadder result. Excellent thriller, has anyone read it?"

A murmur of no's. Do people not read any more? Where was Brian, his fellow aficionado of the art of mystery writing? On his way here, Francisco hoped. But the fog had slowed the world outside to a crawl.

"Back to Archie's Steak House. Oh, I forgot, this was a haunt of Sergeant Everit Cudlipp. And he knew about this victory celebration — two of his men were posted in the front dining area. In any event, the episode was spectacular: an explosion designed to cause the death of many traffickers in narcotics and their lawyers. A great catastrophe which would generate loud headlines. Then the first anonymous letter and more headlines. How better to start rolling the ball? How better to give attention to this…how do you say, mythic creature, the Executor? He was put on display in a blazing fire of publicity.

"I pause. I note that when the grenade exploded one person was safely away from the scene: Miss Rosalind Finch, the secret friend of Sergeant Cudlipp, was visiting the ladies' washroom. Before I forget… let me rewind. The gentleman who delivered the package, a person with a false beard and falsetto voice. What is it he said? 'This is for Mr. Brovak. For all he's done.'"

Brovak drained his whiskey and held up his glass to Goodwinkle. "James, my good man, lighter on the soda this time."

"'For all he's done,'" Francisco repeated. "What had Mr. Brovak done? Exposed Judge Lukey — in a literal sense if I may say — as a client of a young lady of the night. But who knew he had done so? A select group of criminal lawyers. No headlines, no press coverage. Thus we narrow the field."

"Had to be someone who was at the banquet," said Max.

"Who could that be?" Brovak chortled. "What star of what critically acclaimed home movie?"

"Now let us look again at this first note from the Executor. Brovak, Pomeroy and Besterman are named in it. To blow up his plastic dummy of the Executor, to make it life-like, our suspect takes credit for assaults of which he is innocent. He is ready now to send his Frankenstein's monster out to do his bidding. The first target is Eddie Cohn."

"Why was he on the list?" Brovak asked.

"Have patience, John, as I separate the trees from the forest. Mr. Eddie Cohn won a murder charge against an eraser, as you call him. Or is it a rubber? Never mind: a hit man. Mr. Cohn was almost as unreputable as his client. Now let us pause and take note: the point may seem minor, but when was Mr. Cohn entrusted to the defence of this hit man? Approximately a year earlier.

"We turn to the next target: Mr. Martin Wessel, who died in ghastly pain from strychnine poisoning. There was a strange note in his pocket: 'Midnight. E.' I will come back to that note. The sin for which Mr. Wessel was punished was defending a pervert, one Father

Doyle. And how long had he been representing this priest's interests? Three years."

Goodwinkle cleared his throat. "Will there be anything? Drinks to be freshened?"

"We'll help ourselves," said Augustina. "Take a break. Help Mrs. Collins with the dishes."

"I don't normally-"

"Okay, just do whatever you do, James. I'll call when I need you, all right?" The guy was hanging around, listening to everything. He was getting to be too much with his constant clucking.

Brovak had got up and begun to help himself to the scotch. Goodwinkle glanced sourly at him as he left.

"Last but not least, our final target, Olive Klymchuk. Who was she acting for? Kidnappers of babies. She had been their lawyer since June of last year. So. Cohn, Wessel and Klymchuk were all hired by their clients before Arthur Besterman was killed. And the Executor knew this, and as I say, the Besterman and the Pomeroy incidents gave him his inspiration. The hand grenade was only a dressing for the cake. The other three were his real targets. Once the stage was set, all three had to die to make the plan work.

"It is an associate of these three we are looking for. Someone who had dealings with each of them. These conspirators — Cohn, Wessel and Klymchuk — knew their lives were at risk: they were playing a dangerous game. If one of them was, ah, rubbered out, the others would think the Executor did the murder. He was a fantasy figure created to throw everyone off scent so suspicion might not fall on the one person with a motive to kill all three.

"Let us return to the Topaz Hotel. It has been assumed that the killer climbed down some vines to the balcony of the Princess Victoria Suite. I think that not to be the case. He may have been on the third floor earlier, and he may have opened that hallway window to create a false trail. But he was on the second floor when Augustina and Olive Klymchuk returned to their suite. Augustina says she closed and locked the balcony door. I believe her. I think the killer was in the adjoining suite. I think he had a key."

This was coming together rather well, Francisco thought. He had their rapt attention. It was time to discard some of the Executor's own red herrings.

"Let me clean the deck of some of the rubbish. That note, 'Midnight. E.' was placed by someone in Wessel's pocket. A diversion intended to direct suspicion elsewhere."

Wentworth was confused. "The E. *doesn't* stand for Everit?"

"Hold the fort," Brovak said. "What happened to your big theory about Lukey and Cudlipp?".

"I called it a literary hunch. I feel a little foolish about that." He twisted his neck, looked around the room — what was keeping the late Brian Pomeroy? "That mysterious phone tip to Roger Turnbull about the items in the garbage can was another diversion — the Executor knew Turnbull would be suspected, then Lukey. The Executor now seems to be having fun, to be playing with us. But he is making mistakes." He closed his eyes again to concentrate his mind.

James Goodwinkle returned to the parlour door, where with pained expression he watched Brovak mess up his bar making up something Shirley Templish for Leticia.

"The Executor tries to pin it on these others: Cudlipp, Turnbull, Lukey. But how does he know these three men are on the list of suspects? The public does not know. Does a little bird sing these names into his ear? No, he has inside information. Thus, again, we narrow the field."

"A cop," Wentworth blurted. "Someone in C.L.E.U."

Nordquist, still staring out the window, smiled. He knew who it was. So did Max. Earlier, Francisco had bounced his theory off them.

Goodwinkle padded quietly up to the bar, and Brovak gave up control of it to him. He began swabbing it of Brovak's leavings: lime peels and maraschino cherry juice.

"Quickly now, let us skip back to the Topaz Hotel. The key to the case is…the key to the suite that joined Augustina's. The slang for a key is a twirl? A fine word. Who had access to such a twirl?"

Mrs. Collins bustled in to pick up some of the dishes.

"Who?" said Wentworth.

"Hughie Lupo." Francisco opened his eyes to see Mrs. Collins standing above him. "Ah, excellent food, Mrs. Collins. *Bocas*, we call them at home. Little mouthpieces — no, that means something else, does it not? Givers of legal advice, not as tasty. By the way, Mrs. Collins, have you ever seen him with his gloves off?"

The housekeeper turned to him perplexed. "With whose gloves off?"

"I suspect not. Well, it is time to take the gloves off."

That was a good line, but Francisco readied himself for his finest one. Many times would he recount this story to his children.

"I think you will find that the butler did it."

Francisco looked toward the corner alcove and realized Goodwinkle was standing behind the bar. When had he come sneaking back in here? Everyone else had turned to look at him, too. And Inspector Nordquist had his gun drawn and pointed at him.

But when the butler raised his hand from beneath the bar, Francisco found himself looking into the unwavering fat eye of his Colt Cobra .38, Hughie Lupo's gloved finger upon the trigger.

42

Gay
Deceiver

For several heartbeats of deathly quiet, Lupo and Nordquist stood gun to gun. Everyone seemed frozen into place, as if caught in a still frame. Lupo was like a cat, alert, ready to spring. Or shoot.

"Please put your gun down, inspector." The tone was pleasant, even genial in a morbid way. "I assure you that my reflexes are quicker than yours. My eyes are on your trigger finger, and they are very good eyes. We may kill each other, but I'm going to die in Pennsylvania anyway. A bullet or the electric chair, death is death."

Nordquist didn't move. He was standing directly in front of the window, the curtain open behind him about six inches.

"I think I prefer a bullet. I will take others with me if you miss my heart or brain. My gun is aimed directly between your eyes, sir. *Do* check out the angle. I have six bullets, I sincerely want you to believe I will use them all. I *really* mean it."

Still no one stirred. The partners and Wentworth and Leticia were sitting statues. Mrs. Collins stood there gaping, holding a tray of empty coffee cups. Francisco could feel the ache in his leg and he heard the roar of silence.

This wasn't in the script, Francisco thought. The butler wasn't supposed to be in the room during this final scene — earlier, yes, when he tried to deflect Lupo's concern with his red herrings of Cudlipp and Lukey. He had waited until Lupo left before disclosing his real theory. Francisco hadn't seen him return, probably because he'd been self-absorbed, blinded by ego, playing to his audience. While seeking the dramatic build-up to the moment of grand revelation, he had been rashly oblivious to the possibility Lupo might reenter the room. In any event, Francisco's defenses had been down; Lupo had not been carrying his gun earlier. But all evening he'd had it taped under the bar.

"Please lower your service revolver now, inspector, or I will kill you," Lupo said. "Drop it, don't bend down."

Mrs. Collins fainted dead away, collapsing on the rug, coffee cups scattering across the floor. Lupo's eyes did not flicker from Nordquist's, but he saw Augustina start to rise as if to go to the housekeeper's aid.

"I'm sorry, Miss Sage, but please remain seated. No one must move. Inspector, I'll count to three. But I may stop at two."

Nordquist let his gun fall to the floor.

"Now kindly remain absolutely still, sir." Lupo casually stripped some adhesive tape from the butt of his gun. "I believe you have stationed a sharpshooter behind the window. I noticed you drew the curtains apart slightly a little while ago. Now I ask you to turn in such a way as to keep his view of me blocked, and I ask you to close those curtains. Keep your face turned away from his; I will know if you give him a signal."

Nordquist performed the task slowly and deliberately.

"Thank you. Very kind."

Francisco worried about Brovak, whose eyes were shifting about the room, studying what? The dangerous possibilities of physical confrontation.

Lupo picked up a paring knife, weighed it in his left hand. "I have tried to keep fit over the years. I don't think I've lost anything." Holding the knife by the point, he abruptly flipped it end over end, and it stuck neatly into a nectarine on the table.

"That's pretty good," said Brovak, the first of them to speak.

Lupo seemed caught off guard by the compliment. "Yes…well, thank you. And I'm not left-handed."

Brovak decided against hasty action. The correct approach was not to ask this fruit fly whether he preferred to pitch or catch. Unlike his boss, he might not be a ball fan. Brovak decided to bide his time, wait for a chance.

Lupo blew out a big sigh, and began an odd ramble. "Fifteen years of living another life. A toupee, false teeth and coloured contacts. Fifteen years of acting a little…flowerish for the judge's friends. Gays must sure face a lot of intolerance. Was it worth it? I had a pretty good job, a kindly employer, a friendly place to hide. Fifteen years of avoiding the electric chair, I guess that's something."

Mrs. Collins was conscious now, but she continued to lie on her side, her eyes open, breathing hard.

Lupo smiled at Francisco. "I didn't fool you, did I, Captain Sierra? Yes, I guessed something was up when I couldn't find those rubber gloves I left in the garage. You actually got prints off them?"

Francisco heard his own voice: amazingly calm. "Yes, we did," he said.

"That's a good one, I never thought of that. Pull them inside out, out pops a perfect set of prints. Did you read it in a book somewhere?"

"I think I did."

"That was the only thing I couldn't change, the prints. Eddie Cohn took a bite out of a really good pair of gloves; I had to burn them." With his teeth, he gripped a fingertip of the glove on his left hand, and pulled it off. A smear of crimson polish was on the nail of his little finger. "That's a reminder. Like string around your finger, only it doesn't show. Only time I took them off…well, it doesn't matter."

"For the judge's massages," Francisco said.

"Yes, sir. But there was no stuff going on."

"No stuff," Francisco repeated.

"You know. I'm not a…a homosexual."

"Oh, I see. Of course."

"I can talk like them. Womanish."

"Yes, when you called Turnbull," Max said.

"Correct. That was me. I did everything. On my own. And I *really* did more than I should have."

Francisco was trying to get a handle on the man. He could see he wanted to extend things, to talk. He had an idea Lupo wanted some form of recognition for his skills, his accomplishments. A narcissist. Worse, a psychopath, proud and without guilt. Kinky, the FBI had said.

"I thought planting those things in that garbage can was a good idea at the time. I thought it might help Quentin…the judge, get that position in Ottawa he so dearly wanted if all that stuff was found behind his competitor's house. Didn't know the decision had already been made. He should have *told* me."

He shrugged. "Anyway Miss Sage used to tell the judge pretty well everything, and I overheard most of it, so I knew who the suspects were. The judge talked to me about it, too. We're friends even though I'm just his butler. Social friends, that's all. Nothing physical, of course."

"But you put on a great performance, James," Brovak said. "I thought you were some kind of tearoom queen."

Lupo apparently didn't pick up any irony. "As you can see, I'm *quite* normal. By the way, Mr. Brovak, I want you to sincerely know I never intended to kill you. Releasing the pin wouldn't cause the grenade to explode. Only impact would."

"It's a relief to hear that," Brovak said.

"The captain was right. I didn't have any need to hurt you. It was all window dressing for later."

Lupo turned to Augustina. "And Miss Sage, I want to assure you that you were never at risk. The judge loves you too much; I would never do anything to hurt him."

"Of course. I accept that."

His companions, Francisco saw, had covertly joined in playing to the man's bizarre yearning to be liked.

"I truly admire that man," Lupo said.

"Who doesn't?" said Max.

"He was there for me when I needed him most."

"Fifteen years ago," said Max. "When you were on the run."

"Yes." Lupo assumed an almost dreamy expression; his eyes grew soft. Then they became alert. "Oh, but he didn't know who I *was*."

Then the phone rang. "Pick it up, please, Miss Sage. And if you could…just act natural?"

It rang twice more before Augustina managed to get her wobbly knees working, her legs moving. It was Quentin.

"Oh, hello, darling," she said. "Listen, can I call you back? Some friends have just come in. Everything going okay?"

"Yeah, the Jays are ahead four-zip."

She laughed — too nervously — and warbled a goodbye, then hung up.

"You should have gone to Ottawa with him, Miss Sage. Really, I mean staying here at home on his *finest* day. Can I, ah, fix you another drink?"

"Oh." Augustina was startled. "No, thanks." She returned to her seat.

"The judge — he's fine?"

"Yes," she said. "Yeah, he's just fine. Watching a baseball game."

"It's how he relaxes, but it's a waste of one of the truly great minds." Lupo loosened his tie and tugged at his shirt. "That shoulder harness was *really* uncomfortable. The Klymchuk woman had long nails. You should *see* the scratches."

Everyone stirred nervously. Francisco could tell that Inspector Nordquist, who hadn't uttered a word through this ordeal, was also striving to form a picture of the creature they were dealing with. Sitting together on a sofa, Max and Wentworth had their backs to him, but would glance over their shoulders once in a while. Augustina had two cigarettes going. Leticia had her eyes closed, her head bowed, her hands together.

"Anyway, what I want to know, Captain, is how did you zero in on me?"

Francisco thought: how do I handle this? But one must keep talking, keep…making a cool scene, as they say. Stall matters and hope. What was Lupo's plan?

"It was very odd. I, ah, rang the wrong number at first, Mr. Lupo."

"Actually I have got used to Goodwinkle. James, if you like."

"Ah, yes, James. My friend is writing a mystery novel, James, and his murderer turns out to be someone well connected with a judge — a literary hunch, I called it. I must admit I thought at first of Sergeant Cudlipp, the associate of Judge Lukey. Then I thought of you. It was a stab at the darkness really."

Brian — where was he? Would the SWAT members outside stop him from coming in? But do they suspect matters have gone awry here? Their orders were not to enter without a signal from Inspector Nordquist at the window.

"Well, you took those gloves from the garage. It must have been more than a hunch."

A hunch, yes, thought Francisco. But little things had added up: Augustina's nervousness about Russell's reaction to the word blackmail; the butler's absolute devotion to his boss. Nothing, however, could be confirmed until that call from Dr. Schwartz. Nearly a million dollars in a secret fund. This was the blackmail account.

Nordquist had edged away from the window.

"Please stay in front of the window, sir. Facing me."

Nordquist moved back. He, too, wondered what the three SWAT members out there were doing. His closing of the curtain must have been seen by them as a warning sign. He would not have done it unless under duress.

"So what do you think my motive was, Captain Sierra?"

Any answer might be fraught with danger, Francisco realized, providing fission to the latent bomb that was Hughie Lupo.

"Tell him," said Nordquist.

Francisco raised himself on an elbow and looked into Lupo's cool, killer eyes.

"I found certain, shall I say, connections. Mr. Cohn and Mr. Wessel were partners. Cohn had once worked for Judge Russell and had succeeded him as Mr. d'Anglio's lawyer. Olive Klymchuk had served in Wessel's firm. Olive Klymchuk had been Judge Russell's lover."

"The judge had nothing to do with this," said Lupo. "I swear."

A pause. Francisco proceeded quietly. "I think you are not telling the truth, James, out of your respect for him."

Lupo's face hardened. "Tell me what you know, Captain."

"I do not know everything, of course. You can correct me if you wish."

"I *just* may."

"The three intended victims — Cohn, Wessel, and Klymchuk — were blackmailing your employer."

"How do you know?"

"This afternoon, Augustina told us of a piece of land that had been rezoned for a bribe, land which the judge said he turned over for a healthy profit."

Lupo looked reproachfully at her. "Miss Sage, please don't think I'm bold, but was it fair to repeat what the judge said to you in confidence?" He nervously cleared his throat. "I'm sorry, perhaps I am out of turn, I suppose you were put under pressure to do this."

Francisco thought it most odd — the man was clearly uncomfortable in speaking to Augustina with even mild reproof. It was as if he realized he was going beyond his station as her servant in so speaking to her. Francisco caught Augustina's eye. Her nod was barely perceptible.

"The matter was quickly looked into," Francisco said. "Apparently the judge did have this land rezoned, for a profit — but not the vast sum that he claimed was the starting point of his fortune. No, at some point during her romance with Judge Russell, Olive Klymchuk learned a different secret."

"If it's the one you're thinking about, it's not true," said Lupo fiercely.

"What one is that, James?"

"There was nothing between us. Not in that sense."

"I am thinking of a darker secret."

"Well, tell me!"

"Please lower your voice."

Softer: "Just tell me."

Oddly subservient was this judge's...gopher — that is the word gringos use for some reason. A rodent of the fields. Francisco wondered: between servile James and lordly Quentin had there developed some kind of slave-master relationship? A good psychologist could have an enjoyable time with this, more fun than Francisco was having now.

"I assume that Cohn and Wessel took their share of the blackmail moneys in cash," he said. "Miss Klymchuk banked hers for a rainy day. At least a million dollars each, from a tap the judge could not turn off. A plumber had to be sent in to fix it. That was you, James."

"The judge was absolutely clueless about what I was doing."

"I would like to believe that, James, but some fingers point to him. I should say, rather, that Judge Russell was pointing fingers at others. He used Miss Sage to pass word to the authorities that Everit Cudlipp had a motive to kill Mr. Besterman. He prompted Miss Sage to bargain for a low sentence for the kidnappers that would stir up the pot against Miss Klymchuk. When John Brovak hinted about blackmail, he detoured suspicion to Cudlipp and Lukey."

"You are *reaching*, captain. I murdered those…those scum, and I freely admit it. I did it for the judge. But he didn't *know*. He never even knew who I *was*."

Francisco saw that Lupo was losing his poise; he had started to sweat. How to handle this? The man long ago had forfeited his life; an executioner awaited him. Does one keep turning up the heat? When he sees that he cannot save his lord and master and lover, will he wilt in the end…or go berserk?

Francisco realized he might be bungling things. He guiltily cast a glance at Nordquist.

Nordquist picked up his cue. "James," he said, "we can promise you won't be extradited. It would mean a lifetime in prison for you here, but at least you could die of old age."

"What are you asking for in return?"

"Help us out. Tell us what you know."

"About…what?"

"About the murders," said Nordquist. "About Judge Russell —"

"I will *never* betray him," Lupo said with abrupt fierceness, and then he must have realized that by those very words he had done so. He turned white, and started to shake. He spoke again to Francisco, a high, breaking voice: "Tell *me* what *you* know."

Francisco lay back, closed his eyes, and offered a quick prayer, and decided to tell Lupo all. Let him know that Russell could not be saved. Then repeat the inspector's offer.

"Very well, James. On the eve of Miss Klymchuk's murder, you were in Victoria. You did not return to Vancouver that night, but Judge Russell later said you did. He tried to alibi for you." Francisco had made a hasty note of Russell's words, as recited to him by Augustina earlier that day: *I only have Goodwinkle to say where I was Thursday night.* She had thought the chauffeur had returned home on a late ferry.

"It was *all* my idea. I did *everything*, the letters, the executions…"

Francisco ploughed ahead. "But not the murder of Martin Wessel. Poison is a most intimate potion; rarely is it shared among strangers. And Martin Wessel was no stranger to the judge. Often he would phone him, often he would come by to pick up an envelope with cash in it. Wessel was the official go-between. Not Eddie Cohn, who was probably the engineer, the deviser of means and methods. Not Olive Klymchuk, who didn't have the courage to do this on her own, and had taken her secret to her former employer and his partner, the men who would do all the hard work. Miss Klymchuk even hinted to Augustina of the judge's dark past to try to dissuade her from a terrible marriage."

"This is all *quite* ridiculous. It's guesswork, sir."

"Please correct any errors."

Lupo seemed about to say something, but remained mute to this offer. Francisco hoped he was on the right track, and would not be meeting another train head on.

"You had a room at the Topaz Hotel that night. Judge Russell had given you a master key to the hotel. The hope was that Miss Klymchuk would stay there late, celebrating with Augustina — and indeed she spent the night. So you stayed in the adjoining room until they went to bed. You would kill Klymchuk and he would poison Wessel on the same night: if only one is murdered, the other might suspect who the Executor was, and the deck of cards could collapse.

"On the night of Wessel's murder, Judge Russell was alone in this house — he had dismissed the rest of the staff for the Easter Weekend. Wessel arrived that evening to pick up his money, perhaps several million dollars, and when Augustina telephoned here at midnight, he was probably being poured a drink from the very bar at which you stand. Alcohol is an excellent solvent for strychnine."

"This is rich. You are *so* wrong."

"Here is where Wessel died. Judge Russell put that note in his pocket, drove the body to some cliffs, and threw it over. He abandoned Wessel's car and walked home — not far away: two kilometres."

Francisco paused for a spell, his eyes still closed. No shot rang out, no bullet punctured his heart.

He opened one eye. Lupo was shaking more severely; the gun was wavering. Francisco carried on — for better or for worse...

"James, the secret Miss Klymchuk learned had something to do with the judge's wife, yes? Beautiful, wealthy Eunice. Most of the judge's fortune was inherited from her? We will be able to confirm it, of course."

Lupo visibly sagged.

"Fifteen years ago, you arrived on the scene, and she died. How did she die, James?"

"She...she drove over a cliff."

"How did that happen?"

Lupo looked around the room, at the faces looking back. He tried to smile, to tell them he understood the game that was being played, the game to trap the judge.

Nordquist broke the silence with a calm, bold lie: "I think we had better tell you, James, that Olive Klymchuk left a letter in a safe deposit. To be opened in the event of her death."

Lupo did not respond for several seconds. Then his eyes began to tear. Softly, barely audible, he said: "We were worried about that."

"How did you kill Eunice?" Nordquist asked.

Lupo's voice was wooden. "I snapped her neck. I jumped out when I saw the curve coming." A long silence. "She was a bitch. She was sleeping around. She was going to leave him. He didn't love her anyway, not like Miss Sage."

"The deal," said Francisco, "was asylum for murder. The judge was well connected to the Mafia, was approached by them, and offered to hide you out. For your services, he would conceal you forever from the American executioner."

Lupo said nothing. His eyes were damp but not once did he take them from his hostages.

"Would you like to tell us how Olive Klymchuk found out, James?" Nordquist said.

"She overheard me and the judge talking about Eunice one morning. He had a nightmare about...it, about her, and I...I held him, I kept telling him nothing would be found out...We didn't know Olive was standing just outside the bedroom door. We thought she'd left the house. We found out later...He didn't love *her* either. She was *another* bitch."

His voice trailed away. Just muffled sniffles.

"Why don't you put the gun down, James?" said Nordquist.

Lupo wiped his eyes with a bar towel, and seemed slowly to collect himself, and after a few moments he sighed.

"I guess I'm going to die today. I had this idea...the weather's in my favour, I could take a couple of you with me, demand a car." He smiled through the mist in his eyes, and his tone became easy-going again. "But I think I'll kill people instead."

43

Valentine's Day

Brian inched his car through the streets of Point Grey, impatient but joyful. He had just been formally reunited with his wife. After dinner, Caroline had simply stood up, gone to his chair, and kissed him on the forehead, and then they had given in to their longing.

A happy ending and new beginnings...

And he hadn't finished his other ending. He prayed that his jealous muse had not maliciously allowed him to sap his juices for the final thrust, the grand climax of his novel.

The ultimate hero would be Lance Valentine, the character so modestly based on himself. Lance would show up at the last minute and brilliantly save the day.

Night had fallen. He was forced to stop and get out of his car to find the street sign: South West Marine Drive, Russell's house was only a few blocks away. Francisco had seemed ecstatic on the phone earlier today: they had picked up the Executor's tracks. "The game is afoot," he had said.

He almost drove into the fender of Brovak's Mercedes as he pulled into Russell's driveway.

He heard the long low bleat of a distant foghorn. Then the silence shrouded him. He couldn't hear his own footfalls.

He found a railing, the porch. He was surprised to see the front door was open a crack, a few inches. As he stepped up to it, he heard distant murmurings. He was about to ring the bell when he saw, though the opening, a man standing on a wooden chair. Brian sucked air in, and froze.

The man was peering through a narrow aperture between the top of the door and a stained glass transom. He was dressed in black: black pants, black rollneck, black toque. And now he was leaning back, now raising a handgun, now pointing it at the stained glass, now peaking through the aperture again, now aiming…

Though almost nauseated with fear, Augustina was the first to break the silence that followed Lupo's announcement of their impending deaths.

"You're not going to kill anyone, James." She tried to make it sound like an order, but not too brusque. "I'll have that drink after all."

Lupo again changed character: from casual and off-hand to calmly acquiescent. "What would you enjoy, Miss Sage?"

She was startled by his sudden relapse into servility, and took hope from it. "An amaretto."

Working with his free hand, Lupo poured the drink for her, continually flicking glances at the others. Augustina mustered all her strength and got up, and walked in seeming calmness toward the bar, and extended her hand for the liqueur glass.

"Quentin will be very upset if you harm any of my friends. *Very* upset, James. And if you hurt *me*…I don't need to say."

"Do…you love him, Miss Sage?"

"Of course, I always will."

That somehow seemed to satisfy him. In a subdued voice, he said, "What do you think he'll get?"

Nordquist now spoke. "I suspect life imprisonment, James. But you can be with him. He will need you."

"I know. It will be very hard in there for him."

"That is why you should accept the inspector's offer," said Francisco. "Then you can stay in Canada and help him through it."

"It's not a trick?" said Lupo cautiously.

"Give me the gun, James," Augustina said.

The pain seemed about to break Lupo. "How can you stand to see him ruined? How can you *stand* it?"

Then silence, suddenly interrupted by a noise from behind the main door, a startled human grunt, a clatter, a scraping.

"It *is* a trick!" Lupo screamed, turning toward the sound.

The parlour door abruptly swung open, the armed SWAT man falling forward through it, sprawling on top of his overturned chair. Brian Pomeroy's arms were around him, his high, leaping tackle carrying him into the room, where he landed on the officer's back, knocking the air from both of them.

Augustina jostled Lupo's arm as he swung the gun in the direction of the centre of this commotion.

He fired once, and Augustina grabbed his wrist. His second shot hit a Tiepolo etching, shattering its frame.

By now Brovak's springs had uncoiled, lifting him from his chair like a missile. Though Lupo tried to jink him with a swift swivel-step to the side, he was unable to avoid the full impact of Brovak's lunge, and was sent off stride. Max and Wentworth were up now, too, grabbing at his gun hand. Lupo jammed a finger into one of Brovak's eyes, tried to gouge it, but Brovak head-butted him in the mouth so hard that his upper plate broke, and he went limp.

"I don't care about myself," he mumbled though his bloodied mouth. "But you are destroying a great man. A god."

"So sue me," said Brovak, one eye closed and watering.

By then both Nordquist and the SWAT man had a gun barrel in each of Lupo's ears.

Brian sat up, dazed, and watched with the solemn, innocent eyes of the newborn as a bloodstain widened on his shirt front.

44

Suicide Squeeze

Quentin Russell knew he must not act like a cocky rookie on his first day, the kid with the million-dollar contract and coils of gold around his neck. His colleagues had been pleasant, but distant, and would be watching him, maybe hoping this rich and ambitious and rather unelderly upstart would flub an easy fly ball or two.

He might ask one or two questions of counsel, but otherwise no one would know he was there. He would win his benchmates over eventually — not pushy, but he knew a few good jokes — and he'd start by working on that prig Lajoie, whom no one *else* liked, a coy martinet who would surely have flourished in the court of Louis XIV.

Quentin didn't know quite how to handle the Chief. You had to shout most of the time in conversation with him — he refused to get his hearing tested. The old boy had two more years, and God knows why he was hanging on. The one fellow he would steer clear of was Hawrysh, who had an organic brain disorder which was supposedly being held in check with prescribed downers.

All nine judges would be in there today, the whole batting order. Lots of lawyers, too — all ten provinces were represented, and all were opposed to the Senate Reform Bill.

Quentin wondered if he should write his own decision — would that be considered an impetuosity? Or should he just hang on to someone's coattails and concur? If so, probably with Madam Justice Rochfoucauld, a federalist like him, and the brightest of this bunch — excepting perhaps, in all modesty, himself. She also swung a fairly heavy bat around here.

Quentin was alone at his desk in his chambers with a coffee and several kilos of factums. He had read most of them, had managed to grasp the arguments, but had often been distracted from his work by his worries — and by thoughts of Augustina. How open and passionate and free she was, how loyal, how unlike fickle Eunice with her slut's heart and her snideness about his sexuality. His earlier sexual problems had never to do with not *liking* women — the right one simply had never come along.

But something had come between him and Augustina in recent days, something vague that couldn't be grabbed and held. She had sounded so odd when he phoned last night. And when she called back, she seemed too tired to talk, strangely evasive, almost sullen.

Had he not allayed her earlier suspicions? Or had Olive Klymchuk, that shining beacon of integrity, confided too much to her?

Throughout the last few days, Quentin had been pretending to himself that the Senate Reform Bill was more important than any picayune concerns about the investigation in Vancouver. But, trying to block, he'd found himself becoming more and more agitated. Nothing on the news this morning: police had shut themselves off from the press for the last few days, and this had led to speculation that an announcement was pending.

About Turnbull and Calico, he hoped — surely that was it: charges were being readied against them.

But how imbecilic of James to have gone waltzing off on that mindless tangent, depositing the evidence in the garbage of Max Mac Two. He was supposed to have *destroyed* it! Everything!

He tried to stifle the anger welling within him. He thought he had vented most of it in Goodwinkle's cabin. "I thought you'd be pleased." That is what his cowering manservant had had the effrontery to say.

Quentin had observed in his employee, from time to time, hints of a strange willful streak, a rebellion against docility — but he'd never dreamed it would express itself with such gay abandon. A flight of dangerous fancy that had taken off from runway number seven just when it seemed things might settle down.

Quentin suddenly found himself in great distress, the fears he had smothered catching air again, gaining consciousness. He must get control back, or he'd be like Hawrysh in court, infected with the screaming meemies. Maybe he should ask him for a trank or two. Never mind, he had his own, just in case.

It was nearing half past the hour. They would be gathering now; the clerk would be shouting first-inning instructions into the chief's ear. He had better steady these shaking hands, get into judge mode, look wise, assume the correct air of superior passivity.

Quentin stood and examined himself in the mirror. Not too bad. He looked rather royal in red and ermine. He had some colour in his face now, too, sallow though it was. He adjusted his robes. He was starched on the outside, a little soft and doughy within — but he was ready.

Summoning composure from deep wells within him, he emerged from his chambers. En route to the judges' anteroom, he paused at a window. Below him, the Ottawa River, furiously sending to the sea the winter melt of the Canadian Shield. Across the greening laws, the House of Commons, the gothic phallus of the Parliament Building.

But here is where the true power lay, here in this bastille, this ponderous, vulgar courthouse with its dated art deco. Here, bills of Parliament could be voided with an angry swipe of a fountain pen because the Blue Jays lost again the night before.

But he wasn't being fair to himself. You'd be good, Augustina had told him. Yeah, he'd be good. Damned good. Strengthen that Charter of Rights, keep the separatists at bay, try to keep the nation from dismembering into quarreling principalities.

In the anteroom, he joined the others for coffee and soon they were being ushered to the doors.

The clerk shouted at the Chief Justice, drew him away from his newspaper. "We're going in now, sir. They've added Regina versus Milsom to the list, someone wants to speak to it."

"Do we need the whole court for that?"

"Well, everyone is anxious to get going —"

"Never mind. Call the blessed court to order."

Milsom, Quentin thought: the Crown was going to abandon its appeal. No, they couldn't: this was *Milsom's* appeal to restore the acquittal. Now Quentin's head was filled with Besterman, with the Executor who didn't really kill him: Quentin's inspiration but James's creation. Keep anchored, he told himself.

He was the somewhat wobbly tail end of the red-robed procession which straggled into the courtroom, a dark and moody space, back-lit with sickly glowing bulbs. It was fairly full, but mostly with lawyers and their staffs.

The clerk called out, "Milsom versus the Queen."

Lachman, counsel for the Attorney General of British Columbia on the Senate reference, looked around as if he was expecting someone to help him out, but nobody came forward.

"Well," said the Chief, "is no one going to speak to it? Mr. Lachman."

"Ah, yes, sorry. This was put on the list, m'lord, so we could free up some time this fall when we reconvene. I understand the Crown is going to consent to the appeal being allowed."

"Withdrawn, you said?"

"No, m'lord. *Allowed.* I, ah, was actually expecting someone else to speak to it."

Max Macarthur just then charged through the door, quickly and sloppily gowned, no papers or briefcase.

"For the Crown respondent," he said.

Lajoie leaned toward Quentin. "You're our West Coast man, what's this about?"

"Wrong man prosecuted."

"Probably happens a lot more than we think."

Here, coming into court, was someone else Quentin knew: Inspector Nordquist, who, like Max, looked somewhat bedraggled. An overnight flight? For this summary matter?

"Why can't this wait?" the Chief Justice said. "We have a court full of counsel."

"An innocent man is in jail, m'lord," said Max. "We just want to be able to release him."

Quentin could hear the Chief's louder-than-intended words to Madam Justice Rochfoucauld on his right. "Do we have to go through this? We don't have to hear the facts, do we?"

"I think we do," said Roberts from the other side.

Nobody bothered to consult Quentin, but as his fellow judges debated the procedural intricacies, he observed yet another close acquaintance enter the courtroom.

His wife-to-be.

Quentin's reaction was mixed: pleasure, anxiety.

Augustina had decided to surprise him, had flown out on the red-eye express with her partner. But it looked as if she had been... crying? She seemed distraught.

She didn't look at Quentin. She sat beside Nordquist.

Now she was looking at him but was not smiling.

She was looking at him with a venom that bit into his soul.

He heard, distantly, the voice of the Chief Justice: "I think we will recess the court for a few minutes."

Augustina stood and shouted, "Murderer!"

Quentin heard the crack of the bat and watched the ball sail over the fence. The game was over.

During the confusion that followed, most onlookers remained under the impression that Augustina had addressed her accusation to the Chief Justice. They assumed she had something to do with the Milsom case, and was perhaps a sister of one of the stabbed women.

All judges hastily retreated to the anteroom, and, agitated by this strange event, none of them noticed that Russell had left their company.

Augustina was quickly ushered to the security office, where Max and Nordquist eventually managed to intercede with the court wardens, though it seemed to take forever to explain to them what this was about. Max and the inspector showed them the papers, but the implications of a warrant for a Supreme Court's judge's arrest seemed beyond their grasp. One does not just simply walk in and charge such a judge with murder. Calls were made to the RCMP Commissioner, to the Justice Minister.

Everyone had been removed from the courtroom, but now legions of reporters were on hand, milling with the lawyers by the courtroom entrance, a babble of questions and confused answers.

It was a full two hours later when an RCMP superintendent led Nordquist and Max to Justice Russell's chambers door. They found it locked, and no one answered the ringing telephone inside.

They finally found someone with a key. They entered and found Russell sitting stiffly behind his desk, smiling the *risus sardonicus*, with the pungent smell of curry in the air.

45

Postmortem

June 21

Dear Firm Members (and flaccid members, too),

It is the shank of the evening, and Caroline is putting the *niños* to bed. The air is thick with a rumbling tummy sound, black clouds with stomach aches, complaining and petulant, burping up lightning bolts.

We are at the summer solstice, the northern zenith of a sun we have not seen for two weeks — the weatherman continues to sabotage my efforts to prove to Caroline that this joint gives great sunset.

I drove to town today — we are now the owners of a rusted Datsun hiccup truck — and I found your lengthy screed waiting at the post office. Very pleased to know that your lives have settled back into tedious routine, and that ritual and pomp have been restored to the courts. I have been meaning to write, but I've been too busy patching the roof. Caroline bought a bunch of potted plants and stuck them under the major leaks.

The bullet hole below my rib cage has sealed up nicely.

No fungus growths coming from it. All I'm left with as a reminder is a second little belly button off to the side.

Things feel a lot homier here with Caroline and the three little nippers around. Instant family. We are both excellent parental units, and are trying to convince the social workers this is so. Caroline packed a trunk of family how-to manuals down here with us, and she reads them voraciously when she gets a minute or two.

Caroline and I are getting along okay, I guess. She has moods; I have guilt. We argue, we love, we sulk, we laugh, we compete for birds. I think we're going to make it. UBC has granted her a leave until the labyrinthine processes of the Costa Rican adoption laws conclude.

A good business to invest in in this country would be the manufacture of red tape. Endless trips to San José, documents, stamps, and God knows how many interviews with the social workers. They have to make sure we aren't dope fiends or pervs.

Maybe in another ten years we can return to Canada with our three kids. Don't fret, it will all go through — they assure us: no more than three months. I'm aware I'm over-extending my leave of absence, but you guys are obviously raking it in. Brovak has all he can handle with d'Anglio. And now that Wentworth has won Joe Ruff's case against those commie bureaucrats who wanted to bar him from the courts, he has all Ruff's business. That should please the kid.

I knew right away what Ruff had been up to at his oak secrétaire when I saw those RCMP printouts of his carbons. "Little did I know that I had already met the killer face to face." A dead, as it were, giveaway that he was writing a mystery. Gather it's titled *Kill All the Lawyers*. I say, old chaps, wish I'd come up with that.

Wentworth: I'm sorry I'll miss your call next week, but have a drink on me and try not to throw up in the parking lot behind Au Sauterne. The house is yours until we return. One rule: no more witches' seances, if you get my point.

Congratulations, Max, on almost taking the Bronze in the May Day Marathon. You must have maxed out. Pass on my congratulations to your father. I'm sure he'll serve with more distinction than his short-lived predecessor.

I keep having sad thoughts about Russell. To circle the drain in spastic agony — but maybe it was his own way of paying the awful price. It's a loss to the bench, though, let's admit it; sure, he was a ruthless killer, but he was a thoroughly defence-minded judge.

His was a brave and desperate gamble, but I still think he'd have got away with it if Hughie Lupo hadn't indulged his passion for theatre by taking a couple of unscripted initiatives. (And if I hadn't decided to fly Francisco Sierra to Canada to solve the case.)

So it turned out to be a Hugh-dunit.

(Howland knew all along. "Who?" I asked. "Hugh," he said.)

Someone should write a true-crime book: the tale of the haughty master and the naughty slave. I remember being disappointed they didn't find whips and chains in the butler's cottage, but I guess the acts of domination merely involved good old wholesome sex.

Did Mrs. Collins never guess what was going on? All those times Russell trotted over to James' cottage — did she really think he was going there for a massage? I still can't figure out Lupo — not your typical ex-Nam snake-eater. Half-way in the closet, I guess — kind of caught in the door. He must have enjoyed the role of gay pretender. Didn't have to work too hard at it. Thank God he was HIV-negative.

He'll probably squeeze out a few extra years of life with a trial and some appeals before he's extradited to the Quaker State. There our ad-libbing actor will make his final bow and exit. The hot squat. Another victim of America's solemn passion for death and retribution.

I hope you guys will have Francisco's immigration papers cut for him in time for next ski season. Definitely by Brovak's wedding in August, okay? Get Bones to write

a letter, that will speed things up. That big reward should
be more than enough for Frank to open up his own office
as a shoe for hire. Frank Sierra, Private Eye. Might make
for a good series of mysteries. I'll have to give him some
kind of idiosyncrasy — grows orchids, shoots coke, or
something.

He probably won't be casing many stiffs for a while and
will have to start off dicking around with divorce cases, but
maybe our good ol' bosom buddy Abigail Hitchins can send
him some business.

And being reminded of great hooters, how are the owls,
Wentworth? I suppose by now the little ones have grown up
and flown off, hopefully to the security of the Nahanee
Valley, where they can eat Marbled Murrelets to their hearts'
content now that these tasty little birds have been saved
from extinction.

I think it's great that Lukey and Cudlipp have opened a
fishing lodge together. The shark and the narc. I knew they
must have been cooking up something besides hot dogs all
that time over at Lukey's house. What else did you fill me in
on…Oh, Turnbull and Calico — their lawyers think they're
both going to get off? Well, that's justice.

Augustina: I know your emotional wounds will heal
with less scarring than my physical one. You must tell me
more about this insurance appraiser you've been seeing. He
sounds exciting.

My physical wound, by the way, is nothing as compared
to the wound to the soul received last week. The first
rejection slip.

Well, Widgeon prepares his students for this kind of
pain. "Sadly, you will find that many publishers are incapable of recognizing your genius. Do not expect your
manuscript will shoot the lights out at the first house that
reads it. But keep on plugging." I see myself entering the
publisher's office with a gun. Print this book, sir, or I shall
have your life!

(Caroline has reminded me that Widgeon is the name
of a small, somewhat colourful duck, also known as the

Baldpate. I have now developed a picture of the man that will not go away.)

Plugging along,
Brian

September 19

Dear Frank,
   Quick note. A well-respected house says they'll take another look at my book on rewrite. They complain everything is rounded out too nicely. Book needs a final little wriggly twist.
   I've got one. The office just sent me a page of fish wrap from a B.C. trade paper — I don't know if you saw it. Love Among the Planets, by Charity Slough. A $60,000 advance! It's being hyped as "an oddball book by a practising witch."
   Don't try to imagine my unbridled joy. How do you spell dispondant?
   Tell Brovak we're sorry we missed the wedding, but the adoption is taking longer than we expected. Four more months, that's all, they promised. Please let the office know. I can't bear to write them.
   I hear you're getting a lot of the criminal lawyers' business. Don't be afraid to bill them outrageously.
   Caroline and I still await the green flash. She makes a big joke about it, so I'm determined to see it first. If I believe in it, it will come.

My love to you and your family,
Brian

46

The Song Remains
the Same

It was nearly midnight when the painted harlot finally said goodbye
to her friends and left the beer parlour. O.D. Milsom stayed until he
finished his pint of draft. He knew where she lived. He knew where
she hid her key.

A loose woman. Looking for a real man.

Tomorrow he would see it in the newspaper. And on the television.

And if the police asked him about it, he would tell them the truth.
It doesn't matter. They never believe him.